Cursed with a poor sense of direction and a propensity to read, **Annie Claydon** spent much of her childhood lost in books. A degree in English Literature followed by a career in computing didn't lead directly to her perfect job—writing romance for Mills & Boon—but she has no regrets in taking the scenic route. She lives in London: a city where getting lost can be a joy.

Married to the man she met at eighteen, **Susanne Hampton** is the mother of two adult daughters, Orianthi and Tina. She has enjoyed a varied career path, but finally found her way to her favourite role of all: Medical Romance author. Susanne has always read romance novels and says, 'I love a happy-ever-after, so writing for Mills & Boon is a dream come true.'

Also by Annie Claydon

The Doctor's Diamond Proposal
English Rose for the Sicilian Doc
Saving Baby Amy
Forbidden Night with the Duke
Healed by the Single Dad Doc

Stranded in His Arms miniseries

Rescued by Dr Rafe
Saved by the Single Dad

Also by Susanne Hampton

Back in Her Husband's Arms
Falling for Dr December
Midwife's Baby Bump
A Baby to Bind Them
A Mummy to Make Christmas
Twin Surprise for the Single Doc
White Christmas for the Single Mum

Discover more at millsandboon.co.uk.

FROM DOCTOR TO PRINCESS?

ANNIE CLAYDON

THE DOCTOR'S CINDERELLA

SUSANNE HAMPTON

MILLS & BOON

First Published in Great Britain 2018
by Mills & Boon, an imprint of Harper*Collins*Publishers
1 London Bridge Street, London, SE1 9GF

ISBN: 978-0-263-93363-5

MIX
Paper from
responsible sources
FSC www.fsc.org
FSC C007454

This book is produced from independently certified FSC™ paper
to ensure responsible forest management.
For more information visit www.harpercollins.co.uk/green.

Printed and bound in Spain
by CPI, Barcelona

FROM DOCTOR TO PRINCESS?

ANNIE CLAYDON

MILLS & BOON

CHAPTER ONE

THE LEATHER CAR seat creaked slightly as Crown Prince Hugo DeLeon shifted, trying to find a more comfortable position. There wasn't one. He'd only been out of the hospital for twenty-four hours, and the pain in his left shoulder was normal. It would subside in a day or so, and he knew that impatience wasn't going to make him heal any faster.

All the same, he *was* impatient. And if his father thought that he was helping Hugo to get back to normal, then he wasn't.

There wasn't a great deal of choice in the matter, though. The King of Montarino was accustomed to being obeyed, and when he had visited his only son in the discreet private ward of the hospital, he'd made it clear that he was taking no arguments. He'd smiled at Hugo, in much the same way as any father would, and told him that his duty to his country was clear and very simple. He had to get better.

In order to make sure that his son's recovery went smoothly, the King had recruited a doctor who would stay with him at all times over the next month or so. Hugo had still been drowsy from the anaesthetic and his back hurt from having lain still while the pacemaker had been inserted into his chest, but he had got the message. His father didn't trust Hugo to look after himself, and so he was appointing a minder to do it.

He hadn't told Hugo much about this minder, other than that she was a woman, eminently qualified, and that she was due to fly out from London today. The last detail was another smart move on his father's part, because Hugo knew most of the doctors in the small principality of Montarino, particularly those who were well qualified in cardiology. He might well have been able to wriggle out of the arrangement with any one of them, but this woman was an unknown quantity.

He wondered briefly whether she'd come equipped with tranquillisers and physical restraints. And, more to the point, whether she'd been briefed about the requirement for discretion. Hugo assumed that she had, because discretion was one of the codes that his family lived by, and his father never let anyone forget it.

'That'll be her…' His bodyguard sat in the front seat of the car, and had the advantage of an unobscured view. Hugo squinted through the tinted windows, and saw the chauffeur walking across the forecourt towards the airport's short-stay car park. Beside him was a young woman with mid-brown hair and a supple sway to her walk, which made the short hairs at the back of Hugo's neck prickle slightly.

Probably another one of his father's carefully reasoned choices. Hugo had to admit that he wasn't known for saying no to beautiful women, but unusually the King had misjudged the situation this time. A career woman, particularly a doctor, wasn't someone that he could contemplate giving any part of his heart to.

'She doesn't look too formidable.' Ted spoke in English, turning slightly in his seat to display the hint of a smile.

'I wouldn't bank on looks. She's managed to keep

hold of her suitcase, and I imagine that Jean-Pierre did everything he could to wrestle it away from her.' Hugo turned the corners of his mouth down. The first thing his father's chauffeur would have done was to try to relieve their guest of her luggage and wheel her suitcase for her.

'I must be getting slow, I missed that.' Ted had done nothing of the sort; he just hadn't seen fit to mention it. In the five years that he'd been with Hugo, since his retirement from the British police force, the two men had learned to read each other's thoughts and trust what they saw. It had been Ted who had happened to mention that he'd heard that the doctor was being picked up from the airport this morning, and Hugo had made the expected decision to go with the car to greet her. Sizing her up before anyone else at the palace got the chance to speak with her couldn't be a bad thing.

Ted got out of the car, walking to the rear passenger door and opening it. For all the world as if he were according Hugo the respect his position required, rather than helping him with the weight of the door. Hugo climbed out of the car, ignoring the tingle of pain that reached from his chest down his left arm.

Now that she was closer, Dr Penelope Maitland didn't seem as formidable as her old-fashioned name might lead one to suppose. She was all curves and movement, looking almost girlish in a tan jacket over a cream summer dress, creased from travelling. Her light brown hair glinted in the sunshine, and bare, tanned legs gave her the fresh, outdoorsy look of someone going on holiday.

Maybe the gorgeous Dr Penelope was a rare mistake on his father's part. This woman looked as if she was more likely to spend her time here enjoying the pleasures of Montarino, not nagging him about his health. When her honey-coloured gaze met his, there was a spark of recognition and she smiled. A carefree kind of smile that sent tingles down his spine and allowed Hugo to believe that she didn't have it in her to make his life difficult.

Then she stopped in front of him, letting go of her suitcase long enough for Jean-Pierre to grab it and wheel it around to the boot of the car. 'I'm Dr Maitland. I'm told that I shouldn't curtsey.'

Her voice was like honey but her tone was like steel. Clearly Dr Penelope wasn't going to be quite as much of a walkover as her appearance suggested.

'Thank you. I'd prefer it if you didn't.' Hugo held out his right hand, glad that the pacemaker was on the left side of his chest, and didn't hamper the movement of his right arm. Her grip was as firm as her tone. 'Welcome to Montarino. I'm Hugo DeLeon.'

'Yes, I know.' She shot him a questioning look, and Hugo wondered whether she was going to rebuke him for coming to meet her. He mumbled the usual invitation to call him Hugo, wondering if he'd get to call her Penelope. The name seemed suddenly as if it would taste sweet on his lips.

'Please call me Nell…'

Hugo smiled his acquiescence. *Nell* sounded soft and sweet too, even if it was a little shorter.

'You must be tired from your journey. We should be going…' Hugo's discreet gesture to Jean-Pierre prompted him to get into the car.

She raised one eyebrow. 'Yes, we should be going. I'm surprised to see you out and about so soon.'

Her words had an edge to them. If anyone should be feeling tired she clearly expected that it should be him, and Hugo had to admit that he was surprised at the effort involved in making a simple car journey.

'I'm grateful for the fresh air.'

At the moment, the fresh air was making his head spin. Hugo stood back from the open door of the car and she hesitated and then got in, sliding quickly across the back seat before Hugo could even think about closing the car door and walking around to get in on the other side.

All the same, he welcomed the move. On this side, the seat belt wouldn't need to rest painfully on his left shoulder. Hugo got into the car, and Ted closed the door before he could reach for it.

'Have you been to Montarino before?' Hugo had years of practice with small talk.

'No.' Nell shook her head, regarding him thoughtfully.

'It's very small, only eight miles across, but very beautiful. We have one city, half a mountain and, although we have no coastline, there are some beautiful lakes.'

'That's nice. I'll have to come back sometime when I'm not working. I probably won't have much time to see them this time around.' Her mouth was set in a firm line, and Hugo's heart sank. Clearly there was no hope of deflecting the redoubtable Dr Penelope from her intended purpose.

Four days ago, Nell Maitland had ridden home on the night bus, after the farewell party that her colleagues at the hospital had thrown for her. It had been the ultimate failure, after months of trying to work things out with the cardiac unit's new head of the department, and save the job that she loved so much. And now…

She was riding in a chauffeur-driven car, sitting next to a prince. It was an object lesson in how dramatically things could change in so little time.

'I gather you have a strong tradition of attracting the best musicians.' She smiled in response to Hugo DeLeon's indication of the Montarino Opera House, and the car obligingly slowed to allow her a more detailed look.

'We like to think that we can hold our own with the rest of Europe when it comes to our appreciation of the arts. You *do* know a little about Montarino, then?'

Anyone could use the Internet. Although Nell had to admit that the photographs didn't do the grand building justice. Its sweeping, modern lines, rising from the tree-lined plaza that surrounded it, would have made it a landmark in the greatest of cities.

'Only as much as I could read in the last couple of days. In between packing.' Nell wondered whether he'd mind that she hadn't even known where Montarino was before she'd taken this job. It had just been a name, tethered somewhere at the back of her mind, along with a lot of other places that she knew nothing about.

Hugo nodded, smiling. 'That's one of the best things about living here. Most people have few preconceptions, and so we have the chance to attempt to surprise our visitors.'

And it seemed that Hugo DeLeon was giving it his best shot. Nell had been told that he was a doctor as well as a prince, and that her advice would be a matter of reinforcing a message that he was already well aware of. In other words, he reckoned that the physical limits that applied to ordinary people weren't for the likes of a prince, and he needed to be kept in check.

Nell had no idea in which direction they were supposed to be going, but she was aware that the car seemed to be taking a circuitous route past a number of notable buildings, all of which Hugo was intent on pointing out. If he thought that was going to deflect her from her purpose, he was wrong.

'I'm looking forward to seeing the palace.' She smiled brightly, wondering whether he'd take the hint.

'We're nearly there now.' Hugo raised his voice a little. 'Jean-Pierre…'

The driver nodded, turning smoothly onto a wide, straight boulevard and putting his foot on the gas. It seemed that everyone here responded to Hugo's every word, which was the first challenge attached to this new appointment.

The ambassador, who had interviewed her at the embassy in London, had said little but implied a lot. He'd got her medical qualifications and the fact that she spoke French tolerably well out of the way in the first five minutes. Then he'd turned the conversation around to her patient.

'Hugo DeLeon, Crown Prince of Montarino, can be…' The ambassador had paused slightly before coming to a conclusion about how to describe it. 'He can be self-willed.'

Nell had read *arrogant* into his words and had smiled politely. She had experience of dealing with all kinds of patients, and self-willed wasn't a problem. Neither was arrogant.

What the ambassador hadn't warned her about was his smile. It was polite, appropriate, and yet it seemed to hold real warmth. His high cheekbones lent a touch of class, and his shock of dark blonde hair, no doubt artfully arranged to make it appear slightly tousled, added a boyish note. Green eyes gave a hint that Hugo DeLeon was capable of some pretty serious mischief. Nell would have to watch out for those eyes.

But however handsome he was, however his smile made her stomach quiver, Nell had a job to do. Her fingers tightened on the strap of her handbag, which lay comfortingly across her knees. A man had gotten between her and her job before, and no one, not even this handsome prince, was going to do it again.

White knuckles. Hugo was used to looking for the little signs that told him what people were really thinking, and he'd noticed that Nell was clutching her handbag on her lap like some kind of defensive weapon. Despite the firm tone and the clear hints that he shouldn't have come to the airport, there was a chink in her armour. One that he may well need to find and exploit if it turned out that the restrictions she placed on him got in the way of his current plans.

They'd driven through the grounds of the palace and the car stopped at the ceremonial entrance to allow them to get out. She gave the high, pillared archways a glance and then turned to him as the car moved smoothly away.

'My luggage…'

'Jean-Pierre will arrange for it to be taken up to your apartment.' A sudden flare of panic had shown in Nell's eyes, and Hugo almost felt sorry for her. But keeping her a little off-balance, a little over-awed was exactly what he wanted.

'Right. Thank you.'

'Perhaps I can show you around.' The palace was big enough and grand enough to disorientate her even further.

'I think that's best left for some other time.' She was as sweet-smelling and soft as a summer's day, but there was no getting over the determination behind it all. 'This… apartment. I was told that it would be next door to yours.'

'Yes, it is.' If Hugo had had any say in the matter, he'd have put her on the other side of the building, but he hadn't. His father didn't often step into his life, but when he did, he did it thoroughly.

'With a connecting door?'

So someone had told her about that, too. Or maybe she'd asked. Hugo had rather hoped that he could just keep the connecting door closed and that it would never occur to anyone to open it.

'Yes, that's right. It's generally kept locked…' Finding the key was an easy enough matter on the rare occasions that he brought a girlfriend with him to stay at the palace for a few days, but he was sure he could just as easily lose it.

'I imagine someone has the key. Being a doctor yourself, you'll understand the need to have access to your patient.'

'And I'm sure *you'll* understand where your duties begin and end.' Since the pleasantries didn't seem to be working all that well, it was obviously time to make things clear.

'The ambassador outlined them, yes.' She pressed her lips together and Hugo imagined that the British Ambassador had deployed all of the expected diplomacy in the matter. 'The King's letter of appointment, on the other hand, was a little less circumspect.'

Great. So his father had decided that he needed to weigh in on that as well. And even if the tiny quiver at the side of Nell's mouth told Hugo that she was feeling over-awed and nervous, her cool gaze indicated that she wasn't going to let that stop her from doing her job.

'Perhaps we should talk, over some tea.' Since deflection wasn't working, maybe negotiation would. The next step would be outright battle, and Hugo would prefer to avoid that.

'Yes. I think that would be a very good idea.'

CHAPTER TWO

HUGO HAD OPENED the door that concealed the lift, and when she'd seen the old-fashioned gates, she'd slipped in front of him, heaving them to one side. Part of him was grateful, but a greater part decreed that as a gentleman, and her host, he should have been quicker in insisting he open the gates himself. When he motioned her ahead of him into the lift, she hovered annoyingly next to the gates, giving him no opportunity to open them when they reached the third floor.

He showed her to her apartment, leaving her alone to freshen up. That would give him at least three quarters of an hour to rest before he had to submit to another onslaught from her.

Hugo sank gratefully into the chair in his private sitting room and closed his eyes. This morning he had woken feeling invigorated, and it had only been the pain in his shoulder that had reminded him he was unable to move mountains. Wide awake, his body feeling the immediate benefit of a heart that was now paced and doing its job properly, he'd jumped at the chance of getting out of the constriction of four walls, but it had worn him out. His own advice to pacemaker patients—that they might start to feel better almost immediately but must rest and get over the operation first—would be given with a lot more certainty in the future.

Fifteen minutes later, a quiet knock sounded on the main door to the apartment and he shouted to whoever it was to come in, keeping his eyes closed. If someone was here to make the tea or fuss over him, then he'd rather they waited until he was strong enough to smilingly refuse their help.

'How are you feeling?' Nell's voice made his eyes snap open.

'Fine. Thank you.' Hugo's eye's darted to the clock above the mantelpiece. Surely he hadn't been asleep…

Apparently not. She was pink-cheeked, as if she'd just got out of the shower, and Nell had changed out of her travelling clothes and into a slim pair of dark blue trousers with a white shirt, open at the neck and buttoned at the cuffs. She looked businesslike and entirely delicious.

He shifted, wishing that the ache in his left shoulder would go away, and Nell stepped forward. Without any warning at all, she caught up one of the cushions from the sofa and bent over him.

Her scent was… It was just soap. The soap that was placed in all the guest bathrooms at the palace. But Nell made it smell intoxicating. The brush of her hair, one soft curl against his cheek, almost paralysed him.

'Is that a little better?' She'd placed the cushion carefully under his left arm so that it supported his shoulder.

'Yes. A lot better, thank you.'

Nell nodded, looking around the room as if she'd mislaid something. 'Does your apartment have a kitchen? Or do you have to send out for tea?'

'The kitchen's through there.' The desire to stay where he was battled with a strong disinclination to have her make tea for him. Hugo shifted, ready for the effort of standing up, and she reached forward, her hand on his right shoulder.

'I didn't go to all the trouble of arranging cushions for you to spoil it all by making the tea. Stay there.' Her voice was kindly but firm. It occurred to Hugo that if he didn't feel so tired he might have delighted in having Nell be kind and firm with him all afternoon, and then he reminded himself that business and pleasure was a very bad mix.

He heard her clattering around in the kitchen and closed his eyes. Listening to Nell was almost as good as watching her, because he could still see her in his mind's eye. That was another thing that was going to have to stop.

Nell found a set of mugs in the kitchen cupboard. It was a surprise, since she'd expected that a prince would drink only out of bone china, but a good one. She'd been up very early this morning and could definitely do with a decent-sized cup of tea.

She looked in the cupboard for biscuits and found a packet of chocolate digestives. Things were definitely looking up. Next to them was a packet of painkillers, wrapped around with a piece of paper with a typed chart, each dose ticked off neatly. Hugo had taken this morning's tablets but was past due for the lunchtime ones.

He was clearly overdoing things. And her letter of appointment had spelled out exactly what she was supposed to do in response to that likely eventuality. She had to make sure that he took the rest he needed.

She put the tea things on a tray and walked quietly into the sitting room. Large and filled with light, the furniture was stylish but comfortable, allowing the baroque fireplace and the gilded mirror above it to take precedence. Hugo seemed to be dozing, but when she put the tray down, moving a small side table next to his chair, he opened his eyes.

'This is…quite unnecessary.' He seemed quite devoted to the idea that there was nothing wrong with him.

'And these?' She raised an eyebrow, putting a glass of water and his tablets down next to him. 'Pain's generally the body's way of hinting that you should slow down a bit.'

'I thought I'd take them when I got back.' He seemed to be watching her every move as he downed the tablets in one, then took some sips of water. 'Please. Sit down. We really must talk.'

It was almost a relief. It seemed that Hugo wanted to make their relationship clear as much as she did, and it was a grey area that Nell was feeling increasingly uncomfortable with. She put his tea on the table next to him and sat down on the sofa, reaching for her cup.

'The first thing I need to say is that your job here is strictly confidential.' Nell took a breath to protest that she knew all about doctor-patient confidentiality and he silenced her with a flash of his green eyes. 'More so than usual. I don't want anyone to know what your role is here or that I'm your patient.'

Nell felt her heart beat a little faster. 'Is there a reason for that?'

'Yes, there is. A very good reason.'

'I'd like to know what that reason is, please.' She injected as much firmness into her voice as she could.

Hugo smiled suddenly. If he was unused to anyone questioning his decisions, it didn't seem to bother him all that much. 'I imagine you've done your homework and that you know I've been working very hard in the last few years to raise awareness about heart disease and promote early treatment.'

'I know that you're the patron of a charity that has done a lot of work in the field…' How much work Hugo had personally done hadn't been made clear in the article she'd read.

For a moment, it seemed that finally she'd managed to offend him. And then he smiled. 'I'm a doctor and it's my mission. You have a mission?'

'Yes. I suppose I do.'

'Then you'll understand the compelling nature of it. Weakness on my part can only undermine the message I'm trying to give.'

Nell swallowed hard, trying to clear the rapidly growing lump in her throat. 'Or…it might be seen as a strength. That you understand…'

'My job is to make things happen. And I'll freely admit that I'm a prime example of someone who hasn't followed the most basic advice and sought help at the first signs of any problem with my heart. Which is inexcusable, since I have a very clear understanding of what those signs are.'

So he couldn't allow himself this. In Hugo's mind, his illness gave him feet of clay. Nell might disagree, but it was his decision.

'What you choose to share about your own medical issues is entirely up to you. Of course, I'll say nothing.'

He nodded. 'Thank you. I see from your CV that you've taken an interest in the psychological aspects of recovery from heart disease.'

Something about his tone gave Nell the impression that this irritated him. 'Yes, that's right. I did a module on the psychology of recovery at medical school, and when I decided to specialise in cardiac medicine, it seemed very relevant. I co-authored a study on patients' post-operative experiences, in partnership with doctors from five other hospitals.'

'I'd be interested in reading it.' He turned the corners of his mouth down, and Nell felt her muscles in her stomach twist. Maybe he'd decided that questioning whether he needed a doctor wasn't enough, and that he'd take a leaf from her ex-boss's book and undermine her by questioning her professional ability.

She stared at him, wordlessly, and Hugo smiled suddenly. 'I'd be interested to know which category of patient I fall into.'

That charm again. That smile, which seemed calculated to make Nell's head spin and throw her off guard. 'Psychology isn't a matter of putting people into boxes, it's a way of understanding what's there. I'm sure you know that already.'

Perhaps she should mention that understanding exactly why Hugo was so desperate to pretend that there was nothing wrong with him would be a good start in getting him on the road to recovery. Or maybe she should wait until Hugo was ready to voice that idea for himself, even if scraping through the layers of charm and getting him to admit to anything seemed likely to be a long process.

'Yes, I do. And please forgive me if my welcome has fallen short of expectations. Your presence here wasn't my choice, it's my father who thinks I need a minder.'

Nell swallowed down the temptation to take the bait. 'I'm a doctor. If my duty of care to you, as my patient, makes me seem like a minder then…' She shrugged.

Hugo leaned forward, the cushion at his side slipping to the floor. 'Why don't you go ahead and say it? I can take it.'

If he thought that she couldn't look into his green

eyes and say exactly what she meant, he was going to find out differently. Nell met his gaze and felt shivers run down her spine. Okay, so it was difficult to do. But not impossible.

'If you think that I'm here to be your minder, then that says a lot more about your approach to this than it does mine.'

'I suppose it does. But I want to make one thing clear. Duty to my father and professional courtesy to you require that I listen to your advice. But I have specific goals, in connection with a project at the hospital, that need to be met over the next six weeks. I won't allow anything to get in the way of that.'

'Even at the cost of your own health?'

'I can handle it.'

The battle lines had been drawn, and in the heat of his gaze it felt almost exhilarating. Then Nell came to her senses.

In the last three weeks, Hugo had faced a crisis. If that appeared to have had no effect on him, then maybe that just meant he was more adept at covering his emotions than most. He was hurting and unable to trust his own body any more, and if his reaction to that was stubborn failure to face facts, it was her job to get him to a place where he felt strong enough to admit how he felt.

His smouldering green eyes were suddenly too much for her to bear, and she looked away. 'Compromising on the way you get there doesn't necessarily mean you have to abandon your goals. Let me help you.'

He thought for a moment. 'What kind of compromise did you have in mind?'

Nell took a deep breath. This might be the first of many hurdles, but she'd made a start. 'I don't know yet.

I'll need to examine you first and hear exactly what your commitments are. Then we can talk about it.'

'All right.' He smiled suddenly, as if he'd just remembered that he ought to do so. 'I'll make an effort to be a model patient.'

Somehow Nell doubted that. 'I appreciate the thought. But you've a long way to go before you qualify for the title of my most awkward patient.'

This time Hugo *really* smiled. 'Shame. I'll have to try harder.'

'Yes, you will.' Nell rose from her seat, picking the cushion up from the floor and putting it back in place, behind his shoulder. 'You can plan your strategy while I go and get my medical bag.'

Maybe his father knew him better than Hugo had thought. His doctor at the hospital had been highly qualified, deferential, and had treated the whole thing as if it were an afternoon at a health spa. Nell was something different. Honest, no-nonsense and quite capable of cutting him down to size when he tried all the usual diversionary tactics.

Dr Penelope. He didn't dare call her that, she'd told him she preferred *Nell.* Which was charming in its own way but didn't seem to sum her up quite so well. Fierce, beautiful and unstoppable.

It was a little easier to think when she was out of the room. A little easier to remind himself of the flat in London, right at the top of a tenement block, where the lift sometimes worked and sometimes didn't.

A little pang of regret for times that had seemed altogether simpler. The sofa that had creaked slightly under the weight of two people too tired to move and yet happy to just be together. The awful green bedspread that Anna had chosen, and which hadn't matched the curtains but which Hugo had liked because she had. It had been the one time in Hugo's life when duty hadn't weighed heavy on his shoulders. All he'd needed to do was work hard at medical school and love the woman who shared his life.

He'd brought Anna back to Montarino, two newly minted doctors, full of so many possibilities and dreams. The ring on her finger had been replaced by something more befitting a princess, but Anna had always preferred the old one, which Hugo had saved for out of his allowance. It wasn't until she'd left that Hugo had stopped to think that maybe she had been unhappy at the palace.

And that had been his doing. Anna had trained to be a doctor, not a princess. She had fitted the bill well enough, but it hadn't been her mission in life. Hugo had been too intent on pursuing his own mission to see that until it had been too late and Anna had been packing her bags, a ticket back to London with her name on it lying on the bed.

'If you'd just looked, Hugo, you would have seen that this isn't enough for me. I have a career, too.'

There had been nothing that he could say because he had known in his heart that Anna was right. He'd let her go, and had watched from afar as she'd risen to the top of her chosen field, like a cork held underwater for too long and bouncing to the surface of a fast-flowing stream. One that had taken her away from him, and had never brought her back again.

Since then, Hugo had confined himself to women whose career aspirations were limited to being a princess. And if he hadn't found anyone who truly understood him yet, then one of these days his duty would outweigh the yearning for love and he'd marry regardless. It had never made its way to the top of his to-do list, though, and it could wait.

The sound of a chair being pushed across the carpet towards his broke his reverie. It seemed that the doctor was ready for him now.

'Would you unbutton your shirt for me, please?' Nell sat down opposite him, briskly reaching into a small nylon bag to retrieve a stethoscope.

Suddenly he felt slightly dizzy. At the hospital, he'd submitted to one examination after the other, distancing himself from the doctors and nurses who quietly did their jobs while he thought about something else. But Nell was different. She challenged him, demanding that he take notice of what was happening to him.

'My notes are…somewhere…' He looked around, trying to remember where he'd left the envelope.

'I have them. They were emailed through to me yesterday. I'd like to check on how you are now.'

Whether he'd managed to throw any spanners in the works. Her meaning shone clear in her light brown eyes, almost amber in the sunshine that streamed through the high windows.

He looked away from her gaze. Hugo had no qualms about his body, he knew that it was as good as the next man's and that he didn't have to think twice before he allowed anyone to see it. But things were different now. The new, unhealed scar felt like overwhelming evidence of his greatest weakness.

Nell sat motionless opposite him, clearly willing to wait him out if need be. He reached for the buttons of his shirt, his fingers suddenly clumsy.

Hugo was finding this hard. Nell pretended not to notice, twisting at the earpieces of her stethoscope as if she'd just found something wrong with them. The very fact that he seemed about to baulk at the idea of a simple examination told her that Hugo wasn't as confident about his recovery as he liked to make out.

That was okay. Nell would have been more comfortable if she could maintain a degree of professional detachment too, but that wasn't going to work. The main thing at the moment was to maintain their tenuous connection, because if that was lost then so was their way forward.

'What about official engagements?' She'd pretty much exhausted all the things that might be wrong with her stethoscope, and perhaps talking would put him at ease.

'My father's beaten you to it. He's taken care of all my official engagements for the next month. There are various members of the family stepping in.'

'I'll have to be quicker off the mark next time,' Nell commented lightly, trying not to notice that he was slipping his shirt off, revealing tanned skin and a mouth-wateringly impressive pair of shoulders. She concentrated on the dressing on Hugo's chest, peeling it back carefully.

'There's still the hospital project.' He shot her a grin and Nell felt her hands shake slightly. Being this close to Hugo added a whole new catalogue of ways in which he made her feel uneasy. The scent of his skin. The way she wanted to touch him…

'What does that involve?' Nell did her best to forget about everything else and concentrate on the surgical incision on Hugo's chest.

'We're building a new wing at the hospital. It's going to be a specialist cardiac centre, with outpatient services, a family resource department and a unit for long-stay paediatric patients.'

'That sounds like a very worthwhile project.'

'Yes, it is. And there's no alternative but for me to be out there, raising money for it.'

'There's always an alternative...' Nell murmured the words, clipping the stethoscope into her ears and pressing the diaphragm to his chest.

'The work's already started and we've run into some unforeseen problems. There's an underground chamber that needs to be investigated and made safe. With men and equipment already on-site, every day of delay costs money, even without the cost of the new works. If we don't raise that money, we can't afford to complete the project.'

'And you're the only one who can do it?'

'No, but I have the contacts to raise what we need in the time frame we need it. We're looking for large donations.'

Nell frowned. There might be a grain of truth in Hugo's assertion that he was indispensable and couldn't take a break, although she still wasn't ruling out the possibility that pig-headedness and ego were also factors. 'I don't know much about these things but...couldn't your father help out with a loan?'

'I'm sure he would have made a donation, and I would have, too. But the Constitution of Montarino forbids it.'

'Really? You can't give money to charity?' Nell's eyebrows shot up.

'We can and we do, but it's very strictly regulated. The royal family is only allowed to donate five percent of the total cost of a public endeavour, and that ceiling has almost been reached already. You can blame my great-great-grandfather for that—he tried to buy up key parts of the country's infrastructure in an attempt to maintain his influence, and so the legislation was rushed through. For all the right reasons, in my opinion, but at the moment it's an inconvenience.'

'But it's okay if you *raise* the money?'

'Yes. History and politics always make things a great deal more complicated.'

As a doctor, this wasn't complicated at all. But Nell could feel herself being dragged into a world of blurred lines. Hugo's charm, the way her fingers tingled when she touched his skin. That was one line she couldn't cross.

'So you have to rest but you can't. We'll have to be creative...'

Hugo chuckled. 'I'm beginning to like the way you think.'

'Don't start liking it too much. If your health's at risk, I'm going to do everything I can to stop you.'

'Noted. Does that mean I can do everything I can to stop you from stopping me?'

'If that means you're going to get enough rest, and make sure you don't compromise your recovery, then feel free.' This war of words was fast becoming a little too intimate. A little too much like the delicious push and pull of meeting someone who could become a *very* good friend.

But it worked. Hugo nodded, his hand drifting to his chest. 'So what's the verdict, then?'

'Everything looks fine. You can see for yourself.'

He shook his head, and Nell realised that she hadn't seen him look down at his chest once. 'I'll take your word for it. So...the day after tomorrow...'

'What's happening then?'

'It's a lunchtime fundraiser. I get to sit comfortably in the sun and make a two-minute speech. Actually, you could come along if you like.'

'There are spare tickets?'

'I'm your ticket.'

Nell gulped down the realisation that she'd be there as his plus-one. What mattered was that she'd be there, which meant that Hugo would have a doctor, and hopefully a restraining influence, on hand.

'Okay. Let's see how you are tomorrow and make the decision then.' Twenty-four hours and a night's sleep might just be enough time to get her head straight.

'Fair enough.' His green eyes seemed to see right through her. And it was worrying that when he turned his gaze onto her, his lips twitched into a smile.

CHAPTER THREE

NELL HAD SPENT as much of the afternoon as she could unpacking. Laying things into neat piles and hanging dresses in the large wardrobe. Smoothing the already immaculate covers of the great bed, which would have dominated a smaller room but here was simply in proportion. It had been an exercise in restoring order, pushing back the chaos that seemed to follow Hugo like the scent of expensive aftershave.

He seemed intent on playing the host, inviting her for dinner in his apartment. Over a beautifully cooked and presented meal, Hugo talked about the charity that seemed so close to his heart. How they'd raised awareness about heart disease and increased the number of people who had regular 'healthy heart' checks. How they wanted to move forward and provide a centre of excellence, which would cater to both inpatients and outpatients, for all the people of Montarino.

It was a dazzling vision. And yet here, at the centre of it all, was a man who felt the need to risk his own health.

She returned to her apartment tired but unable to sleep. A long bath didn't help, and neither did reading a book. Nell scarcely registered the words in front of her, because Hugo seemed to fill her mind, chasing everything else away. He'd said that he would be going straight to bed after she left, but when she went out into the darkness of the hallway she could still see a sliver of light escaping under the connecting door to his apartment.

She could hear Hugo's voice, distant and muffled behind the heavy door. Either he was talking to himself or there was someone there.

Someone there. There were pauses, as if he was waiting for an answer and as Nell pressed her ear to the door she thought she heard another voice, this one too low and quiet for her to be even sure whether it was a woman or a man.

Whoever it was, they shouldn't be there. It was midnight, and Hugo should be asleep by now. Nell's hand trembled as she took hold of the door handle. Walking into his apartment and telling him to go to bed might be one step too far.

But they'd had an agreement. He'd promised. And Nell had believed him. The feeling of empty disappointment in him spurred her on.

'Hugo…' She opened the door an inch, and heard the soft sound of classical music, coming from the room beyond. 'Are you still up?'

Silence. Then the door handle was pulled out of her grip as Hugo swung the door open, standing in the doorway and blocking her view of the sitting room.

'This isn't the time, Nell.' He spoke quietly, as if he didn't want the person behind him in the room to hear.

He obviously wanted some privacy and the thought struck Nell that his companion might be a woman. She felt her cheeks flush red. The last thing she wanted to do was come face-to-face with a girlfriend, who for some reason Hugo hadn't seen fit to mention.

'I'm…sorry, but we had a deal, Hugo.'

'I'm aware of that. Something came up.'

'That's not good enough…' Nell stopped herself from telling him that he should be in bed. In the circumstances, that might be a catalyst for even more exertion on his part. She felt her ears begin to burn at the thought.

'It's not what you're thinking, Nell.'

'Really? What do you think I'm thinking?' If she really was that transparent then things had just gone from very bad to much worse.

'What I'd be thinking. But on this occasion, we'd both be wrong.' He stood back from the doorway, allowing her to see into the room. Two seats were drawn up to a games table, which had been set up by the fireplace, and an elderly man sat in one of them. He wore immaculately pressed pyjamas and held himself erect in his seat. When he turned towards Nell, his milky blue eyes seemed not quite to focus on her.

'Jacob, we have a visitor. This is Nell.'

'A pleasure, miss.' The man spoke quietly, in heavily accented English. Despite his neat appearance, there was something vulnerable about him.

'It's a pleasure to meet you, Jacob.' Nell went to advance into the room, but Hugo stepped back into her path.

'Nell can't stay…' He threw the words over his shoulder, turning painfully to Nell and motioning to her to comply. She didn't move.

Hugo took a step forward, and she took a step back, instinctively avoiding touching him. He pulled the door half shut behind them.

'Jacob is…fragile.' He was whispering, but Nell could hear both urgency and fatigue in his voice.

'I can see that. But you need your sleep.' Whispering back seemed rather too conspiratorial for Nell's liking but having Jacob hear what was going on didn't seem like a good idea.

'I'll take him back to his apartment as soon as I can.'

'No, Hugo. You said we'd take things as they came and that you'd accept my help. Let's give that a trial run now, shall we?' Hugo hesitated and she glared at him. 'I'm not going to walk in there and order him out.'

Silently he walked back through the doorway, and Nell followed him. Jacob turned to Hugo, a fond smile on his face. 'Hugo, my boy… What's going on?'

'Nothing. It's all right, Jacob. I've asked Nell to join us.'

'Very good.' Jacob seemed to approve of the plan, gesturing towards the draughts, which lay on the chequerboard tabletop. 'You play, miss?'

'Not very well.' Nell smiled at him.

'Jacob taught me to play thirty years ago.' Hugo went to pull up a chair for Nell and thought better of it, allowing her to move it across to the table. 'I used to sneak downstairs when my parents were out in the evening, and we'd play draughts and drink hot chocolate.'

'Hot chocolate!' Jacob's eyes lit up suddenly, and he gestured towards the pot that lay on the coffee table, along with two gold-rimmed cups and saucers. 'I remember now. Would you like some, miss?'

Maybe that would bring the evening to a close. 'Thank you. I'll get another cup, shall I?'

Nell glanced at Hugo, and he nodded, resuming his seat opposite Jacob. His smile barely concealed his fatigue and he was moving as if he was in pain. The sooner they could end, this the better.

As Nell walked to the kitchen, she heard the two men talking quietly in French behind her.

'Who is she, Hugo?'

'She's a doctor, and her name's Nell.'

Hugo repeated the words, no hint in his tone that this wasn't the first time he'd told Jacob.

'A doctor? What does she want?' Jacob's voice took on an air of perplexed worry.

'She's here for me. Not you, my friend.' Hugo's tone was smooth, reassuring.

'Where's she going?'

'Just to get another cup. We're having hot chocolate.'

'Ah, yes. Hot chocolate and draughts…'

Jacob's memory had become fragmented by time. Some things were still clear in his mind, but he was groping in the dark, trying to make sense of others. It was common in patients who had dementia, and it was clear that Hugo was trying to reassure Jacob by re-creating the sights and sounds of things he did remember. The sound the counters made on the draughts board. The taste of hot chocolate. But that was all coming with a cost to him.

She fetched the cup and re-joined the two men, wondering whether Hugo knew that she'd heard and understood their conversation. Smiling, she poured the hot chocolate and sat down. Jacob moved one of his pieces and Hugo chuckled quietly.

'You have me…' He made the only move possible, and Jacob responded by taking four of his counters in one go.

'Another game?' The old man still seemed wide awake, and Nell wondered how long this was going to go on before he tired and they could take him back to wherever he'd come from.

Hugo nodded, and Nell shot him a frown. He couldn't do this all night, but it appeared that he was perfectly capable of trying if it kept Jacob happy.

'Will you teach me, please? I know how to play, but I don't know the tactics.'

'Of course, *mademoiselle*.' Perhaps Jacob had forgotten her name again, but he remembered how to play draughts, and that was the way that Nell could keep him occupied while Hugo rested.

Hugo stood, giving Nell his seat, and retreated to the sofa. As she and Jacob set out the pieces, ready to play, he seemed to be dozing.

At least Hugo was relaxing, now. As they played, Jacob became animated, suggesting better moves to Nell, slipping from French into English and then back again, sometimes in the course of one sentence. Finally he began to tire.

'Hugo's tired. He's ready to go to bed now.' Nell nodded towards Hugo. If Jacob had known him since he was a boy, then he would also remember taking care of him, and some part of that relationship would still exist somewhere in his head.

'Is it time?' Jacob glanced around the room and then at his own attire. 'It must be. I'm wearing my pyjamas.'

That posed a second problem. Nell had no idea who Jacob was or where he'd come from. But Jacob turned, calling softly to Hugo.

'Wake up, lad. Time to go to bed.'

Instantly, Hugo's eyes were open and he roused himself. Jacob clearly came first, however tired he was. 'Let's go.'

Nell was perfect. Hugo had been prepared to exert his authority and order her out of his apartment, but she'd realised Jacob's situation very quickly and had played along. More than that, she'd taken charge, allowing Hugo to relax and get comfortable. Despite all his efforts to conceal it, he had to admit that he was very tired.

He led the way through the quiet corridors of the palace, Nell and Jacob arm in arm behind him. As he ushered them through one of the back doors and across the small courtyard towards the neat row of cottages used by palace employees, he wondered whether she'd be quite as gentle and understanding when Jacob was no longer within earshot.

It took Celeste a while to answer the door, and when she did so she was bleary-eyed, pulling on her dressing gown. Looking after Jacob was becoming a twenty-four-hour-a-day task for her, and she'd clearly been fast asleep when Hugo had texted her to say that Jacob was with him. He waved away her apologies and said goodnight, hearing Nell's voice behind him echoing the sentiment.

The door closed and he turned to Nell, watching as the smile slipped from her face. That capable, no-nonsense expression didn't fail to send a tingle down his spine, even if he was far too tired to make the best of whatever conflict was brewing.

'So, Jacob wanders at night?' She walked next to him back across the courtyard.

'Yes. I'd appreciate it if you didn't say anything about it.'

He couldn't see the flash of her eyes in the darkness, but imagined it there. 'This place is full of secrets, isn't it? How long do you think you can cover this up?'

'I don't need very long. Before I went into hospital, I was talking to Celeste about getting a carer for him at night so that she could get some sleep. I contacted her after I was taken ill and she said that things were okay and she was managing on her own.' He turned the corners of his mouth down. Clearly things hadn't been okay, and Celeste had just not wanted him to worry.

'Celeste's his daughter?'

'Yes. Jacob came to work here at the palace when he was sixteen, it's the only home he knows. My father's always said that he and Celeste have a place here for as long as they want.'

'So why all the secrecy?' Nell frowned, clearly bothered by it.

'When he heard that Jacob had been wandering at night, my father went to see Celeste and mentioned to her that a nursing home might be the right place for Jacob, and offered to pay the bills. Celeste took that as a royal command...'

'But he was really just trying to help.' Nell gave Hugo's father the benefit of the doubt. Maybe Hugo should, too.

'I'm sure he was. But Celeste doesn't think it's the right thing for Jacob and neither do I. Like I said, this is his only home and he'd be even more disorientated than he is now in a new place.'

'Okay. Let me get this clear.' Nell stopped suddenly in the middle of the courtyard, and Hugo felt the hairs on the back of his neck stand up. They were in full view of the palace, and he didn't take anonymity for granted the way that Nell obviously did. He saw a light flip on, and then back off again. Probably nothing.

'Your father thinks that the best place for Jacob is a nursing home, and you think it's best for him to stay here.' Hugo dragged his attention back to what Nell was saying. 'So instead of talking to him about it, you're going to get a night carer in, see if that works and then tell your father about it.'

When she put it like that it didn't sound the best way of doing things. But then Nell didn't know his father. 'Yes. That's essentially it.'

She held up her hands in a gesture of resignation. 'Okay. You have an agency in mind, where you can get this carer?'

'Yes...' Hugo had wondered how he was going to

break the news to her that tomorrow he'd be busy making those arrangements.

'Right. Give the details to me. I can do an assessment of Jacob and talk to Celeste about what she thinks is best in the morning, and we'll get things moving. If we can get someone in for tomorrow night, then Celeste can get some sleep and think better about her long-term options.'

Her tone brooked no argument, which was generally like a red rag to a bull where Hugo was concerned. But Nell was right. And although he'd only known Nell for a matter of hours, he trusted her. She'd take good care of his old friend.

'Thank you. I'd appreciate that.' He started to walk towards the back door of the palace, where they'd be out of sight of anyone who happened to be traversing one of the rear corridors.

'That, of course, is dependent on your not taking advantage of my being busy elsewhere to do something you shouldn't.' Nell caught up with him.

'Of course.' He opened the door for her and she walked through.

'I'd feel happier if you said it.'

He could see her face now, shining in the dim light of the corridor. A little humour mixed with the kind of determined compassion that he reckoned must make her a very good doctor.

'My mother's intending to cheer me up over lunch tomorrow. You can hand her the keys to the ball and chain if you want.' Nell raised her eyebrows and he sighed. 'If you'd be good enough to see Jacob in the morning, you have my word of honour that I'll rest.'

A stab of guilt accompanied the thought that he'd been a little hard on Nell. For the last two weeks, he'd gritted his teeth and submitted as gracefully as he could to the authority of his doctors and nurses and the limitations his own labouring heart had put on him. Yesterday morning, when he'd arrived back at the palace, he'd resolved to leave all that behind. He had to get back to normal as quickly as possible if he was to achieve the goals he'd set himself.

None of that had anything to do with Nell, though. She had a job to do, and when she smiled at him, everything else seemed to retreat back into obscurity.

'Thank you.' She gave him a *now we're getting somewhere* smile. Maybe they were.

CHAPTER FOUR

HUGO LOOKED RESTED and relaxed. Like someone who had spent yesterday in his apartment doing nothing in particular while Nell assessed Jacob and made all the arrangements for a carer to come and help Celeste. Which was just as Nell wanted things to be.

But today was sure to bring new challenges. Hugo had wished her a good morning, and Nell had responded by picking up his car keys and giving him a lecture about staying within his limits. Ted, his bodyguard, had flashed her a quiet smile and got into the front passenger seat of Hugo's car, while she fiddled with the driver's seat, pulling it forward.

'Remember to drive on the left.' Hugo's quiet voice had sounded from the back of the car, and she'd ignored him, slipping off her high sandals and starting the car.

Ted directed her through the morning traffic to a large house, set back from the road and gleaming white in the sunshine. She'd followed the ushers' signals and parked the car between two others, which would have cost her the approximate value of her own flat had she been careless enough to scratch them.

'You look very nice.' Hugo bent towards her as they walked together to the circle of awnings laid out behind the house.

'Thank you.' On the basis that she couldn't compete with anyone here, Nell had decided on a plain dress with no jewellery. That seemed to fit well enough with Hugo's approach, a grey suit with a white open-necked shirt. No signet rings, no diamond tie pins. He really didn't need that kind of thing, he was striking enough already, tall and tanned, with an easy manner that marked him out as someone who would always be acceptable in any social setting.

She was introduced to their hosts, and Hugo kissed the lady of the house on both cheeks. A drink appeared magically in her hand, and Hugo shook his head when he was offered one, obviously feeling that the juggling of drinks and handshakes would be too much for him to accomplish while taking care not to compromise his recent surgery.

'Prince Hugo!' A middle-aged woman marched up to him, and Hugo responded to her greeting with a hug. His face and body showed no signs of the pain that it would have caused him, but Nell knew that his left shoulder must be pulling at the movement. Then someone brushed against his left side, and this time he jumped imperceptibly.

This was no good. Nell carefully slipped in between Hugo and the people on his left side, curling her fingers around his left elbow. She knew exactly which angle his arm would be the most comfortable at, and she made a show of seeming to hang on to his arm, while making sure that it stayed immobile.

A nod, and a smile in her direction. And then, just for her, a mouthed *Thank you*.

'Nell's here from London. A friend of the family.'

The woman who was with him smiled. 'What do you do?'

'She's in between jobs.' Hugo had obviously decided to speak for her, in case she got their story wrong. 'Taking a well-earned holiday.'

'I'm particularly interested in the work of Hugo's charity.' Nell decided that taking Hugo's arm could be forgiven, under the circumstances. Acting like a glove puppet couldn't.

'Ah…' The woman nodded. 'Well, he's risen to the occasion yet again. Are you going to make a bid for him in the charity auction? So generous of His Highness to donate a trip with him on the royal yacht as one of the lots!'

Nell gave her brightest smile. 'He didn't tell me that there was going to be an auction after lunch until yesterday evening. It would be rude of me not to put in a bid for him.'

The woman laughed, and Hugo smiled graciously. Nell gritted her teeth.

A seemingly endless amount of small talk was cut short by their hostess, and everyone found their places at the tables. Champagne was served, and Nell leaned towards Hugo.

'What happens if the amount I have to bid for you goes over the limit you can donate to the project?' She hadn't thought that would be possible last night, but now she wasn't so sure.

'You over-estimate my desirability.'

'Not really. These women all look as if they can spend a large amount on just a whim.'

'I'm suitably crushed.' He put his hand to his heart, not looking even slightly crushed. 'Remember this was your idea.'

'Were there any other options?'

'There's always another option. But your solution was the best.'

'So you weren't looking forward to entertaining some lucky girl on the royal yacht for the weekend?'

'What makes you think it's going to be a woman? The trip on the yacht is the point of it all—a family with children would enjoy it, too.'

Right. Nell would bet a pound to a penny that there wouldn't be any men bidding for this particular lot. But telling him that would only add to the chorus of appreciation that surrounded him, and Hugo already seemed to be under the misapprehension that he could get away with almost anything.

'What's Montarino doing with a royal yacht, anyway? It's completely landlocked.' Nell hadn't thought to ask last night.

'It's moored in France. Montarino has an ancient treaty that allows us safe harbour there. Unfortunately the treaty doesn't mention bills for the marina, so we have to pay those.'

'So you were intending a three-hour drive to the coast, in addition to swimming and sailing and...whatever else you do on a royal yacht? You do know that you're not supposed to be driving for six weeks.' Last night this plan had seemed a matter of pretending to pay a nominal amount to get Hugo out of a fix. Now the stakes were looking a lot higher.

'I won't be doing any of that, though, will I? Not if you win the bidding.'

The look that she gave him made the large hole that this afternoon was going to make in his bank balance seem more than worth it. Hugo could have changed his contribution to this afternoon's auction to something that demanded a little less activity on his part, but the programmes were all printed, and somehow the idea of having Nell stake her claim on him publicly had made him lose touch with the more sensible options.

Lunch was eaten, and a frisson of excitement ran around the tables when the auctioneer climbed up onto his podium. Nell's hand moved to her bidding card.

'You're sure there's no limit?' She smiled suddenly and the sunlight playing on the ornamental fountains, on each side of the group of tables, dimmed in comparison.

'I trust you.'

'That might just be your first mistake…'

She was enjoying this. It occurred to Hugo that Nell might be about to teach him a lesson, and the idea didn't fill him with as much dismay as it should have done.

Premier tickets for a football match, courtesy of Montarino's one and only football team. Seats for a hotly anticipated rock concert. Some silver jewellery, from an up-and-coming new designer, who had cannily decided that it would do her no harm to have her work seen by the guests here today, was snapped up after a bidding war.

'That's a beautiful piece. It'll really suit her.' Nell was completely caught up in the proceedings, leaning over to murmur the words in his ear as she watched the winner talking excitedly to her husband.

'Would you like one? I can have another made…' The abstract curves of the silver necklace would actually suit Nell far better than they would Monique LaTour.

'Don't you dare!' She turned to him, a look of reprimand on her face. 'For what she's just paid, she deserves to have something unique.'

Hugo thought about telling her that Jacques LaTour was a multimillionaire and that Monique had enough jewellery to fill a wardrobe. But he doubted the information would make any difference to Nell, and anyway her attention was back on the auctioneer's podium now.

'Now, a special treat, ladies and gentlemen. Hosted by His Royal Highness Crown Prince Hugo DeLeon, a weekend trip on Montarino's royal yacht.' A gratifying buzz of excitement ran around the tables. Hugo smiled in acknowledgement, and then glanced at Nell. Her champagne flute was in her hand, and she'd just downed the whole glass in one.

Ted would have to drive back, or they could call for the chauffeur. Nell was sure that something could be arranged, and she needed something to calm her nerves. Bubbles hit the back of her throat and she almost choked.

This was it. She was about to spend an unknown sum of Hugo's money just to have his company for the weekend and ensure he didn't over-exert himself, something she was being paid to do anyway. The doctor's common room would have had a field day with that, but suddenly she couldn't have cared less. This felt like an adventure, one that might wipe away all the slights that had hurt her so over the last year.

As soon as the bidding started, three women held their cards up. The auctioneer managed to come to a decision over who had bid first, and as his finger moved briskly to and fro the price began to rocket upwards.

Nell saw Hugo's head turn towards her, and caught a glimpse of his worried expression. Then she held up her card, waving it to attract the auctioneer's attention.

'Two thousand from the lady on the right…' Nell felt slightly giddy at the idea that she was spending this much money.

There were many more rounds of determined bidding and one by one her rivals shook their heads. When the auctioneer rapped his hammer, an unexpected burst of exhilaration made Nell catch her breath. A few people looked round at her as Hugo leaned towards her, smiling.

'I thought for a moment you were going to let me down. Do I detect an element of risk-taking in your approach?'

Let him think that. If this was an exercise in each keeping the other off-balance, it couldn't do any harm. Nell gave him a smile and reached for her glass, which had been refilled at some point during the bidding. Clearly one of the attentive waiters had thought she might need it.

Hugo's lot was the highlight of the afternoon. There were a couple more, to round things off, and then the ring of a silver spoon against a crystal glass called for quiet as their hostess got to her feet. She thanked everyone for being there, and introduced Hugo.

He got to his feet, smiling, and Nell saw more than one person smile back. Taking a sheet of paper from his pocket, Hugo scanned it and then tore it in two.

'Ladies and gentlemen, I had a speech prepared, but I find that there's little more I can do to add to this afternoon.'

Nell took a sip of her champagne. This sounded pretty much par for the course. This afternoon was all about delighting in smoke and mirrors, not getting to grips with the serious issues.

'First, I'd like to thank Yvette, our hostess today…' He paused as a round of applause ran around the tables, and Yvette nodded a smiling acknowledgement. 'Second, I'd like to thank you all for your generosity.'

He paused. Five seconds' silence, which was enough to catch everyone's attention. Hugo's timing was impressive.

'You all deserve to know what that generosity means. Under your placemats, you'll find a leaflet…' He held up a glossy trifold, and Nell looked under her place mat and found one just like it. 'We're not in the business of bricks and mortar, or of reputation, although we're rightly proud of Montarino Hospital's record of excellence. We deal in people.'

Hugo's gaze dropped suddenly to the trifold in his hand. Almost against her own will, Nell opened her own copy of the leaflet, seeking out the photograph inside that he seemed to be studying. A little girl in a pink dress, cuddling a battered teddy bear. She was smiling, reaching for someone or something behind the camera.

'I'll let these photographs tell you how much your kindness means. Thank you, ladies and gentlemen.'

Hugo sat down abruptly, seeming to be almost overcome by emotion. Applause ran around the tables, followed by a buzz of conversation, which seemed to be centred around the leaflets in everyone's hands.

It was a great speech. Short and to the point, and tugging nicely at the heartstrings. Nell had noticed that he'd put the paper he'd torn in half safely back into his pocket. She wondered vaguely if there had ever been anything written on it.

It didn't matter. If Nell had seen the reality of heart disease, and knew that it wasn't all smiles and teddy bears, that wasn't what today was about. She'd lost count of the amount of money that had been raised, and it seemed the auction was just the tip of the iceberg.

A middle-aged man in a silk suit had approached their table, and Hugo had turned in his seat to talk to him. He pressed a folded cheque into Hugo's hand.

'Thank you, Henri. We'll use this well.'

The woman standing next to Henri spoke. 'Next time, I insist on being the hostess, Your Highness.'

Hugo hesitated. 'You're too kind, Justine. Think about it…'

'No, I don't need to think about it. I've thought about things for too long and it's about time I did something.'

'I'll have Nathalie contact you, then. She'll talk through all the options with you.'

'I think I have an idea that will be perfect.' Justine brushed off any other options with a wave of her hand.

Henri smiled suddenly. 'We must be going. It seems that my wife has a plan that needs my attention.'

'You shouldn't work so hard, Hugo…' Justine frowned suddenly at Hugo and caught Nell's eye, reverting to English. 'Take him away, my dear. He is neglecting his responsibilities to you.'

Nell smiled, not knowing quite what to say, and Hugo bade the couple goodbye. When he turned, his face was suddenly ashen and drawn. This was the first time that Nell had seen Hugo betray any weakness, and he was obviously tired.

Nell leaned towards him, speaking quietly. 'We're going. Now.' She injected as little room for argument into her tone as possible.

'I think you're right… Yvette will wrap things up.'

Nell glanced across at their hostess and saw that she too was accepting cheques, tucking them into a small designer clutch bag that lay on the table in front of her, which seemed to contain little else.

'I'll…go and make our excuses…' Maybe something would spring to mind on the way over to Yvette's table.

'That's all right. I said we might have to leave a little early.' Hugo reached for an auction programme, taking a pen from his pocket and scribbling something on it, then beckoning to one of the waiters. The note was carried to Yvette, who read it and smiled over at them.

Whatever he'd written, it seemed that their hostess was now happy to allow them to leave with as little fuss as possible. Nell bit back the thought that they should never have been here in the first place. Perhaps this would serve as a lesson to Hugo, and he'd respect his own limitations a little better from now on.

He swayed a little as he stood, wincing in pain. Nell hung on to his right arm, supporting him as well as she could and ignoring the glances and smiles from the people who crossed their path on the way back into the house. If they wanted to jump to the conclusion that there was something between her and Hugo, then let them. She imagined that she was just the latest in a very long list, which had the virtue of rendering her unremarkable.

Ted appeared out of nowhere, and Nell breathed a sigh of relief. 'Would you be able to bring the car round, please, Ted?'

'Yes, Doctor.' Ted flashed her a conspiratorial smile and hurried away.

Hugo almost stumbled at the bottom of the steps at the front of the house, and when she put her arm around him to steady him, Nell found herself almost in an embrace.

'I'm sorry.' He made to pull away, but Nell held him tight.

'That's all right. We'll just get home, shall we?' She could see his car now, moving towards them, Ted at the wheel.

He nodded, and she felt his arm curl around her shoulders. 'Yes. Thank you.'

CHAPTER FIVE

HUGO HADN'T QUITE been feeling fine, but he had at least been in charge of himself. And then suddenly he'd hit a wall. The one that he told his own patients about and reassured them wouldn't be there for ever.

If Nell hadn't been there, he wasn't sure how he would have managed. But she had, and he'd felt her next to him, holding on tight as he'd walked what had seemed like a marathon to get to the car. Somehow, her scent had strengthened him and stopped him from just sitting down right where he was and not getting back up again.

Ted had helped him back up to his apartment and Nell had fussed around, taking off his shoes and jacket and loosening the collar of his shirt, then making him lie down on the bed. He'd protested and she'd ignored him, and then suddenly a wave of fatigue had pulled him into sleep.

When he woke, the room was in semi-darkness. He could make Nell out, sitting by the window, reading in the last rays of the sun.

'Do you want me to say it?' When he spoke, it felt as if his mouth was full of cotton wool.

She looked up from her book. 'You can if it makes you feel any better.'

It did. Hugo pulled the bedspread down from his chest,

sitting up slowly. 'I overdid it today. I felt okay and I was sure I could manage it but…I couldn't.'

She smiled and suddenly overdoing things and proving Nell right didn't seem such a bad thing after all.

'You know, of course, that this happens. After the shock of being taken ill and then going through a surgical procedure.'

'Yes. Primitive instincts. We fight to survive, and then, when the danger's passed…'

She nodded quietly. 'And now you have to come to terms with it all.'

'What if I don't want to?' The words escaped Hugo's lips before he had a chance to stop them.

Nell shrugged. 'That's just too bad. You can command it to go away all you like, but it's not going to listen.'

Maybe. But if he couldn't rule his own feelings, then he could return the favour and not listen to them. Not let anyone know his weakness.

He swung his legs slowly from the bed. They seemed strong again. All he'd needed had been to sleep for a while.

'You're getting up?' Nell was looking around the room as if she was trying to figure something out.

'I feel much better now. What are you looking for?'

'Your wardrobe.'

'Through there.' Hugo nodded towards the door to one side of the bed, and Nell got to her feet. It seemed she'd decided to lay out a change of clothes for him. The idea that she might stay and help him into them didn't seem quite as deflating as it had when the nurses at the hospital had done it.

'Oh…' She'd opened the door and put her head inside the dressing room. 'Sure you have enough to wear here?'

'I go out a lot.' Hugo chuckled. 'Casual is on the left, at the end.'

She disappeared inside the dressing room, and Hugo heard her opening drawers and closing them again. Then Nell reappeared, with a dark polo shirt and a pair of pale chinos over her arm. 'Will this do?'

'That's great, thanks.'

'Bathroom?'

'Through there.' Hugo indicated another door, staying put. He wondered how far Nell intended to go with this.

She disappeared into the bathroom and he heard the sound of water running. Then she popped her head around the doorway. 'I'll take a look at your chest and then leave you to it.'

Hugo heaved himself from the bed and walked into the bathroom. She'd moved the shower chair in front of the basin, and motioned him to sit down.

'How do you really feel?' She bent down, unbuttoning his shirt.

He wanted to say that he felt fine. Hugo *meant* to say that he felt fine, but in her quiet, fragrant presence he couldn't.

'As if I've been hit by a truck.'

Hugo closed his eyes, feeling her slip his shirt from his shoulders and carefully threading it off his left arm. Coming to terms with the piece of cutting-edge technology that was now implanted in his chest was the easy part. It was the thought that he was somehow flawed that he just couldn't shake.

More flawed. He hadn't been perfect to start with.

He felt her carefully remove the dressing over the surgical incision. It was hard not to shiver at the touch of Nell's cool fingers.

'It's looking good. A little bruising, still, but there's no infection and it's starting to heal. It's a nice job.'

Nice job. She'd said that before and he'd wanted to turn his back on her and tell her that he didn't need that doctor-to-doctor reassurance. If he'd still had a gaping wound on his chest, a scar that would never heal, it might reflect the way he felt a little better.

'Take a look.'

Hugo had purposely *not* removed the dressings to see what was underneath. But it seemed that parts of his body answered to her and not him, and his eyes flipped open. The first thing he saw was her face, composed in a reassuring smile, and even though he knew that smile was probably something she wore for all her patients it did its job. He smiled back.

'What do you think?' She stepped out of the way, and Hugo found his gaze on the mirror above the basin.

'It's…' Hugo tried for a shrug, and felt his left shoulder pull. 'You're right. It's a neat job.'

She nodded and turned to the basin, leaving him alone for a moment with his own reflection. Hugo didn't like the way it made him feel and he concentrated on watching Nell instead.

Her hands were gentle but capable as they dipped a flannel into the basin, twisting it to wring out the excess water. In his experience, that was only a short step away from tender. She laid the flannel over his shoulder, her entire concentration on what she was doing. It felt warm and comforting.

'That feels good. Thank you.'

She nodded, removing the flannel and dipping it back into the water. Wiping it across his skin, careful not to allow any drops of water near the wound. He'd seen this so many times before at the hospital, and had always felt that this was one thing that no amount of technology or learning could replace. When the nurses washed a patient, there was a tenderness about it that spoke of the kind of care that only human beings could give one another.

And now he felt it. The warm touch of water against his skin calmed Hugo, and the suspicion that everything would be all right floated into his consciousness, with all the reassurance of a forgotten friend.

She leaned towards him, rubbing the flannel across his back. Stopping to rinse and then repeat, her movements slow and thoughtful, like those of a craftsman plying his trade. Hugo closed his eyes, not ready to let go of this feeling just yet.

She finished with the flannel and gently patted his skin dry with a towel. Then he felt her fingers on the top of his left arm, gently massaging. He knew what Nell was doing. He wasn't supposed to lift his left arm above shoulder level for six weeks, and it was common to get a frozen shoulder during that time. It was just straightforward care, but it felt like so much more.

'Would you like help to shave?' He opened his eyes and saw that Nell was now opening one of the sterile dressings from the box that lay on top of the bathroom cabinet.

It had been a while since he'd let a woman shave him, and then it had been purely for pleasure. Anna had done it, but since then he hadn't let a woman get to know him that well. Hugo regarded the shaving cream on the shelf above the mirror and decided against it.

'Thanks, but I'll go with the designer stubble.'

Nell gave him a half smile. 'It suits you.'

It was the one thing she'd said that betrayed some kind of emotion locked behind the caring, and it sent tingles down Hugo's spine. Nell checked that the new dressing over his wound was firmly anchored, and then turned abruptly, leaving him alone in the bathroom.

If it worked, then it worked. Society lunches and bidding for a weekend in the presence of a prince wasn't a strategy that Nell had been called on to adopt before, and neither was washing a patient. But talking to someone, learning what made them tick and suggesting ways of coping was. And if the sudden closeness with Hugo had left her wanting to just touch his skin, simply for the pleasure of feeling it under her fingertips, then that could be ignored in the face of a greater good. Her job here was not really to look after him in a medical sense but to get behind his suave, charming exterior, and find out what drove him so relentlessly that he was willing to risk his health for it.

Nell rang down to the palace kitchen, wondering if anyone was there at this time in the evening, and found that not only was the phone answered immediately but there was a choice of menu. She ordered a salad, on the basis that it was probably the least trouble to make.

Apart from raiding the fridge, of course. Nell had suspected that the top-of-the-range fridge in Hugo's kitchen was pretty much for show, and when she'd opened it, she'd found a selection of juices and other drinks. Nothing that involved any culinary activity other than pouring. She could have made him a milkshake, but that was about all, and a decent meal would help him recover.

The formal dining room in his apartment seemed a little too much like keeping up appearances, when that was exactly what she was trying to encourage Hugo not to do. A small table on a sheltered balcony was better, and she opened the French doors at the far end of the kitchen and arranged two chairs beside it. It would have made an excellent place to cook and enjoy food, and it was a pity that Hugo's gleaming kitchen didn't look as if it saw too many serious attempts at cooking. Nell wondered what he would say if she expressed the intention of baking a cake, and smiled to herself. Maybe she'd try it, just to see the look of bewilderment on his face.

Their meal arrived, and Nell directed the young man who carried a tray loaded with two plates and various sauces and condiments through to the balcony. He looked a little put out that she'd laid the table herself, and adjusted the position of the knives and forks carefully.

She called Hugo, and he appeared from the bedroom, looking relaxed and rested. When Nell had chosen his clothes, she been considering comfort, and hadn't spared a thought for how well they might fit or how her eye was drawn along the hard lines of his body. Chest. Left arm. It was permissible to allow her gaze to linger there, on the grounds that she was checking up on him. The strong curve of his shoulder, the golden skin of his arm, which dimpled over bone and muscle, were both visual pleasures that Nell could pretend not to have seen.

'Thank you. This is nice.' Hugo pulled one of the seats away from the table, waiting until Nell sat down before he took his own place. Even now, he couldn't quite let go and let her look after him.

'I just made a call down to the kitchen. Is someone always there?'

'No, not always. My parents are hosting a dinner party tonight.' He smiled at her, and in the muted lights that shone around the perimeter of the patio his face seemed stronger. More angular and far more determined, if that was even possible.

'So calling down for a midnight snack is usually out

of the question.' Nell picked up her fork, stabbing at her food.

'Yes.' He grinned. 'If I want a midnight snack, I usually have to walk all the way down there and make it myself. Life at the palace can be unexpectedly hard at times.'

Nell couldn't help smiling in response to the quiet joke. Hugo knew exactly how lucky he was. Maybe not exactly, he probably hadn't ever battled his way around the supermarket on a Saturday morning, but he understood that he was privileged.

'If we'd been at my place, this might have been cornflakes. With chocolate milk if you were lucky.'

'You think I haven't done that?' Hugo looked slightly hurt. 'I trained as a doctor, too. You're not the only one who's eaten cornflakes with chocolate milk at three in the morning then fallen asleep on the sofa.'

Probably a nicely upholstered sofa, and not too much like the lumpy one that had been in Nell's shared digs, when she had been training. She wondered if Hugo's memories of medical school were quite as good as hers were.

'Where did you stay in London?' Holland Park, perhaps. Somewhere near the embassy.

'Shepherd's Bush. We had a flat over a pizza place for a while, and it always smelled of cooked cheese. Then we moved to Tottenham. That was a great flat, in a high-rise. You could see right across London.'

Perhaps his experience had been a little more like Nell's than she'd thought. 'It must have been a bit of a culture shock for you.'

He laid down his fork. 'People are people. That's what every doctor learns, isn't it?' He said the words as if he was explaining a simple concept that Nell had somehow failed to understand.

'Yes, of course. But some people find things easier than others.' Waiting lists. Doctors who had enough time to see to the physical needs of their patients but not always the opportunity to talk for as long as was needed… The list could go on.

'You met Justine and Henri earlier today. What did you think, that they were a couple of privileged people who like a nice lunch?'

'They…' Yes, that was exactly what Nell had thought. 'They were very generous.'

'Yes, they always are. They lost their son to heart disease when he was only two years old. Justine became very depressed and it was years before she would even talk about him. Holding a lunch event is a massive step for her. It's not all about the money. Yvette lost her father to heart disease when she was fifteen.'

Nell felt herself flush. 'I'm sorry. I did think less of what they were doing because they're rich, and that was wrong of me.'

Hugo shook his head. 'You're not entirely wrong. A lot of the people who were at the lunch today were there because they wanted to be seen in the right places. But many of them have a real and personal commitment to what we're trying to do.'

'The little girl in the leaflet. She's really a heart patient?' Nell had had her doubts, wondering if the leaflet was principally an exercise in PR. It was important now, to know whether she'd been wrong.

'Yes, she is. One of my patients, in fact. She had her ninth operation a few days ago. She wanted to help me build her new clinic.'

Nell laughed. '*Her* new clinic.'

'Yes, it's hers. She might let a few other patients in if she likes them. No boys. And she wants it to be completely pink, like a giant marshmallow.' He was smiling now.

'Sounds like my kind of hospital.'

'So what *are* you doing here?' He asked the question quietly. 'You don't strike me as the kind of person whose ambitions lie in the direction of keeping errant princes in check.'

Hugo had a way of dropping the charm and cutting right to the chase. It was uncomfortable. 'I'm…in between jobs at the moment.'

'I saw your curriculum vitae. Someone with your talents isn't usually in between jobs unless she wants to be.'

He'd seen what the employment agency hadn't, and there was no explaining it away with clichés. Nell wanted to tell him the whole truth, but that probably wouldn't be all that wise.

'My last job was challenging, both professionally and personally. I want to spend six months looking around for another that will…'

'Just be challenging professionally?'

Nell caught her breath. How did he know so much about human nature, when he seemed so protected from it? 'Something like that.'

'So you thought that one patient might be a bit of a holiday.' He was taking her apart, piece by piece, and Nell felt powerless to stop him. 'But I imagine you're someone who gets a little bored on holiday.'

She could feel her cheeks heating up. She wasn't going to give Hugo the satisfaction of admitting that he was absolutely right. He held her gaze for a moment longer, and then leaned slowly back in his chair. Maybe he'd already seen what he wanted to see, and her reply was unnecessary.

'Then maybe I should consider diversionary tactics. To keep you from feeling that you're wasting your time here.'

He reached for the bottle of water on the table, and Nell took it from him. 'How can I be wasting my time when there are bottles to be opened?'

If he could hide his innermost feelings under a layer of charm, then so could she.

CHAPTER SIX

THE SUMMONS HAD arrived first thing the following morning, and Nell had followed the messenger to the King's study. Despite the early hour, he was already working at his desk. He had offered her a cup of coffee and then pushed the morning paper towards her.

The King hadn't expressed the horror that Nell had felt when she'd looked at the pictures on the front page. It was just one of those things, an innocent action could be misinterpreted under the glare of scrutiny that the royal family were subjected to. But he had taken issue with a number of other things.

Nell had felt her heart close. Unable to look at him, she'd given no reason as to why she and Hugo had been seen at the back entrance to the palace at one in the morning. How could she? She'd promised to keep silent about the business with Jacob and Celeste until Hugo had had a chance to approach his father.

The King moved on to why exactly she'd been seen bidding for Hugo's company at the auction yesterday. This time Nell did have an answer, even if it wasn't a very good one.

'It was my idea. I thought that...well, it's too much for him to be hosting a weekend like that so soon after the operation. And Hugo wouldn't back out.'

'And you didn't consider how it might look?' The King's tone wasn't unkind, but it was very firm. He tapped the paper with one finger. 'My real concern though, is that it's clear to me that this photograph does not show an embrace, as the papers seem to believe, it shows Hugo leaning on you. Your one responsibility was to ensure that he didn't take on too much, and damage his health.'

Nell nodded her assent, her hands clasped tightly in her lap. How could she object to the King's request that she submit a written account of Hugo's activities and medical condition every day, when she had already failed so spectacularly? And how could she complain when he hinted that unless things changed, he would be finding another doctor for Hugo.

She was trembling by the time the King dismissed her. Hurrying back to her apartment, Nell blinked back the tears. They were her own business, fit only to be seen by the four walls of her sumptuous bedroom.

Nell sat down on the bed, gulping for breath. She was just being stupid. The King had every right to ask questions, and if he'd been unfair, it was because he didn't know about Jacob's visit to Hugo's apartment, and Nell hadn't enlightened him. This *wasn't* a re-run of all that had happened in her last job.

All the same, it had a similar sting to it. Nell had rejected Martin's advances, and he'd taken advantage of his position as her boss to deliver payback. She'd come to dread seeing him on the ward, because there had always been some barb or put-down. And she'd learned to sit in silence when he'd called her to his office, because replying to his catalogue of her faults and flaws had only made things worse. She'd thought his anger might subside over time, but if there was one thing that Martin knew how to do, it was hang on to a grudge.

This wasn't the same. In some ways it was worse, though. The King had been painstakingly correct, and in his own way he'd been almost kind, but his concerns were justified. She couldn't put his criticism down to spite, the way she'd been able to with Martin. And she'd hardly looked back when she'd left the hospital, but leaving Hugo…already he was quite a different proposition.

There was nothing else for it. She had to get the crying over and done with, pull herself together, and do better.

She was expecting the knock on the connecting door between their apartments. Hugo would have finished his breakfast, and would be ready for another battle of wills over whether he was well enough to do whatever he pleased. Nell had dried her tears and was ready for him.

She opened the door, trying not to look at him, just in case he happened to be smiling. Hugo's smile was his most effective weapon.

'You did too much yesterday. You need to rest today.'

He raised one eyebrow. 'All right. Now that you've got that off your chest, would you like to join me for coffee?'

Maybe she could have waited a little longer than two seconds to say it. 'Yes. Thank you.'

'You've had breakfast?' He moved away from the door, leaving Nell to follow him into his sitting room.

'No, I…' Saying that she felt sick with apprehension wasn't the best way of appearing strong. 'Coffee's fine.'

'Right.' The tray was standing ready on the table, and he filled two cups, watching silently as Nell added milk to hers. 'What's the matter?'

'Nothing.' She smiled breezily at him, and he frowned.

'So I'm going to have to make a guess, am I?'

Nell puffed out a breath. Maybe she should tell him, he'd probably hear about it anyway. And perhaps Hugo would respect his father's wishes better than he did her advice.

'The King called me to see him this morning. He's not happy.'

'He isn't happy about a lot of things. Ignore him.'

'I can't ignore him. Apart from the fact that he happens to be the King, he's also my employer.'

'I'm Crown Prince, don't I get a say?' Hugo grinned, and Nell ignored the temptation to forgive him anything and everything.

'This isn't a game, Hugo. If you want to bait your father then go right ahead and do it, but don't put your own health at risk just because you won't admit that he's right.' Nell pressed her lips together. She could have put that more tactfully, but right now she wasn't in the mood to do so.

He was suddenly solemn, his gaze searching her face. Nell felt herself redden, the tears that she'd only just managed to control pricking at the corners of her eyes.

'What did my father say to you?'

'He heard about you being up so late the other night. There was nothing I could say to him in response, without telling him about Jacob.'

'So you took the blame yourself.' His frown grew deeper.

'What else could I do? He heard about my bidding at the auction as well. And there are photographs of me supporting you to the car in this morning's papers.'

'He can't hold you responsible for that.' Hugo pressed his lips together, obviously aware of the conclusion that the papers had drawn.

'He doesn't. But he holds me responsible for the fact

that you're doing too much. He says that things have to change and that from now on I have to submit a daily report to him.'

'Nell, I'm sorry. I'll make it right.' His jaw hardened into a determined line.

'No, you won't. You can't. But if you're reckoning on carrying on like this, then tell me now, because I'd rather leave than be fired.'

'No one's going to fire you, Nell.'

She shook her head silently. Hugo didn't understand, he'd never been squeezed out of a job or bullied by a boss. He was the golden boy, who everyone wanted.

Even Nell wanted him. Despite all her exasperation, she'd started to enjoy their battles, almost to look forward to them. And in doing so, she'd forgotten the reason why she was here.

'There's a meeting arranged for this afternoon at my charity's offices. It's only going to be for an hour, the construction company is going to update us on how things are going. If I asked everyone to come here instead, I'd find it less taxing.'

Hugo's tone was almost contrite. When Nell looked up at him, there was a trace of concern on his face.

This was a start. 'That sounds like a good idea, Hugo.'

Shame was something that Hugo usually tried to avoid. If he worked hard, and met the standards that he set, he generally found that he could live with himself. But now he felt thoroughly ashamed.

Being ill had made him crazy. It had stripped away the feeling that he was in charge of his life, and he was struggling to find the man he'd once thought himself to be. But in trying to pretend that it hadn't happened, he'd hurt Nell, and that was unforgiveable.

He knew exactly where his parents would be during the week, they were creatures of habit. As he expected, he found them sitting at the twin desks, placed back to back to allow murmured conversation and smiles while they completed their correspondence for the day.

'Mother…' He smiled, and his mother rose for a hug, made awkward by his lame shoulder.

'Hugo, darling. How do you feel today?'

'Much better, thank you.' Hugo's relationship with his mother was an effortless synergy of respect for her position and warmth. The one with his father involved rather more effort. 'I'd like to speak with Father.'

His mother sat firmly back down, waving her hand towards his father, who had looked up from the papers in front of him. Her smile told Hugo that she knew exactly what all this was about, and she wasn't going to give either of them the chance to argue in private.

'Go ahead, darling. He's right here, in case you didn't notice.'

Right. Hugo turned to his father, and found himself locked in the familiar combative stare that was their usual greeting to each other. He sat down, knowing that it probably wouldn't defuse the situation. Pacing up and down wasn't going to help much if he wanted to imply that he was taking things easy.

'It's not Nell's fault, Father.'

His father turned the corners of his mouth down. 'I'm inclined to agree with you. It is, however, Dr Maitland's responsibility to make sure that you rest.'

'And she's doing that.'

'I disagree, Hugo.'

The silence between them wasn't broken by his mother's voice. Usually her intervention avoided conflict between father and son, neatly suggesting a solution that everyone could live with. But this time there was just a silence.

'My behaviour isn't her fault. Nell's a good doctor, and…she's exactly what I need at the moment. In the future, I'll follow her instructions.' This was a climb-down of gargantuan proportions. But Hugo had seen humiliation and rejection in Nell's face this morning, and they haunted him.

'So things are going to change, are they?'

'They will. Don't punish her in order to get to me.'

His father leaned back in his chair. 'You've seen the papers this morning?'

'It'll blow over. How many other young women have been photographed in my company in the last year?'

'Goodness only knows. I don't know where you get the time,' his mother interjected suddenly, and both men turned on her, frowning. 'It's just an observation, darling. It would make things a great deal easier if you decided that your health wasn't such a secret.'

'I want it to remain private.'

That was one of the few things that Hugo and his father had agreed on lately, even if it was for different reasons. His father had always drawn a line between his family's personal lives and their public duties, and that had allowed Hugo to grow up outside the glare of publicity. For Hugo, it was more a matter of not wanting to be seen as irrevocably flawed.

King Ferdinand nodded. 'You know I have no argument with you there, Hugo. But you have a duty…'

Hugo nodded impatiently. 'I know what my duty is. To be strong enough to serve the people.'

His father nodded. 'I assume from your presence that Dr Maitland *wants* to stay.'

'I have no idea. But *she* gets that choice.' Hugo felt his

heart quicken and he ignored it. He would have to stop gauging everything by the beat of his own heart.

'There's only one person who can make sure that Dr Maitland keeps her job. That's you, Hugo.'

Hugo got to his feet, making an effort to swallow his anger as he turned to his mother. He bade her goodbye, omitting the same gesture towards his father, before turning and walking out of the room.

Hugo had been oddly compliant all day. It was as if he'd suddenly come to his senses, or at least decided that it was more politic to appear to have done so. He'd spent the morning reading through the reports from the construction company, and the meeting was a short one. Nell had been able to relax a little and take an interest in the plans for the clinic. She could see why the project excited Hugo, and why he was willing to give up almost anything to see it come to fruition.

'What did Celeste say?' Nell had gone to speak to Celeste alone, while he stayed in his apartment.

'She said that last night, when the carer was with them, she got the first good night's sleep she's had in months.'

Hugo nodded. 'That's something. It's working, then?'

'It's early days. But, yes, I think it'll work very well.'

'Good. I'll speak to my father…'

'Not yet, Hugo. I… I've already taken the blame for the other night, and I'm still in one piece. Let's wait a week and make sure that the arrangement's working for Celeste first. Then you can speak to him.'

'He should know now. That you weren't to blame for that either.'

Either? 'You've already spoken to him, haven't you?'

'Yes. I told him that yesterday was entirely my fault and that it wouldn't happen again.'

The sudden feeling of warmth in Nell's chest caught her by surprise. Nell didn't dare wonder if she was really that important to Hugo, that he'd comply with his father's wishes for her sake.

'You didn't need to do that… But thank you.'

'My pleasure. There are always plenty of other options when it comes to defying my father. You'd be surprised at the scope his position affords.'

He was making light of it, but the look in his eyes said something different. That she could trust him and he'd be there for her.

The sound of the bell, at the front door of the apartment broke the silence. It couldn't have come at a more inopportune time, and Nell willed him to ignore it, but he didn't, rising from his seat. Maybe he was glad of the interruption.

She heard voices in the hallway, and jumped to her feet when Queen Margaux entered the room. She was more casually dressed than in the pictures Nell had seen on the Internet, wearing a pair of tan trousers and a matching shirt, but she was still immaculate.

'I'm glad to see that you're here, resting, Hugo.' Queen Margaux bestowed a smile on Nell that seemed to indicate she thought Nell had something to do with that. 'Penelope. I'm very glad to meet you.'

'She prefers Nell, Mother. Nell, meet my mother.'

Nell wondered whether she should curtsey, and remembered she didn't know how. Queen Margaux held her hand out and gave Nell's a surprisingly firm shake.

'I'm very glad to meet you, Your Majesty.' Nell hoped that was something close to the right form of address.

'Margaux, please.' The Queen dropped a slim file that she was carrying onto the table and sat down.

'Would you like some tea…?' Hugo's mother was obviously here to speak to him, and it was a good means of escape. It might be rude not to address the Queen by name, as she'd instructed, but Nell couldn't quite bring herself to call her Margaux.

'Thank you, but no. I've come to speak with both you and Hugo.'

'What about? If you're here to try and talk some sense into me, Nell already has that covered.'

Margaux flashed another smile at Nell. 'Then I won't go to the trouble. Anyway, this is far more pressing. I think you should both read this.'

She slipped two sheets of paper from the folder, holding them out. Hugo took them both and started to read.

'What is it?' Nell reached across, and he threw the papers down on the coffee table.

'It's rubbish. Outrageous… You don't need to see it.'

'If it's rubbish then it can't do any harm to look.' She picked up one of the sheets.

'You have to understand, Nell, that the papers will pay for stories, and people will make things up. It gives them a misplaced sense of importance.'

'All right. Let me read it, will you?' How bad could it be? Nell turned her attention to the paper and started to read. She immediately recognised the name involved. Three sentences in, she realised that it was worse than she could have possibly imagined.

'This is a request for comment.' Queen Margaux's voice broke through her horror. 'It's from one of the more responsible papers, and if I speak to the editor I can refute the claims and at least delay publication. If they can't get any corroboration then it'll stop it completely. But if the man making these claims goes somewhere else, that might not be so easy.'

'Is…there any indication he might?' Nell felt her cheeks redden at the thought.

'I had my secretary examine his social media pages, and it seems he's already shared the story that was in the paper this morning and made a few comments. Nothing of any substance, they're more of the *I know something you don't* variety, but it shows an intention. But you know this man, Nell, he's your ex-boss. What do you think?'

'I don't think he's going to give up.' Nell shook her head miserably. The one thing that neither Hugo nor Queen Margaux had asked yet was whether the allegations were true. It didn't appear that Hugo was going to, and his mother was clearly taking his lead.

She took a deep breath. 'I want to say…that it's not true. I didn't make any passes at my former boss, he was the one who propositioned me. And I'd never offer sexual favours in return for covering up my mistakes. The previous Head of Department knew me well, I worked for him for three years, ask him—'

'Don't, Nell.' Hugo interrupted her. 'You shouldn't have to defend yourself.'

'I want to. It's the truth.'

Queen Margaux turned to Nell, laying her hand on hers. 'I didn't doubt it, Nell. But thank you for clarifying things. This is a situation where we must be clear and direct in all of our dealings.'

'Yes, we can be clear and direct in completely refuting these allegations.' Hugo's brow was still dark.

'Of course, Hugo. But if you'd read the whole piece, you'd see that there's a reference at the end to a romantic entanglement between the two of *you*. If Nell's real relationship with you were known, then it might well defuse the situation.'

Nell shook her head. 'I'm sorry but…no. I'm Hugo's

doctor, and it's my responsibility to make sure that if he wants to keep the details of his medical condition private, that's what happens. I can't allow it.'

'Nell, that's up to me.'

If Hugo was about to make an abrupt about-turn on the question of his own privacy, Nell wasn't. 'You've already expressed your wishes, Hugo, and while I don't altogether agree with them, it's my duty to uphold them. I won't have it.'

'But—'

'There's always the Royal Agreement,' Queen Margaux cut her son short.

'That doesn't apply here, Mother.'

'It might. Since the papers seem already to be jumping to conclusions…' Queen Margaux reached for the folder, taking off her reading glasses. 'I'll leave you both to consider the options. But in the meantime, Nell, I want you to understand that you have my full support in this. We will do whatever it takes.'

Nell stammered her thanks, and Hugo rose to see his mother out. While they were gone, Nell concentrated on keeping breathing. Because it appeared that was about the only thing that Martin could never take away from her.

CHAPTER SEVEN

'I HAVE TO EXPLAIN.' Hugo had returned to the sitting room and was regarding her silently.

'No, you don't. I don't make a habit of explaining what the papers say about me...' He broke off, seeing the tears that ran down Nell's cheeks.

'I do...really.'

Hugo came to sit next to her on the sofa. 'If you *want* to tell me something about this, then I'll listen. All you *need* to say is that you want this stopped.'

'It's good of you to say that. I want to tell you.'

'Okay.' He was sitting close, but still not touching her. The temptation to ask for Hugo's comfort was almost too much to bear, but Nell couldn't do that. Not until he knew all the facts, and he believed her.

'When I was a student, Martin was a visiting lecturer. He was brilliant, he has a very fine mind.'

'Okay. I'll take your word for that.' Hugo didn't look very convinced.

'I went to speak to him after the lecture and he asked me for coffee. One thing led to another...' She glanced at Hugo and he nodded. 'I was dazzled. He was older than me, of course, and very handsome. He knew about loads of things that I didn't. Introduced me to a lot of new experiences.'

She expected Hugo to nod and understand. Instead, he rolled his eyes. 'I've seen that type. No feeling of self-worth, so he has to pick on someone in a subordinate position to impress.'

His words chipped away at the dream. The feeling that Martin had been all-knowing and that it was she who'd done the wrong thing. She *had* done the wrong thing, and maybe Hugo would think a little differently when she told him.

'He was based in Newcastle, and he came down to London every couple of weeks. I saw him then and I used to count the days…' Nell shook her head at her own stupidity. 'It went on for six months and then he told me that he was married. He said it didn't matter, that he and his wife had some kind of understanding, but I broke it off immediately.'

Nell looked into Hugo's face, wondering if he could understand. 'I thought he loved me. And even though I loved him, I couldn't do it.'

'Sounds as if you were the one who was the adult in that relationship.'

He thought so? Nell had always considered herself as the silly little girl, blinded by love. Slowly Martin was developing feet of clay.

'I don't know about that. But I stuck to it, even though he contacted me a few times afterwards. Finally he left me alone, and I reckoned that it was just a life lesson and I should chalk it up to experience. I graduated, and got a job at the hospital and things were going well. Then the head of department retired, and…' Nell felt herself start to shake. That feeling, that she couldn't escape and that her mistakes would always come back to bite her, had turned out to be about the only true thing in this whole business.

'And when the new head of department showed up, it was him?' Hugo was filling in the gaps now. 'Any reasonable man would have spoken to you privately, admitted that he'd acted very badly and hoped that you might find the goodness of heart to draw a line under the whole business. I'm guessing he didn't do that.'

Nell shook her head, finding herself smiling grimly. 'No, he didn't. There were a couple of weeks of extreme awkwardness, and then I couldn't bear it any longer. I spoke to him and apologised…'

'*You* apologised?'

'It seemed reasonable. I had been one very willing half of the affair.'

Hugo let out a short, sharp breath. 'Are you saying it was all your fault?'

'No, I…' In truth, after the last six months, Nell had been reduced to not knowing what was and wasn't her fault.

'We talked a bit and I thought we'd come to an understanding, but the following day he said he wanted to talk a bit more and could he meet me for coffee that evening.'

Nell still didn't understand how she could have been so stupid. But when she looked at Hugo, there was no sign of reproach in his face. Perhaps he was just waiting to hear everything before he made a final decision on that.

'I went, and he started telling me about how his marriage had broken up because his wife had found out about our affair. I don't know if that was true, but I was horrified. Then he said that the least I could do was give things another try. I said I didn't think that was a good idea and he offered to take me home. He walked me to my door and then he told me he knew I wanted it really and pushed me inside. Somehow I fought him off…' The words had tumbled out, and Nell was suddenly breathless with shame.

'I hope you hurt him.'

'I… Actually, I had a copy of *Welman's Clinical Procedures* in my bag. I managed to get free of him and hit him with it.'

Hugo grinned suddenly. 'Good girl. The full edition, I hope.'

'Stop it, it was the abbreviated edition. It still hurt him, though. He made some comment about my obviously not being in the mood tonight and left.' She was shaking. Not so much as she had that night, but she still couldn't stop.

'Did you report him?'

'No, I…' Nell shrugged miserably. 'I was the one who asked him in. And it wasn't as if we'd just met, we had a history.'

'No means no. Nothing trumps that.'

It seemed so simple when he said it like that. Hugo's sense of honour made it simple. She wished that he'd reach out to her, but knew that he wouldn't. As far as Hugo was concerned, one touch now would make him as bad as Martin and she wished she could find a way to tell him that wasn't true.

She had to finish the story. Get this over with as quickly as possible. If she could do it without breaking down, that would be a bonus. Nell squeezed her hands together in her lap, feeling her nails dig deep.

'He…tried it on a few times after that. I rejected him and started to make sure we were never alone together. Then one day he called me into his office, and went through a very comprehensive list of all the things I was doing wrong. All from a clinical point of view, there was nothing personal.'

'Payback time?'

'Yes. That went on for a few months, and I started to wonder whether there really was something wrong with the way I did my job. Then he blocked my promotion.'

'On what grounds?'

'He said I was an excellent doctor but that realising my full potential meant staying in my current post a little while longer.' If Martin had criticised her performance, Nell could have fought it. But this had been impossible.

Hugo thought for a moment. 'He's done this before.'

'What? What makes you say that?'

'He always put you in a position where you felt you were in the wrong, he was married, then his divorce was because of his relationship with you. And he was always in a position of power, your teacher, and then your boss. I'm not saying he engineered all that, but he exploited it. He's an abuser, and he probably didn't just do it to you.'

'But…' Nell had thought she was alone. The idea that Martin might have done this to other women was horrific, but it did make her feel as if it wasn't so much her fault. 'Maybe you're right.'

Hugo got to his feet, starting to pace. 'We're going to stop him, Nell. My mother will refute the allegations and we'll release the details of my operation. That'll keep the papers busy for a while, and in the meantime we'll find a way to shut him up permanently.'

'No, Hugo. I know that's not what you want, and this is *my* battle. You shouldn't be dragged into it…' The heat in her heart, at the idea that Hugo was prepared to defend her, was burning too hot and threatened to consume her. He couldn't be allowed to do this.

'It's what works.' Hugo had obviously made his mind up about this.

'No, it won't work. Martin will just find another way

to make these allegations…' If Hugo was so determined to make this sacrifice, Nell needed to find a different approach.

'If he does, then we're in a good place to refute them.' A grim smile quirked his lips. 'You underestimate the power of good contacts.'

'It's not about having power, Hugo, it's about what's right and wrong.'

He shook his head slowly. 'It's about picking a side, Nell. Allow me to pick mine.'

She stared at him. Hugo was on her side. The thought that he would protect her washed every objection she had to the idea away for a moment. He took full advantage of that moment, turning and walking out of the apartment.

It was done. Hugo had spent an hour with his mother and the palace press advisor, and a call had been made to the managing editor who had contacted them for comment. The promise of a press release within the next twenty-four hours had oiled the wheels, and Martin Jarman's story was suddenly dead in the water.

'I'm proud of you.' His mother had stopped him as he'd gone to leave, murmuring the words.

'It's a matter of principle.' Hugo had been telling himself that. He was doing this for everyone caught in this kind of situation, and not just for Nell. Not because he wanted to hold her close and keep her safe.

'Yes, it is. Anyone in your position has a duty to defend someone who…' His mother paused. 'You are quite sure that Nell is innocent of these allegations, aren't you?'

'Of course I am. I'm perfectly capable of noticing when a woman is trying to seduce me. Nell's a good doctor, and she acts appropriately.' His thoughts might touch on the delights of the inappropriate from time to time, but that was his business.

His mother nodded. 'Your judgement is always sound, Hugo. And whatever you say, I'm still proud of you.'

That was something. Hugo reflected that he wasn't all that proud of himself at the moment. The idea of having his most humiliating secret blazoned across the front pages of the papers was something he was trying not to think about. While he was still obviously recovering, people might look at him with sympathy. But sooner or later, they'd come around to seeing him as a hypocrite. How could he advocate for a heart clinic when he—a doctor no less—hadn't seen the signs of his own heart issues?

That was just something he'd have to put up with. Maybe Nell was right. Maybe an admission that he'd made the mistakes that he was urging others not to make would emphasise his human side. But right now Hugo's human side was cowering somewhere in a corner, and it felt far more comfortable to pretend that there was nothing wrong with him.

He walked back to his apartment, pondering the question. Things had to change—there would be no more battles of will with Nell, no more creative solutions. Even though the alternative sounded dull in the extreme, their relationship from now on would be entirely professional. If he were blameless, that would give Nell the opportunity to prove herself blameless, too.

Nell had waited for Hugo in his apartment. She'd made a cup of coffee, leaving it untouched while it had gone cold, and then emptied and washed the cup. Then she'd retreated to her own apartment, leaving the connecting door wide open, and switched the television on, hoping it might drown out the clamour of her own thoughts.

This was wrong. She'd been unable to say conclusively that she was entirely blameless in the business with Martin, but Hugo was different. No part of this was his fault, and yet in defending her he was the one who would feel humiliated.

Nell thought for a long time. When he came back, she'd put a stop to all this.

She heard the front door of his apartment close quietly, and hurried to the connecting door, stopping short at the threshold. When Hugo walked into the sitting room and saw her, he smiled.

Nell imagined that this was the smile he reserved for the most formal of occasions, devoid of any emotion other than the one he wanted to project. 'It's done, Nell. I'm going to…get some rest now.'

Normally she would have applauded the sentiment. Now, keeping Hugo awake until he'd told her exactly what had been done, and how it could be unravelled, seemed far more important.

'What's done?'

'Our press officer has stopped the story. We've promised a press release on another matter during the next twenty-four hours.'

Things had moved faster than Nell had thought they might. But it still wasn't irrevocable. 'We can undo it then. I can find another way.'

He paused for a moment, just long enough for Nell to wonder whether he was reconsidering. But he was just choosing his words. 'As I said, Nell, this is my battle too, and you don't have to find another way.'

This was too much. Standing, yards away from each other, trading appropriate conversation. They should be past this by now, but somehow Martin had inveigled his way in between them, and Hugo no longer felt comfortable with the relationship they'd started to build.

It was obvious that Hugo wasn't going to ask her into the apartment, but she couldn't say what she wanted to say from the doorway. Nell took the initiative, walking over to the sofa and sitting down.

'What did your mother mean by the Royal Agreement?' Hugo had dismissed the idea quickly, but maybe this was an alternative.

He shook his head. 'It doesn't apply here. When my parents were first married, they were keen to bring up their family without the constant press attention that my father had when he was young. They made an agreement with the press, and until I was eighteen, the only news stories published about me were official press releases from the palace.'

Nell frowned. That didn't seem to apply, but Queen Margaux had obviously thought it did. 'There's something you're not telling me.'

'My mother showed a great deal of foresight in negotiating certain extensions to that protection. My grandmother was allowed privacy during her final illness. And an engaged couple can expect the same privacy.'

An engaged couple?

What was the Queen thinking? Nell swallowed down her own objections to the plan, because it was something, anything, that would provide an alternative to what Hugo was planning to do now.

'So your mother's suggesting that…if we got engaged then there would be no difficulty in stopping this and other stories about us.'

'Yes, that's exactly what she's suggesting. But I won't put you through that…'

'You make it sound as if you're committing me to the palace dungeons. It's not as bad as that, is it?'

The flicker of a smile crossed his face. 'No. Not quite.'

'Well, can't we consider it? I don't have to actually marry you, do I?'

'No, you don't. We'd have to make a show of being together for a few months, but after that we'd break the engagement off quietly… But look, Nell, your career is at stake here. There's no point in saving it, only to have it ruined by being engaged to me.'

He had a point. Leaving her job and getting engaged to a prince might not look great on her CV, but it wouldn't be as disastrous as having Martin's story in the papers, and it wouldn't hurt Hugo as much as his current plan would.

'I don't have to spend all my time just pretending to be engaged, do I? I could do some work with your charity, if that's okay with you.' He shook his head and Nell puffed out a breath. 'This isn't doing my ego any good, Hugo. Is it that bad to have to pretend you're engaged to me?'

He laughed suddenly, all his reserve dissolving in his smile. 'I'd be very honoured to be engaged to you. Even if I was just pretending.'

'Then stop this nonsense about having to release the private details about your surgery. It's not necessary, we can find another way.'

Nell had started to boss him around again and his resolve to keep her at a distance had melted. But at least she didn't seem so beaten and dejected as she had when she'd recounted how she'd been treated by her last boss.

He'd begged her not to go through with this, and had told her that it was no sacrifice to allow his own medical details to be released to the papers instead, but she'd seen straight through him. So he'd called his mother, hoping that she might regret her mention of the Agreement, and talk some sense into Nell.

Fat chance. His mother had made a comment to the effect that she wished he'd make up his mind, and had gone on to embrace the idea. She appeared at the door of his apartment within minutes, and it seemed that she saw eye to eye with Nell over this compromise solution.

The details were worked out over a glass of wine. Nell insisted on giving up her employment, which seemed only sensible to Hugo. He insisted on her being involved with his work for the clinic as much as possible, so she'd at least have something to show on her CV later on. Even if that hadn't worked out so well with his real engagement to Anna, it seemed that it could at least be accomplished in the context of a fake engagement.

'This will work well, Hugo. You're obviously already good friends.' His mother's habit of not leaving before she'd made some private comment about the situation could be trying, even if it did usually elicit her real thoughts.

'We're...' Hugo shrugged. '*Good friends* doesn't happen in the space of four days.' Even if it did feel as if he'd known Nell for much, much longer than that.

'You want to protect her. She wants to protect you.' His mother turned on her heel, leaving Hugo to think about the implications of her statement.

He was too tired to think about anything very much. Nell cleared away the glasses, and thankfully skipped any examination of the healing incision on his chest. Perhaps she knew that the intimacy would be too much for him to bear tonight, when he was fighting to remain detached, now that they were alone.

He slept deeply, not remembering his dreams. In the

morning, a package sent from his mother set the seal on the agreement that had been made last night, which was itself the stuff of crazy dreams.

He tore open the package and, looking inside, found a short handwritten note from his mother.

Treat her with the greatest respect, Hugo.

Right. He didn't need to be told. He reached into the envelope again, finding a bundle of tissue paper wrappings and another note. He looked at both briefly, before putting them in his pocket.

CHAPTER EIGHT

NELL HEARD THE knock on the connecting door between their apartments, just as she was putting the last of her clothes into her suitcase. When she answered it, Hugo was looking rested, which was a great deal more than she felt.

'You've had breakfast?' He grinned at her and she felt her stomach lurch. That would have been entirely appropriate if the engagement they were planning wasn't all a fabrication.

'No, I've been packing my bags. I was going to get that done first.' They'd agreed last night that it would be best for them both to leave the palace. Hugo's house in the country had no staff and was small enough that Ted and his team could maintain close security.

'Would you like to join me, then?'

She nodded. 'Yes. That would be nice, thank you. Just toast...'

An awkward silence accompanied the arrival of the tray from the kitchen, and Hugo motioned towards the balcony table, indicating that the tray should be set down there. Nell sat down, reaching for the coffee and pouring it.

'You still want to go through with it?' He didn't need to say what.

'Yes, I do. I'm even more sure this morning.'

He nodded, taking a tissue paper package from his pocket, undoing it and laying four rings in a line on the table. 'These are my mother's. She'd like you to have something nice to wear.'

In Nell's book, *something nice* didn't necessarily have to cost as much as the average house. 'They're real?'

'Yes, of course they are.'

'I can't wear any of these, Hugo, they must be worth… I can't even think how much they might be worth. Can't I wear a fake?'

He shook his head. 'No fakes, Nell, please. This engagement may not be real, but I want to say to you now that my promise to protect you is. I believe that you want to protect me, too.'

It wasn't the proposal that every girl dreamed of. But suddenly Nell felt that there was something real about this. Hugo was a better man than she'd thought he was, not just a spoiled prince who could destroy her if he wanted, the way that Martin had tried to.

'I will protect you, Hugo. I promise you that.'

He nodded. 'Then I'd like it if you would choose whichever ring you like the best.'

That sounded like something she could put her heart into. She looked at the rings, not daring to touch any of them. One had a massive ruby at the centre, and it looked far too opulent. The other three were all large diamonds.

'That one…' She pointed awkwardly to a diamond solitaire that flashed blue-white in the morning sunshine.

'That's a very good choice. It's the best stone.'

Nell went to protest that the only thing she'd seen was that it was the smallest stone, and he silenced her with a laugh. Picking up the ring, he held it out towards her. 'Will you wear it now?'

'The announcement hasn't gone out yet. I shouldn't wear it until tomorrow, should I?'

'We've made a promise. I'd like it if you would wear the ring now, because that's what it is to us. You can wear it on your right hand until tomorrow.'

Still he wouldn't touch her. It was as if this new arrangement had blotted out any possibility of an innocent touch, and anything physical was now laden with some kind of meaning. Nell reached out, putting her hand in his.

'Then...would it be appropriate for you to put it on for me, please?'

'I think that would be entirely appropriate.' His voice sounded inappropriately husky, and Nell avoided his gaze. Looking into his eyes wasn't necessary.

She felt him slip the ring onto her finger, twisting it a quarter turn to get it past the knuckle. 'It looks nice.'

Nice was a bit of an understatement. It looked amazing, and far too good for Nell.

'It's beautiful. I'll take care of it and return it to your mother in good condition.'

He wrapped the remaining three rings in the crumpled tissue paper, and then put them back into his pocket, withdrawing a piece of folded notepaper. He handed it to Nell and got to his feet. 'I'll leave you to read that.'

Nell read the note. Queen Margaux would be most grateful if she could accept whichever ring she and Hugo chose, as a gift. It would be a symbol of gratitude and of enduring friendship between them.

Nell put the letter down on the table. It was too generous, and she'd have to ask Hugo if there was some way she could express her gratitude to his mother, whilst refusing the gift. She had the feeling that wearing it after the arrangement was over wasn't going to be a particularly comfortable option.

But while she had it on her finger, she'd do her best for Hugo. She'd take care of him, and help him raise the money he needed for the clinic. That was a promise.

Hugo was aware that this arrangement had to be treated with the utmost delicacy. He must show how much he valued Nell as a friend. Slipping into anything more would be horribly easy, and something that he had promised himself he wouldn't do.

All the same, their departure from the palace seemed like the start of something new and exciting. With the top of his convertible rolled back, and Nell at the wheel, it felt as if he was making an escape with a beautiful woman at his side. Who knew what might happen when they were finally alone, away from the bustle of the palace?

Ted's voice from the back seat jerked him back into reality. 'Left-hand side…'

Nell obligingly swerved to the left of the palace driveway, and came to a halt, waiting for the palace guard to open the gates.

'Thanks. I nearly forgot.'

She waved to the guard, the ring flashing bright on her finger. Then she turned out of the gates into the anonymity of the busy city on a warm summer's morning.

Their destination was only half an hour's drive away, which was about as far as anyone could go from the capital of Montarino and still remain within its borders. There was no suburban sprawl, just a sudden change from houses to open countryside. And the countryside in Montarino *was* beautiful.

Hugo directed Nell through rolling hills and around

the edge of a wide, blue lake. Another mile and they reached a high wall, built of weathered bricks, driving the length of it until they reached an archway, protected by a heavy wooden gate.

The gate swung open and Ted got out of the car, speaking briefly to the man who had opened it. He waved the car through, and Nell drew up outside the house. It was small by the standards of the palace, built in stone and shaded by trees. A small garden at the side was overlooked by arches, the weathered stone now housing state-of-the-art single sheets of glass.

'It's lovely. This has been in your family for a long time?'

Hugo quirked his lips downwards, shaking his head. 'No. I bought this place with my doctor's salary. Since I have almost everything else provided for me, it seemed like a good idea to have my own bolthole.'

Nell wondered what it must be like to have to take your own independence that seriously. She took it for granted that everything she had was the product of her own work, but Hugo seemed to need to make a distinction between what he'd been given and what he'd earned.

Inside, the house was light, airy and simple. None of the folderols of the palace, just plain furniture in neutral colours, exposed wooden beams and a utilitarian kitchen. Upstairs, there were three bedrooms, one of which was clearly Hugo's. He directed her towards a second, which commanded stunning views of the hills stretching off into the distance.

'I suppose I'll have to keep away from the windows when the news breaks.' Nell wasn't exactly sure what to expect.

'Not really. Because of the Agreement, the paparazzi won't be able to sell any pictures they take, so it's not worth their time. And Ted's team will make sure that no one disturbs us here.'

'You usually have this much security?' Nell had counted four men outside.

'No, it's usually just Ted, and he generally doesn't have all that much to do. He stays in the guest house at the back.'

Nell walked over to the window, looking out. Beyond the garden, and shielded by trees, was a small cottage, nestling against the perimeter wall.

'It all sounds reassuringly normal.'

'Not quite. But we try to make it so.' Hugo was watching her speculatively. 'There is one thing I want to ask you.'

'What's that?'

'Nadine, the little girl in the brochure, wearing a pink dress. I told you she'd had an operation recently…'

'Yes, I remember.'

'Dr Bertrand, the head of department, is the only one there who knows that I've been ill—everyone else thinks I'm taking a leave of absence for fundraising. He told me that he'd have me removed by security if I went in to see Nadine earlier than seven days after my own operation.'

Nell grinned. 'He sounds like a good man…'

'He's a very good man. You'd like him.'

'And since this is the seventh day, you'd like to go and see Nadine.'

'It would be best to go today. After the news of our engagement breaks, my turning up on the ward might cause a bit of a stir.'

'Where is the hospital?'

'On this side of the city, so it'll only take twenty minutes to get there. I'm feeling better every day, and I'd really like to see Nadine.'

If this was normal, then it was a new normal that Nell hadn't experienced before. Hugo asking her whether or not he could do something. 'It sounds like a lovely idea. May I come along? I'd like to see the hospital.'

Hugo smiled. As time went on that smile was surfacing more and more, and it convinced Nell that everything was going to be all right. 'I was hoping you might. You'll have to drive.'

CHAPTER NINE

No one seemed to notice Hugo's presence as they walked through the reception area at the hospital. He exchanged smiles with the receptionist at the main desk, who waved him through in much the same way as she probably would have done with anyone else she knew. Here, Hugo appeared to shed the mantle of royalty.

He led her through a maze of corridors, mysterious box in hand, and a high-speed lift took them to the seventh floor. Hugo punched a code into a keypad at the entrance to one of the wards and the doors opened automatically, allowing them through.

This might just be Hugo's greatest test. Fooling a group of luncheon diners that there was nothing wrong with him was one thing. Fooling a senior nurse was quite another, and just such a person had looked up from her conversation at the nurses' station and was heading straight towards them.

'Hugo. This is unexpected.' The woman spoke in French.

'I've come to see Nadine. This is Dr Nell Maitland, she's a cardiac specialist from London. Nell, this is Senior Nurse Adele LeFevre.'

Adele smiled, holding out her hand to Nell and switching to English. 'I'm pleased to meet you. I hope you see much that you like here.'

'I have already. This is a beautiful hospital.'

'Thank you. We are proud of it. When the new cardiac unit is built, we will be even more proud.' Adele's English was almost perfect, like that of so many of the people of Montarino. And she was keeping hold of Nell's hand, staring at her.

'I called Dr Bertrand to let him know we were coming. Is he free?' Clearly Hugo didn't expect everyone here to drop what they were doing as soon as he arrived.

'He is finishing his rounds.' Adele barely seemed to glance at Hugo. 'Ten minutes.'

'Very well. May I show Nell around, and then go to see Nadine?' He had the grace to ask that as well.

'Of course.' Adele flashed Nell a smile and turned back towards the nurses' station.

They walked through the cardiac unit, and Hugo showed her the light-filled wards, exchanging greetings with some of the nurses as they went. There were treatment rooms and a small sitting room with a dining room to one side for ambulatory patients. Everything was gleaming and state of the art, but Nell could see that the unit was working at its full capacity, with no empty beds in any of the wards.

'Why is everyone staring at me?' Nell whispered to Hugo as he punched a number code into a keypad next to the door at the far end of the ward.

'This is the first time I've ever brought a friend here.' He turned to her, looking a little sheepish.

So this was a first taste of the interest that would be shown in her, then, after the press release went out. Nell had anticipated something of the kind, but she hadn't expected to feel so exposed, as if she wanted to cling to Hugo for shelter.

'I suppose…if they're staring at me, then at least they're not looking at you. A lot less chance of anyone noticing that you're still recovering from an operation.'

'There is that.' He leaned closer, his arm moving protectively around her but not touching her. 'There's still time to change your mind. The press release won't go out for another couple of hours.'

Maybe this was why he'd wanted her here with him. To give her one last chance to back out of the engagement.

'I'm not changing my mind, Hugo. I've got the ring now.' She'd be wearing it on her left hand and not her right tomorrow. But today it meant the same as it would tomorrow, a symbol of their agreement to protect each other.

'Thank you for wearing it…' He reached out, as if to take her hand, and Nell heard a stifled giggle coming from somewhere behind them. Two young nurses were at the other end of the corridor, staring at them. Adele bore down on them, shooing them back to work, and then shot a smile in Nell's direction.

Hugo ushered her through the door and one look told Nell that this was the children's ward. There was a riot of colour on the walls of the reception area and an open door revealed a play area, where young patients were being supervised by play leaders in bright tunics.

Hugo led Nell into a small ward, nodding a greeting to the nurse. Nell recognised the little girl who lay in one of the beds, as well as the teddy bear at her side.

'Hey, Nadine.' He dangled his fingers over the safety rail on the side of the bed, tapping the back of her hand, and she opened her eyes.

'Uncle Hugo.'

'I told you I'd come. I brought you something.' He opened the box he was carrying and drew out a beautiful silk flower, dangling it over the rail so that Nadine could see it.

'Thank you, Uncle Hugo.'

Nadine smiled, but didn't reach for the flower. Nell saw concern in Hugo's eyes and she knew what he was about to do next.

'Speak to Dr Bertrand,' she whispered in his ear and he ignored her.

'How do you feel, sweetie?' He reached forward to brush her forehead with his fingertips.

'I'm all right, Uncle Hugo.'

Hugo went to reach for the notes at the end of the bed, and Nell bowed to the inevitable and fetched them for him. 'I'm just reading about you.' He smiled at Nadine and she gave him a smile back.

He studied the notes carefully, and then checked the monitors by Nadine's bedside. From what Nell could see, everything was completely normal, and Nadine was just a little drowsy.

Hugo wasn't giving up, though. He reached for the sheet covering Nadine's body, pulling it back slightly to reveal her shoulders and a large plaster over the right side of her chest.

'No, Hugo. You are not to examine that child. You're on sick leave.' He'd probably survive, but goodness only knew what kind of medical liability issues it might raise.

'There's clearly something the matter with her.' He reached for a pair of surgical gloves from the dispenser on the wall, wincing slightly.

'Then we'll call for a doctor.' Nell beckoned to the nurse, asking her in French to fetch someone.

'I'm a doctor. Nadine is my patient.' She could hear

the pain in Hugo's hushed voice, and Nell wondered what she'd do in his shoes.

'All right. Out of the way, I'll do it.' She grabbed the surgical gloves, pulling the heavy ring from her finger and putting it into his hand. Nell wasn't entirely sure what kind of liability issues that might also raise, but at least she was officially fit and well. And the thought that Hugo knew Nadine, and his instinct told him there was something wrong, was nagging at her.

'Thank you.' His green eyes flashed with warmth, and he turned to Nadine. 'Sweetie, this is Dr Nell. She's my friend.'

He stepped back but Nell could feel his eyes on her as she carefully moved the sheet that covered Nadine's chest further down. Everything seemed fine. The dressings were clean and there was no blockage that Nell could see in the surgical drain. When she gently touched Nadine's skin, it was cool.

All the same, she took the thermometer from the cabinet by the bed, inserting it carefully into Nadine's ear. The little girl was watching her solemnly. Nell looked at both her hands, and even her feet, for some sign that something might be wrong.

'I don't know, Hugo. I can't find anything.'

'Okay. We should try Claude.' He nodded towards a teddy bear propped up at the side of the bed.

Nell picked up the teddy bear. 'Hey, Nadine. Is Claude all right?' She spoke slowly, in French.

Nadine shook her head.

'No? Will you tell me what's wrong with him? I'd really like to make him better.'

'He has a pain.'

It was too much for Hugo. He moved in close and Nell shooed him back, out of the way. She leaned over the bed, holding Claude where Nadine could reach him. 'Where does Claude have a pain, Nadine?'

'There.' Nadine traced her finger over Claude's chest. Out of the corner of her eye, Nell could see Hugo flipping through Nadine's notes again.

'She's been having pain relief regularly. Not as much as she might, and my guess is that she's been telling everyone that it doesn't hurt. Nadine will do that.'

'Don't the nurses know?'

'They should. But the nurse who usually looks after her is on holiday at the moment. I was supposed to be here.' Nell heard Hugo's voice crack suddenly.

There was no answer to that, other than to remind Hugo that he'd been under orders to stay away. Nell smiled at Nadine. 'Uncle Hugo's going to find someone to make Claude better.'

'Thank you, Dr Nell.' Nadine spoke slowly, her eyelids drooping. Nell arranged the sheet carefully back over her and stripped off her gloves. When she turned to follow Hugo, she found that he was already gone.

She caught up with him, deep in conversation with another doctor, an older man. This must be Dr Bertrand. Nell wondered whether Hugo was admitting that they'd carried out a brief examination of Nadine, and guessed he probably wasn't. Dr Bertrand was nodding, and he turned to walk quickly back to the ward with Hugo.

It was all worked out in the space of a couple of minutes. Dr Bertrand examined Nadine, listened to what she had to say about how Claude was feeling and spoke to one of the nurses, who hurried away.

Dr Bertrand gestured to Hugo, motioning him out of the ward. He clearly had more to discuss, but Hugo seemed reluctant to leave Nadine.

'I'll sit with her.' Nell plumped herself down on the

chair next to Nadine's bed, holding her hand over the guard rail and feeling the little girl squeeze her fingers. Hugo shot her a smile, and followed Dr Bertrand out of the ward.

By the time Dr Bertrand returned, a nurse had given Nadine the extra medication, and she seemed a little happier, declaring that Claude felt better now. He spoke briefly to Nadine and then pulled up a chair next to Nell.

'I gather that you too are a doctor.' Dr Bertrand spoke in studied, careful English.

'Yes, that's right. I'm sorry, I know that this is highly irregular…'

Dr Bertrand smiled. 'I have known Hugo for some years. His talent for being highly irregular, when circumstances require, is what helps make him one of my best doctors. This little one is feeling better now, and I have made sure that this will not happen again. Her nurse says that she was not in pain twenty minutes ago, on her last half-hourly check.'

'We just came at the wrong time, then.'

'No, it was quite the right time. If we can spare Nadine ten minutes of discomfort, then we are grateful. I have told Hugo that I cannot have him working while he is certified as sick.'

'How did he take that?'

'He has apologised and the matter is closed.' Dr Bertrand regarded Nell thoughtfully. 'He has many responsibilities, and is under a great deal of pressure. More than most men would be able to deal with.'

'Do you have any advice for me, Dr Bertrand?' Nell wanted to hear what this kindly, perceptive man had to say.

He leaned forward, as if he was about to impart some gem of wisdom. 'No. I do not.'

Nell had to think for a moment before she got the point. 'We all have to find our own way?'

'If anyone can, Hugo will.'

'Thank you.' Nell got to her feet, shaking his hand. 'May Hugo come to say goodbye to Nadine? He'll be no more than five minutes, I promise.'

'You will give him five, and he will take ten. And that is quite all right.' Dr Bertrand smiled at her.

One of the nurses directed Nell to Hugo's office and she found him sitting behind the desk, staring out of the window. She sat down and waited for him to say something.

'You don't need to tell me. I know I was wrong.' He didn't look at her.

'Yes, you were. For all the right reasons, though.'

'I know that Nadine's well cared for…' He swung his chair around to face her, and Nell saw that his face was full of anguish.

'But you can't help feeling that this is all your fault. For not being here.'

'I know it doesn't make much sense.'

'What happened, Hugo? When you were taken ill?'

'You know what happened. It's all in my notes.'

'I want to hear it from you.'

He frowned. 'You're psychoanalysing me?'

'No, I'm off duty, on account of an impending engagement.'

'Same as me, then. On account of not following my own advice.'

'So what happened?'

Hugo sighed. 'I knew my heart rate was lower than it should have been. And when I was in bed at night, I could…feel an irregular beat. I thought it might just be stress or overwork.'

'But it wasn't.'

'No. Surprisingly enough, despite being not only a doctor but also a prince, I couldn't just snap my fingers and tell myself to get better.' His voice was laden with heavy irony.

'And then you collapsed,' Nell prompted him for the next part of the story.

'Yes. Pretty much as detailed in my notes.' He shot her an exasperated look. 'Apparently my heart started beating again of its own accord, but when I was monitored overnight in the hospital, they found that it was beating too slowly and actually stopped every now and then.'

'How long for?'

'You know that, Nell. Up to three minutes. Which was almost enough to kill me if it wasn't corrected.'

'So they inserted a pacemaker. Which will help you live a completely normal life.'

'I don't *feel* normal, Nell.' He shook his head. 'It seems I'm not that good at coming to terms with my own flaws.'

'A pacemaker isn't a flaw, it's what makes you well.' So many pacemaker patients connected their device with the illness that had made it necessary. It was an obvious piece of logic, but it didn't help much when it came to accepting that their heart now needed a little help in order to function properly.

'I don't *feel* well. My shoulder aches still, I run into a brick wall whenever I try to do more than take life at a snail's pace… I can't even be at work, Nell. You see my desk? They've cleared it and given my cases to other doctors.'

'So you got sick. And you need a bit of time to get better. You're not superhuman and you're not perfect. Welcome to the world, Hugo. It's a place where pink marshmallow hospitals get built for little girls because only an imperfect world has the imagination to create that.'

Nell stopped, a little breathless. She wondered whether she might be accused of bullying a sick man, in a hospital of all places. You could probably get struck off for that kind of thing.

'You're sure about that?' He was looking at her solemnly.

'Yes, I'm sure. We're going to get the money you need.' Somehow, somewhere Nell had found a commitment to that.

He felt in his pocket, bringing out the ring. With everything else that had been going on, Nell had forgotten about it, and she was glad he hadn't lost it. She held her right hand out and he slipped it onto her finger.

'I feel… Sometimes I can't help listening to my heart, just to see if it's still beating. I'm not sure it's even possible, but I'd swear I feel the pacemaker kick in at times. It's as if my body isn't quite my own any more.'

He'd found a place where he could voice how he felt. There was still a journey ahead, but he'd found the starting point. 'That must be really hard for you. But in time, I promise you'll forget you even have it.'

Hugo nodded, slowly. 'I'm being an idiot, aren't I?'

'Yes, since you mention it.' Nell looked at her watch. 'You have five minutes to say goodbye to Nadine. Then you're coming with me.'

CHAPTER TEN

HUGO LAY ON his bed, staring at the ceiling. He had slept a little after their return from the hospital and then lain awake, thinking mostly about how Nell was both magnificent and unstoppable when she was angry.

He could hear her clattering around in the kitchen downstairs. Hugo got up, walking slowly into the en suite bathroom to splash his face with water. The scar on his chest was still there, but the stitches would be out soon. It seemed somehow to be fading already.

'I think I might cook this evening.' He made sure that he spoke while he was still a good twenty feet away from her so as not to make her jump. All the same, she did jump, turning around and flushing a little when she saw him.

'You can cook?' She smiled suddenly.

'Of course I can cook. I know how to deal with all the appliances in this house. Even the vacuum cleaner.'

'Well you're not dealing with that for a while, vacuuming requires too much reaching. Although it's something I'd really like to see as soon as you're well enough.'

Hugo chuckled. Everything was going to be just fine. 'I *can* cook, though. You can help if you like, and get things out of the cupboards.'

'What were you thinking of cooking?'

'I do a mean lasagne. I asked Ted to get the ingredients when he went shopping this morning.'

'Okay. I do a pretty mean lasagne myself, so let's see what yours is like.' She grinned as she threw down the challenge. 'Perhaps Ted can give us his opinion.'

'I'll give him a call when dinner's ready.' Hugo opened a drawer and took out an apron. A number of people had said he was a good cook, but no one had ever accused him of being a tidy one.

Nell walked across the kitchen, taking the apron from his hand and unfolding it. Then she reached up, putting it over his head.

'Thanks.' Hugo wasn't sure he could reach behind him to tie the apron, and he wondered whether Nell would do that for him as well. And whether she'd do it the way a fiancée would, reaching around from the front, or whether she'd prefer to do it from the back, the way a doctor might.

She reached around from the front. Somehow she managed to do it while hardly touching him, but she was so close that Hugo caught his breath.

'I was thinking…' She'd tied the bow in the apron strings but she didn't step back.

'What were you thinking?' he encouraged as she tailed off.

'That… Well, if I were called upon to kiss you, in light of our announcement…'

If she felt able to do that Hugo wouldn't object in the slightest. 'You're not going to be called upon to do anything you don't want to, just for the sake of appearances. We'll just do the same as we've been doing up till now.' He wasn't in the habit of pawing women in public anyway, and the thought that Nell might not welcome it made it a complete no-no.

'So no kissing?' It was extremely gratifying that Nell looked almost disappointed. Hugo supposed that a woman might close her eyes and kiss someone while overlooking their other physical flaws.

'I'd be extremely happy if you kissed me. And extremely unhappy if you felt in any way pressured to do so.'

'I don't.' There was a mischievous glint in her eyes, which made Hugo's heart beat faster. 'I just wouldn't like to do it for the first time in front of a crowd of people.'

Before Hugo could think of a suitable reply, she'd raised herself up on her toes, planting a soft kiss on the corner of his mouth. For a moment, she stared up at him and then lowered her gaze shyly.

He wanted so badly for her to do that again. It had been just a moment and it hadn't felt real, but it still felt special. 'May I...put my arm around you?' Hugo decided that asking first would be the best course of action.

'Yes. I'd like that.'

He put his right arm gently around her waist, resisting the temptation to pull her hard against his aching body. Then Nell reached up suddenly, putting her left arm around his right shoulder, her fingertips touching the back of his neck.

It was delicious. If she'd thrown all her clothes off it could hardly be any more arousing than this. He felt himself trembling at her touch, all the more powerful because she was touching so little of him.

He saw her pupils dilate suddenly, and that small reaction almost made him choke with desire. Nell kissed him again, this time on the centre of his mouth, lingering just long enough for him to return the kiss.

Neither of them needed to say anything. Nell had to know how much he liked this. And it was very clear that she was enjoying it, too. Too far gone to even worry about whether she might feel his arousal if she got any closer, he tightened his arm around her waist.

She melted against him, as if it were the most natural thing in the world. Chemistry wasn't going to be a problem. Not kissing her again was…

It happened again, almost of its own accord. One moment their lips were tantalisingly close and the next Hugo was kissing her, and Nell was kissing him back. Soft and slow, as if to imply that perhaps there was control over it.

He thought he felt her lose control, her fingers tightening suddenly into a fist against his chest. Her heart beat against his and… That sudden feeling, as if the pacemaker had just kicked in to accommodate the screaming urge to take this as far as it would go, and then further. It reminded him that he couldn't. Not yet, and very probably not ever.

Hugo drew back slowly, planting a last kiss on her waiting lips. 'This is a role I'm not going to have any trouble with at all.' This was special, even if it did promise nothing.

'Me neither. I think we're good with that part of it.' She gave him a luminous smile as Hugo released her from their embrace, and turned back to the kitchen counter. 'Now. How about something a little more practical? Let's see if you really *can* cook.'

It was as if Hugo had swept her up and they'd danced together through the last ten days. Nell had reorganised his diary, and although Hugo had put up a few token objections, they'd always come to an agreement. Even the round of golf was made easier for him by giving up his own opportunity to play in favour of teaching his new fiancée.

She'd stayed close to him in public, the obvious implication that they were in love disguising the fact that she kept to his left, always protecting his arm and shoulder. When she leaned across to whisper in his ear, the words she breathed were questions about how he felt, and his smiling answer was often accompanied by the brush of a kiss.

Hugo's manners were impeccable, always making sure she was seated before he was, his hand guiding her when she was faced with a crush of people and didn't quite know which way to turn. And they managed to waltz through seemingly difficult obstacles. When a particularly heavy door blocked their path, and Nell stepped forward to heave it open, a smile flickered on Hugo's face. He bowed to her, catching her hand up to kiss it, and Nell made a mock curtsey. It seemed like the relaxed playfulness of new lovers, and not a concerned doctor making sure that Hugo came to no harm.

The ring on her finger still felt odd, but Nell was getting used to it. She was getting used to always being watched. And she was beginning to understand how Hugo felt. Living his life, all the highs and lows of it, at the centre of everyone's attention must be hard.

And now there would be another test. A private dinner at the palace, attended by the royal family of Montarino and visiting French and German ambassadors. It was an important occasion, and Hugo was expected to be there, which meant that Nell was expected to be with him.

The morning dawned fresh and clear, and they were on the road as soon as Nell had gulped down a cup of coffee.

'I'm a bit worried about this dress…' Nell frowned as she drove out of the gates of the house.

'It's no big deal. My mother's got it in hand.'

'That's what I'm worried about.' The thought of being

closeted with the Queen and a personal stylist from the largest store in Montarino, who would be bringing a selection of suitable gowns for the evening, was frankly terrifying.

'They'll help you pick something nice. And my mother will have the jewellery to go with it, she's got something to go with everything.'

'I'm going to feel foolish, Hugo. I'm not used to wearing a lot of jewellery.'

'Fine. No big jewellery. Just tell them.' He grinned. 'Anything else you don't want?'

'No sequins. And no frills. Definitely no bows.'

'Sounds good to me. I doubt my mother will have frills or bows in mind either, she generally goes for a more classic look. You might have to mention your aversion to sequins, though. What about colour?'

Nell sighed. Hugo didn't sound as if he was taking this as seriously as she was. 'No pink. And definitely no yellow.'

'Right, then. You've practically picked your dress already.' He stretched his long legs into the footwell, obviously ready to move on and enjoy the drive.

Driving *did* calm Nell a little, but as soon as she reached the palace car park, her fears returned. Hugo seemed intent on hustling her through the corridors to his parents' apartment as quickly as possible.

The apartment was larger than his, and more lavish. His mother greeted them both with a kiss, and Hugo followed them through to her dressing room, sprawling onto one of the cream silk upholstered chairs.

'Hugo, darling. You have something to do…' Queen Margaux fixed him with a determined glare.

'Nothing that I can think of.'

'I'm sure you might think a little harder, then.' The

Queen took the words out of Nell's mouth, and Hugo ignored her.

A rail-thin, elegant woman appeared, a couple of assistants behind her wheeling a rack full of dresses. In any normal circumstances, she looked as if she might have chased Nell away from the confection of silks and satins that were far beyond her purse, but she greeted Nell obsequiously.

An analysis followed of Nell's colouring and figure, both of which were apparently perfect. Nell shifted awkwardly from one foot to the other, and out of the corner of her eye she caught Hugo's grin.

'I think it all goes without saying, *Madame*, that my fiancée is perfect in every way.' He got to his feet, advancing towards the rail, and Queen Margaux shrugged, dropping into a seat to watch. Clearly the preferred course of action when Hugo was in one of these moods was to wait a while, to let it all blow over.

'Of course, Your Highness.' *Madame* smiled beatifically at Nell.

'Let's have a look at these…' He was shuffling through the dresses. 'No…no…no… What about this one, Nell?' He held up a dark blue dress and then shook his head. 'No, it's got a bow at the back.'

'Detachable, of course, Prince Hugo.'

'Oh. What do you think, Nell?' He turned to Nell, suddenly still. Somewhere, deep in his eyes, she saw that maybe this wasn't going to be as excruciating as she'd thought.

'It's…very nice.'

'Watered silk, Miss Maitland.' *Madame*'s voice held a tang of disapproval. Clearly *very nice* wasn't the right reaction.

'Hmm.' Hugo peered at the bow at the back of the

dress and shrugged. 'Well, perhaps that can go on the "possible" pile.'

He looked around, obviously trying to decide where to put the dress, and *Madame* clicked her fingers. One of her assistants sprang to attention, wheeling an empty rail forward and taking the dress from Hugo.

'This one, Prince Hugo?' *Madame* tried to reassert herself, grabbing a fuchsia-pink sequined gown.

'My fiancée is a doctor, *Madame*, not the Christmas Fairy.'

'Hugo!' Queen Margaux had been watching quietly, but now murmured a reproach.

'Apologies, *Madame*. What do you think, Nell?'

'It's...not really my style.' Nell smiled apologetically at *Madame*, who pursed her lips. 'What about this one?'

'Very plain.' *Madame* took the dark green velvet dress from the rail. 'Of course, with Queen Margaux's emeralds, it would be most striking.' Nell's heart sank as *Madame* held the dress up against her.

Hugo shook his head. 'Better without. What is it you say, Mother, wear the dress and don't let the dress wear you?'

Queen Margaux stifled a laugh. 'Yes, exactly. When did you become so interested in women's couture, Hugo?'

'Nell's been teaching me all kinds of things,' he responded dryly, and his mother smiled. 'Let's put that with the "possibles" and leave the emeralds for later.'

They'd whittled the dresses down to four. Three blue and the green one, which *Madame* was obviously regretting putting on the rail to bring to the palace. Hugo was questioning *Madame* closely on the latest trends in menswear, which gave Nell a chance to slip away alone to put the first dress on. When she returned, *Madame* practically ran over to her, tugging unnecessarily at the bodice.

'Perfect...perfect.' She turned to Hugo as if Nell didn't exist, looking for his reaction.

'You like it, Nell?' Hugo's gaze found hers.

'It's...it looks beautiful.' Nell looked at her own reflection in the mirror. Was that really her? 'It's a little tight.'

'Form-fitting...' *Madame* murmured the words.

'I'd recommend breathing over form-fitting. Can you breathe, Nell? On a scale of one to ten.'

Nell grinned at him. 'About three and a half. Maybe only three if I'm sitting down.'

'Well, go and take it off quickly. Before I have to resuscitate you...'

The dress was chosen. Hugo had somehow managed to infer that the diamond earrings and bracelet that his mother was lending to go with it were all *Madame*'s idea, and she'd left, trailing the scent of slightly mollified disapproval in her wake. Queen Margaux had asked Hugo whether he was going to interfere when the hairdresser arrived, and he'd shrugged. Nell had laughingly told him that she thought she could manage alone.

'It's a matter of knowing your power.' Since the choosing of the dress had been accomplished in record time, they were now free until three o'clock, and Hugo had taken Nell for a stroll in the palace gardens.

'I'm not sure I have any power, do I?' Nell looked up at Hugo. Caressed by the sun and relaxed in the warm breeze, he seemed the epitome of a handsome prince.

'Of course you do. You know, when you're a prince, people will tell you that you're the one in charge. And then they tie you up in knots over all of the things you can and can't do.'

'Like having to accept your own private doctor?' Nell knew now that Hugo's studied avoidance of her advice hadn't been just a game. He'd been fighting to express his own feelings over his surgery.

'Well…that worked out. And you were right, I did need to rest a little more. And I needed to be told that I'm not indestructible.'

'You needed to accept that for yourself. Not to be told.'

He chuckled. 'Yes. Big difference. And you don't need to be told which dress you like, so remember that next time.'

'There probably isn't going to be a next time.' Nell had to remind herself every day that this wasn't permanent. That she wasn't really Hugo's fiancée and that in a few months' time she'd be leaving.

'No. I suppose not.' Suddenly the space between them seemed to grow. Their leisurely pace was the same, but they were just taking the same path through the gardens, not walking together.

'Thank you for stepping in, though. I'm not sure what I would have ended up with if you hadn't been there.'

'My mother knows how to handle *Madame* and her entourage. It might have deteriorated into a squabble, though.'

'A squabble? Surely not!'

Hugo chuckled. 'They've known each other for years. *Madame* has access to all the best dresses, but she's not that flexible in her approach. There have been a few full and frank discussions.'

'I didn't realise…'

'That's what I mean about taking your own power. People like *Madame* love to tell you what to do, but if you stand up to them, they've got nothing.'

'And you take a lot of pleasure in standing up to them, don't you?'

He didn't answer. The complex politics, the unspoken expectations of the palace must be hard to live with. Being a doctor seemed suddenly a lot simpler.

'I've been thinking. About Martin…'

He raised an eyebrow. 'Yes? You do that a lot?'

'Not all that much.' The last ten days had been busy. And full of the kind of achievement and joy that didn't naturally bring Martin to mind. But that respite had served to consolidate Nell's thoughts.

'I'm glad to hear that.' There was a note of possessiveness in Hugo's tone.

'I checked his social media accounts. He's been very quiet recently.' Nell had wondered whether Hugo had had anything to do with that.

'The email that our legal team sent him might have had something to do with that.'

'So you *did* do something.'

'Nothing very much. They simply made contact and made a polite request that any future public statements be copied to them, as a courtesy.'

'But coming from an eminent law firm, with the backing of the palace… That sounds like a threat to me.'

'There were no threats. All bullies are cowards, don't you know that? If Jarman backs off because you have powerful friends, that's his business.'

'I was thinking maybe…that I might make him back off by myself. I'm considering lodging an official complaint with the hospital.'

Hugo nodded. 'If that's what you want. It won't be easy, though. Our lawyers can support you through the process.'

'I know, but I don't want that. I thought about what you said, about him probably acting that way towards other people. I'd been so bound up in my own problems that I thought I was alone, but if there *is* anyone else…'

'You want to support them.' He clearly approved of that wholeheartedly.

'Yes, I do. And I want him to know that I did it alone. That I have the power to fight back by myself.'

'Okay. Does that mean I'm not allowed to help?'

'As a friend?' That was a far more demanding proposition. One word and he could have the weight of highly placed contacts and a hotshot legal team crashing down on Martin's head. It would take a lot more input from him to support her through the process as her friend.

'Yes. Always.'

'If I wrote everything down, would you be able to look through it? Give me your opinion?'

His hand drifted to hers, and he tucked it into the crook of his elbow, his thumb brushing against the ring on her finger.

'Yes, of course. Partners.'

'Thank you. I'd like that.' The ring meant one thing to everyone else who saw it and quite another to her and Hugo. That they couldn't love each other but they could be friends, who protected each other.

CHAPTER ELEVEN

HUGO HAD LET her go, and Nell had set off for his parents' apartment with a hint of determination in her step. Whatever happened with her hair and make-up, he was pretty sure that Nell would have a say in it.

He took more time than usual dressing, his left arm still hampering him as he sorted through his wardrobe to find a waistcoat that was exactly the shade of the dress she'd chosen. He'd never done that before, not for any woman, but Nell… They were of the same mind. Beneath all their differences they were cut from the same cloth.

He heard her let herself back into his apartment and rose from his chair to meet her. A little thrill ran up his spine, tempered by a reminder to himself that he shouldn't expect too much.

And then, not expecting too much became irrelevant. He couldn't possibly have expected her to look this stunning. The slim-line green dress traced her curves, the hem high on her ankle. A slender row of diamonds at her wrist and neck and a pair of high-heeled, strappy shoes balanced the look perfectly.

'What do you think?' She was pressing her lips together, and Hugo realised that his over-awed silence had left Nell waiting a little too long.

'I think the dress is very nice.' He wanted to touch the

soft folds of material, but instead he allowed his hand to trace the shape of her waist, just millimetres away from it. 'The diamonds are just right for it.'

She gave him a nervous smile and he permitted his fingers to follow the curve of her chin. Still not touching her. Somehow not touching was almost as sensual as feeling the softness of her skin. 'They'd be nothing without you, though. *You* are exquisite.'

'You think...it's all right?' She was smiling now.

'It's so much better than all right that...no, it's not just all right.'

Nell nodded, obviously pleased, walking over to where his jacket hung across the back of the chair. Picking it up, she helped him on with it, smoothing her hands across his shoulders.

'Will I do?' He smiled down at her.

'For an everyday, handsome prince? You'll definitely do.'

He made her feel good. Clinging to his arm had become a matter of each supporting the other now. Nell protected him from being bumped and jostled, and he protected her from the enquiring heads that turned to look her way.

Everything glittered, from the magnificent chandeliers high above their heads down to the jewels of the assembled company. The great and the good of Montarino, along with delegations from their neighbouring countries. Hugo passed effortlessly between them all, his arm always there for her, the place by his side always reserved for Nell.

The King and Queen led the way into the grand dining hall. Queen Margaux shone in a canary-yellow dress, which complemented her blonde hair, and King Ferdinand was upright and gracious beside her. Everyone was seated, and Nell looked around nervously, feeling Hugo's fingers brush hers under the snowy tablecloth. She looked into his smile and nodded an answer to his unspoken question. As long as she waited and followed his lead in picking the right one from the array of silver knives and forks in front of her, she'd be fine.

Hugo had taken charge of the conversation at their part of the table, asking questions and including everyone. Soon their group was animated and laughing and even Nell began to relax. Underneath the fine clothes and the magnificent surroundings, they were just people getting to know each other.

'Would you like a break?' As they rose from the table, Hugo bent towards her, murmuring in her ear.

'Can we…? Don't you have to stay with your guests?'

'My parents have it covered. Just for ten minutes, so that you can stop having to keep smiling.'

That would actually be nice. Nell's jaw was beginning to ache a little. She followed Hugo as he slipped through the open French doors and out onto the stone-flagged terrace. A number of people seemed to have had the same idea, and Hugo led her out of the circle of light cast by lanterns that were positioned around the terrace, down the steps and into the garden.

'You're *sure* we won't be missed?'

He chuckled. 'This is Montarino, not England. Protocol practically demands that a newly engaged couple disappear for at least ten minutes during the course of the evening.' Hugo walked slowly along the paved path, which was flanked by a sculpted hedge.

'Ten minutes. Not much time, then?' She grinned up at him.

'Something else you need to learn about Montarino. We know how to make very good use of just ten minutes.'

Suddenly ten minutes seemed like ten hours. Out here in the warm evening breeze, the lights and noise of the house were beginning to recede behind them. Nell shivered at the thought.

'Cold?'

'No, it's nice to be out here. It was beginning to get very hot inside.'

Their leisurely pace grew more leisurely, until they were standing together. She had to touch him. Nell ran her fingers down the lapel of his jacket and felt Hugo's hand resting lightly on her waist.

'So…while everyone thinks we've escaped to do what every engaged couple does…' Hugo chuckled.

'We could read the paper?'

'We could. Or play a game of cards.'

'Not enough time.' Nell reached up to touch his face. There was only one thing she really wanted to do right now. And since tonight was all about their public personas, an engaged couple who were naturally very much in love, maybe that one thing was permissible.

'No. You're right.' His gaze never left her face as he raised her hand to his mouth, kissing her fingers.

They could have stopped there. But Nell didn't want to, and she knew that Hugo didn't either. Ten minutes.

His lips were almost touching hers. This wouldn't be the formal kiss, planted on her cheek or hand, to delight the people around them. This was just for her.

Hugo's arm tightened suddenly around her waist and she felt his body tighten against hers. 'Who's there?'

There was a rustle in the bushes behind her. Hugo pulled her away, facing the hurried whispers coming from the darkness. And then a shape detached itself from the deepest of the shadows, followed by another.

'Who's there?' Hugo asked again, his tone demanding an answer.

'The necklace…' A low voice, full of menace, spoke in French and Hugo pushed Nell behind him. Not a good idea, even if he had been in full health. Nell kicked off her shoes, ready to run, clinging to Hugo's arm.

'All right.' He held one hand out in a gesture that was clearly intended to calm the situation.

'Quickly!' The man spoke again, taking another step forward. He was holding something in his hand, and Nell wondered whether he was armed.

This must have been so easy. Any one of the women here was wearing jewellery that would fetch a high price. The men had only to get through high railings at the perimeter of the palace, conceal themselves in the garden and then wait.

'Nell. Give me the necklace.'

'What?' Queen Margaux's diamond necklace. She'd promised herself to take good care of it. But if giving it up was unthinkable, the alternative was even worse.

She fumbled with the catch at the back of her neck, but it was too firmly secured for her trembling fingers. And she'd hesitated for a moment too long. The man lunged towards her as if to tear the necklace from her throat, and she felt Hugo's body pushing her back and taking the brunt of the impact.

'No…Hugo!' He was stumbling to one side and Nell cried out in terror. 'I'll give it to you.' She pulled frantically at the necklace, trying to get it off.

But it was too late for that. She felt a gloved hand close around her wrist, trying to get at her bracelet, and then she was free again as Hugo let out a great roar, tackling her assailant. The man lashed out at Hugo, and she saw a spark. In the silence, broken only by the sound of the wind in the trees, the clicking sound seemed to last for a very long time, even if it was just a few seconds. Then Hugo screamed in pain, dropping to the ground like a stone.

'Hugo!' There was no possibility of just giving the men what they wanted and letting them go now. Nell yelled for help at the top of her voice, hoping that if the assembled company in the palace didn't hear her, there would be a security patrol in the grounds that did.

The men were running now, and Nell dropped to her knees beside Hugo. He was still groaning and gasping for air, and she grabbed his arm, feeling for his pulse.

'Uh…' He tried to speak, but couldn't. All Nell could do was to hold him, as if that might absorb some of his pain into her own body and spare him.

'I know. He had a stun gun. They're gone now.' Nell knew that a jolt from a stun gun could disable the strongest man. It dealt excruciating pain, rather than injury, but a recent operation and a pacemaker complicated things.

Hugo knew that as well as she did. 'You're okay, Hugo. I can feel your pulse.'

His body relaxed a little, but there was still fear in his eyes. 'You're…sure?' His voice sounded thick and strange, and his free hand drifted to his chest.

'I'm sure. I feel it beating, Hugo. Strong and steady.' Fast. But who could blame it for that?

A noise behind her made her jump and Nell looked round to see three men from the palace security team. People were running down the steps of the terrace and Nell could see the King at their head, no longer the stiff monarch but a man of action like his son.

'I'm a doctor. Stand back, he's all right.' She waved the security men back, and they formed a triangle around them, keeping watch. Nell clung to Hugo, trying to comfort him, as he rolled painfully onto his back, his head in her lap.

'Hugo!' The King practically skidded to a halt, bending down, his questioning gaze meeting Nell's.

'He's been hit by a stun gun. It's very painful but it'll pass. The jolt from a stun gun shouldn't affect a pacemaker.' Her words were for Hugo, as much as they were for the King. It must have been terrifying, feeling only pain, his body out of control. Knowing that the pacemaker was there in his chest and wondering whether his heart had already stopped beating.

The King knelt down, suddenly just another father. 'You hear that, son?'

Somehow Hugo managed a smile. 'Never contradict a lady...'

'No. That's right.' King Ferdinand flashed a tight smile at Nell and reached for his son. Hugo took his hand, gripping it tight.

The King had asked one of the men who came running towards them to tell the Queen that Hugo was all right and then his attention was for Hugo alone. He hardly seemed to notice the security guard who had approached and was standing at a respectful distance, waiting to be acknowledged.

Nell caught the guard's attention, keeping her fingers on Hugo's pulse. Now wasn't the time to interrupt the King. 'You have something to report?'

'We've apprehended the two men, and called the police.'

'Thank you for acting so quickly. I'll tell the King. Do you have the stun gun?'

'Yes, ma'am.'

'Would you find out the make and model for me,

please?' Obtaining the information would stop the guard from hovering here, and finding out exactly what Hugo had been hit with couldn't do any harm.

'Yes, ma'am.' The guard turned and hurried away.

Maybe she'd overstepped her authority, but there was no trace of reproof in the King's face when he looked up at her.

'Thank you, Nell. Should we move him, now?'

'I'd like to take Hugo to hospital. It's just a precaution, but I want a pacing check done, and he should be monitored for a little while. Just to be on the safe side.' Scar tissue hadn't had a chance to form around the newly implanted leads yet, and they might have been dislodged by the scuffle or the sudden convulsions of Hugo's body.

'I think that's wise.' The King nodded, looking down at Hugo. 'What do you say, Hugo? Still in no mood to contradict the lady…?'

'No mood at all.' Nell had been sure that Hugo would protest, but he just nodded. This had frightened him even more than she'd thought. 'You should go back to our guests, Father.'

For a moment the King seemed torn. Then he shook his head.

'He'll be all right. And I'll keep you and the Queen informed.' It seemed wrong to break the new bond that had surfaced between father and son in the heat of this emergency, but Nell was beginning to understand that duty was a hard taskmaster.

'Every step of the way?' The King's voice was cracked with emotion.

'Yes, I promise.'

The King bent over his son. 'You know we'll be there, Hugo. Your mother and I…'

'Yes. Just give me a bit of space.' Hugo's words were clearly a fond joke, and his father laughed quietly.

'Perhaps you'll help me get him up on his feet and we can walk him over to the car.' Before now, Nell would never have asked the King to do such a thing. But he seemed to need this, and Hugo clearly did, too. It had taken a stun gun and a lot of pain before the two men had been able to bury their differences, but maybe it was worth it.

CHAPTER TWELVE

ALTHOUGH THE JOURNEY to the hospital was a short one, the car was starting and stopping in the evening traffic. Ted had been fetched from the palace kitchen and arrived stony-faced, clearly annoyed with himself that he'd done what had been expected of him and relied on the security measures at the palace to keep Hugo safe for the evening. He sat in the front seat of the car, next to the chauffeur.

'I feel fine now. There's no need for the hospital. Ted…?' Hugo appealed to the back of Ted's head from the back seat of the car, where he sat with Nell.

'You know what I think.' Ted didn't turn around, and Hugo looked across at Nell in a silent appeal.

'We're going to the hospital.' Nell glared at him. If he thought that she was an easier touch than Ted, he had another think coming.

'Yes, ma'am.' Hugo settled back into his seat. 'Only I'll prove you wrong when I get there.'

'That's exactly what I expect you to do. And it's never wrong to be on the safe side.'

She heard Ted chuckle from the front of the car, and Hugo rolled his eyes.

By the time they arrived at the hospital, the cardiac surgeon who had implanted Hugo's pacemaker had been roused from his bed. Nell quickly told him what had happened and he nodded in agreement with her assessment. She left him alone with Hugo for a moment, and found Ted brooding outside the door.

'He's okay, Ted.'

'I know. But *I* should have been there. A stun gun hurts like the blazes.'

If Ted had been on duty, she and Hugo would have found a way to evade him. The sweet promise of those moments with Hugo, alone in the darkness, made Nell shiver. 'You can't be with him all the time. You were off duty.'

Ted knew that she was trying to make him feel better, and flashed her a wry smile. 'He knows what to do if there's an incident. He should stay back and shout for help.'

'He was protecting me.' Nell had been feeling just as guilty as Ted obviously was.

'Understandable.' The creases in Ted's forehead relaxed slightly. 'Maybe I'm getting a bit too old for this.'

Nell laid her hand on his arm. 'He trusts you, Ted. And Hugo needs people he can trust right now. I don't think age has anything to do with the fact that you can't be in two places at once.'

'Maybe…' Ted didn't look convinced, but at least he was thinking about it.

'Why don't you go and get a cup of tea? I'm sure there'll be somewhere…'

Ted nodded. 'The café on the ground floor is open all night. Would you like me to get you something?'

'No, I'll stay here and talk to his doctor. I'll call you when we've finished and you can see him.'

'All right.' Ted went to turn, and then stopped. 'Thanks.'

* * *

Hugo was lying in bed, a heart monitor by his side. His smile was back in full force, as his coping mechanisms kicked in.

'Don't you think this is a bit over the top? People get hit with stun guns all the time, and they get up and walk away.' He'd waited to come up with his objections until the door had closed quietly behind the cardiac surgeon.

'Yes, they do. But they're generally people in good health who haven't just had surgery. Give it a rest, Hugo.'

'I *am* in good health. Reasonable health, anyway. I'll feel better when I can get back into the gym.'

Nell rolled her eyes. 'Don't give me that, Hugo. This might be just a precaution but it's one that I believe is warranted, and your cardiac surgeon agrees with me.'

'I know what the risks are as well as you do…'

He broke off suddenly, seeing the tears that were filling Nell's eyes. This time she'd made no effort to hide them from him. Why should she? Nothing else seemed to get through to him.

'I'm sorry, Nell. I know you must have been really frightened tonight.'

'Yes, I was. And the bit that frightened me the most was hearing you scream and seeing you hit the ground.' She grabbed his hand, holding on to it tight.

He twisted his mouth down in a show of embarrassment. 'I heard that everyone cries like a baby when they're hit with a stun gun. I know why now…'

'Stop it, Hugo! Stop trying to make out that you weren't afraid. And don't pretend that your first thought wasn't that your heart had stopped, or that you needed your father and he was there for you.'

'Please… Don't cry.' His voice was suddenly husky.

'Well, someone's got to. Ted's maintaining a stiff upper lip, while wrestling with the idea that he should have been there. Your father was really cut up about letting you leave without him, but he had to put on a brave face for his guests. He really cares...'

'Yes, I know. I do too, we just... Sometimes we lose sight of that.' Suddenly he reached for her, shifting a little in the bed.

'Come here. Please... I need you, Nell.'

There wasn't a great deal of room on the bed but there was enough. Nell slipped off her shoes, lowering the bed a little and then climbing carefully up beside him. What the hell, if anyone found them like this, they were supposed to be engaged, weren't they?

He put his arm around her shoulders, holding her close. 'I couldn't protect you, Nell. I'm sorry.'

'I couldn't protect you either. And I'm sorry about that.' She nestled against him. Suddenly everything seemed all right.

They lay together for long minutes. No more words needed, just the silence and the feel of her heart beating. His, too. Finally Nell felt Hugo move, and when she looked up at him he brushed a kiss against her forehead.

'Much as I love having you here, you should go.'

'You're sending me away?' Perhaps Hugo felt he'd admitted a bit too much, and he wanted some time on his own to reconstruct his armoured exoskeleton.

'I can't sleep with you next to me. And you're going to need some sleep, too...'

'Me? I'm all right.'

Hugo chuckled. 'Don't you start. I'm all right enough for both of us. But I need you to do something for me.'

'What?' Right now, she just wanted to stay here and hold him. Or if that would keep him awake, she'd go and have a cup of tea with Ted and then creep back after Hugo fell asleep and sit in the chair next to his bed.

'If I'm going to be here for the next twenty-four hours, I need someone to fill in for me at the meeting tomorrow afternoon. I thought you might do it.'

'Me? But I can't!'

'Why not? You know all the issues, and I think that the clinic means as much to you as it does to me.'

'Yes, it does. But it's *you* they want to see. We can put it off…'

'That's not going to be so easy, the arrangements have already been made. And you'll be speaking directly for me.' He moved his left arm stiffly, catching her hand, his thumb moving across the ring on her finger. 'That gives you the right.'

'That's just a pretence, Hugo.'

'You want the same things I do. I trust you to speak for me. That's not a pretence.'

'Is it what you really want?'

'Yes, it is. Isn't it what you'd want?'

In his place, she'd do exactly the same. She'd want Hugo out there, working for the thing that was most important to her, instead of cooling his heels, drinking tea at the hospital. Even if the prospect of going to the meeting alone was terrifying, Hugo seemed to think that she could do it.

'Okay. I'll stay a little longer…'

'No, you'll go now and get some sleep. Ted will take you to the meeting, and he'll point you in the right direction, who to greet first and so on. You'll knock them dead.'

'You really think so?'

'Yes, I do. Go. Although if you could get me a phone first, I want to call my father.'

'I'll find Ted, you can use his.'

'Thanks.'

Nell climbed off the bed, pulling her dress straight. It seemed to have survived the evening tolerably well, which was a tribute to its quality. She fussed with it, aware that she was putting off the moment of leaving.

'I'll…call you. In the morning.' She picked up her clutch bag, checking unnecessarily that the diamond necklace and bracelet, which she'd finally managed to take off in the car on the way to hospital, were still safely inside.

'Wait…' Hugo was grinning now. 'You were thinking of leaving without kissing me goodbye? Just on the cheek, I don't want the monitor to register anything that gives my doctor pause for thought.'

Nell laughed, bending over him. 'First you tell me how you really feel.'

'Dreadful. I ache in muscles I never knew I had.'

'Good. You'll be well cared for here, and I'll be back tomorrow, after the meeting. Think you can be awake for me?'

'I'll do my very best.' Hugo pulled her down for a kiss that set Nell's heart thumping. Goodness only knew what was going on with the monitor, and she didn't dare look. 'Go. Before I decide I'm feeling a lot better now and I need another one of those…'

Having Nell walk away had been more difficult than he'd thought. Hugo kept it together until Ted had come and then gone again, and then there was nothing to prevent his thoughts from ranging wherever they wanted to go. However much he craved having her with him now, this was what he wanted her to do. He wanted Nell to walk out of that meeting tomorrow feeling the exhilaration of having taken it by storm. She'd been bullied and made to feel ashamed for much too long.

Maybe if he'd done the same with Anna, given her some way of taking her own career forward while she was with him, then things might have been different. But he doubted it. Anna had told him that she lived in his shadow even when he wasn't there, and that she couldn't handle it. Things were working with Nell because, despite what everyone thought, they weren't in love. He should remember that, just in case he felt any temptation to fall in love with her.

It wouldn't be all that hard. She was beautiful and brave, and when she was there he forgot all about whether or not his heart would keep beating. He knew that it would, just so he'd be able to spend another moment with her. But if he fell in love, things would change. However hard he tried, Nell's career would have to take second place to the duties that he'd been born to.

His limbs felt heavy, and he could hardly keep his eyes open. Hugo realised that the tablet he'd taken from the nurse, not even thinking to question what it was, was probably a sleeping pill. As he drifted into sleep, he wondered briefly what it might be like to fall asleep with Nell at his side.

Nell had called him before going into the lunch meeting, her nerves jangling in the cadence of her voice. When she called him again, a little more than two hours later, she sounded quite different.

'I did the presentation, just the way you did last time. They really liked it, Hugo.'

'I'm sure they did.' Hugo leaned back against the pillows, smiling.

'They're going to help us.'

Hugo grinned. 'It didn't occur to me for one moment that they wouldn't.'

'Well, it occurred to me. I thought they might chase me away and say that they'd come to hear you, and I just wasn't good enough.'

'When are you going to realise that you're always good enough, Nell?'

There was a pause, and Hugo imagined Nell frowning, the way she did whenever he complimented her.

'I'm not sure how you can say "always" good enough. There are a lot of things you haven't seen me do yet. But I was good enough today.'

That was something. If large oaks could grow from little acorns, then one of these days Nell was going to stand up and command the attention she deserved. Until then, Hugo would just keep pushing, one inch at a time.

'Did your parents come to see you?'

'My father did. Mother obviously decided that it was safe to allow us in the same room unsupervised.'

'And was it?'

'We disagreed on a few things. Patched it up again. We're good.' Better than they had been for a very long time. Hugo wondered whether Nell knew that it was her influence that had made that possible.

'Are you getting out this afternoon?'

'Yes. I've been pronounced none the worse for wear and I can go as soon as you can collect me.'

Nell laughed, the sound of pure happiness reaching him despite the less-than-perfect phone connection.

'That's great. We're on our way now.'

She almost danced into his room a little later. Nell was wearing a red summer jacket over a red-and-white printed dress, and Hugo began to wish that he'd been with her at the luncheon. But then she would have sat quietly beside him, supporting him but hardly speaking up for herself. She could do so much more than that.

'Are you ready? Before we go, I have someone who'd like to see you.'

Hugo just wanted to go down to the car and get home. But then Nell ducked outside the doorway, appearing again with a wheelchair.

'Uncle Hugo!' Nadine beamed at him.

'Nadine. What are you doing here?'

'I came to see you, silly.' Nadine wrinkled her nose at him and he laughed.

'That's very kind of you. Who told you that I was here?'

'Dr Nell. She said you were ill but you're better now.'

'Yes, that's right.' Nell pulled up a chair and Hugo sat down, facing the wheelchair and leaning forward towards Nadine.

'Are you *all* better?'

'Yes, every bit of me. And what about you? You look much better than when I saw you last.'

Nadine nodded. 'Mama and Papa are taking me home soon.'

'That's good news.' Hugo flipped his gaze up towards Nell, and she nodded, smiling. Clearly she'd taken a moment to find out how Nadine was, and the little girl was recovering well.

'Were you lonely?' Nadine looked around the room that Hugo had occupied. He supposed that the exaggerated quiet of the private wing of the hospital must seem a little lonely to her.

'Yes, I was a bit lonely. But I was only here for one day.'

Nadine nodded, tugging at the teddy bear that was squashed down beside her in the wheelchair. A little tattered now, Claude had accompanied Nadine through most of her stays at the hospital. When she stretched out her hands, offering him to Hugo, he felt his eyes fill with tears.

'Are we going to see how Claude is?' How many times had he pressed his stethoscope to Claude's chest to dispel a little girl's fears? He knew something about those fears now, the unspoken shadows that defied everything he'd learned as a doctor.

'How *you* are.' Nadine was growing up. She knew that Claude was just a way of talking about her own difficulties, and she was offering him to Hugo in the hope that he might speak for him, too. Hugo's hand automatically reached for the stethoscope that wasn't in his pocket, and decided instead to just press his ear to Claude's chest.

'I hear it…' He nodded, hearing only the pounding of his own heart. 'That's very good…'

'Perfect.' Nadine echoed the word he usually said when he listened to Claude's heart. It had been on the tip of Hugo's tongue but somehow he'd been unable to say it in connection with himself. Hugo nodded, giving Claude a hug and then passing him back to Nadine.

'It's time to go back now, Nadine.' Nell spoke in her careful, studied French, but the warmth of her smile was unmistakable. 'Your mother will be here to see you.'

Hugo couldn't let her go yet. This little girl who had been through so much but had still found it in her to offer him the comfort of a teddy bear. 'Would you like me to come with you?'

Nadine nodded, and Nell flashed him a querying glance. Hugo realised that his jeans and casual shirt weren't his usual attire for the hospital, but that didn't seem to matter right now. He got to his feet, releasing the brakes on the wheelchair.

Hugo had breezed past the nurses, smiling as he went but not stopping to receive his printed discharge papers. Nell had collected them for him, and followed him through the building to the children's section of the cardiac unit. A couple of the staff obviously noticed that he was dressed particularly casually today and might have wondered, but Hugo didn't seem to care and neither did any of the children in the ward. Nadine was settled comfortably back into her bed, and Hugo spent time talking and playing with her and all the other children.

He seemed to light up when he was around them. After an hour, it still didn't seem that Hugo was about to leave and Nell stepped in, dragging him away. He'd had enough for one day and there was no question about whether Hugo would be back soon, despite the fact that he was still on leave of absence from the hospital and had so very recently been one of its patients.

'They've been through so much. I feel like a complete fraud.' He murmured the words as he got into the back seat of the car, next to Nell.

'You need to stay strong, Hugo. Who's going to champion them if you don't?' This afternoon had brought exactly what she and Hugo were doing into sharp perspective. If the endless meeting and lunches had seemed less important than being on the wards, it would make a huge difference to both the patients and the doctors and nurses who worked here.

He laughed suddenly, taking her hand, even though no one was looking. 'And who's going to champion *me* if you don't?'

'I expect you'll find someone.' Every time he got too close, she instinctively drew back. Then kicked herself for it, because being close to Hugo was the best thing that she could imagine.

The car slowed a little and Hugo nudged her. On the pavement a couple of women were waving at them, and Hugo waved back.

'Wave…' he murmured to Nell.

'They're not interested in me.'

'No?' He turned to her in disbelief. 'Try waving and see what happens.'

Ted had obligingly bought the car almost to a halt. Nell leaned across and waved at the women, feeling rather stupid, but they reacted by waving even more enthusiastically. A small boy standing next to them on the pavement started to jump up and down, catching their excitement.

Hugo caught her hand up, pressing it to his lips, and the women laughed, nudging each other. Ted waited a few more seconds and then applied his foot to the accelerator.

'That's nice of them.' Nell watched through the back window as the car moved away.

Hugo nodded. If only the women knew that this was all a sham. Nell sat back in her seat, suddenly feeling dispirited.

'By the way, I've postponed my meeting for tomorrow. We can fit it in next week.' Perhaps he felt the same. Hugo seemed keen to change the subject.

'Are you sure you're feeling all right?'

'I feel fine. But another day's rest couldn't hurt.'

Nell had assumed that as soon as Hugo got out of hospital he'd be as unstoppable as the last time. 'Have you got something up your sleeve, Hugo? You're not going to tell me you're going paragliding or something?'

'No. Seems you've got me under control…'

Nell snorted with laughter. 'Right. That's never going to happen, Hugo.'

CHAPTER THIRTEEN

HUGO HAD TO admit that these few days' rest had done him good. He felt stronger, less fearful, and less of a slave to the imagined beat of his heart.

But now it was time to get back to work, and Nell accompanied him to a presentation to the board of directors in the most prestigious of the few high-rise offices in Montarino. It was one of their most important meetings so far, and Nell seemed to dwindle into the background, hanging on to his arm and supporting him. It wasn't until he'd got up to speak that the idea in Hugo's head became a reality.

He thanked everyone for being there, and reiterated the importance of the project that they were being asked to help sponsor. Then he introduced Nell, and sat down.

She kicked him so hard under the table that he jumped. But she got to her feet, smiling. She made a charming apology for any shortcomings in her French, making a joke about having to learn so that she knew what her fiancé was up to. Everyone laughed, and then the lights went down and the first of the images from Hugo's laptop appeared, projected onto the wall. She then proceeded to make a presentation of such vigour and freshness that even Hugo felt he would have given anything that she asked of him.

She waited until they were in the car again before she turned on him. Hugo shifted his feet away from her, just in case she decided to kick him again.

'What are you doing, Hugo?'

'I'm doing the best I can for the clinic. You had them eating out of your hand.'

'You!' She pointed at him accusingly. 'They wanted you, not me.'

'Maybe they went in wanting me. Unless I'm very much mistaken, by the time you'd finished with them, they'd forgotten about tax deductions and publicity, and they wanted a clinic.'

'You might have told me first.'

'Yes, you made that plain. I'm sorry, I was improvising.'

'Well, don't do it again, Hugo. Next time you *tell* me what you're about to do.'

The pink of her cheeks, Nell's passion, and her unerring sense of how to capture hearts. He'd do anything not to see that subsumed into the quiet, submissive woman who had walked next to him into the building.

'All right. So that means you'll do the next presentation?'

'This is *your* project, Hugo. You're the boss.'

He didn't want to be the boss, in Nell's eyes. He wasn't someone whose opinion of her might drag her down and make her feel any less than she was. But on the other hand, being the boss did give him the opportunity to build her up, and he decided to let go of the question of who was supposed to be telling who to do what.

'So I'm making a decision. You do it better than I can.' He leaned forward, hoping for some support. 'Don't you think so, Ted?'

Ted was keeping his eye on the road and didn't turn. 'I didn't catch that…'

Right. Ted was keeping out of it. Wise move, probably. But if Hugo was venturing where angels feared to tread, he wasn't going to back down now. It meant far too much to him.

'So you'll do the presentation tomorrow?'

Nell was trying to glare at him, but she couldn't quite conceal her pleasure. 'I'll think about it.'

Hugo closed his eyes, trying to conceal *his* pleasure. Things were going in the right direction.

'Ted… Ted, look…'

'I see it.' The car slowed suddenly, and Hugo opened his eyes. For a moment he remembered the pain from the stun gun, and almost threw his arm protectively across Nell before he realised that they weren't under any threat.

At the side of the road, a car had veered off the road, breaking through a fence that bounded a field. Another car, which had stopped at the side of the road, was crushed at the front right-hand side and a young man was climbing slowly out of it.

Almost before Ted had brought the car to a halt, Nell had the door on her side open and was climbing out. Wobbling a little on her high heels, she ran over to the man, calling to him and then changing direction, making for the car that was in the ditch.

'We're going to need the first aid kit, Ted.' Hugo climbed out of the car, knowing that Ted would follow him with the medical kit they carried in the boot. He ran over to where Nell was sliding precariously down a grassy slope towards the stricken car.

This time, he supported her. Reaching out with his right hand, he grabbed her elbow to stop her from falling as they both hurried towards the car. As they approached, Hugo could hear the sound of a baby crying.

Nell carefully pulled the driver's door of the car open. A woman was sitting inside, trapped by the crushed dashboard and steering column. Mercifully, it seemed that she was just unconscious.

'I'll take her.' Hugo knelt down on the grass, reaching in with his good arm to find a pulse. 'You get the baby out.'

'Right.' Nell opened the back door of the car, reaching in towards the baby carrier in the back seat. It was still firmly strapped in, and that seemed to have saved the child from any injury if the noise it was making was anything to go by. But the angle of the car made it awkward to get to.

She crawled inside without a moment's hesitation. Hugo felt a flash of regret, wanting to be the one to go inside the car but knowing that Nell was the better choice right now. He bit back his feelings, turning quickly to the woman in the front seat.

Behind him, he could hear Ted calling for an ambulance and a fire and rescue truck. Then another voice came to his ears.

'Is she all right?'

The man from the other car was standing right behind him, blood beginning to trickle down the side of his face. Ted ended his call and stepped forward, ushering him away. He would check him over for any signs of serious injury, and with the information that Hugo had now, he had to concentrate on the woman. He could see blood beginning to pool under the seat but couldn't see where it was coming from. She was pinned down by the infrastructure of the car, and even if she hadn't been, Hugo was loath to move her until the ambulance arrived with the proper equipment.

The woman was breathing but still unconscious. Carefully he pushed his fingers between the seat and her legs, but there was no blood there. The bleeding must have been further down, and he couldn't see her lower legs. Quickly checking her chest and stomach, Hugo turned his attention to craning inside, cursing quietly as he felt his left shoulder pull. There was no time to think about that right now.

Nell climbed inside the car, sliding across to where the baby was secured on the back seat. Fumbling with the nylon mesh straps, she found that one of them had become caught when the front passenger seat had been forced back a few inches in the crash.

But it seemed that the baby was unhurt. Quickly she crawled backwards out of the car, opening the medical kit that Ted had brought and searching for a scalpel. It registered at the back of her mind that as car medical kits went, this one was particularly well-stocked and it looked as if Hugo might need it. The woman in the front seat of the car still wasn't moving.

She climbed back inside the car, cutting the straps around the car seat with the scalpel and carefully pulling the car seat free. Laying it down on the grass, she examined the baby for any signs of injury.

'Okay?' Ted's voice behind her sounded as if he was fighting with a lump in his throat.

'Yes, I can't see any injuries at all.' The baby was still screaming, tears squeezing their way down its crumpled little face, and Nell tried vainly to comfort it. 'How's the driver of the other car?'

'Okay. Cut on his head. Someone else has stopped and they're sitting with him.'

'Right. Let me know if things change. Can you…um…

do anything…?' She gestured towards the carrier. If the baby and the other driver were all right, she should help Hugo.

'Yep.' Ted leaned over the car seat, his thick fingers suddenly tender as he smoothed the child's head then brushed his finger against the palm of its hand. It opened its eyes, still grizzling fitfully.

'Great. Nice one.' Nell assumed the manoeuvre wasn't in any royal bodyguard's manual, so it must be in the one that came with being a father of three girls. Ted nodded, picking up the seat and carrying it over to their car.

'How is she?' Hugo was bending down awkwardly, trying to see into the footwell of the car.

'Airways are clear, and I can see no signs of internal bleeding. She's injured somewhere, though, and I think it's her lower legs.'

'Let me see.' Nell pressed her lips together. Implying that he couldn't do his job was a bitter pill for Hugo to swallow, but right now their feelings didn't matter. They had to make the right decisions for the woman in the car.

Hugo stepped back immediately. 'Can you see anything?'

'No, not from this side. I'll see if I can get to her from the passenger seat.' Nell straightened up and started to walk around the car. Hugo couldn't do this. He was bigger than she was, and although his shoulder was improving, it still hampered his movement.

'Be careful…' He shot her an admonishing glance and Nell nodded.

It was a struggle to get the passenger door open, but she managed it. Climbing inside, she bent down, trying to see through the twisted metal.

'I can see her legs. She's pinned but…yes, I can see where the blood's coming from.' Nell stretched out, gripping the woman's leg just below the knee, and the blood that was coming from a large gash on her lower leg began to ooze slower.

'Can you reach the wound?'

'Just about. Pass me some dressings, would you? I think I can pack a temporary dressing around it, just to stop the bleeding a bit, until they get her out.'

Hugo leaned in to pass the dressings to her. 'Give me the ring. If you get it caught on something…'

'Yes. Thanks.' Nell had seen de-gloved fingers, where rings had been caught in machinery, during her stint in A & E, when she'd been training. She pulled the bulky ring off and put it into Hugo's hand. 'How's she doing?'

'Vital signs seem steady.'

Nell wriggled forward, leaning down to apply the dressings to the woman's wound. It was awkward work in the confined space, and she ended up half on the seat and half lying in the footwell. As she finished, she saw the woman's foot twitch.

'She's moving, Hugo. Might be coming round…' Hugo would need to try and keep her still, and that wasn't going to be easy.

'Okay. I've got her.'

Nell heard the woman moan, and what sounded like an attempt at words. Hugo's arm across her legs was keeping her relatively still, and he was talking to her, replying to her incoherent cries.

'Your baby's safe and well. I'm a doctor and we'll have you out of here soon. Try to stay still for me.'

The woman's leg moved a little and she screamed in pain. Hugo quieted her and Nell heard the sound of weeping.

'All right, sweetheart. Hold on to me.'

A siren, which cut off abruptly, heralded the arrival of

the ambulance. Then voices, telling Hugo to move back, which changed their tone considerably when he turned around and the ambulance crew recognised him. He updated them on the woman's condition and asked what analgesics they carried with them. After some conversation he turned back to Nell.

'I'm giving her a shot of morphine. Are you all right down there?'

'Yep.' Nell's back was twisted uncomfortably and her arm was beginning to ache. But she didn't dare move in case the dressings were dislodged and the woman started bleeding again.

After what seemed like an age, but was probably only a few minutes, Nell heard another siren. She heard Hugo talking to someone and squeezed her eyes closed, concentrating on holding the dressings in place and ignoring the ache in her back. Hugo would take care of things. He would deal with it, and the woman would be brought safely out of the car.

'Okay… Nell, are you still with us?'

'Yep.'

'Good job. They've decided to take the roof of the car off.'

'Right.' Nell had expected that. It made it easier and safer to move someone who might have a spinal injury. And the Jaws of Life should make short work of the car's structure and allow the rescuers to peel the car roof off.

'It looks as if once that's done, they'll be able to free her legs easily. Shouldn't take too long.'

'Good. That'll be good.'

'Tuck your legs in a bit. They'll be using a shield to protect you both from the broken glass.'

Nell moved her legs, tucking them under her as well as she could manage, without letting go of the dressings.

‘That’s great. Hang on in there, honey.’

Nell felt the car move slightly as it was propped and steadied. Then the sound of the mechanised cutters and the breaking of glass. She concentrated on the woman’s leg. It looked as if it needed attention soon.

Hang on in there, honey.

Hugo was always kind and encouraging towards his patients. And perhaps he was, even now, keeping up appearances—she was supposed to be his fiancée. But there was a note in his voice that no one could counterfeit.

The words were just for her, no one else. She repeated them over and over in her head as she felt the rough brush of a gloved hand against her ankle, moving her leg a little in the constricted space and sending showers of pins and needles down it.

Sunlight filtered down into the footwell as the rescuers peeled the roof off. Then Hugo leaned into the car, his gloved hand over hers, taking over the pressure that she was keeping on the wound.

‘Got to stop meeting like this.’ His grin and the murmured words were for her too, despite the quiet, concentrated work going on around them.

‘Have you got it?’ Nell slipped her hand out from under his, and he nodded, his gaze flipping up to somewhere above and behind her.

‘Okay, someone’s going to help you out now.’

Someone gripped her waist firmly, pulling her backwards. Her leg muscles began to cramp painfully and she grimaced, trying not to cry out as she was hauled out of the car.

‘Ça va?’ A tall fireman was looking down at her as she sat on the grass, rubbing her leg.

‘Oui.’ Nell pulled her rumpled skirt down. Not all

that demure for a wannabe princess, but as a member of the team who'd just spent the last fifteen minutes in an awkward, half upside-down pose, flashing a little leg could be forgiven. She wondered briefly which one the fireman saw her as.

The latter, clearly. He turned away, leaving her to it, and got on with his job. Nell watched as Hugo and the paramedics quickly ascertained the woman's condition a little better, and Hugo gave the signal for the fire and rescue team to remove the twisted metal that was holding her legs down.

As soon as Nell could stand, she hobbled out of their way and sat back down on the grass, watching. It was a quiet, professional operation, everyone updating everyone else on what was happening, the woman in the car the centre of their attention. The paramedics backed off, leaving Hugo with the woman, as the fire and rescue team made the last, careful removal of pieces from the car. Then they closed in again, carefully lifting the woman from the car and securing her onto a stretcher.

Hugo was still directing operations, speaking briefly to Ted, who climbed into the ambulance with the baby, still in its car seat. Hugo followed him, obviously intent on a last examination of the woman and her child, to make sure that they were ready for the journey to the hospital. Nell sat alone and unnoticed, watching the fire and rescue team pack up their equipment.

Then Hugo climbed down from the back of the ambulance and the driver shut the doors. He walked across the grass towards her and sat down stiffly.

'How is she?' Nell looked up at him, knowing that the answer would be written on his face.

'Her legs are broken and she's lost a lot of blood. No sign of spinal injury, and although she's drifting in and out of consciousness, which is a worry, I don't see any head trauma either. They'll do a CAT scan…' He lapsed into silence, realising perhaps that his face had already told Nell what she wanted to know. There was every reason to be optimistic.

'Good. And you're okay?'

'Yes. I knew there was a reason for the last couple of days' rest.' He chuckled, and then saw Nell's hand, still absent-mindedly rubbing her leg. 'Cramp?'

'Yes. It just aches a bit now. Ted's going with them?'

Hugo grinned. 'He's going to see that the baby's all right and handed over to its family.'

'Good.' Nell chuckled. 'Think he'll give it up that easily?'

'They might have a bit of a struggle on their hands. He's bonding fast.'

They sat together in silence as the ambulance drew away, followed by the fire and rescue truck. The other driver was standing by a police car that had arrived at the scene and was parked a couple of hundred yards along the carriageway, and the people who had stopped had got back into their cars and resumed their journeys.

It was suddenly quiet. In between the swoosh of passing vehicles, Nell could hear birds singing and the sun was warm on her face. If it hadn't been for her own crumpled dress and the spots of blood on the rolled-up sleeves of Hugo's white shirt, it would have been a fine day for a walk in the countryside.

'Have you seen my shoes?' A thought struck her.

'Ted put them in the car.' Hugo turned his face up to the sun, as if he were thinking the very same thing. It was the quiet after a storm, in which they both began to move from the urgency of a wrecked car by the roadside back into the other reality of their everyday lives.

Or back into Hugo's reality. However much he tried to involve her, it seemed as if he was just giving her something to do, making her feel as if she wasn't just an accessory on his arm. But in truth, that's what she was. This was Hugo's country, and his mission, and Nell was just helping him out for a while. She'd be back in London, reading about him in the newspapers, before very long.

'Why so glum?' Nell turned to find that he was looking steadily at her.

'Nothing. I was just hoping that the woman will be all right.' She got to her feet, flexing the still-sore muscles in her leg, watching as Hugo stood. He was holding his left arm loosely by his side, not moving it but seeming to have suffered no ill effects from his exertions.

He opened the back door of his car, motioning her inside, and Nell stood her ground. 'If you think you're going to drive…'

'No, I don't think that.' He reached into his pocket, drawing out the car keys and put them into her hand. 'Just get into the back for a moment.'

Nell got in, shifting over to let him follow her. He closed the door and then turned, reaching for her ankle and propping her leg up onto his lap. 'Looks as if your leg's still sore, which gives me a marvellous opportunity to return the favour you've been doing me.'

The look in his eyes wasn't anything like Nell hoped that her demeanour was when she massaged his shoulder. But his face was the model of propriety. She sat still, feeling his fingers on the back of her leg, just above the knee.

'Ah!' For a moment, all she could think about was his touch. And the way that the sore muscle at the back of her leg was reacting and then relaxing as his fingers pressed a little harder. 'That's it. A bit higher?'

It sounded a little bit like sex, and felt a lot like it, too.

Rather than stare into his eyes, the way that she wanted to, she squeezed them shut.

'Right there?' Even his voice sounded like the honey-smooth tones of a lover.

'Yes, you've got it. That's much better.'

Her leg felt a great deal better. The rest of her body was beginning to ache for the same touch. Very slow, and as sure as the careful progress of his fingers on her leg. Closing her eyes hadn't been such a good idea after all, she could practically see Hugo making love to her behind her eyelids.

'Thanks. That's fine now.' When she opened her eyes, she thought that she saw the hint of a smile on his face. The dark echoes of what she'd been imagining in his green eyes.

'Wouldn't want your foot to slip off the clutch...' His fingers kept massaging.

'This is an automatic.'

'Ah, yes. Silly me.' Hugo let her go and Nell pushed her skirt back down to her knees. Feeling in his pocket, he brought out the ring. 'Don't forget this.'

Nell smiled, holding out her hand. Whenever she took the ring off, he always put it back on her finger again. She liked that, even if it was only temporary and didn't mean what everyone thought it did.

He leaned towards her, as if he were about to kiss her. But something attracted his attention and Nell turned to see one of the policemen strolling towards the car. Hugo grinned at her, getting out of the car and walking towards the man.

He seemed to have a sixth sense about that. Hugo was always on guard, aware of who was around him and what they were doing. Nell supposed that came from living his life in the spotlight, never being able to walk down the street alone and unnoticed. It was why he guarded his secrets so carefully. He had to know that something was private.

He exchanged a few words with the policeman and Nell climbed into the driver's seat of the car, pulling the seat forward. In the rear-view mirror, she could see him walking back towards her. Relaxed, stains on the knees of his trousers from having bent down beside the injured woman, but still handsome. Still so perfect that Nell could hardly bear it.

She started the car, waiting for him to get in beside her. It was time to get back on the road.

CHAPTER FOURTEEN

HUGO COULD FEEL his strength returning. The bruises were long gone, and the red gash on his chest had knitted well. It would heal into a fine white line, as barely noticeable as the slight change in the contour of the skin above the pacemaker. It was there but rapidly becoming hidden.

He needed Nell less and less each day. He could make his way through a press of people now, without wanting to shy away from them and protect his shoulder. He'd be able to drive in another few weeks, and the exercises that he did every morning, to prevent his shoulder from freezing, could become a little more strenuous.

Nell had thrown herself into raising money for the clinic, and they'd decided that, working apart, they could cover twice as much ground as working together. Hugo missed having her with him, but he knew she enjoyed it, and as time passed, her confidence seemed to be growing.

The best part of the day was always the morning. Dressed in a T-shirt and sweatpants, her hair scrunched on the top of her head, and without a scrap of make-up, Nell was the most beautiful woman he'd ever seen. They'd have breakfast together, discussing their respective commitments for the day. Then he'd put a suit and tie on, and Nell would put on a dress and her engagement ring, and they were ready for the day, their public faces firmly in place.

'So...how would you like a day off?' Hugo had been thinking of broaching the subject for a while and had decided that there wasn't much to lose by doing so. The worst that could possibly happen was that she could say no.

'A day off?' She was sitting in the sun, the breakfast things in front of her on the patio table. One leg was curled up beneath her, and there was a smudge of marmalade on her thumb. Hugo tried not to look as she licked it off.

'Yes. Remember I still owe you a trip on the royal yacht.'

'That was just for show, Hugo.'

'It doesn't mean we can't go. Take a weekend off, we've both earned it.'

'Isn't there...? Don't you want to spend the time somewhere else?'

Nowhere in the world that he could think of. 'We're supposed to be engaged. I wouldn't dream of spending a weekend anywhere other than with you. And I paid enough for the pleasure of your company.'

Hugo winced. He hadn't meant that quite the way it had sounded and from the look on Nell's face, the joke had fallen flat. It had been a long time since he'd been this tongue-tied when asking a girl out.

'We're not really engaged, remember,' she said quietly.

'I can still enjoy spending time with you, can't I?'

'You don't have to say that here. No one's listening.' There was an edge to Nell's voice now that cut away at Hugo's heart. Suddenly the morning sun seemed harsh and altogether too bright to sit here for any longer.

'Of course. I'm sorry.' He stood up, reaching for his

diary, which lay with hers on the table. 'I have an early start this morning. I'll see you this evening.'

She hadn't needed to say it, not like that at least. Nell sat on the patio, wondering whether Hugo would forgive her, and when she heard the front door open and then close, it seemed that he hadn't. She ran to the front window and saw him, immaculate in his suit and tie, getting into the car, while Ted waited at the wheel.

A weekend with Hugo. Sun and the sea, a chance to relax. It had sounded too wonderful to be true.

And in Nell's experience, that usually meant that it was. Beneath all the excitement and glamour, beneath the very real relationship that was growing between them, Hugo was still a prince. He could buy whatever he wanted, and even though there was no contract of employment between them any more, he was as much in control of her future as Martin had been. And she'd allowed that.

She had to get ready. She was due to speak to a women's club at noon, a talk that was designed both to educate them about the signs of heart disease and ask them to spread the word about the plans for the clinic. That was what she was here for, a shared goal and an agreement, which protected his secrets and her reputation. She needed to remember that whenever it started feeling too much that her rightful place was on his arm.

'Nell, I'm so sorry.' Hugo marched into the sitting room, clearly gripped by the urgency of being on a mission. Nell jumped. She hadn't heard him come in.

'You took the words right out of my mouth.' The magazine lying open on her lap had gone unread, while she'd mentally rehearsed her apology.

'I...' He looked suddenly perplexed. Clearly he'd been rehearsing too, and his speech wasn't going entirely to plan. 'You have nothing to apologise for. And since I do, I'm going to break the ladies-first rule.'

'Okay.' When Hugo was in one of these moods, there was no stopping him. Nell had learned to just go with the flow.

He took a breath, as if reorienting himself back on his trajectory. 'I'm really sorry about this morning. It was just a joke and...all I meant was that money pales into insignificance in the face of the pleasure I'd take in spending a weekend away with you. You owe me nothing, and there's no obligation on your part to join me.'

'I know. It's all right, Hugo, I never thought that was the case. I was just being a bit over-sensitive.'

'No, you weren't. I know you have good reason not to mix business with pleasure, and any implication that I—'

'Please stop, Hugo. Let's just say we're okay, shall we?'

He nodded, bringing out a glossy paper carrier bag from behind his briefcase. 'I was going to bring you flowers but decided on this instead.'

What was this? The carrier bag looked as if it had come from an exclusive store somewhere, and when Hugo handed it to her, Nell saw an embellished cardboard box inside. Too big for jewellery and too heavy for underwear. But in this situation, they'd be gifts that an unsubtle man would bring, and Hugo was never that.

She took the lid off the box and smiled. Perfect. 'Chocolate! Thank you, Hugo.'

He grinned, finally taking his jacket off and sitting down. Nell proffered the box. 'Would you like one?'

'You first.'

The chocolate was delicious, with a centre of dark

brandy truffle. 'Mmm…these are gorgeous. You should try one.'

'Thanks… One can't hurt, right?'

'No. One can't hurt.' Even though he had no problem with cholesterol, Hugo's diet was strictly balanced and healthy. Perhaps too much so. Nell had never seen him eat sweets or sugary foods, even as a treat.

Hugo loosened his tie, leaning back on the sofa, taking a moment to appreciate the forbidden chocolate. 'That's good.'

They were friends again. Clearly Hugo didn't care about receiving any apology from Nell, but she cared about giving it.

'Hugo, I'm sorry, too. I didn't mean to infer that you were being in any way insincere. This is just…a difficult situation. I don't know quite how to act sometimes.'

'You're doing just fine. You should never apologise to me, because it's my weakness that's put you into a difficult situation.'

That assumption, again, that he was somehow flawed. Hugo seemed to take it for granted, as if it were beyond argument, and a given thing.

'You're weak because you have a pacemaker? Is that what you say to all your pacemaker patients, that they'll never be the same again?'

'No, of course not…' He broke off, as if the incongruity had only just occurred to him.

'Then why say it to yourself? You know it's not true. Why keep it such a secret?'

He shook his head. 'I don't know, Nell. I feel…different somehow. Less than what I was.'

'But you don't mind relying on a watch to tell you the time. You don't mind relying on your phone to keep you in touch.'

'That's not the same thing. I'm not relying on either of them to keep my heart beating, that's a bit more important.'

'Yes, it's a great deal more important. But what happens if the pacemaker fails? Your heartbeat will probably slow up, but it's not going to stop completely. Most of the time, your heart's beating just fine on its own, the pacemaker only activates when your level of activity increases and you need a little extra help. So the worst that can happen is that you have to stop and sit down. You *know* all this, Hugo.'

'Yes, I do. I…' He looked at her suddenly. 'You're pushing me, aren't you?'

'Yes, I'm pushing you. Because what you know up here…' Nell reached forward, tapping his forehead lightly with her finger '…isn't what you actually feel inside, is it?'

He shrugged. 'No. But I can't change that.'

'You could look at the reasons. Why you blatantly disregard everything your head is telling you.'

'Is this your usual psychology chat?' He narrowed his eyes, and Nell could see that he was only half joking.

'No. This one's just for you.'

Nell had a habit of asking all the questions that Hugo didn't want to answer. He supposed that on some level, he must have known that she'd get around to this sooner or later. Perhaps on some level he'd wanted her to.

'I can't fall short, Nell. I've been given a great deal in life, and it's my duty to repay it.'

'What makes you think you aren't?'

'You've seen the kids at the hospital.' He knew that Nell would understand that.

'Yes, I have. And I know you're doing your best for them. We can't do any more than our best.'

'And my best may not be good enough.' Hugo's greatest fear was right there, on his lips. As if somehow Nell had managed to entrance it, and coax it from its hiding place.

'It's all we have. And we're allowed to take some time out and have a life, to have holidays and take some time off when we're sick.' Nell frowned, and Hugo braced himself for whatever was to follow. He knew that look.

'I can't believe that you don't have someone to come home to at night. That you're so sure you won't that you can commit yourself to a fake engagement for the next few months.'

Hugo had got used to coming home to Nell at night, and it was almost a shock to be reminded that it wasn't real. But he'd made that decision a long time ago.

'That's not as easy as you think, Nell.'

'It's never as easy as anyone thinks. I know that.'

Suddenly he wanted to explain. It was the first time that he'd felt that someone might understand, as a friend.

'I did have someone once. I was going to get married. Anna and I met at medical school in London, and we lived together for a couple of years. I told her that I wanted to come back to Montarino and she wanted to come with me, but when we got here…'

Nell nodded him on.

'I had a new job and got caught up in that and the round of engagements that the palace had planned for me. I was happy to be home and…I didn't look closely enough at what was going on within our relationship. I didn't see that Anna was feeling trapped on the sidelines.'

'She didn't have a job?'

'Everyone expected that she was going to be a royal

bride. She was offered a lot of roles as patron of various medical facilities, which would take effect after our marriage, but she didn't want her success to come through me. Anna was worth a great deal more than that, and leaving me and going back to London was the best decision she ever made. She has a fulfilling career now, and a husband who doesn't take up so much space that she can't breathe.'

'It seems a bit unfair to give yourself all the blame.'

'I knew what my life was going to be like, I should have seen that it wouldn't be enough for Anna to live through me. I could have followed her back to London but I didn't, because I felt it was my duty to give whatever I could back to Montarino. That's what I have now, and I feel I'm failing.'

'You're not failing, Hugo. You're just recovering from an operation.'

Hugo looked for the understanding he craved, and found it in her eyes. Suddenly it was too much to bear and he got to his feet. 'Is that our chat done, then? I'll go and make dinner...'

'No, it's not done. I'm not finished with you yet.' She called the words after him, but there was humour in Nell's tone. Maybe she knew that the burden of his duty was feeling a little heavy at the moment.

'What are you going to do?' He chuckled, turning on the tap to wash his hands. 'Find me someone who doesn't mind trailing around after me and playing princess?'

'Are there women like that?' Nell professed just the right amount of surprise, before turning her attention to the box of chocolates. He wanted to walk back into the sitting room and hug her, but right now it was probably better to keep his distance.

'Plenty of them.'

'That sounds a bit boring.'

And that was it, in a nutshell. A career woman, someone like Nell, would always want their own life, free of the constraints of his life. Women who wanted him just because he was a prince generally weren't that interesting after the first couple of dates.

It was a catch-22 situation that held him in limbo. There was no way out that Hugo could see, and he suspected that Nell couldn't either. If she could, she would have mentioned it.

The invitation to spend a weekend on the royal yacht had been given again, and this time Nell had accepted it straight away. If his admission that he felt no woman would want the life he offered her was horribly sad, it also neatly let Nell off the hook. There were no expectations from him, and she could match that by allowing no expectations to infiltrate her own thinking.

They set off early. As they crossed the border into France, the sun came out and Hugo retracted the roof of his convertible. A warm breeze and a handsome prince beside her.

As they approached the motorway, Nell took over the driving, and Hugo lounged in the front seat of the car, enjoying the journey. Dressed in a pair of shorts and a sweatshirt, his short hair ruffled in the breeze, he seemed to finally be getting it into his head that they were on holiday.

It was almost midday when they reached the small, bustling French port where the yacht was moored. Hugo took his place at the wheel again, negotiating the narrow streets of the old town, before driving along the quayside and into the marina.

He drew up alongside a young man in pristine white

shorts, with the name of Montarino's royal yacht sewn across the sleeve of his white shirt. He stepped forward, opening the passenger door of the car before Nell could reach for the handle.

Hugo gave him an affable grin. 'Thank you, Louis. How are you?'

'Well, Your Highness. It's good to see you.'

Hugo got out of the car, taking a draught of sea air into his lungs, as if it felt easier to breathe here. 'It's very good to be back. How are your studies going?'

'I've just been sitting my exams. They went well, I think.'

Hugo nodded, tossing the car keys to Louis. 'Let me know when you get your results.'

'Will do, Your Highness.' Louis got into the car, driving it towards the car park, leaving Nell and Hugo standing on the quayside.

'Which one is it?' Nell surveyed the boats moored around the marina. Smaller yachts were tied up against the piers, which extended out into the water, and larger ones were anchored further out.

'That one.' Hugo pointed towards one of the yachts. It wasn't the largest of the boats there, but it seemed the most elegant, glistening white, and bobbing gracefully on an azure sea.

'It's beautiful. How do we get to it?'

He grinned. 'This way.'

Another man in the same uniform as Louis's helped her down into a motor launch. She looked around for her luggage, but it didn't seem that they were going to be waiting for that. As soon as Hugo was on board, the engine was started and they began to speed way from the land.

'This is wonderful.' Hugo's arm was slung across the

back of the seat and she had to move a little closer to him, so that he could hear her over the noise of the engine. 'I already feel spoiled.'

'That's exactly how you're meant to feel.' Hugo's lips brushed against her ear.

She was helped up a set of steps onto the deck of the yacht, Hugo following. Waiting for her was a man who bore the word 'Captain' on the sleeve of his shirt.

'Welcome, Dr Maitland.' He stepped forward, holding out his hand. 'I'm Captain Masson.'

'Thank you.' Nell shook his hand, looking around her. The yacht looked just as white and gleaming close up as it had from the land. 'This is a beautiful vessel.'

'Thank you, ma'am.' Captain Masson beamed at her. 'Where would you like to go?'

Nell turned to Hugo and he shrugged. 'Your call. We can dock somewhere for a little shopping. Or if you prefer swimming there are some nice places to stop off.'

Nell thought for a moment. It seemed a little bit of a waste to spend time shopping and swimming when she could enjoy being here on the yacht. 'The sea. I'd like to go…somewhere on the sea if that's all right?'

'A short trip along the coast perhaps, ma'am?'

'Yes, I'd like that.' Nell glanced at Hugo, wondering if that was what he'd had in mind.

'That's an excellent idea. Thank you, Captain Masson.' Hugo smiled.

'Very well. We'll be on our way very soon, we just have to wait for your luggage. In the meantime, drinks have been laid out on the main deck.'

The captain gestured to his right, and Nell took a couple of uncertain steps in that direction. She felt Hugo take her arm and followed his lead, walking towards a short flight of stairs that led up onto a deck, shaded by awnings and dappled by the sun.

'It's…very formal here.'

Hugo nodded. 'This is the royal yacht, my parents bring important visitors here. The crew don't call the captain by his first name, and neither should I. When we're at sea, his word is law, and it's his responsibility to keep us in one piece if we run into a squall.'

'Are we going to run into a squall?' Nell looked up into the blue, cloudless sky.

'I very much doubt it. Captain Masson will have already looked at the weather forecasts all along the coast, and he'll be counting on giving us a smooth ride. It's just a principle.'

He led her onto the main deck, where a table was set out, with champagne on ice and canapés. Nell ignored the seats arranged around the deck in both the sun and the shade, preferring to lean against the wooden-topped rails to watch as the motor launch sped back towards the land and then returned with Louis and their luggage.

As the muted sound of the engines reached her, and the yacht began to move slowly, Hugo joined her, leaning with his back against the rail. 'What do you think?'

'This is wonderful, Hugo. A real treat, thank you.'

CHAPTER FIFTEEN

HUGO WAS HAPPY. Nell was happy, and shining with excitement as he showed her around the yacht. She expressed surprise at the size of her cabin, insisting on looking through each of the portholes to ascertain whether there was a different view from any of them. She explored all the decks, leaning over the rails to see as much as she could.

When the expected message came from Captain Masson, inviting her to the bridge, she ran after Louis's retreating back, seemingly determined to deliver her acceptance of the invitation herself.

He watched as she asked questions about all the instruments and examined the navigation charts that were brought out for her to see. When she was accorded the singular honour of being allowed to take the helm for a while, Captain Masson talked her through making a small corrective manoeuvre, rather than simply letting her hold the wheel, and Hugo saw the helmsman smile. If they weren't careful, the crew would be renaming the yacht after her.

'I hope I didn't take up too much of Captain Masson's time.' The yacht lurched suddenly and she almost stumbled down the steps from the bridge. Hugo caught her arm to steady her.

'All right?' She'd stopped, clutching the handrail, one hand on her chest.

'Yes…yes, I'm all right. I felt a little bit queasy just then. It's passed now.' She squinted out towards the horizon. 'Are the waves getting bigger?'

'A little, yes. You'll get used to the motion of the ship soon, but if you feel sick we've got a full stock of medication to choose from.'

'No, thanks. I'm fine now. I think my sea legs are kicking in.'

Hugo nodded, watching her down the remainder of the steps. It was probably best to take her mind off the idea of being sick, and mention to Captain Masson that a smooth ride would be appreciated.

'The captain doesn't let just anyone take the helm, you know.' He took her arm, strolling towards the main deck so that they could sit in the afternoon sun.

Nell's cheeks regained their colour suddenly. 'He's very kind. And it's all so interesting. I wonder if he'd let me watch when we stop for the evening and put the anchor down. I'd keep out of the way.'

'I'd be very surprised if he hasn't already got that in mind.' Nell didn't seem to care much for the prestige of being here, but she loved the yacht and wanted to know everything about it. Captain Masson and his crew had seen that, and Hugo reckoned that the dropping of the anchor would be carried out under Nell's command.

And that was the difference. The one that meant that Nell was beyond his reach. She didn't care to spend her days off in the usual leisure pursuits, she wanted to know how things worked. He'd seen her out in the garden at his house, questioning the gardener about how the mix of planting gave year-round colour and helping him weed. She threw herself into her work with the same gusto. Her life had purpose, a life that should never be squashed by his.

But for today and tomorrow, he had her here with him. That had to be enough, because it was all he dared take from Nell.

At dusk, they came to anchor outside a coastal town, and Nell watched the lights begin to come on, growing brighter as the sky became darker. Then stars appeared in a sky that looked as if it were putting on a show just for her.

Dinner was in the open air on the main deck. Candles on the table, protected from the warm breeze by glass shades. And Hugo, looking far more handsome than he had any right to, in a white open-necked shirt.

'Tonight's a night for dancing.' They'd had their after-dinner coffee, and all that Nell could think was that he was right. Tonight *was* a night for dancing.

She rose, smiling, wondering where the music would come from. Hugo took her in his arms, humming the snatches of a tune and moving her to its slow rhythm.

Perfect. On a perfect night like this, it seemed quite natural that he should kiss her. When he did, it felt as if she were melting into him. As if together they could be at one with the stars and the breeze and just be, without needing to think about the consequences.

'I wish…' They were still moving, dancing together as they kissed.

'What do you wish? If it's anything that I can grant, it's yours.' He whispered the words, leaving a kiss behind them.

'I wish that there was nothing to stop us.'

He knew what she meant. Every line of his body

hinted that this could so easily be a seduction, if they'd only let it.

'Is there anything? What happens at sea might be persuaded to stay at sea.'

'We're not exactly at sea.' Nell clung to the last vestiges of her sanity. Even if stars were dancing in the sky, the lights of land were closer than that.

'We're not on dry land either. We might be able to see them, but they can't see us.'

It was tempting. *Very* tempting. Surely she and Hugo could leave everything behind, just for one night?

'I can't leave myself behind. I brought my baggage with me, and you brought yours.'

'You're right. As always.' He kissed her again, warm and unhurried, as if to show that being right didn't mean that she could escape his tenderness.

'Thank you for a wonderful day, Hugo. And a wonderful evening…' The thought that this wonderful evening might so easily become a wonderful night was tearing at her resolve. Nell broke free of his arms. She had to go now, while she still could.

What…*what*…had he been thinking? Hugo put his head around the galley door to thank the chef for his efforts tonight, and walked to his cabin.

It had seemed so natural. Taking her in his arms, letting the breeze take them with it, away from the land and into a place where only desire mattered. But Nell was always the more sensible of the two of them. He should heed her judgement, and remember that there was no possibility that they could make a future together, however tantalising tonight might be. He sat down on the bed, slowly unbuttoning his shirt.

And there was another thing. Hugo rose, walking into

the en suite bathroom, pulling his shirt to one side, as if seeing the scar could finally convince him. However many times Nell told him he wasn't, he still felt flawed. And Nell deserved only the best.

A knock sounded, and he dragged his gaze away from the mirror, closing his shirt before he opened the cabin door. Hugo froze.

'You'll keep me standing here?' Nell smiled up at him. Her hair was still gathered up around her head, stray curls escaping around her face. Her eyes were as bright as the moonlight, as if she'd brought a little of it below deck with her.

'No! Come in.' He stood back from the door and she walked into his cabin. For a moment, all he could think was that her feet were bare, and that she walked as if she were floating on air.

Hugo closed the door behind her and leaned against it, as if somehow that might stop this dream from escaping.

'I came to ask you if you'd like to come to my cabin. We could…see the sunrise tomorrow.'

He reached out and touched the sleeve of the ivory-coloured wrap that covered her body. Even that seemed unbearably erotic, since it was clear that she had little else on.

'I would love to come to your cabin. Although I can take or leave the sunrise.'

She nodded. 'Me, too.'

Suddenly she was in his arms, and Hugo found his strength again. He kissed her, tracing his fingers across the soft, silky fabric of her wrap. It was so thin that he could feel her response, the heat of her skin and the sudden tightening of the muscles of her back. He could do this. He could make her cry out for him.

Wordlessly, he wrapped his arm around her and

opened the door, looking out to make sure that no one was in the corridor outside then hurrying her forward to her own cabin door. When they were inside, she turned, twisting the lock. The sharp snap seemed to echo through his senses.

'I'm at your mercy now.' Hugo could feel that his own body was ready for hers, and if it let him down, then he knew she'd be kind. Nell was always kind.

'And I'm at yours…' She began to undo the knot in the sash at her waist, leaving the last twist in place, as an obvious invitation for him to finish the job. Hugo stepped forward, taking her in his arms and pulling the sash open.

It seemed unlikely that Nell could be prey to the same madness that he was, but he felt it. Her whole body was trembling, moving against his. When he pulled the wrap from her shoulders, finding a narrow lace strap underneath, she let out a little gasp and he heard the same need as he felt.

Moonlight slanted across the bed. He wanted so badly to be a part of that moonlight, making love to her in its cool gleam. No sooner had the thought occurred to him than he felt Nell's hand, bunched in his shirt, pulling him towards the bed.

His heartbeat seemed to ramp up, leaving him almost breathless. Suddenly she was still.

'It's okay, Hugo.' She laid her hand on his chest. 'It's not going to let you down.'

It was Nell who wouldn't let him down. Always knowing, always understanding. He kissed her, feeling the thump of his heart against hers. And suddenly it didn't feel like a precursor of doom. It felt good.

'Your heart and mine, Nell. Beating together.'

'That means we're both alive.' She smiled up at him. 'I feel more alive than I have for a long time…'

Hugo sat down on the bed, spreading his legs and pulling her close, kissing the wide strip of flesh between the open fronts of her robe. He felt her hands on his shoulders, and heard her cry out when he ran his tongue lightly across her stomach. He could see now that the robe had concealed ivory lace underwear, and he felt another jolt of longing. More time, more pleasure involved in taking that off.

She sank down onto his knee, and he held her close, kissing her and gently working her free of the wrap. It slid down, draping around his leg.

'You are so beautiful, Nell.' He heard his own voice, thick with desire.

'You are, too. I want you to make love to me, Hugo.' She was working on the last few buttons of his shirt, pulling it from his shoulders.

A stab of self-doubt cut through the desire. It was impossible that she couldn't have felt it, he was hers already in as many ways as he could think of. She ran her fingers lightly over the scar on his chest, and he shivered.

'It'll be okay.' She laid her hand on the side of his face, kissing him on the lips. 'Believe me, Hugo.'

Suddenly he did. He let her pull his shirt off, and as she ran her fingers across his chest, he gave himself up to her caresses.

They were both so aroused already that even the smallest gesture seemed to provoke a reaction. When Hugo brushed his fingers across the lace that covered her breasts, Nell felt a sharp tug of desire. When she laid her hand on his belt buckle, she felt him tremble, as if just the thought, just the implication of an action, was as potent as the deed itself.

Undressing each other slowly was an expression of a shared need, which demanded that they take each moment and make it last. The leisurely rocking motion of the yacht seemed to follow their pace, as unstoppable as the movement of the ocean.

And Hugo was all hers. No more fears, no looking over his shoulder. He took pleasure just as wholeheartedly as he gave it, smiling up at her when she found herself on top of him, astride his hips.

'Doesn't anyone ever call you Penelope?'

'No.' On his lips, her given name seemed to sparkle. 'You like it?'

'Yes, I do.'

'I like hearing you say it.' This was something that she could share, just with him.

He chuckled, pulling her down for a kiss. 'Penelope.'

He said it again, gasping it when she lowered her body onto his, taking him inside her. When he gripped her hips, pushing her further towards her own climax, he may have said it. By that time, Nell was a little beyond thought. But he did say it again as she clung to him, turning her over to explore every angle of their lovemaking.

He was her heart. Even that thought didn't seem out of place tonight, because there *was* no tomorrow.

'I loved the lace…' They were sprawled together on the bed, whispering the quiet minutes of the night away. 'Is that what you usually wear?'

Nell grinned. She'd hoped he *would* like it. 'It's my body armour.'

'Really? Can't say it worked too well in that regard.' Hugo kissed the top of her head.

'I noticed. But a good friend always used to say that if you're feeling a little under-confident, nice underwear helps.'

'You've been feeling under-confident?'

'I'm not as used to standing up in front of a lot of people as you are. Or having people notice me on the street, or seeing my face on the front pages of the paper.'

He laughed quietly. 'Okay. So you were wearing lace when you first met me?'

'No, if you remember I was fresh off the plane. I was dressed for comfort.'

'So when we talked, that first time at the palace?'

'Yes.'

He sighed. 'At the luncheon? When you bid for me?'

'Of course. What part of that day did you think wasn't a challenge?'

'If I'd known…' His hand went to his forehead, as if he'd just realised an irrefutable truth. 'Actually, if I'd known I wouldn't have been able to get a word out. Probably best that I didn't.'

'I don't imagine you as ever being lost for words, Hugo.'

He rolled over, covering her body with his. Kissing her, with more than a hint of the desire that had filled them both tonight. 'Maybe you should consider the idea. You leave me speechless.'

Hugo felt whole. Wholly happy, more than wholly satisfied, and…just whole. He hadn't felt that way since he'd first felt the signs that his heart might not be working as well as it should. Nell had somehow seen something different in him, and had never shown any doubt about his ability to recover and lead the life that Hugo had thought he'd lost.

That had been his mistake. He'd wanted to put his illness and his operation behind him so badly that he'd tried to rush it. Hugo saw a lot of things differently now.

And one thing that he saw with complete certainty was that tonight wasn't going to be enough.

Nell was sleeping now and Hugo fought the temptation to watch her sleep. If he wanted to keep everything that he'd found, he needed to be strong.

Opening her eyes came with a sudden burst of nausea. The whole cabin seemed to be pitching and rolling, taking her stomach with it. Nell closed her eyes, and then opened them again quickly when the feeling that she might be about to die washed over her.

She wasn't about to die. She was just going to be—No. Not now. Please, not now…

Her stomach wasn't listening. Hand over her mouth, Nell rolled off the bed, half staggering and half crawling to the bathroom. The door banged shut behind her, and the whole world lurched.

'Nell…?'

She heard Hugo's voice, but even that couldn't stop her from being sick. Trembling, she called back to him.

'I'm okay. Go away…' Naked and being sick in the bathroom wasn't the best way to wake a lover. The lock on the bathroom door seemed about a mile away and rocking dangerously.

And he ignored her, dammit. She felt him wrap a towelling robe around her trembling shoulders.

'All right. Try to relax.'

How could she? Humiliation wasn't conducive to relaxation. 'Go away!'

'Be quiet.' His voice was firm, and Nell reckoned that begging wasn't an option. Another bout of sickness chased any further thoughts away.

'I'm sorry. I'm so sorry…' She moaned the words, wishing that she could be somewhere else. Anywhere else.

'It's okay. You're just seasick.'

'Uh. Just…?'

'You'll feel better in a minute.'

No, she wouldn't. She felt so ill that she was almost glad that Hugo was there. In between wanting him to go away and somehow forgetting that this had ever happened.

'Is that everything?'

Maybe. Nell wasn't sure, but she felt cold now, instead of burning hot. Hugo seemed to think so because he was gently guiding her to her feet.

'Come…'

'No!' At least she'd made it to the bathroom. Now she was here, she wasn't taking any chances. Hugo reached for the large, well-stocked bathroom cabinet. It seemed that in addition to condoms, which she'd found in there earlier in the evening and made use of later, the cabinet was also prepared for seasickness. Hugo took out a cardboard dish and gave it to her, collecting a bottle of ginger tablets.

He walked her through to the cabin, sitting her down on the bed. She felt a little better. Just well enough for embarrassment to take a better hold around her heart.

'The sea's a little choppier now than it was earlier.'

'Yeah? Thought it was just me.' Nell groaned as another wave of nausea took hold, but this time, she managed to quell it.

'No, it's unusually rough for this harbour. Try looking at the coastline, that might help orientate you a bit.'

Nell looked at the lights, still shining around the bay. They seemed a long way away at the moment, and enticingly still. 'Can't we…dock or something?'

'I'm afraid not. There's nowhere *to* dock.'

'Oh-h-h…!' Nowhere to run. Nowhere to hide. This was turning into a nightmare.

He supported her gently through to his cabin, saying that it was further back and so the roll of the ship would be less. If it was, Nell couldn't feel it. He let her sip water, sitting with her as she looked through the porthole, trying to tell her brain which way they were moving before her stomach reacted to it. Gave her ginger tablets to chew, but they just made her sick again.

'Drugs, Hugo…'

'Yes. I think so, too. Do you have any allergies?'

'No… I need the drugs…' Surely he wasn't going to make her go through the preliminary questions. But he did, and Nell responded automatically to his calm, gentle tone, trying to distance herself from what was happening.

He was good at this. Even the injection was accomplished with the minimum of indignity.

'That's going to work pretty quickly now.'

'Yeah… Quickly…' Thinking was suddenly like wading through treacle. All Nell could feel was Hugo's arms around her and the sudden feeling of drowsiness.

CHAPTER SIXTEEN

SHE WOKE TO half light. A slight breeze was playing through the cabin, and the sun must be shining outside the closed curtains. Nell's first thought was that she didn't feel sick any more.

Her second thought was for Hugo. He was sitting quietly in the corner of the cabin, looking the way a lover should in the morning. Freshly showered, not yet shaved, wearing a pair of shorts and a polo shirt. She wondered if he had fresh coffee somewhere and decided her stomach wasn't quite up to that.

'I'm so embarrassed.'

He didn't even pretend to shrug it off. 'Want me to show you my scar? We can feel embarrassed together.'

In an odd way, it was the nicest thing he could have said. Saying it didn't matter would have been ridiculous. Sharing the way he felt was oddly comforting.

'Your pacemaker isn't as messy as being seasick.'

He shrugged. 'You have excellent aim, which must be entirely intuitive, since you clearly weren't up to thinking about it.'

Nell smiled. 'Glad to hear it.'

'Feeling better now?'

'Yes, much. If I'd known, I'd have taken something before I came on board.'

'I should have mentioned it. But then we doctors can be trusted to look after our own health so well.' He quirked his lips down, to give the obvious lie to the statement.

'Don't we just.'

She almost wanted him to come back to bed. Actually, she *did* want him to, but she wasn't going to ask, not after last night. Maybe that wasn't such a bad thing. It made the transition, between lovers and friends, a little easier. Something that might be laughed about even, when the sting of embarrassment had lost its bite.

We slept together, then I got seasick and he had to give me an injection. Yes, right there...

'Can you face something to eat? Toast, maybe?'

That sounded like a good idea. Something to get her back on her feet and put this behind her.

'I'd love some.' Nell was still wearing the robe that Hugo had wrapped her in last night. She pulled back the bedcovers, finding that standing up was hardly even a challenge.

'Stay here. I'll go and get a tray.' He rose, stopping to curl his arm around her shoulder to give her a hug. Hugo was clearly pretty good at this morning-after *we're still friends, aren't we?* thing. She felt him kiss the top of her head, and then he turned and walked out of the cabin.

By lunchtime, Nell felt well enough to eat some more, and then take another trip to the bridge, so that Captain Masson could demonstrate the complexities of getting back into the marina without hitting anything. She said her goodbyes, and the motor launch took them back to land, where Hugo's car was waiting for them.

Something had happened last night. Something outside the obvious.

It wasn't just the amazing sex, or the look in Hugo's green eyes when he'd given himself up to her. He'd met her embarrassment with his own shame, and somehow that had created an understanding. Acceptance in the face of what each of them was most afraid to show.

They could be friends now. They *must* be friends, because anything less would be a tragedy. As they walked towards the front door of his house, and Hugo turned the key in the lock, this seemed like a new beginning. One that would see them both succeed in the dream that Nell had so recently begun to share. The clinic.

They left their bags in the hall for later, and walked through to the kitchen. Hugo opened the fridge and took a can of ginger beer out, and Nell laughed.

'No, thanks. I think I can manage without it. Would you like a cup of tea?'

'Love one.' He was suddenly still. The man who had moved through today with the ease of a practised diplomat was suddenly unsure of himself.

'Nell…?'

'Yes?'

'Last night. I…'

She could handle this. Nell took the can from his hand, putting it down on the countertop. He looked at it for a moment and then his gaze moved to her face.

'I had the very best night. And then the very worst. I'm glad you were there for the best part, and sorry you had to be for the worst.'

'I'm not sorry…' he started.

She laid her hand lightly on his chest, and he fell silent. 'I'm very grateful you were there to look after me. That's the advantage of sleeping with a doctor. And, like you say, what happens at sea stays at sea. We have a clinic to build.'

He nodded. 'And you don't feel you can work with me and sleep with me? I can understand that, if that's what you're saying.'

At some point, she'd become a different person from the one who had been taken in by Martin, and then bullied by him. Nell wasn't quite sure when that had happened.

'I'm think I'm still working that one out.'

'Then...are you somewhere that might allow a bit of flexibility? On the working together and sleeping together thing?'

It was as if someone had opened a door, letting sunlight into the room. All the knowledge of chemical reactions in the brain didn't make it any less a work of magic.

'What kind of flexibility?' The sudden desire to be wooed flared in her chest, making Nell's heart beat a little faster.

That smile of his was a very good opening salvo. The way he stepped a little closer, not quite touching her, made Nell's head begin to reel.

'I want to touch you again. I know I can't keep you for ever, but it doesn't make it any the less sweet that you're here now.'

Nell reached up, brushing her fingertips against his cheek. 'I want to touch you, too.'

He reached for her, pulling her close. When he kissed her, she could feel all the tension buzzing between them. Last night hadn't even begun to sate it; instead, it had only made it grow.

'Upstairs.' He whispered the word, but it still held all the promise of a command.

'Yes. Upstairs.'

It was odd. Before they'd been sleeping together, no

one had doubted their devotion to one another. The papers had used the official photographs taken to celebrate their engagement and painted a rosy picture of a couple who were completely in love. But now…

Hugo was laughing on the phone with his mother as he walked her from the car to the front door. He walked into the kitchen, pulling a carton of juice from the fridge, and Nell fetched two glasses.

'Yes, I'll give her your love… Love you, too.' Hugo had seemed more openly affectionate with his mother in the last few weeks, and he'd even taken to chatting with his father on the phone.

'What was that all about?' Nell picked up her glass, taking a sip from it.

'Apparently we're cooling off.'

'Really?' Nell raised her eyebrows. She hadn't noticed anything of the sort. The last two weeks had been all heat.

'My mother was talking to a friend of hers who was at the gala we went to at the weekend. She said that I hardly looked at you all evening.'

Nell grinned. 'Perhaps we'd had an argument.'

'Perhaps. Maybe I was just looking the other way, trying not to imagine what you were wearing under that dress.'

'Oh. So you can do that, can you? Look the other way and get your imagination under control.'

'No, not really.' He took a step towards her, laying his hand on her waist. 'What are you wearing under this dress?'

'What if I said long johns?'

He laughed, taking the near-empty glass from her hand and putting it on the kitchen counter. Nell backed away from him and he followed, closing in on her.

'Long johns would be fine. Just as long as you're in them.' He wound his arms around her waist, pulling her against him, his body suddenly taut.

'Ah. What about something in stout cotton? Plenty of buttons and safety pins.'

'Wonderful. They'd take a bit more concentration to get off. I might just faint from anticipation while I do it, and then you can revive me.'

Nell laughed. Hugo loved the act of undressing her. Made an art of it, as if he were slowly unwrapping something precious. She loved it, too. It was one of the ways he made her feel special.

'I've been wanting you all day...' Every time she touched Hugo, she wanted him. That was probably why she studiously avoided touching him in public.

'I'm glad to hear that. You want me now?' His hand slipped beneath her jacket, moving towards her breast. Nell began to tremble and she felt his lips curve into a smile against hers. 'You *do* want me. I can feel it.'

'Come and find out how much...'

Nell couldn't remember being any happier than she was now. Hugo was becoming stronger and the scar on his chest was fading. It felt as if maybe the scars in Nell's heart might be finally fading, too.

They reached their fundraising target, and celebrated it with champagne in bed. All that mattered in these early days of their heady romance was that every moment spent alone was spent in each other's arms.

They sat on the patio, eating breakfast, and Nell tore open the thick envelope, drawing out the heavily embossed paper. Hugo was watching quietly. He knew it must be a letter from the legal team he'd persuaded Nell to use in her complaint against Martin.

'What do they say?' He gave her time to read, hope kindling in his eyes when he saw her smile.

'Four other women have come forward and said that Martin made persistent and unwelcome advances towards them. Apparently one of them had the presence of mind to record him on her mobile phone.' She grinned at him. 'He used exactly the same phrases as I wrote in my complaint.'

Hugo chuckled. 'Open and shut case, then.'

'I think so. The hospital have suspended him, and there may be criminal charges in connection with one of the complaints.' She slid the letter across the table so that Hugo could read it all. 'Thank you.'

He shook his head, laughing. 'You did it all. I just… watched and admired.'

'Well, thank you for watching and admiring. You do it so well.'

They finished breakfast and drove to the hospital. Hugo had a planning meeting to attend, and Nell had decided to spend the time in the ward, helping the children's play specialist.

'It'll be great when we have more space.' The young red-headed woman grinned at Nell.

'Did Dr Bertrand tell you? We have the money now, and the work can go ahead again. There should be some progress during the next few weeks.'

'Yes, he did. We'll be able to watch it go up. I'll take pictures for you every day, so you can see what's happening.'

It was a nice thought, but Nell wondered why Louise thought she wouldn't be able to take pictures for herself.

'Thanks. I won't be here every day, so it would be good to have those.'

'You won't be here at all, will you? What about the celebrations?'

'I forgot about those,' she hedged. Maybe this was something that Hugo hadn't told her about?

'Well, once you've been, you won't forget them for next year. Montarino's royal anniversary fortnight is a bit special, there's always lots to do. I expect you'll be really busy.' Louise's voice rang with anticipation.

'Mmm. Well, yes. It would be great if you could take some photos. While I'm busy.' Nell turned her attention to the little boy who had just been wheeled into the play-room by one of the nurses, gathering up some bricks and putting them on the table in front of him.

'Montarino's royal anniversary fortnight.' Nell couldn't help keeping the sharpness from her voice. Over the course of the day, she'd made discreet enquiries about it, as well as looking it up on the Internet. Apparently the whole royal family took part, and there were concerts, exhibitions and other events over a full two weeks. Why hadn't Hugo told her about it?

A small voice at the back of her head told her why. But Nell was trying to ignore it.

'Ah. Yes.' Hugo put his car keys down on the table. 'I was going to mention that.'

His tone had a guilty ring to it. The small voice got louder.

'Okay. It's just that one of the play therapists at the hospital mentioned it. She says it's really good fun.'

'Yes, it is.'

'And that the whole royal family takes part?'

'Yes, we do. It's a tradition dating back hundreds of

years. It's said there used to be a banquet that lasted two weeks, but we've skipped that bit now.'

'And it's in two weeks' time.' Nell was getting a very bad feeling now.

'Yes.' He paused, frowning. 'Nell, I think… Maybe we should give it a miss.'

'That's entirely up to you, Hugo. But shouldn't you be with your family?' Hugo seemed to be getting on so much better with his father these days. They still occasionally had their ups and downs, but Nell had encouraged Hugo to voice his affection and respect for his father. No doubt under similar pressure from his mother, Hugo's father had begun to voice similar feelings about his son.

'Well… I'll have to go to some of the events. Now that I'm back to full health, I should start taking on some of my royal duties again. I may have to stay at the palace for…a few nights. Maybe more.'

This wasn't like Hugo. He was usually so decisive. Nell knew for sure now that something was up. 'Hugo, just say it. What's going on? Don't you want me to go with you? You know I'll support you, in whatever you want to do.'

He sat down at the kitchen table, tracing his fingers across its surface. Then he seemed to come to a decision. 'I don't want you there.'

'Okay. Fine.' Nell swallowed the feeling that suddenly the world was turning in the wrong direction. It was making her feel a little sick.

'It's not that I don't want you with me. I just…' He shrugged, letting out a sigh. 'I don't want you involved with my official duties. These two weeks are always really busy and… I promised you that you'd never be just the woman on my arm. That you'd always have your own career.'

Nell didn't remember him promising her that. Maybe he'd just promised it to himself. 'I can see why you'd say that. But I don't mind. If you want me to be there, I'll happily support you. That's what we do for each other, isn't it?'

'Yes, it is. And my way of supporting you is to draw that line and stick to it. You…you've only been to one official function and that seemed…stressful for you.'

'Yes, it was stressful. You got hit with a stun gun.'

Hugo shrugged. 'I meant the bit before that. The dress and everything…'

'It was my first time, of course I was a bit stressed.' Nell frowned. 'This isn't about me, is it?'

'It's all about you, Nell. It's about my not taking you for granted, and giving you the room to have your own career.'

'It's about Anna.' His *real* fiancée. Nell felt a sudden stab of jealousy, knowing that the ring she wore was the symbol of an agreement, not of love.

'Anna's in my past. We've been finished, in every way, for a long time.'

'Yes, but what happened isn't finished. You can't let go of the idea that Montarino is your duty, and that you can't escape it. Or that your duty is incompatible with having a partner who has a career.'

'No, I can't. Because that's the truth of it, Nell. Believe me, I've tried and it doesn't work.' His voice was suddenly cold. Nell knew that she was pushing Hugo too far, into places that she'd resolved never to go with him. But if that could break them apart then maybe it should. Because it was an issue that they could only avoid for so long.

When had she started thinking about the long-term? Their engagement was one of convenience, and they'd agreed that three to six months would be enough. They'd decided to part after that.

But that was before they'd slept together. They'd promised that it would change nothing, yet it had changed everything. And suddenly Nell saw that while Hugo was kind and honourable, and Martin was neither, she would still always have to play the mistress with Hugo. His first loves were his work and his country, and he would never truly believe that there was room for her in that situation.

Nell deserved more than this. At the very minimum, she deserved his honesty. Hugo had almost deceived himself into thinking that it could work between them, but in truth he'd been careful to show her only one side of his life. Just as their engagement had sheltered her from the press, he had sheltered her from the realities of sharing her life with a prince.

Much as he wanted to, he couldn't do this to her. He couldn't take away her independence, and her career, and watch her fade and wilt in the bright light of his responsibilities.

'Nell, we agreed.' He didn't want to say it, but he had to.

'Yes, we agreed. A three-month engagement and then we go our separate ways.' As usual, she was ahead of him. The connection between them, which up till now had been a conduit for love, seemed now to be pushing them inexorably towards a parting.

'I'm fit and well now. And you're safe from the lies.' Was that really all there was to their relationship? A convenience? It had started out that way, and it seemed that it was going to end that way.

'So you'll go back to your life, and I'll go back to mine.'

'I think that's best for both of us.'

She turned away from him suddenly. As if she didn't want to even look at him any more. 'Fine. We'll do that, then.'

'Nell…' He hadn't wanted things to end like this. Maybe he should have thought about that when he'd first reached out to touch her. 'Nell, you can stay here for as long as you want. I'll go to my apartment at the palace…'

She faced him, her cheeks flushed red. Even now, if she had cried, Hugo could never have let her go, but she didn't. 'I'm not your employee, Hugo. You don't have to give me a notice period, I can leave whenever I like.'

Anger started to mount in his chest. If that was the way she wanted it. 'Fine. I'm going to the palace anyway.' He picked up his car keys and walked back outside to the car. Starting the engine, he pulled out of the driveway and onto the road.

CHAPTER SEVENTEEN

HUGO BROODED ON the matter for two weeks. Then he got on a plane and flew to London.

Nell's flat was in a nice road, with trees on each side of it. As he got out of the taxi, he noticed that her front gate needed mending, and that the brass on the front door had been recently polished. It felt as if everything had suddenly shot into sharp focus.

A young woman answered the door and stared at him blankly.

'I'm looking for Nell. Nell Maitland.'

'Oh. She's not here any more. Sorry.' The woman made to shut the front door and Hugo wondered if he should put his foot against the frame. Probably not, it might scare her.

'Please…' The door opened again, and Hugo breathed a sigh of relief. 'Do you know of any way that I might contact her?'

'No, I'm sorry. We've been here for three months and we've just signed another lease. The agent said that she was going abroad again.'

'I don't suppose you know where?'

'No. She didn't go back to…' The woman clicked her fingers, trying to recall the name.

'Montarino.'

'That's right. The agent did say that she wasn't going back there.'

Okay. That was Montarino ticked off the list. It was a start. All Hugo had to contend with now was the rest of the world.

'Would you be able to give me the name of the agent, please? I'm trying to get in contact with her.'

The woman looked him up and down, seeming to come to the conclusion that it would be okay. 'It's Green's in the High Street. You know it?'

'No, I'm sorry, I don't. Which way is that?'

'End of the road, turn left. Walk down to the very end of that road and then turn right along the High Street. You can't miss it.' The woman shrugged. 'There's a big green sign.'

'Thank you.' Hugo smiled. It seemed as if this was going to be a long journey, but this was at least the first step.

The woman smiled suddenly. 'Good luck.'

'Thank you.' He was going to need it. He had to fly back to Montarino tonight, but he had time enough to speak to the estate agent and if Nell was still in London, he might be able to see her today.

This was Nell's third job in a few weeks. Maybe this one would be a keeper.

She'd told her employment agency that she'd take any job anywhere, as long as it wasn't in London and they would guarantee absolute discretion as regards her whereabouts. They'd taken her at her word. The first job had been a week or so as a supply doctor on nights in a busy Huddersfield A & E department. The second had taken her to Manchester for a few days, and the third had brought her to Northern Germany, where she was helping an overworked and understaffed clinic that had been set up to cater for refugees.

It might be classed as overkill, but you didn't just walk away from Hugo. He had contacts everywhere. If he missed her one quarter as much as she missed him, he might try to get in contact. And if he did, she couldn't trust herself not to respond.

It was better not to give him that chance. Not face the dilemma of his having tried to find her, and not to feel the heartbreak if he hadn't. This way she could draw a line under their affair and find a way to start again. Let him start again, and have the life he deserved.

The clinic was hard work. Nell's German wasn't up to scratch yet, but it was improving every day, and her French and English were both useful. The families under her care tore at her heart, but it was work that was important. The director of the clinic had already asked whether she was available for another month, and she hoped that might be extended even further.

It was late, almost nine o'clock, when she finally packed up her things and grabbed her coat. Tomorrow was her one day off per week, and she might just spend that sleeping and eating, since she hadn't had a great deal of time for either in the last couple of days.

'I'll see you on Thursday.' She smiled at the receptionist, who nodded back. Pulling her coat around her against the first chill of winter, she walked outside, nodding to the security guard at the gate and making for her car, which was parked some way down the road.

He was under a lamppost, next to her car. Huddled in a thick jacket, pacing back and forth to keep warm. Hugo must have been waiting a while. Nell had one moment to escape, but then he saw her. She saw his face in the light of the lamp, and there was no running away now. He waited, suddenly still, as she walked towards him.

'Hugo.'

'Nell.' His voice was thick with emotion. It carried with it the long weeks of running and the inevitable search he must have made to find her. And suddenly that was all nothing. She wanted to fall into his arms and kiss him.

'It's cold.' There wasn't any point in asking him what he was doing here, that was obvious. And Hugo was shivering.

'Yes. They wouldn't let me into the clinic.'

'Security's pretty tight there. How long have you been waiting?'

'A couple of hours.'

Nell unlocked her car and opened the passenger door. 'Come and sit in the car.' If she switched the engine on, the heater might warm him a little.

'Would you mind coming to mine? I'm parked just around the corner.' He gave a hesitant smile. 'Heated seats.'

He'd found her. He'd come for her and had stood in the cold for hours, waiting for her. And despite everything, that unspoken connection between them was still as strong as it had ever been. This was like walking on the edge of a precipice in the darkness, but Nell couldn't stop herself. She took his arm, and Hugo started to walk.

'What's the clinic like?'

'It's tough. There are a lot of kids who are sick and have been through a lot. Adults, too. Any progress is hard won, but it's rewarding work.'

'Do you think you'll stay?'

If what he meant was would she forget about all this and come back with him to Montarino, the answer was no. Not to see their relationship crumble once more and feel that heartbreak all over again.

'Yes, I'm thinking about it.'

'Good. I'm glad you've found this.'

What did he want? To sit in the car and reminisce about old times? It didn't really matter, whatever it was, Nell knew she'd see it through to the end. He stopped beside his car and opened the passenger door. Nell got in.

He was cold, and the long wait had given all his fears the chance to settle heavily around his heart. But Hugo had found out what he wanted from life, and he wasn't going to give it up without a fight.

Nell's warmth hadn't changed. He still felt it, binding them together the way it always had. If her voice was tempered with sadness, it was the sadness that he felt in his own heart, too.

She pulled off her knitted hat, putting it in her lap with her gloves. She was staring at the steering wheel, as if that was safe middle ground. Not straight ahead, Nell was never that cold. Not at him, because he'd broken her heart. She didn't need to say it; he could see it in her eyes.

'Nell, I've thought about this a lot, and there are only four things that truly matter.'

She glanced at him, turning her gaze away quickly. 'Four?'

'Yes. That you follow your calling as a doctor. That I follow mine. That's two. The third, and most important, is that I love you.'

'But...you don't want me.'

'I've always wanted you, Nell. I sent you away because I thought I couldn't have you without you having to sacrifice number one. Now I know better.'

She turned suddenly, wide-eyed. 'And the fourth?'

'That's up to you. If *you* love *me*, then we can work everything else out.'

Her lip began to quiver. If she cried now he wouldn't be able to stop his own tears. Maybe that was just yet another proof of the connection that he felt with Nell.

'What about Montarino?'

Hope thumped almost painfully in his chest, and he ignored it. It was just his heart beating, and that was proof that he could live long enough to show Nell how much he loved her.

'There are people who will oversee the building of the clinic, just as well as I can. The royal calendar can do without me from time to time, my parents have it all pretty well tied down. Montarino doesn't need me, it was me who needed Montarino. I needed something to dedicate myself to.'

'And you don't now?' She frowned, shaking her head. 'Hugo, you love the place.'

'Yes, I love it. It'll always be my home. But you're the one and only love of my life, Nell. You're a lot more important to me.'

Her gaze searched his face. Then one tear dropped from her eye, tumbling down her cheek. 'You're the one and only love of my life, too.'

He reached for her, wishing that they were somewhere less cramped so he could hold her properly. But it didn't matter. Hugo knew what really mattered now, and that was being able to look into her eyes. Wipe away her tears and brush a kiss onto her lips.

'Where are you staying?' Finally she broke the warm silence that curled around them like a blanket.

'At the Grand.'

'That's right across town!'

'I booked it from the lamppost. There wasn't a great deal of choice.'

Nell chuckled. 'Okay, so we can drive across town and have room service, or it's ten minutes to mine. Fifteen if we stop for pizza on the way.'

'Pizza sounds great.'

Crown Prince Hugo Phillipe DeLeon, only son of the King of Montarino, had to carry the pizza up three flights of stairs because the lift was broken. He looked around her flat, which didn't take long, because there were only two rooms and a bathroom, and pronounced it delightful. He kept his coat on while the heating took the edge off the chill in the sitting room.

They ate pizza and drank coffee, and her small flat became the centre of the world. The one place where they could both be happy, because it was the place they were together. Curled up on the sofa together, talking about plans and dreams, futures and possibilities.

'That's what we'll do, then?' The sun was rising but Nell didn't feel tired any more.

'You're sure that's what you want?' Hugo leaned over, kissing her.

'I'm sure. You're sure you really *can* take a holiday for the next month? So that I won't let the clinic here down?'

'Positive. I'll be waiting here for you every evening with a smile on my face and a tasty meal in the oven.'

Nell snorted with laughter. 'You will not. If you're staying here, you can earn your keep. I'm sure the clinic will take you on, they could do with more doctors. And being a prince has its advantages.'

'They don't have to pay me?'

'Yeah, they don't really have the funds for that. You'll spread a little happiness, though.'

'That sounds great. Can't wait to start.' Hugo got to his feet, stretching his limbs, and walked over to the window, looking out at the glow on the horizon. 'Come with me.'

'Where are we going?'

'See that little park down there? It looks a nice place for an early morning stroll. We can watch the sunrise.'

They pulled on their coats, tiptoeing down the stairs so as not to wake any of the neighbours. Across the street and through the park gates, into a cold, fresh morning. Hugo seemed to know exactly where he wanted to go, and Nell followed him over to a small playground, sitting next to him on the swings.

He grinned, feeling in his coat pocket. Then he opened a box, holding it out for her to see the ring inside, flashing bright in the new day. 'Nell, this is a symbol of love between the two of us. That you'll love me, and I'll love you. That we can make happen the things we both want.'

He'd said almost those same words before. This time it was real. Nell began to tremble with excitement, as he fell onto one knee in front of her. 'Will you marry me, Nell?'

'Yes, Hugo.' She leaned forward, kissing him. Holding on to him tightly, in case this was just a beautiful dream.

'This isn't a royal jewel. If you'd prefer one of those, there are plenty to choose from…'

'No. No, Hugo, this is much better. I want this one, please.' It wasn't some anonymous jewel. Hugo had chosen this just for her. It was exquisite, a gold band with square cut diamonds set all the way around it. Clearly expensive, but not so bulky that it would tear a pair of surgical gloves.

'You don't need to take this one off when you're at work.' Hugo had obviously been thinking exactly the same as she was.

'Hugo, thank you for coming for me. Thank you for

believing in me. I'll never take it off.' Nell could feel tears streaming down her cheeks. He pulled at her glove, tugging it off, and she held out her hand.

'I'll be taking it off on our wedding day. Just for long enough to slip your wedding ring on.' He kissed her, sliding the ring onto her finger.

'Come home with me, Hugo. I have a three-quarter-sized bed, and I want to see how well you fit into it.'

'I'll fit. Particularly if I have you in my arms. Are you tired?'

'What? No, I'm not tired. Are you?'

'Not even slightly.' He got to his feet, wrapping his arm around her shoulders. Then Nell walked her prince back up to the tiny flat that now contained every dream she'd ever had.

EPILOGUE

THEY'D STAYED ON at the clinic in Germany for two months, working for nothing so that other doctors could be recruited and paid. Hugo bade the little flat goodbye with more regret than he'd ever left anywhere before. It held the best memories of his life.

But there was more to come. Nell was a quiet force to be reckoned with, planning a wedding and a reception that didn't follow any royal protocol that Hugo had ever heard of. The idea was received with hardly a murmur from his father, and warm approval from his mother.

Everything went off without a hitch. Nell's father and his had become friends over a shared interest in gardening, and Hugo's mother had finally managed to persuade Nell's mother that her outfit was perfect for the occasion. They were married in the presence of close family and friends in a small private ceremony. Nell looked more beautiful than he could ever have imagined, wearing a knee-length fitted dress in cream silk, her only concession to royal splendour being a small diamond tiara, which held a shoulder-length veil in place.

There was nothing but love. When he recited his vows, and she said hers. When he slipped the ring onto her finger. But the moment that made Hugo proudest was the one when his new bride took his arm and he walked into the children's cardiac unit at the hospital. She sat with each of the children, letting them hold her bouquet and even taking off the tiara so that the little girls could try it on.

Then there was cake in the children's playroom, which for some reason that Hugo couldn't fathom had candles on it. It turned out that one of the children had a birthday today, and Nell duly helped her to blow out the candles, to cheers and clapping from the parents. The nurses supervised the cutting and distribution of the cake, while Nell managed to retrieve the tiara, finding a handkerchief to wipe the sticky finger marks off it.

'Oh, dear.' She held it up to the light, twisting it back and forth. 'It's got icing on it.'

'Probably the best use it's ever been put to.' Hugo grinned, sitting down next to her on one of the plastic chairs that lined the ward. 'I dare say my mother will know the best way to clean it.'

'I can't give it back to your mother like this. She's already been so good about delaying the start of the reception so that we could come here first.'

'I thought it was rather a good idea. Gives everyone a chance to put their feet up and loosen their ties.'

'Like you've loosened yours?' Nell gave him a mischievous look. 'What *will* people say?'

'They'll say I've married the most beautiful woman in the world. The most dedicated doctor and…' Hugo brushed a crushed petal from her dress '…the best person I know.'

'And I've married the most handsome prince in the world. Actually, I should widen the scope a bit. The most handsome *doctor* in the world.'

'I like that a lot better.' Hugo kissed her hand, and heard a camera shutter click. He turned and smiled, his arm around his new wife. A picture for the hospital scrapbook.

'I'm so proud of you, Hugo. Last week, a man told me how much your speech about having a pacemaker had meant to his wife. She said that if it was good enough for you, then it was good enough for her.'

'And I'm proud of you, too. Your project is going to make a big difference to a lot of people.'

He and Nell had decided that they would work together, but each concentrate on different special projects. Nell had already formed a partnership between the hospital in Montarino and the London hospital where she'd worked, to create a joint initiative to promote research and care for elderly patients with heart disease.

'I hope so. It's early days yet.'

'We have plenty of time. All our lives.'

Nell smiled at him. 'I'm so happy, Hugo. You're my one true love.'

'And you are mine.' Hugo kissed his wife, and a cheer went up around the room.

'Do it again!' a child's voice piped up from somewhere, and everyone laughed.

There was nothing else he could do but kiss Nell again.

* * * * *

THE DOCTOR'S CINDERELLA

SUSANNE HAMPTON

MILLS & BOON

To my Father.
You gave me unconditional love.
You encouraged me to pursue my dreams.
You wanted me to be the best version of myself.
You are my hero, looking down from heaven.

And to Helen Mckerral for encouraging me to write
this story and believing that I could do it justice.
Thank you.

CHAPTER ONE

MOLLY MURPHY WAS sad and irritated in equal amounts and she was barely awake. Clanging sounds followed by thuds in the street outside had woken her from a deep and much-needed sleep. Soft frown lines formed on her forehead as she rolled over and pulled the pillow around her ears but the harsh sounds continued. She gave up trying to block them out. The pillow was far too thin and no match for the noise.

It was officially the first day of winter in Australia and unrelenting rain had been teeming down for five days straight. Molly could hear that hadn't abated overnight. The tin roof was still being hammered by the downpour but the other sounds were even louder. She rubbed her eyes, then closed them again as she contemplated whether she should get up. Her alarm hadn't sounded so she decided to stay put.

Pleasant dreams were hard to come by for Molly and she wasn't happy that one had been cut short as it had been far better than her reality of late. As she lay in the cosiness of her bed, her immediate recollection was a little scattered but it had included a sun-drenched, sandy beach, a cocktail with a tiny paper umbrella…and no overdue bills on the kitchen counter.

Suddenly her musing stopped as she peeked through

her heavy eyelids in the direction of the window. Winter sunlight was streaming in through kinks in the ageing venetian blinds. The intensity of the light saw irritation turn to panic. Even half-asleep Molly knew her room should not have been that brightly lit at six-thirty. It was the first of June. It was officially winter and it should have been dark outside. Feeling her heart begin to pick up speed, she anxiously reached over for her mobile phone on the nightstand. The screen was black. The phone was flat. The alarm was never going to sound. She tried to focus on the clock hanging in the hallway opposite her door. It was almost eight o'clock. She had overslept by an hour and a half.

'Oh, God…no, no, no, not today…'

Her reality was now even further from dreams of a cocktail on a beach.

Molly sat bolt upright in her bed. Only to collapse back down again in pain. Her head had collided with the ridiculously placed wooden bookcase that jutted out from the vinyl-covered bedhead. Hideous decorating from the sixties had sent her crashing back onto her pillow. Her knees instinctively lifted up to her chin and she rocked as her fingers gently rubbed the smarting skin underneath her mop of messy curls. Through tired and now-watering eyes, she looked upwards at the heavy wooden structure inconveniently protruding only twelve inches over the top of her bed.

'Damn you,' she spat as a few tears began spilling from her eyes and trickling down her cheeks. Molly surmised her crying was partly from the shock of hitting something so hard, partly from the pain that followed and maybe more than a little from what had led her to be sleeping in a bed with such a goddamn ugly bedhead.

Love. Naive, stupid love.

Molly had lost almost everything because of it.

And she still blamed herself.

But the new, resilient, heart-of-stone Molly Murphy would never fall in love again. Not ever. It hurt too much.

Taking a deep breath and wiping away the tears with the back of her hand, she attempted to calm herself. She didn't have time for self-pity, not even a few minutes of it. She had to put on her big-girl panties and get going because she was running late. Very late. And since she had been sleeping in the same bed for close to a year with the horrific bookcase bedhead hovering over her, she had no choice but to assume at least part of the responsibility. Each time she had knocked her head on the oak eyesore, and there had been numerous times, she had vowed not to do it again. But then, half-asleep, she would go and *do it again*. If the house were hers, she would have ripped the monstrosity of a bedhead from the wall. But as a tenant she had no choice but to be the victim of it. And that unfortunately happened with annoying and painful regularity.

Insomnia had been her only bedtime companion since her fiancé had disappeared into the night without warning. He had just scribbled a five-line note that, after stripping away the narcissistic wordsmithing, had explained nothing. It had also provided Molly with no inkling of the mess that she would be left to face alone, including the last-minute cancellation of their winter wedding.

Since that dreadful day she had been tossing and turning alone in her bed, so the evening before the anniversary of the day on which she should have been walking down the aisle, she had gone to her room early. Trying desperately not to throw herself a full-blown pity party, she had listened to her female empowerment playlist on her mobile phone. Hours of the edgy, no-holds-barred lyrics had finally allowed her to fall asleep under the security of the heavy woollen blankets. And had also allowed her phone battery to go flat. If it hadn't been for the relentless clanging of each bin being emptied into the truck then dropped back to the kerb in her narrow rain-soaked street, she might well have slept until midday. The sound of the trains shuttling past so close to her tiny home that her windows rattled had become white noise over the months and something she could easily sleep through. And she now knew the rain pelting down had joined the same category.

The sharp pain on the crown of her head quickly replaced the threat of melancholy thoughts as she climbed hurriedly but still a little gun-shy from underneath the weight of her warm covers. Still mumbling to herself, Molly switched to fight-or-flight mode as her feet touched the chilly floorboards of her bedroom. The tiny home was close to ninety years old and there were little gaps between the aged planks that allowed a draft into her room anywhere in the house where there wasn't time-weary linoleum. But that morning Molly barely noticed the icy landing. She was in too much of a rush.

There was no time to wash her hair. In fact, there was barely enough time to run a brush through the short curly brunette bob as she ran into her tiny bathroom, jumped under a two-minute shower and then dressed in the semi-darkness of her room. Molly knew there was a hard rubbish collection as well as the bins so the council workers would be collecting the bins on both sides of the street and she didn't want to be their early morning floor show, so she hurriedly pulled the curtains closed over the broken blinds.

Reaching for the light switch, she found the single light globe hovering over her head had blown. Mentally taking stock of the morning up to that point, she decided it was disastrous and apparently getting worse by the second. The clock was ticking. The next bus would be pulling up at the nearest bus stop in eight minutes and she couldn't even resort to the flashlight on her phone.

She pulled a skirt and shirt from the wardrobe, hoping they matched or at least came close, and her fingers felt around manically under her bed for her shoes. She didn't have time to open the curtains and begin her search. Her heart was beating a little faster than usual as her anxiety levels had peaked. She needed this job as she had few savings left and she had health insurance due the following week, along with the rent and utilities. Molly was well aware that her landlord was not the understanding type. His eldest son and right-hand man, Joel, on the other hand, would offer leniency, accepting part-payment at a price Molly would never pay. He knew she was single, struggling financially and he made his terms very clear. The very thought made her skin crawl and her stomach heave. She would rather live in a tent than give in to him.

Still shuddering with the revolting image of Joel when he delivered his disgusting proposition, Molly raced into the kitchen, on the way calling out to her younger brother, Tommy. Quickly she realised with the lack of a response that he had already left for work. She was grateful that at least one of them had headed off on time. After grabbing a muesli bar from the pantry for breakfast and tossing the phone charger into her bag, Molly threw on her heavy overcoat and hurriedly closed and locked the front door behind her. She navigated puddles down the cracked pathway of her yard, noticing the grass on either side was covered with a layer of overnight frost. Winter was there to stay, she decided as she ran in the rain-dampened cold morning air for the bus stop only two streets from hers.

She had forgotten her gloves so she secured her bag on her shoulder and pushed her hands inside the deep pockets of her heavy overcoat. She had, according to her calculations, two minutes to make it to the stop.

Still catching her breath as she rounded the corner, Molly watched in horror as the fully laden bus pulled away from the kerb. The windows were foggy with the warm breath of the early morning passengers all cramped inside and holding on to the ceiling straps so they didn't lose their footing as the bus muscled its way into the fast flow of traffic. She stopped in her tracks, huffing and puffing and staring helplessly as it drove away. Never before had she wished so much to be crammed uncomfortably against strangers as she did at that moment. Never before had she worried that two minutes could potentially change the course of her life and put her on the unemployment line.

A feeling of resignation that she had no power to change her sad state of affairs washed over her as she walked towards the bus stop and waited in line for the next bus. She could make it to her temp assignment if the next one was on time, but if it was late then she too would be late and there was the risk that the practice would call the agency and request another temp and she would be down a month's steady income.

That couldn't happen, she thought as she looked around her at the crowd building in anticipation of the arrival of the next early morning bus. Was she the only one who had slept in and was at risk of eviction if the bus was late? Was she the only person whose life had been tipped upside down and had still not righted itself, despite how hard and how long she tried to get herself back on track? Was she the only one who couldn't afford to hail a cab even if she could get one to stop, which she doubted as they would all be taken on a day like this?

The cold breeze gained intensity, cutting through Molly's coat. She pulled her arms closer to her body and tried to stop the shivers taking over. Chilled to her core, and waiting in line for a bus that she prayed would arrive in time, she looked around at the others also huddled around the bus shelter. There were schoolchildren of various ages and heights in different uniforms but all with raincoats and backpacks; office workers with briefcases; a construction worker in his high-vis vest, carrying his metal lunch box and hard hat; and an elderly couple holding gloved hands, their faces a little contorted by the frosty elements but no doubt, Molly thought, warmed by each other's company. She had no such comfort or company.

Within a few minutes, and with no warning, the ominous grey clouds that were threatening a downpour opened their floodgates. Hurriedly Molly reached back for her hood but there wasn't one. Both of her black winter overcoats were on the hall stand and naturally, in keeping with the tone of the morning, she had chosen the coat without a hood. There was no room as her fellow travellers rushed for the already oversubscribed shelter and moments later it became obvious her umbrella was not in her oversized handbag.

It couldn't get worse, Molly decided. She would arrive resembling a drowned rat and more than likely late for a much-needed new job. She allowed herself a few seconds to once again indulge in the state of her life, which at that moment was quite dreadful. Then she took a deep breath and settled her thoughts. Until she looked down at her rain-splattered feet and almost laughed out loud.

'Really? Who does that?' she mumbled. With the noise of the heavy traffic rushing by on the wet roads no one could have heard her mutterings but Molly no longer cared if they had. It didn't bother her if the world thought she was mad because at that moment she felt awfully close to it anyway. In her fluster and the darkness of her tiny bedroom, she had slipped into odd ballet flats. One navy and the other black. The black one had a small velvet bow and Molly felt quite certain that unless her work colleagues were short-sighted they would notice. It would be an embarrassing beginning. Then something deep inside reminded her that it was the beginning of something new. A new start, she thought. A rebooting of her life, she told herself as the rain trickled down her temples and inside the collar of her coat.

With that thought, her soggy chin raised a little. It was the beginning of Molly Murphy's new life. The old debts were finally paid in full. It had taken her eleven months to repay everything. The man who had destroyed her credit rating and almost destroyed her life was gone. And she had a new job. The new, resolute Molly was ready to build a new life...but one without a man. She might have a terrible address at that moment and no long-term, well-paid career prospects, but she had done the best she could.

Hindsight would have seen her make very different financial decisions. But hindsight was like that. It was wise and sensible. And she had been neither when she'd met the man she'd thought would be her happily ever after. She had rushed in and believed every word he had whispered in her ear. Hung on every promise he'd made in the warmth of the bed they'd shared. Trusted every dream he'd told her as she'd smiled at her beautiful diamond engagement ring. She'd thought her life was turning around after the sadness of losing her parents. She'd believed she had found the one. The man who would make her dreams come true. The one who would make her life whole again.

But all of it was a lie. A well-planned, brilliantly executed lie.

And one she had willingly and naively bought into and lost almost everything she had in the process. But fortunately, not everything. She still had her most treasured, shining ace.

She had Tommy.

Looking up into the falling raindrops, she didn't know whether to laugh or cry. And so, she did neither. Instead she let the water run over her face, waking her up completely, while her icy fingers felt around in the bottom of her bag for her makeshift breakfast. She unwrapped it and unceremoniously wolfed it down in three bites. At least the pain in her head was subsiding and while she was quite powerless to change much about the morning, she could at least prevent her stomach growling with hunger. The very first day of winter was testing her mettle but she would get through it. She had Tommy and together they could face whatever life threw at them. They had already proven that.

Suddenly the thought of her younger brother warmed her heart and went a little way to quelling her rising anxiety. He more than made up for the wreck the other parts of her life had become. And on the days when she felt herself spinning a little close to the edge, knowing they had each other kept her grounded.

And that day would be no different.

Whatever the world threw at her, she would face it head-on.

She had to do that for Tommy.

CHAPTER TWO

'YOU'RE PRETTY.'

Molly lifted her bright blue eyes from the keyboard at the reception desk that had been officially hers for four hours. Her lips instinctively curved upwards to form something close to a smile at the unexpected compliment. It was the last thing she'd expected to hear. Pretty was nowhere close to how she felt. In her mind, bedraggled would have been a more accurate call but she was trying not to think about her appearance and just get on with the job at hand. She was warm and dry and that was an improvement on the start of her day. Grooming had not been a priority that morning but hearing the young woman's compliment definitely lifted her spirits.

'Thank you. I think you're very kind to say something so sweet,' Molly told the young woman who had fronted the desk. 'I think you're very pretty and I love your red boots.'

The young woman, just like Molly's brother, Tommy, had been born with Down's syndrome and just like Tommy, she appeared to be relatively independent, by virtue of her attending the surgery without a caregiver by her side. Molly noticed she was wearing designer jeans and a red jumper under her checked woollen overcoat that also looked as if it had been bought at a high-end store. Her short blonde hair was in a bob style and the flat red ankle boots completed the outfit. She was quite the young fashionista.

'Thank you. Red is my favourite colour in the world.'

'I must agree. Red is lovely,' Molly told her, then continued. 'May I have your name, please?'

'Lizzy Jones,' the young woman said. 'My boyfriend likes red. He didn't like red before he was my boyfriend. Now he likes red.'

Molly smiled at the thought of the young man changing his favourite colour to match his girlfriend's taste. Young love was so sweet and naive and something to be treasured as it rarely stayed that perfect. When the rose-coloured glasses came off the real man was rarely as perfect as he once seemed. She hoped for Lizzy's sake her boyfriend remained as lovely as he was at that moment.

'Do you have a boyfriend?' Lizzy asked, breaking Molly's train of thought.

'Um…no, no, I don't.'

'You should have a boyfriend. It's nice. You can share lunch and hold hands.'

'I will give it some thought,' Molly said politely, all the while thinking quite the opposite. Boyfriends, fiancés, they were all the same. They brought heartbreak and disappointment and she was not going back there. Not ever.

'My dad doesn't know I have a boyfriend.' Lizzy giggled then covered her mouth with her hand. 'I will tell him maybe next week or maybe at Christmas.'

'It's a long time until Christmas,' Molly told her with her eyebrow arched slightly.

'Mmm…maybe next week. I don't know.'

'That might be a good idea to let your father know you have a boyfriend. He might like to meet him. I'm sure he's very nice.'

'Shh,' Lizzy said with her fingers at her lips and looking a little anxious. 'You can't tell when you see him.'

'Don't worry, I won't, I promise,' Molly replied with a smile, wondering if Lizzy's father was parking the car or running late to meet her. Whatever the case she hadn't hesitated to reassure the young woman. She had become visibly agitated and needed reassurance that her secret was safe. Molly could see no purpose in announcing to a complete stranger that his daughter had a boyfriend when it might be nothing more than puppy love. And none of her business.

'Okay,' Lizzy said before she crossed the room and made herself comfortable on a waiting-room chair.

Molly sensed Lizzy was quite at ease with being in the practice, almost as if it were a second home to her. She checked the appointment schedule. Forty-five minutes had been allocated for Lizzy Jones, which was unusual considering the pace of the morning, and there was no reference to patient notes available online. She wasn't listed as a new patient but she wasn't in the records management system either. Molly found all of it unusual and decided she would raise it with Ryan later.

There were no other patients waiting as they had been running early and the previous patient had just left. Molly glanced up periodically and noticed Lizzy had taken off her overcoat and neatly placed it on the chair beside her. She was happily swinging her legs and glancing around at the paintings on the wall. Sometime in the ensuing minutes while Molly was processing correspondence Lizzy made her way back to the reception desk.

'Are your shoes red?' Lizzy asked excitedly.

Molly jumped with the surprise of having the young woman upon her again without warning. Then she cringed at the thought of her mismatched shoes. As a knee-jerk reaction to feeling more than a little self-conscious she placed one foot on top of the other. Quite purposely squashing the solo bow on her left foot.

'Umm...'

Before she had a chance to finish her reply a deep male voice came from somewhere close behind her.

'Well, Lizzy, I'm looking at them now and they're definitely not red. Actually, it would appear that Miss Murphy couldn't quite decide whether to wear blue or black shoes today...so she chose one of each colour and threw in a bow of sorts...but only on one of them.'

'That's funny,' Lizzy said with a wide grin that further lit up her happy face.

'Well, funny's one way to describe it,' the male voice countered. 'Another would be odd. Quite literally.'

Molly didn't turn. She was only too well aware it was her boss of four hours. The far too perfect Dr Ryan McFetridge. Charcoal-eyed, raven-haired, six-foot-two, sole general practitioner to the wealthy and privileged who happened to need a temp office manager at the same time that Molly needed a job, any job. It was her only option to ensure she and Tommy were not evicted by the week's end. And that morning as she had stood in the rain watching the bus pull away a tiny part of her had feared that might happen.

'Do you like to mix it up?' the deep voice continued, bringing Molly back from her unsettling thoughts.

Molly drew a deep breath, plastered on a smile and spun to face her boss. His perfect smile made the picture even more ridiculous. And made her feel even more self-conscious. She was bedraggled and he was standing so close with his leading-man looks, not to mention a voice as smooth as melted chocolate. She knew the type. He had playboy written all over him. But he didn't impress her. Not in the least. Molly Murphy had sworn off men… and nothing was going to sway that vow.

'Or was it a case of dressing in the dark?' he continued as he stepped to the side a little and, opening one of the filing cabinets, began sifting through old hard-copy case notes. After finding what he wanted, he returned his gaze to her but said nothing.

'Actually, you nailed it,' she responded without expression in her voice or on her face. 'I did dress in the dark this morning, quite literally.'

'Power outage?'

'Of sorts,' she replied, not liking the fact he hadn't broken eye contact. For some unknown reason, despite her showing no emotion, he was unsettling her. It wasn't his line of questioning. It was his proximity to her. Through his clothes and her own, she could almost sense the warmth of his body. It was as if her own body was adjusting its thermostat to his and she was enormously relieved when he stepped away.

'That would explain a lot.'

Molly wasn't sure what the comment alluded to but assumed it was her previously wet hair and clothes. Before she could take him to task on the meaning behind his remark, he popped the patient record under his arm and then asked Lizzy to follow him to the consulting room.

As the two of them disappeared, Molly was angry with herself. Why the hell was she reacting to him being so close? She should be angry with him but instead she felt a warm wave wash over her and suspected her cheeks might be flushed. She was appalled and surprised.

Molly had met Ryan briefly when she had first arrived, flustered and rushed. She accepted he was an extremely good-looking man but their meeting had been brief, and from a distance across the office as he'd taken an early arriving patient into his consulting room. She had been more interested in settling into the job with the assistance of the young nurse, Stacy, who was there arranging influenza shots and bloods. Molly just wanted to stay under the radar and unnoticed herself, rather than noticing too much about her employer. But suddenly, now, she had noticed far too much about him.

The handsome medico was dressed straight from a men's designer store, the kind of store filled with expensive leather shoes and every imported suit hanging an equal distance from the next on the rack, all covered with shoulder protectors, and assorted silk ties dressing shirts that were housed in open mahogany display cabinets. She knew the stores only too well. A year before, she and her fiancé had been regular customers of them. Her fiancé was quite the clothes horse and she had unwittingly been footing the bill. Ever since, the stores and the people who shopped there had held no appeal to her.

And there was Dr McFetridge's elegantly decorated consulting rooms in one of Adelaide's most affluent eastern suburbs. The leafy side streets were lined with large, opulent, double-storey homes with return driveways and at least three imported cars while Molly's home had no driveway, which was fine as she had no car to park in one anyway. She had sold it along with her jewellery to cover the bond on her home and buy some simple furnishings. And she could get by just fine without it. Except for this morning, when a car would have been very handy.

Everything about Ryan was impeccable. She assumed his designer underwear would match his socks too. Black and more than likely the finest imported woven silk…

She stopped mid-thought and shook herself mentally. What had got into her? And why on earth was she even thinking about her employer's underwear? It had to have been the knock to her head. Or perhaps being celibate for a year was affecting her reasoning, she decided. But it hadn't until that moment. The need to have a man in her life was below the need to match the colour of the bin liner to the trash can. Of no importance and not worth a second thought. And a man like Dr McFetridge was not on her wish list; no man was.

Perhaps it was the significance of the day that was making her react. That had to be it, she told herself, and the next day would be different. She wouldn't be having the melancholy thoughts and she wouldn't give her boss even a second thought.

But she begrudgingly admitted to herself that she did like his cologne. The fresh woody fragrance was still lingering. Fragrance had not been her priority that morning. She was lucky to get close to soap and nothing about her lingerie matched. Molly's stomach dropped and she moved in her seat to confirm in her rush she had remembered underwear. She breathed a sigh of relief when she could feel the elastic of her knickers. Thankfully she had grabbed one of the three pairs pegged to a coat hanger to dry over the bath the night before. She cringed momentarily.

If they had not been hanging in her line of sight would she be wearing any?

Just as quickly yet another unsettling thought swept into her mind. She pushed it aside. They were on and she didn't need to dwell on what might or might not have been. It had been a ridiculously rushed start to her first day but with a smidgen of Irish luck, from her father's side, she had made it with five minutes to spare. Although after seeing the consulting rooms she wondered just how long he would keep her on staff. It was only too obvious to Molly that appearance certainly counted with him. His dress sense, his rooms, all of it was immaculate.

And she was not. Well, not at that time. She had previously dressed well and taken pride in her hair and make-up, but equal amounts of money and sleep deprivation meant both had gone to pot. And nothing much about that was going to change overnight. But she was clean and efficient. Like the pitch to sell a small imported car, she thought.

Her mind was jumbled and she had to stay focussed. It couldn't be that difficult. He was just another tall, dark, good-looking man and she was not interested in men, tall, short, dark or fair; she was not interested in being used and lied to again. And stripped of her faith in humanity…and her worldly possessions…in one fell swoop.

She opened her eyes just as quickly and, looking around at everything, she was reminded that, while she no doubt looked out of place in Ryan McFetridge's practice, her skills should ensure she stayed put as long as possible and enable her to meet the rent and avoid Joel's advances.

Despite her decision not to bite back too fiercely, Molly could not roll over and let another man think his looks would allow him to act in a way that was just wrong in her book. While it was only her shoes, she had to put a line in the sand and retain a little dignity. She had made it to work on time and he had no idea what she had been through to get there. So what if her shoes didn't match? As if it mattered in the scheme of things—her feet were hidden behind the desk and it didn't make her less competent, she reminded herself, all the while feeling quite ridiculous and uncomfortably exposed. Although she did not truly feel the level of bravado she was trying to exude, she would do her best to let her temporary employer know where she stood.

Twenty minutes later, Lizzy and Ryan reappeared. He placed the notes on the reception desk, and Molly couldn't help but notice he patted the dog-eared records almost affectionately. She was even more confused.

'I'll need you to make another time for Lizzy in four weeks with Dr Slattery. His details are on the notes here. And can you make it a time that I can attend with her so block out ninety minutes in my calendar too, please, Molly, to allow for my travel time.'

'Certainly,' Molly replied, then, wondering why Ryan would be accompanying his patient to see another medico, added, 'Is this for a second opinion?'

'No, it's not a second opinion. Lizzy is Dr Slattery's patient.'

'Okay, I'll call his rooms and make that time now.'

Molly didn't quite understand but decided not to question him further. However, she did need to address something. His remarks about her shoes were playing on her mind. She wanted to be clear in what she would tolerate and what she wouldn't and wanted to address it before Ryan disappeared back into his room.

'I'll make the time right away, then after that I could take a lunch break, go home and collect matching shoes if you think they're an issue.' Molly's tone was not confronting but it was firm and resolute. She was respectful of Lizzy's presence and aware she was witnessing everything.

There was silence for a moment. Molly watched as Ryan's eyebrow raised but she quickly sensed amusement rather than annoyance in his expression. It was almost as if his eyes were saying *'bravo to you'* but his lips hadn't moved, not even twitched.

She was incredibly confused and that had not happened to her in a very long time. For the last year she had felt confident that she could size up a man quickly. There were two categories: not to be trusted and those over sixty-five.

'That won't be necessary,' he told her. 'You look perfectly fine just as you are.'

Molly was taken aback by his response but didn't have time to say anything as he continued.

'Lizzy, I don't think you've met Molly. She's my new office manager and she'll be here for the next month. You'll see her whenever you call in to visit me.' Ryan paused again for a moment, his eyes darting between the two women, as if deep in thought. Then he continued, 'Molly, I'd like you to meet my daughter, Elizabeth, who prefers to be called Lizzy, and the aforementioned red shoes are her favourite.'

Molly almost fell off her seat. She had not seen that coming at all. Dr McPerfect had a teenage daughter. She suddenly understood why Ryan wanted to attend her appointment with her general practitioner and why Lizzy wasn't on the record management system. Lizzy was his daughter, not his patient, despite having a different surname. And if Molly had heard correctly, he wanted her to stay on for the length of the assignment. He apparently wasn't about to fire her for rushing in at the last minute looking as if she had been plucked from a downpipe.

Ryan was not the man she had imagined at all.

Watching the way Ryan walked from behind the reception desk and over to Lizzy, putting his arm around her in such a loving way, made Molly's heart soften just a little. Suddenly Molly saw him as just Lizzy's father, although he didn't look old enough to have a daughter Lizzy's age. She felt her heart almost skip a beat. There was something in the way his dark eyes smiled as he pulled his daughter protectively to him that to her surprise took Molly's breath away. It was an unconditional love he had for her. And she knew that feeling so very well. It was exactly how she felt when Tommy gave her a hug goodnight. And it was the feeling that kept her going when everything else in her life was turning to mud.

Molly had thought she had men safely locked away. They were not to be trusted. Period. Suddenly Ryan was testing her bias. Suddenly she realised that she had been the one casting judgement on her boss because she was afraid of being judged. Dr McFetridge was keeping her on staff even though she had assumed she did not fit his vision of perfect. Perhaps it was her idea of what perfect should look like that was skewing her outlook. Everything about the previous five minutes had taken her aback. She had been the one guilty of assuming the book was the total of the cover.

Molly was quickly being forced to accept that perhaps there might actually be more to Dr McFetridge than handsome packaging.

CHAPTER THREE

RYAN HAD WANTED uninterrupted father-daughter time to discuss the medical issues at hand and then link via a telephone conference to discuss the prognosis and potential treatment plan with Lizzy's GP and the specialist.

A choice would need to be made but Ryan had no intention of rushing into a decision that didn't sit well with his daughter. He had removed his own GP hat and had worn his father hat during the conversation. There were a number of considerations moving forward. How his daughter felt about each and every one of them was paramount to Ryan. With the options clearly explained, Ryan wanted to sit and talk more with Lizzy before making their joint decision and visiting her doctor.

Finally, a driver arrived to collect her. Ryan waved goodbye and walked his next patient into his consulting room and closed the door. He sat down opposite the older woman and leaned in towards her slightly.

'Tell me, Dorothy, how are you and how is the adjusted medication level coming along?'

'Not too bad, Doctor.'

The elderly lady's reply didn't convince Ryan as he watched as her softly wrinkled hands fidgeted with her handkerchief. She was twisting the delicate lace-edged linen nervously.

'Not too bad?' he replied. 'That's not what I was hoping to hear and it's not the same as good. I would like to hear that you're feeling very well, Dorothy. You're the most energetic and engaging octogenarian I know. What's bothering you?'

He didn't take his eyes away from hers. Ryan was not going to let her leave without an explanation.

'Well.' She paused for a moment then took a considered breath and continued. 'My sugar readings are all around six or seven, which you told me is fine, but the headaches are still there. Every day I have one. Some days I even wake up with one and, on those days, they are particularly bad. I don't like taking painkillers but George says I must take them or I'm like a grumpy bear. He makes sure I do every four hours and gets quite cross if I don't want to take them. I don't want to upset him and I would hate to be a grumpy bear but I'm taking twelve of those tablets a day and that can't be good.'

Ryan's displeasure with George's behaviour towards his wife, insisting that she take the tablets rather than solving the problem, showed in his frown. 'George is not qualified, Dorothy. And you should not need that level of medication, so let's get to the reason for the headaches.'

He did not further push his annoyance that George was encouraging the painkillers without consultation with a professional. Dorothy Dunstan, in Ryan's opinion, was as far from a grumpy bear as one could get. Even in pain. The eighty-one-year-old was a slightly built woman, with a mass of white curls, stunning blue eyes and the sweetest smile. He had no doubt she would have been very beautiful as a younger woman and her prettiness would more than likely still turn heads in the upmarket retirement village where the couple lived.

Her husband, George, on the other hand, also a patient

of Ryan's practice, was a solidly built man with a gruff demeanour and very much closer to a bear's disposition on the best of days, particularly when his diverticulosis flared up and he blamed everyone around him. Ryan was upset that the man would force his wife to take medication just to keep her happy around him.

'Let's trial a break of your current medication. That may help with the headaches. No guarantee but it's worth trying that route.'

'Really, Doctor? But what about my diabetes?'

'The surgery to remove your gall bladder last November also removed the chronic infection. That would have been stressing your body and as a result a number of organs were not functioning properly and your blood sugar level became elevated. I have been lowering your dose each month, as you know, but now I would like you to stop taking your medication completely for one week.' Ryan paused and looked Dorothy in the eyes with a serious expression dressing his face. 'But, Dorothy, you must maintain a diet without any added sugar as the dietician advised. None. No chocolates or other sugary treats. That means no cakes or biscuits with your cup of tea…and no scones, jam and cream either.'

'I promise, Dr McFetridge, but I do love Devonshire teas and it has been very hard to say no to my friends when they make scones. And George buys us both cake with our coffee after lawn bowls and I don't like to say no to him.'

George's selfish and ignorant attitude was testing Ryan's patience but he controlled his desire to tell Dorothy what he thought of her husband. 'I know, but you also want to stay healthy and drug free so it's worth the sacrifice and I'm sure that your friends and George love you enough to understand. But you must tell them and you must be firm.'

Dorothy nodded in response.

'And I want you to call through your blood sugar reading every day to my nurse. Any raised levels and I need to see you straight away. Don't try to persevere if the levels change. I can't reiterate this enough. Diabetes is a serious condition, but as it only occurred after your illness we may be able to control it with a sensible diet from here on in. But it will mean ongoing monitoring and food restrictions.'

'Really? You mean I may not need to take the medication again, ever?'

'Let's hope so. In some cases, an adjusted diet is all the treatment a patient needs and I hope you are one of the fortunate ones. Would you like me to tell George that he should refrain from buying the cake and the painkillers?'

'Oh, Lord, no. He would have a fit if he thought I'd told you that.' Dorothy's disposition was suddenly flustered.

'You can rest assured that I won't say anything, then, Dorothy, but you need to be firm with him. And I do mean firm. You can't eat the cakes just because your husband has bought one for each of you.'

'I'll just tell him I'm not hungry.'

'You can tell George whatever you like, that is not my business, although I would have thought telling him the truth about your condition would be better, but again that's not my place to advise you how best to manage George. However…' He paused and his voice became increasingly deep and more serious in tone. 'Whatever you tell him, you must not waver under pressure. It's your long-term health that we are talking about here. And George would most definitely want a healthy wife.'

She nodded her agreement to Ryan's terms then continued. 'If I stop the medication and avoid the temptation of the sweets, do you think my headache will finally go away?'

'That's what I'm hoping,' Ryan told her as he stood.

'Then that's wonderful news and worth the sacrifice of a few cakes…'

'*All* cakes, not a few cakes.'

'That's what I meant.'

Ryan smiled as he reached for Dorothy's arm and lifted her to her feet and walked her out to the reception area, asking Molly to make an appointment for the following week.

He left Dorothy with Molly, then turned and smiled in her husband's direction. 'How are you today, George? Keeping dry and out of the cold as much as you can, I hope.'

George grunted and made a dismissive gesture with his hand. 'Damned appointments all day. After this I have to go home, pick up Dorothy's darned cat and get her to the vet. Fur-balls again. If it's not one thing it's another. So much for retirement. I never get a day at home in peace. And the cat doesn't like me anyway. It either hisses at me or ignores me. Typical woman.'

Ryan wasn't sure quite what to say. The elderly man was healthy for his age, with relatively few ailments, but his demeanour was another story. He behaved as if he had the weight of the world on his shoulders, and nothing appeared to make him happy. Ryan had initially suspected a level of depression but that was quickly ruled out by a referral to a clinical psychologist. George had retired from his successful fishing charter business in the lower Eyre Peninsula town of Port Lincoln a very wealthy man. He had a very sweet wife, the two of them had taken numerous extended overseas holidays and were active for their age, and their four daughters had provided them with half a dozen healthy, happy grandchildren. If only, Ryan thought, there were a medication to remedy a glass-half-empty outlook on life. George's cup was chipped, stained and the handle missing most days and he truly had no idea how fortunate he was to have the love and devotion of a woman as wonderful as Dorothy for over sixty years.

Ryan knew that he would never have that same unconditional love and, in his heart, he knew why. He would never trust anyone to get that close to him again.

Ryan walked back into his office leaving Dorothy Dunstan speaking with Molly. He hoped that she had listened to his instructions and would adhere to the strict diet, and the headaches would in time subside. There was of course a very good chance that the cause of her daily headache was George, and if that was the case there really was no medicinal cure. The only cure would be to leave him. And a woman like Dorothy would never consider that an option.

As he closed his door, Ryan's thoughts unexpectedly turned from Dorothy to Molly. Molly, with her uncontrolled mop of brown curls and contagious smile. And feisty attitude. The agency had told him Molly Murphy would be temping at the office to replace Maxine, his office manager of six years who had slipped and broken her arm in her Zumba class. Immediately he had formed a picture in his mind of a pleasant and efficient Irish woman in her late fifties or early sixties to replace his very efficient but now injured gym junkie and almost sixty-year-old office manager. With an image of the Irish replacement having a love of home knits, wonderful cooking skills and a slight brogue accent, Ryan felt confident the woman would meet the needs of the family-focussed practice for four weeks. She would be the wholesome motherly figure like Maxine whom his patients would like and adapt to quickly.

Then Molly had arrived and she didn't come close to his vision. In her mid to late twenties, she had no Irish accent, and she didn't seem the type to sit home knitting. She had shot his clichéd assumptions out of the water. She certainly was a conundrum. And more than a little difficult to read. He had observed her open and comforting rapport with patients during the morning and decided that her chosen path in a medical support role matched her natural affinity with people and his patients would quickly warm to her, but there was something that didn't add up. Her administration skills appeared more than competent but her medical expertise appeared more aligned to that of a doctor or nurse. He had overheard her speaking to more than one patient and the level of detail she provided exposed the true depth of her knowledge. The agency had not provided a résumé as his request had come at short notice but Molly came highly recommended and very quickly Ryan could see why.

He couldn't deny he was curious about her. There was definitely more to Molly Murphy than met the eye.

At odds with her empathetic nature was a woman who had come out fighting like a cornered alley cat when he'd mentioned her dubious footwear. He was grateful that he hadn't raised the matter of her arriving drenched to the bone with only minutes to spare.

He shook his head a little as he crossed to his desk and opened up the emails on his computer. Not many people surprised Ryan McFetridge any more. He treated most people with a level of distrust until they could prove otherwise and he believed that he could fairly easily and accurately sum them up. But he didn't feel his usual level of confidence about his summation of Molly. He wasn't sure what he felt but it did unsettle him that he felt something.

He closed his emails. There was nothing of interest, just a reminder about a medical association event he had agreed to attend the next evening and some pharmaceutical promotions. Running one hand through his short black hair, he opened the afternoon patient roster as he routinely did after every morning's appointments were completed. He did a double take and, far from being annoyed, his interest was piqued when he saw changes to the layout of the next day's patient listing. He hovered the cursor over the first name and the medical history and purpose of the appointment appeared. He tried it again on the next patient and again the function allowed him access to the notes of the previous three visits without going into each patient's records. It was an abbreviated medical history with a link to archived notes. He smirked. Molly Murphy had been doing some upgrades. The reference to these details was an impressive feature and a function of the software package that he had never accessed because he hadn't been aware it existed. Molly certainly knew the program well. And Ryan was more than impressed. He had not asked for improvements, nor had the busy schedule provided her with additional time on her hands to do this out of boredom. Molly had used initiative to make improvements. Again, she had surprised him and that never happened. Not any more.

Molly Murphy, he thought, you might just be the perfect for-ever woman...*for my practice*, he quickly qualified.

Ryan McFetridge had no need for a for-ever woman in any other area of his life. And particularly not a woman like Molly. She appeared very different from the women with whom Ryan kept company. Her manner with patients was genuine. The empathy showed a warm heart beneath her shapeless clothes. The women Ryan preferred wore clothes that hugged their shapes but underneath there was no sign of a heart. And that suited him. A night of mutual satisfaction with a woman who was not wanting or expecting more was all he wanted.

Because Ryan McFetridge had nothing to give. Nor did he want anything back.

He rested back in his large black leather chair, a touch of melancholy colouring his mood as he swivelled to look out through the rain-spotted window to the overcast streetscape. It was cold and miserable, with few people in sight, but for some inexplicable reason Ryan felt different. His mood was lighter. And Ryan had not felt anything close to that in a very long time. He brushed aside the coincidence of his mood lifting on the same day that Molly had started work. It was just that. A coincidence. It couldn't be anything more.

His sole focus outside his work was his daughter. She was his motivation to keep going. To build a legacy to ensure she never needed or wanted for anything. That responsibility weighed heavily. And he would never let her down.

Or ever let anyone hurt her.

Ever again.

Swivelling back on his chair and returning his focus to his computer screen, he realised Molly Murphy knew her stuff and he couldn't help but wonder about her background and her qualifications. And why she was working in a role that Ryan suspected was far less than her capability. He knew so little about her. He had to admit to himself he had noticed she was not wearing a wedding ring. He didn't know why he'd even looked. But with Molly he was curious to know more. Although the absence didn't mean there was no significant other in her life. And he reminded himself that she could potentially have children, although they would be relatively young.

But none of it mattered, he continued to remind himself. She was his office manager. Nothing more. Nothing less. But it still didn't stop thoughts of her occupying his head. She was pretty in an almost fragile way but she had spunk and clearly knew how to take care of herself. And now his practice. There was something about Molly that reminded Ryan of the weather outside…unpredictable and challenging.

And Ryan McFetridge had always loved winter.

He drummed his fingers on the edge of his mahogany desk. It was inlaid with a deep burgundy leather and not in keeping with the rest of the more modern decor but it had been a graduation gift from his parents. As they had both since died not long after he'd opened his practice in Adelaide, he loved having something to remind him of them every day. His childhood had been happy and filled with love and encouragement and one of Ryan's many regrets was that Lizzy had never met her paternal grandparents.

He rested his chin on one hand as he began to scan through his emails. He needed to get back on track and stop being distracted by random thoughts, especially those of his new staff member. Pondering the unknown was pointless and wasting time. He reminded himself firmly that Molly Murphy's past, present or future after the immediate four-week placement was not his business. With common sense born from the realities he had faced over the years since Lizzy had come into his life, Ryan knew, no matter what effect Molly was or wasn't having on him, he had to keep it purely business.

Despite her best intentions, Molly's own curiosity continued to niggle at her new-found peace of mind. Lingering doubts were replaced by an unsettling and growing interest in knowing a little more about her temporary boss. As much as she also tried to push thoughts about Ryan away as she sipped on lunch, they kept returning. While she felt secure in the knowledge that she had ongoing employment for a month, she felt concerned about why she wanted to know more about her employer. And his daughter. She wondered if Lizzy was using her mother's surname or maiden name. Not that any of it mattered. She was not naturally curious but now, for some inexplicable reason, she wanted to know more than was necessary to carry out her job.

Why did he have to be so damned attractive and, from all appearances, a loving father? she thought as she pursed her lips. She gently blew on her spoonful of soup in an attempt to cool it slightly. She had not been interested in men since her engagement ended. And she had to keep it that way. He was a man giving her employment for a month. And in her financial situation it was not unlike a rope to a drowning man. A godsend. She couldn't confuse gratitude for anything more than that. She couldn't afford to romanticise the situation.

Molly felt sure that she had reconciled the situation in her head and definitely quelled any thoughts stirring in her heart. It was relief and gratitude turning her emotions upside down. Nothing more, she decided as she continued eating her lunch, glancing occasionally out through the rain-splattered window. The weather was still dismal and, on top of the rain, she had discovered when she'd dashed out to find lunch that the bitterly cold breeze had not abated. A patient had told her that falling branches and trees had knocked down power lines in the foothills. It was only slightly better in their location as a powerful gust blowing down the street cut through her thick coat during her mad dash out, once again chilling her to the bone. An arctic freeze, one patient remarked.

She was grateful she had taken the earlier dampness out of her hair with the hand-dryer in the restroom and borrowed an umbrella from Stacy or she might have brought the stirrings of a winter head cold back to the practice with her. But climate aside, Molly's day had insurmountably improved from the rocky start. A month's employment was everything she needed at that moment. She knew rent would be covered and she could save a little for unexpected bills. Finally, she could exhale if only for a few weeks and that brought her great comfort. As did her warm surroundings that she studied in a little more detail.

The lunchroom was brightly lit, with a round white wooden table and four matching chairs with red cushions and an arrangement of fresh red and yellow gerberas, which she knew must have been imported at that time of the year; a well-stocked wall-mounted magazine rack that was female friendly in choices; and the usual kitchen amenities, including a red enamelled espresso machine and red mugs. Molly had wondered if Lizzy might have had input into arranging the pretty room since there were many not so subtle splashes of red in the decor.

A few moments later Ryan made his way into the lunchroom, slightly startling Molly. She had assumed he had left the practice for his home rounds. There were five visits that afternoon and Molly discovered Ryan, unlike many GPs, didn't use a locum service to meet his patients' needs. He called in personally to monitor those who were housebound by various short- and long-term medical ailments, including those patients who had been admitted permanently to nursing homes. He seemed more like a country-style, hands-on GP.

'Molly,' Ryan said as he made his way to the refrigerator and collected milk. 'I wondered if you might be in here.'

'Just grabbing a bite to eat.'

'Ah, soup,' he said, peering into the bowl as he passed by. 'Is it home-made?'

'No, the local shop,' she mumbled as she swallowed and pointed in the direction of the local bakery across the road. 'I didn't have time to think about breakfast this morning, let alone packing lunch.'

Ryan smiled in reply and made his way to the espresso machine. 'I'm not much of a breakfast person, slice of toast on the way out of the door if I'm lucky, but I never go without my coffee. I'm addicted to caffeine, I can't lie.'

'It's not a serious vice,' she returned, happy their conversation was light and casual and he was on the other side of the room. Her emotions were in check and he was just a handsome doctor making chit-chat. It was easy, she told herself. She had clearly overreacted before to being in a new environment.

'I agree, there's worse,' he said as he turned his back on the machine and faced Molly with his arms folded across his chest. 'Before I head off for the afternoon, I wanted to say thank you for the changes that you made to the scheduling.'

'You're welcome. I like the software and you hadn't been utilising all of the features.'

'It's great. I had no idea the software had that capability.'

'I've seen it at a number of practices, and even some small country hospitals use it. The bigger ones not so much.'

'So, you've done some country placements in admin too, then?'

'As a nurse, I accessed the software for patient notes and was impressed so I looked into it further.' As the words slipped from her lips she realised she had said more than she intended. 'Keep it simple and short' had been her plan. Since the break-up Molly just wanted to keep her life a closed book. Information to be provided on an as-needed basis. But again, she felt safe. Ryan was just her boss and things were professional and she didn't need to worry.

Ryan swung around to collect his coffee, then back to Molly. 'Nursing background? Now it makes sense.' He nodded to himself. 'I heard you speaking earlier to a patient, Jean Burton, and the level of detail in answering her questions about her blood-pressure medication was so much more information than an admin assistant or receptionist would, or for that matter generally could, provide.'

'You haven't seen my CV, then?'

'No. The agency told me you were highly recommended but no in-depth details. To be honest I didn't have the time to look through CVs last week. With Maxine's accident I just needed a replacement asap so I had to trust them…and I'm glad I did,' Ryan said as he pulled up a seat and put his freshly made coffee on the table before him. His long, lean fingers were comfortably wrapped around the hot mug.

It was at complete odds with how uncomfortable Molly was suddenly made by his decision to sit down with her. Everything she had told herself about him having no effect on her was being negated quickly.

'Are you a registered nurse?'

'I'm…I'm actually an anaesthetic nurse.'

'Any reason you specialised in anaesthesia?'

'I did a Theatre placement during my second year and realised that was where I wanted to be after graduating, so that's what I did.'

He sat back in his seat, releasing his hands from the cup. 'Then you are a very long way from home, Dorothy.'

His smile was wide and Molly sensed genuine. But it was also making her pulse pick up speed. She had to get it under control. She wasn't sure how but she suspected distance might help.

'Not so far, really,' she said matter-of-factly. 'I'm still working in the field of medicine…'

'You are and, believe me, I'm not complaining,' he cut in as he once again leaned forward.

To Molly's horror he made the distance between them even less. His forest-fresh cologne brought a sudden tingling sensation to her skin.

'Your medical experience is a huge benefit to my practice, but may I ask why you stepped away from Theatre?'

'Long story and I won't bore you. Just say that the temp hours suit me better.'

'I shouldn't imagine the remuneration would so much,' he said matter-of-factly with a frown forming, replacing the previous light-hearted expression. 'I suppose we stand a chance of losing you, then. I mean, if a better-paid gig came along in line with your experience, with the hours you want, then I couldn't, and I wouldn't, blame you for leaving.'

'You don't have to worry about that happening,' she said, hoping her racing heart wasn't making her blush.

'If I make a promise or commitment I always keep it. This suits me just fine.'

'In the interim perhaps, but long-term maybe not so much—'

'Let's not fudge words,' Molly cut in, wanting to end the conversation. 'I'm barely dry after four hours and my typing speed is twenty-nine words a minute. The average for a temp is over eighty. My strength is my medical background and you're offering good hours. So, if you're happy, I'm happy. It's a great trade-off for both of us.'

'I think you're selling yourself short. While I have to agree you arrived a little soggy—I couldn't help but overhear the hand-dryer running for ten minutes straight earlier on,' he told her as he leant back on the chair, his long legs stretched out in front of him, giving her the space she suddenly realised she needed. 'But I need more than a great typist in this practice and I think you'll fit in extremely well. I'm astute enough to see what you've accomplished in a couple of hours. You've made changes I didn't know were possible.'

'It's hardly rocket science but I'm happy you like what I've done. I've been here four hours so it wasn't too difficult to make the changes. You had the software capability, it just needed to be utilised,' Molly answered as she stood up. She had to create the space between them herself so she collected her bowl and cup, and made her way to the sink. She rolled her eyes at the way she had reacted having him so close. She dropped her bowl into the sudsy water in the sink. The unexpected effect he was having on her was absurd…and disconcerting. She wasn't about to be swept off her feet. It was ridiculous. And risky. She had more to lose than gain by thinking that way about a man, let alone her boss, and she would never take a risk again.

'Whether it's been four hours or four weeks, you instinctively searched for ways to make improvements. It was like a four-hour quality-improvement audit. I never asked you to do that and no previous office manager has, no matter how long they were with me. But it was exactly what I needed. You, Molly Murphy, are exactly what I need and I would like to make it worth your while. In fact… I have a proposition for you.'

CHAPTER FOUR

A PROPOSITION?

Molly's eyes darted about as she repeated the words in her head. What on earth could he be talking about? She felt quite sure it wasn't the type of proposition that her body might be silently willing, if he got too close again.

It had to be business, but what? She had a job for a month. Once Maxine's cast came off she'd return to work and Molly would leave. The practice was busy but not enough to warrant two in administration.

She turned around knowing she wore a curious look but she couldn't hide it. His expression appeared serious and, damn, it made him look even more handsome. He was making her question so much about him and herself and it didn't make sense. She was becoming even more unsettled and didn't trust her reaction so she turned back to the sink. Grabbing for the sponge, she washed her cup and her bowl before she rinsed them both and placed them in the otherwise empty dish drainer. She needed something else to keep her busy and delay her turning back to him. Reaching into the warm shallows of the sink, she searched under the bubbles with her fingers for her spoon. Finding it quickly, she washed it thoroughly and rinsed it with the same attention before she put it in the drainer with the other things. Unfortunately, there was nothing else to wash and nothing else to do. There was effectively no way to stall.

She had no choice but to turn back around to the man who was stirring emotions she forgot she could feel. And those she never wanted to feel again. Hoping the feeling was fleeting and born from a mix of her initial job insecurity and gratitude to be in the role for a few weeks, Molly had hoped it would disappear as quickly as it had appeared. But looking at Ryan she knew it hadn't gone or even dampened. It was still there. It felt a little like butterflies...and a lot like...she wasn't sure. But she was confused. It didn't make sense. She barely knew the man and she had sworn herself to a life without one. Men, particularly handsome, confident men like Ryan, brought only trouble into her life and she didn't need any more. She also knew how bedraggled she appeared but for some reason the way he looked at her at that moment made her feel unexpectedly beautiful.

She quickly decided her mind was playing tricks on her. How could she possibly see something in Ryan other than as her boss within a matter of hours of meeting? That didn't happen in real life. That was the stuff of movies. He and she were so very different. He was clearly established and on track with his life, and hers had derailed and she wasn't sure when or even if it would ever truly be travelling in the right direction. Thanks to the man who she had planned to marry.

And she didn't need to have her heart broken again.

Once was more than enough.

She noticed his jaw flick as his eyes slowly pulled away from hers. She sensed he hadn't wanted to look away and that made her confusion grow and those damned butterflies in her stomach flutter manically. It was more than ridiculous. He was her employer, for goodness' sake. Molly had noticed the absence of a wedding ring although she didn't know why she'd registered that fact. She no longer cared about a man's marital status. They were all off-limits in her mind. She couldn't go there. She couldn't let her feelings get the better of her. There was only room in her life for one man and that was Tommy. He had to be her sole focus. No one would ever get close enough to ruin their lives again. Her mind was racing and she appeared to have no control over her thought process.

Without warning, and with purposeful steps, he moved closer to the exit.

'Molly, I can see you're preoccupied, and I've got to get to my home visits, but I want to let you know that I'm proposing a thirty per cent pay increase immediately, I'll call the agency from my car and let them know. And they're not getting a cent of it—it's all yours. You earned it and I hope that might keep you on board and not head-hunted. I think you could make a real difference here. If I have anything to do with it, and if I can stop you from getting bored, you might just be with me long after this assignment.'

With that Molly watched Ryan walk from the kitchen as relief and confusion washed over her in waves. Huge waves.

While the logical side of her brain was happy, in fact over the moon, with the pay rise and the idea that the job could be ongoing, her heart, for some crazy, unexplained reason, was even more elated by the prospect of being with him long after the assignment.

Her emotions could not have been more jumbled at that moment. And she had no control and that worried her. Hadn't she learnt her lesson? She had been resolute in her determination to keep men at arm's length and out of her life and suddenly she was overjoyed by both aspects of his *proposal.*

It was a mix of stupid and ludicrous in equal amounts, and she knew it, but, no matter what her logic and reasoning were reminding her, her heart was definitely beating a little faster than normal and her tummy was doing gentle somersaults. Romantic nonsense. It had to be from the excitement due to the pay rise, the security of a long-term job. Whatever it was, it was immaterial. She had to get a grip and ignore the happiness that was growing inside. She had to think logically. Her clothes were dry and she had a job that could potentially go far longer than the month. Tommy was settled in his job and they had a roof over their heads. She didn't need anything else.

And she didn't want anything else.

She had an outcome to the day she could never have imagined from the soggy start. Brushing the crumbs of bread roll from her skirt, she gathered her wandering thoughts hurriedly as she made her way back to the desk. Ryan had just given her a thirty per cent pay increase so she would forget the sausages and mashed potato she had planned. Molly would be buying Tommy's favourite fish for dinner that night, and if the long-term position was realised then she could potentially look for a new home for the two of them. Goodbye Joel and his advances and the derelict accommodation that she and Tommy had been forced to call home.

If she could just get her heart to slow down and the butterflies to leave, her life would be close to perfect.

Tommy was dropped home fifteen minutes after Molly had raced from the bus stop in the drizzling rain. She'd had enough time to change into her comfortable stretch jeans and a thick baby pink sweater and dry her hair, which had been rained on again on the way home, before she heard her brother putting his key in the door.

Tommy's job didn't pay much at all but it made him happy and that was more than enough for Molly. He couldn't wait to get to work every day and was at the front door early, dressed in one of his two pairs of favourite jeans, a brightly coloured shirt, and in the colder weather he would add a sweater and jacket. He also wore an expectant smile. He liked routine so every day into his backpack he placed a lunch box in which he'd packed a sandwich and a piece of fruit the night before, and which he'd put into the refrigerator. Each morning the bus arrived promptly at seven forty-five, filled with his equally excited friends and work colleagues. Molly and Tommy's house was the last pick-up before the driver finished his round and headed to the workplace with his eager fellow passengers.

Molly had noticed over the previous few weeks that Tommy was beaming a little more than usual as he waited by the door. He spent just a few extra minutes combing his hair and always checked he didn't have his breakfast down the front of his shirt or his trousers. She suspected that as he grew older, Tommy wanted to do his best to be independent. She was so proud of everything he managed on a daily basis and she encouraged him to try new tasks. Each one he accomplished brought him added confidence.

During the previous four weeks, his demeanour had been a mix of excitement and nervousness as he'd waited and she hadn't been completely sure she understood why. But had decided not to ask. As long as he was happy and looking forward to each day, then Molly was happy too. Whatever the impetus for his new-found joy, she knew in time he would tell her. Her baby brother had something in his life that made him feel a level of happiness that Molly had been scared he would never feel again when they had lost their home.

That morning she hadn't heard the driver beep his horn to let Tommy know they were waiting outside, nor had she heard his deep voice calling out to her to say goodbye. Not even the front door being slammed closed as Tommy had run to the gate had disturbed her. He must have been so excited to get on the bus that he'd forgotten to hug her goodbye. He had been a man on a mission.

And Molly had slept through all of it. The worry of finances had kept her counting bills, not sheep, into the early hours. It was a worry she couldn't halve by sharing it with him. His happy disposition didn't need to be brought down by seeing her concerned so Molly kept a brave face until he was in bed.

He had told her he was saving his money to buy a ring and a house when he found a pretty girl to marry. Then he'd changed his mind and said they could all live together because he didn't want his sister to be alone. Molly hadn't been entirely sure when or if her younger brother would find the right girl to fill or appreciate a heart as big as his, but loved the fact he had included her in his plans. He was the sweetest brother a girl could ever hope to have and she felt blessed every day.

She had signed up to a temp agency knowing it would assist in the short-term. The long-term prospects were potentially dire if she couldn't return to her nursing, but the long shifts were close to impossible to manage in her current situation. At least now, with the pay rise, for the time being she could relax. Her life that had been wound very tightly had now slightly loosened.

Leaving Tommy to arrive home to an empty house, cook and eat alone at night had not been an option so she had chosen a lower-paid role to ensure she was home when his bus pulled up each night. After dinner, he would happily watch television with her or sometimes he would go to his room and watch one of his favourite shows in bed.

The remuneration as an office manager up to now hadn't been close to that of an anaesthetic nurse with Molly's skills, but it had meant she wouldn't be caught up in Theatre in a longer than expected operation and not be able to be there for Tommy. The stress of that occurring was too much for her to deal with on a daily basis.

'How was work today, Tommy?' Molly asked as she plated their special dinner of grilled salmon and steamed vegetables courtesy of Ryan's generous offer.

'Good,' he told her as he tucked his napkin into the belt of his trousers and sat waiting at the table for two in their small but clean home. The structure was old and worn but the atmosphere was always happy. The table was set with a pretty floral tablecloth, two glasses of water and a small basket with some sliced bread. The butter was nearby and Tommy had already buttered one slice for himself and one for Molly. 'I like it. I have lots of friends.'

They had an agreement. Molly cooked and Tommy would wash up afterwards. It worked out well. Tommy loved his sister's cooking and he clearly felt good about contributing by cleaning up the dishes that he very carefully washed and dried.

Molly smiled as she carried the plates to the table and Tommy dropped his head closer to smell the hot food on the plate she had placed in front of him.

'Yum,' he said with a big grin. 'My favourite.'

'I know,' she replied as she sat down, put her napkin on her lap and gave a little sigh of relief to have survived a day that had begun so terribly. 'I bought enough for two nights so we can have it again on Wednesday.'

'Wow, we must be millionaires!'

Molly laughed. 'Not quite, but I did get a pay rise on my first day.'

All was good in the world, she thought as she looked over at her brother, who was enjoying the food she had prepared. He was eating the vegetables first as he always did so he could save the best for last. Conversation was at a standstill as Tommy was concentrating on the task in front of him. Sitting in the happy silence they shared, Molly knew that there was nothing she would change except to one day provide a larger home for them both.

At that moment, the six-forty-five train raced past so close the windows rattled and she amended her plan to ensuring their new larger home was in a quiet suburb and out of earshot of a train line.

The next morning as they both left on time for work, Molly noticed Tommy watching her intently as she locked the front door. It was still bitterly cold and they were both rugged up against the chilly morning air, but at least it wasn't raining.

'Is everything all right? Did we forget to pack something?' she asked with a bemused look.

'No,' he told her without hesitation.

'Is there something you want to tell me…or ask me?'

'I have a girlfriend.'

Molly spun on her heels to face him, completely blindsided but thrilled by his announcement. Suddenly it made sense. That was the reason Tommy had been paying more attention to his appearance and so excited to get to work. She wasn't sure what the title *girlfriend* exactly entailed or how serious it was, but her brother was obviously very happy so she wanted to tread carefully.

'That's wonderful.'

'Honey's pretty.'

'I bet she is and she has a very pretty name.'

'She's clever. We eat lunch together every day.'

'That's lovely.'

'She's not tall but I don't mind.'

Molly smiled as she slipped the house keys in her handbag, zipped it closed and together they walked to the gate. 'She doesn't need to be tall. I'm sure she's just perfect.'

'She is perfect.'

Their steps were a little slower and she playfully pulled his shoulder closer as she became acutely aware that her brother was a young man apparently falling in love. He was a loveable and wonderful young man and she prayed the young woman was just as sweet.

Suddenly she felt an unexpected ache in her chest as she realised perhaps it wouldn't just be Molly and Tommy in the future. It was bittersweet and she was so happy for Tommy. Perhaps her brother had found a sweetheart to share his life. It made the moments they shared even more precious. She had been through some heartbreaking times with Tommy and their bond had become even stronger. Because they had each other to lean on they had survived and she had not considered a future without him right by her side.

But now she had to think about it. With all her heart, Molly hoped that his feelings were reciprocated. She was thrilled that Tommy might have found someone to love and he deserved that. Everyone deserved to feel loved.

With the beeping of the bus horn by the waving driver, Molly was snapped from her wandering and somewhat jumbled thoughts. Maybe for Tommy it was just a simple infatuation, not a lifetime commitment, she reminded herself. She really was getting ahead of herself.

Molly readjusted his backpack. She couldn't stop herself from fussing over him the way she always had.

'I'd love to meet her one day.'

'I will bring her home for tea. Maybe lamb chops,' he said, not bothered at all by his big sister's fussing. 'She looks like a princess.'

'She sounds lovely.'

'I know her favourite flower and her favourite colour,' he told her before he leant in for Molly to kiss him goodbye. He didn't kiss her back but he did allow her to plant her lips on his ruddy cheek. 'Bye, Molly.'

'Have a lovely day, Tommy,' she called out as she watched him climb onto the bus and take his seat.

Molly tried to peer through the window to see if he was seated next to the lucky girl, but Tommy had taken a place on the other side so whether his girlfriend was on the bus or not she wasn't sure. But the moment he had stepped inside the bus she couldn't help but notice that he was smiling from ear-to-ear.

Walking briskly to her bus stop, she thought ruefully that perhaps one of the Murphys would be lucky in love after all.

And the other one had a well-paid job for at least a month.

CHAPTER FIVE

'OF COURSE I don't mind if you buy a new dress. You're my date at the AMA dinner tonight and I want you to have whatever you want. Buy two if you like and get some shoes and a bag too. I put my credit card on your bedside cabinet this morning. You were still asleep when I left.'

As she hung her heavy winter overcoat in the closet near the kitchen, Molly felt a tug at her heart hearing Ryan speaking so warmly on his phone to the woman he was apparently taking to dinner that night. It was Friday, her fifth day working in the practice, and, as much as she didn't want to admit even to herself, with each day her admiration for her boss had been growing; realising that Ryan had a woman in his life had an unexpected effect on her.

She had kept her distance in an effort to control the way she had reacted to him in the kitchen that day. She knew any stirring feelings she had would lead nowhere. While her body was reacting to him, she was resolute that she didn't want to ever get involved or make herself vulnerable again. She wouldn't survive another heartbreak so she wasn't interested in even thinking about a relationship.

Standing there in the hallway, she couldn't help but

wonder, if all of that were true, then why did she feel a twinge of jealousy?

She had made small talk but kept it to a minimum and kept him at arm's length so she had more control of her emotions, but still hearing him speaking that way to another woman had affected her.

While she could try to label her feelings as an appreciation of him as a doctor, she knew she had stepped outside those boundaries. She couldn't deny it.

He worked long hours and after he finished consulting at the practice, and he had visited all his home rounds, she noticed on his calendar that he had two hours put aside from eight to ten o'clock three nights a week to provide medical services to a residential care facility for single mothers. For a young, eligible medical practitioner, his life could have been very different, but instead of leading a hectic social life, Ryan appeared to be dedicated to his profession and providing services to those who needed him most.

Molly realised it was more than simple admiration and she didn't want to feel that way, particularly as she overheard the conversation that morning. She hadn't wanted to eavesdrop but she couldn't hang her coat anywhere else and she had hoped to make a coffee before she started for the day. She heard him laugh and wondered about the woman's response.

The woman with whom he'd obviously shared the previous night as he'd dropped his credit card beside her bed while she'd still been sleeping.

Molly pulled the knitted woollen cap from her head and absent-mindedly ran her fingers through her hair, all the time wondering what his date would look like. Against her better judgement she let her thoughts wander. She mentally pictured the woman lying across satin sheets, in her silk lingerie. Perfectly waved, long blonde hair, no doubt. Beautifully manicured nails. She felt fairly confident she knew the type of woman who would be the perfect match for Ryan in looks and sex appeal.

The antithesis of herself, she thought with a sigh as she self-consciously flicked her slightly frizzy curls away from her face.

She no longer even window-shopped at high-end boutiques. The variety of stores she frequented had nice neat clothes, they were simple, with hundreds of the same style hung in racks all over the city in every size, but they were new and clean. She had different priorities. Designer clothes and accessories weren't included.

'My tux is at the practice, so I'll change here and whizz by about seven to pick you up,' Molly heard him say. She did wonder if she wasn't moving more slowly than needed so she could hear just a little more about her boss and his date. She knew that, against her own will, Ryan was having an effect on her, and it was borderline masochistic to hear him talking to another woman but her curiosity was piqued. Where was the elegant soirée to be held? She knew that AMA was the Medical Association dinner so no doubt it would be at one of the city's five-star venues and the ladies would be dressed as if they were to meet royalty. Like a twenty-first-century Cinderella ball. But there was no fairy godmother for Molly and the only pumpkin she would see was in the soup she and Tommy would be having for dinner that night along with home-made shepherd's pie.

Maybe it was good to hear the banter, she reminded herself, as it also made her realise he was taken or a player, which either way set the boundaries for her. And with her feelings escalating for the man little by little each day, she needed the reality check. Ryan McFetridge was never going to be more than her boss.

'No. Of course, I don't want to rush you. Sure...uh-huh... okay, I'll pick you up at seven-fifteen so you have time to get back from the hairdresser and get dressed.'

Of course I don't want to rush you... You must go to the hairdresser, Molly repeated in her head as she rolled her eyes.

She cringed as she shut the closet and made her way to her desk, shaking her head. She didn't resent the woman, or want to be her, she reminded herself sternly. But as she shuffled down the corridor the sinking feeling that wasn't subsiding made her wonder if that was true.

Life for Molly was getting back on track but there was something about the way Ryan made her feel whenever he was close that she needed to manage. And hearing conversations like that should have made it easier. But for some reason it hadn't.

Her day would have to begin without caffeine as she didn't want to intrude further on the intimate conversation. There was no doubt in her mind that there might be some parts she didn't need or want to hear before she started work. Molly had lots to do that day and listening to any more discussion and giving any more thought to the woman's preparation for the evening she was going to share with Ryan was just too much to handle.

The first two hours went smoothly with most of the patients arriving and leaving on time. Molly had continued to make small changes to the appointment scheduling to make the process even more time efficient. She felt confident as she listened to the patients call in that she could schedule sufficient time for each consultation so that Ryan wouldn't be running late, but not so much that she would waste any of his day. She doubted Ryan would have noticed if he was running either late or early as his mind seemed to be elsewhere. More than likely on his date that night, she surmised.

'Tell me a bit about yourself, Molly. Apart from being an anaesthetic nurse who wanted a role with better hours, I know nothing.'

Molly almost jumped out of her skin. She hadn't seen Ryan standing by the window as she'd walked into the kitchen for a glass of water.

She softly coughed to clear her throat. 'There's not much to know, really.'

'I don't believe that.' His arms folded across his broad chest and his look was one of curiosity. 'There's not a hospital within this state, or this country, that wouldn't snap you up in an instant. May I ask if your desire to have regular hours is due to a child or ailing parent?'

'Neither.'

'I appreciate your right to privacy in your personal life, so if my questions are intrusive, we can just leave it there.'

Molly studied the man standing so close to her that she could quite literally reach out and touch him. He was handsome, intelligent and the love he had for his daughter was palpable. She wasn't sure if having a teenage daughter meant that Ryan was hiding his age well or he had been a very young father. But it didn't matter. It was none of her business. Dr Ryan McFetridge had a close, loving relationship with his daughter, was wonderful with his patients and…had a hot date for dinner that night, she reminded herself. But she didn't want to be rude and not answer the man who had freed her from Joel's lecherous plans.

'It's family,' she replied. 'The reason I need a position with regular nine-to-five hours is my brother, Tommy.'

'He's young, then?'

'No, Tommy's twenty-five, but, like Lizzy, he has Down's syndrome and I'm his sole caregiver. He likes routine and he's happiest when I'm home before he is dropped off from work each night, so I need a job that allows me to give him that.'

Ryan didn't say anything for a moment but Molly watched as he nodded his head in a knowing way.

'I had no idea, but then again, why would I?'

Molly shrugged in response. Silently she agreed. Why would he? Molly's life outside the practice bore no interest to Ryan. He had a daughter, a full professional schedule and a girlfriend, so the frizzy-haired temp's life would hardly be of any concern to him.

'I understand completely. I'm all the family Lizzy has too so I pretty much work around her needs. I guess we have a lot in common.'

'I suppose we do,' Molly replied politely, all the while thinking they had very little in common.

'But I wouldn't change it for the world,' he added. 'She's a blessing and I'm so grateful to have her in my life.' He drew a deep breath and looked intently at Molly. 'No doubt you feel the same.'

'Yes, I do,' she told him as she looked down at her food to avoid his gaze. He was much too close and the room suddenly became much too warm. 'Knowing that I will be there every night when his bus pulls up makes him happy. He doesn't like changes or surprises. Lizzy no doubt doesn't like surprises either.'

'Hates them,' he said, rolling his eyes. 'She has to know everything, days ahead.'

Molly nodded. 'I found that if I can reassure Tommy

that nothing will change, then his anxiety levels don't rise and he more than copes—in fact he exceeds all expectations put on him.'

'You clearly understand how to manage the challenges he faces on a daily basis.'

'Not all of them, but I do my best. Tommy is the most loving brother a girl could have and I feel lucky to have him.'

'I'd say he is very lucky to have you. He chose his sister well,' Ryan said, then paused, deep in thought. 'Well… I'd best get back to work.'

'Ditto, I have quite the pile of correspondence that I need to process.'

It was just before twelve when Ryan came and perched casually on the corner of her desk. There were no patients as he was running a little early.

'I have a huge favour to ask you,' he began.

Molly spun on her nicely padded leather chair. She was enjoying the quality of her seat, as it certainly was an improvement from the last temp assignment that had seen her perched on a rickety stool that had seen better days. She wished immediately that she had not turned to find him so close yet again. His face, freshly shaven, was almost irresistible. Her eyes traced the line of his chiselled jaw down to the cleft in his chin then up to the softness of his lips.

Damn, why could he not have been the wrong side of seventy instead of the right side of everything?

'And what would that be?' she enquired while dragging her gaze back to the computer screen. She couldn't allow herself to be drawn into his eyes.

'I'm going out to the AMA dinner tonight.'

'Yes, I know…' Molly blurted out, then blinked nervously at her admission to overhearing a private conversation. 'I was hanging up my coat this morning and briefly heard something about it.'

He paused for a moment in silence. Molly noticed that the leg not supporting him began casually swinging.

'My *date* for tonight is struggling to find anything to wear and I was wondering if you might meet her in the city and help her to find something.'

Molly's face turned back to his and she stared at him in gobsmacked silence for a moment. She couldn't mask her surprise and only barely her displeasure with the idea.

'Really? Me?'

'It's the Australian Medical Association annual dinner so I want something classic, timeless yet fun and age-appropriate.'

Age-appropriate? Was he dating a college student? A hideous suggestion suddenly became monumentally worse. Molly had to find a way to diplomatically decline the request to assist. It wasn't part of the job description so he could find someone else to do it. Perhaps the campus counsellor could accompany her, she decided with heavy dose of sarcasm colouring her thoughts.

'It's fairly obvious to say that I'm not a fashion plate. I think you could find someone much more suitable for the task.'

'But she asked for you.'

'Me? Why on earth would she ask for me? I don't know your girlfriend.'

Molly watched as Ryan's lips formed a smirk and he began shaking his head and almost chuckling. She did not like that he found it amusing, when she found it more and more disconcerting.

'For your information, Molly, my date tonight is not a *girlfriend*. I'm taking Lizzy to the AMA dinner. I thought she would have told you that when you were chatting about her shoes…and *yours*,' he said, referring to her first day's odd choice. 'Anyway, you made quite the impression on her that day and I feel, after our chat about Tommy, that Lizzy would be very safe in your hands. She's taken a real liking to you, which she never does that quickly. You know the challenges she may face and you can help her through them if they arise—perhaps she senses that. You definitely have a rapport.'

Molly was momentarily speechless, almost wanting to kick herself for thinking and saying what she had. She had not considered Lizzy could be his date. Her version of the story was based on nothing much but her own wild, and slightly jaded, imagination.

'You would make such a difference and I would really owe you if you'd agree,' he continued. 'I left my credit card beside her bed this morning while she was still sleeping but she had no one to go with her to the stores. She's worried she won't find anything and she's getting very upset. She took a cab to the local shopping mall about forty minutes ago and she's struggling. Her grandmother couldn't go with her today and Lizzy doesn't cope well with making decisions on her own and I don't want her to get overwhelmed and decide not to go tonight. It's happened before.'

Molly felt so silly. Once again, her assumptions about her boss were so far from accurate.

'I completely understand, Molly, if you don't feel comfortable with the idea. You have a lot on your plate and I don't want to add to it. Honestly it's not in your job description so I'll call the store and ask them to send a few things to our home and she can make a choice there.'

'No,' Molly cut in.

'It's fine, honestly, Molly. It was wrong of me to ask…'

'No, I didn't mean to hesitate. I'd love to help Lizzy to find something very pretty and age-appropriate for tonight.'

'You're sure?'

'Yes. I assume you've checked with the boss, and he's okay with me taking time off from here,' Molly added with a smile. Was she smiling because Ryan hadn't been speaking to a love interest earlier? She wasn't sure, but something was making her happy.

Ryan returned the smile. 'Perfectly happy and very grateful. I've already checked with Stacy and she's happy to stay on for the afternoon. She's finished her influenza immunisations for today and is not needed at the other practice so it's all set...with your approval.'

'It seems like you covered everything so I'll head off, then,' Molly said as she stood up.

'Not quite,' he said, reaching into his pocket. 'Take these.'

Molly watched as he handed her his car keys. The fact he would entrust her with his car was pleasantly surprising but her heart began to race when the warmth of his fingers touched her hand ever so briefly.

'I'll cab it home after I finish here and then Lizzy and I can drop you off at your place on the way to dinner.'

'There's no need, really,' she replied, very aware of her pulse quickening.

'I'm being a little presumptuous here—I'm hoping after you find Lizzy her outfit you might drive her to the hairdresser at three-thirty as she might get distracted and not make it there on time without company. She's pretty good generally but it's a lot to fit into one day.'

'Of course,' Molly told him. 'I'm happy to take Lizzy to have her hair done and then get her back to your place. Where exactly is your place?'

'Thirty-four Lincoln Avenue, Unley Park. I'll send it in a text to you.'

Molly sighed. Of course it was in Unley Park. One of the nicest suburbs in Adelaide, filled with palatial homes, manicured gardens and tennis courts.

'That sounds great. I'll need to get home by five o'clock, which is well before you'll be leaving for the dinner. That's when Tommy gets home.'

'Of course,' he said. 'I don't want you to be late home. I'm incredibly grateful that you're helping out and I don't want to cause any anxiety or problems for your brother.'

Molly noticed Ryan staring at her but she didn't feel judged. She actually felt appreciated and it had been a long time since she had felt that. She could see that, along with everything else, Ryan was a good and kind man by the consideration he was showing towards Tommy. Her fiancé had never been understanding of Tommy's needs, or hers for that matter. She acknowledged Ryan's response with a smile that was coming from her heart but once again worrying her head immensely.

Their eyes locked for the longest time in silence and Molly was not sure where the conversation would lead. Finally, Ryan broke the spell she felt herself falling under.

'I guess it's time you took off if you're to help Lizzy.'

'Yes, of course,' she answered as she reached down to the drawer to collect her handbag. 'I will try to bring the car back in one piece…'

'I would hope so. I only picked it up from the dealership two weeks ago.'

'Then I will try extra hard,' she said, with her lips forming a soft smile as she headed to the closet and collected her coat.

Ryan followed close behind.

'Where is Lizzy exactly?' she asked as she opened the back door to the staff car park.

'She's at the Eastern Hills Mall and she'll be at one of these boutiques,' he said as he handed Molly a piece of paper and then headed back in the direction of his office. 'I wrote down the names and the phone numbers for you. They know Lizzy well and usually make it easy…apparently just not today, for some reason. But I'm sure, once you arrive, she will relax and find some lovely things. And, Molly, if you need to leave before I arrive home, please book a cab from my place to yours and charge my card. It's the least I can do for you,' Ryan called down the hallway to her.

'Sounds perfect.' Molly was relieved that Ryan and Lizzy wouldn't see where she lived. It was on the very wrong side of the tracks and she didn't want their pity as they dropped her off before heading to their black-tie dinner.

Looking down at the keys in her hand, Molly smiled. She closed the door and made her way to the shiny new BMW in the car park feeling happy. Not with the car, although it was very nice; it was the trust and confidence that Ryan showed in her to help his daughter. They would have fun, she felt certain. And Lizzy would look gorgeous.

'Molly. I can't find a dress. Dad will be sad if I don't find a dress.' Lizzy was clearly distraught when Molly arrived. Ryan knew his daughter only too well.

'Hello, Lizzy,' Molly said as she drew closer to a very desolate young woman sitting by the change rooms of an exclusive boutique. 'That's why I'm here. I'll help you find a dress. And a very pretty one.'

Lizzy scratched her head nervously. 'There's no red dresses.'

Molly bent down and, dropping her voice, she said, 'There's other stores here—perhaps one of them will have a red dress. We don't have to buy a dress from here.'

Molly noticed Lizzy's frown soften and the hint of a smile forming. 'Will we find one?'

'I think we will,' she told her. 'And it will be the prettiest dress in Adelaide. Shall we get shoes to match?'

'Uh-huh,' Lizzy said as she climbed to her feet. Molly thanked the sales assistants for their help, explained the need for a red dress and, together with Lizzy, left the small store.

It didn't take too long before they found another boutique with a wider selection of after-five wear. Floor-length gowns, some that skimmed the calf and a few sparkly mini-dresses were all in the store window. 'This looks perfect,' Molly said as she led Lizzy inside.

'May I help you?' the sales assistant asked as she approached.

'Yes, Lizzy's looking for a gown for a black-tie dinner tonight. And she would love one in red.'

'Mmm…I think I may have something for you. Are you about a size fourteen?'

'Yes,' Lizzy replied, coyly. 'I like sparkles too?'

'It's a little sparkly, but not too much,' the older woman replied with a warm smile. 'I'll go and fetch it from the back and you can let me know if it's sparkly enough. It was on hold for two days but that time was up at nine o'clock this morning. You're welcome to take a seat or look through the other gowns. I'll be right back.'

The woman disappeared, leaving Molly and Lizzy in a sea of gowns decorated with sequins, lace and faux fur.

'You should buy a dress,' Lizzy said to Molly as she sat down on a high-backed gold velvet chair. 'But not red.'

'I'll look to fill in time, but I won't buy anything.'

Molly admired the stunning gowns. And she tried not to gasp when she saw the swing tags. Each one seemed to be more expensive than the last. Her eyes fell upon an emerald-green halter gown with the most delicate beading. She pulled it out and swung it around as if she were dancing with it. Lizzy laughed as Molly swayed and dipped in time to non-existent music.

'I have that in your size,' the second sales assistant said.

Feeling a little silly that she had been seen by someone other than Lizzy, Molly came back to her senses. 'Goodness, no,' she said, shaking her head as she hurriedly put the dress back on the rack and sat down beside Lizzy. Molly Murphy knew that she could not afford to buy a dress costing anything close to nine hundred dollars. She hadn't spent even a tenth of that on anything for herself in a very long time. 'I'm here to help Lizzy find a dress. I'm not looking for anything for myself.'

At that moment, the older woman returned carrying a pretty red dress with a scooped neckline, cap sleeves and red and silver beading on the shoulders. 'I knew we had something in red,' she announced, not hiding her pride in recalling the dress that matched Lizzy's description. 'Please come with me and I can help you to try it on.'

Lizzy jumped up with glee. Molly was so very happy to see the expression on her face. They made their way to the elegantly decorated change rooms and the woman hung the dress up and unzipped the back. Molly smiled at the sight of the reproduction antique chair with black satin upholstery adjacent to the floor-to-ceiling mirror. Next, she noticed a gold-framed Kandinsky print hanging near the clothing rail. She knew the piece, it was from 1920, and one of her favourite pieces by the artist. Her gaze then dropped to two pairs of black patent leather heels on a small shoe rack. It was the perfect change room indeed. The type the Molly of late saw in her dreams.

'And you try on the green one, Molly.'

'No, Lizzy. I'm not trying on a dress. Today is about you, not about me,' Molly replied as she backed out of the room and headed to the blue velvet sofa. She was going to put her feet up for a moment while Lizzy changed. She hoped the dress fit as Lizzy really did have her heart set on red and sparkly.

'Pleeeeeeease try on the pretty green one,' Lizzy pleaded. 'Then we will both be princesses. Please.'

Molly smiled. Lizzy's honesty was so sweet, just like Tommy's. No hidden agendas, no game-playing, just saying exactly how they felt.

'But you are pretty so you should have a new dress,' Lizzy told her. 'Then you can find a boyfriend.'

The older woman arched her eyebrow and looked at Molly with a smirk. 'I think you may not have much of a choice. Can you let me know which one…?'

'Here it is,' the second assistant said as she swept past them with the stunning gown draped over her arms and placed it in the adjacent change room. 'I saw you dancing with it earlier.'

Molly cringed at the thought of how ridiculous she would have appeared dancing with the gown but she was impressed with the woman's customer service. No doubt she had great sales figures, the way she moved so quickly to place the dress in Molly's possession. Pity the poor woman, Molly thought, because, despite her nimbleness, there would be no sale. Molly had neither the intention nor the money to make the dress hers.

And on top of that Molly Murphy would have absolutely nowhere to wear a dress like that.

'Fine… I'll try it on…' Molly faltered. 'But after this we are going to find shoes and a bag for you, Lizzy.' Molly tried to make her voice a little stern and serious. Ryan had entrusted Molly with the task of finding his daughter a dress, shoes and bag and that was exactly what she would do after she tried on the gown waiting for her in the equally elegantly decorated change room.

Her chair was upholstered in beige satin and two pairs of nude patent leather heels were beside the mirrored wall. And the artwork, *Mountains and Sea* by Helen Frankenthaler, complemented the colour palette of the tiny space perfectly. Molly loved abstract art and apparently so did the store interior decorator. Everything about the store was perfect and for the first time in a long time Molly thought her life was heading that way too.

'We need to find you a dress—that's an order given to me by your father. We need to remember he's my boss, so I can't let him down.' She smiled as she closed the door, then took a deep breath as she looked at the softly draped fabric that would be against her skin for only a few minutes.

A few glorious minutes.

'My goodness.' The sales assistant gasped. 'That dress was made for you.'

Molly shook her head in response as she stepped out of the change room. She was unaccustomed to compliments. Lifting the hem of her dress so she didn't catch her heels, she made her way to Lizzy's door. One of the two pairs of the shoes were in her size so she had slipped them on and it made the hem skim the floor perfectly, but she was still a little nervous of catching the expensive fabric.

The dress felt wonderful against her body but she knew the feeling would be fleeting. 'Hardly made for me. I'm more your jeans and T-shirt type.'

'Well, you should seriously consider broadening your wardrobe choices,' replied the older assistant. 'You look simply divine and the gown fits you like a glove.'

Molly ignored their flattery. The dress momentarily made her feel special but she could not afford to be swept away by it.

'Do you need some help with the zipper, Lizzy?' Molly asked as she knocked on the door to Lizzy's room.

'Uh-huh,' came the reply and the door opened enough for Molly to slip inside.

A moment later Lizzy stepped out in her red dress with the sparkles and did a little hesitant twirl, holding the sides out as if to curtsey, and the three women gasped with delight. The dress skimmed her ankles so it was still formal but wouldn't need any adjustment to the hem. Molly had worried that, with Lizzy being just over five feet tall, there might be some very hurried alterations to anything she chose.

'You look just like a princess,' Molly said in delight.

'Beautiful, just beautiful,' the other women cried in unison.

Then the younger assistant added, 'And I have a silver beaded bag that would be just perfect.'

'Do you like it?' Lizzy asked Molly, then continued without taking a breath. 'I like it a lot. My boyfriend will like it too.'

'I think you will be the prettiest girl in the prettiest dress tonight.' Molly walked back to her dressing room and quickly emerged with the credit card Ryan had given her. 'Please charge Lizzy's dress while I change so we have time to find shoes.'

'You look so pretty, Molly. Will you buy that dress?' Lizzy asked excitedly.

'Not today.' Molly smiled and thought with a price tag like that she wouldn't buy the dress that day nor any day in the future.

With Lizzy's dress carefully wrapped and slipped inside an oversized carry bag, along with the beaded clutch that Lizzy also liked, the two shoppers left the store and went in search of shoes, but not before Lizzy made a call to her father and told him all about the red dress. Molly stepped away so they could have a private conversation. She heard Lizzy giggling and it made her heart sing to know how happy the young woman was with her purchases. She watched her nod a few times and then hang up the phone and walk over to her with a skip in her step.

'So, your father's happy you found a dress?'

'Uh-huh,' Lizzy replied with a broad smile and then, holding on tight to her special purchase, she walked over to a store with some pretty shoes in the window.

Molly followed behind quickly and together they stepped inside the upmarket boutique with designer shoes and beautifully groomed sales assistants. Lizzy picked three styles and sat down while the store assistants disappeared in search of the shoes. Suddenly Molly noticed a worried expression replace Lizzy's happiness.

'I don't feel well. I want to go home,' she announced as she stood up and left the store. Molly quickly followed her to a seat in the shopping mall. Lizzy's face was flushed and she was very agitated. A change had swept over her with no warning.

'Of course,' Molly said, sensing the young woman was

overwhelmed. 'I'm sure you have pretty shoes at home you could wear tonight anyway.'

'I'm not going.'

Molly sat down beside her and patted her hand affectionately. 'Maybe after a rest you'll feel better.'

'I can't go. I need medicine for my tummy,' Lizzy said and inched her hand away.

Molly tilted her head a little, confused by what Lizzy had said and her abrupt change in demeanour.

'I'll take you home, then, and you can get some rest.'

'I want Dad. Dad knows what I need when I get the pain.' Lizzy's voice was beginning to spike. Her anxiety was palpable.

Molly stood up and reached around for her phone within her handbag. 'Of course, he does,' she said softly as she dialled the surgery number and Stacy put her through to her new boss.

'Hi, Molly, did you find everything for Lizzy so she's all set to attend the dinner?'

'Yes, and no,' Molly began, then lowered her voice as she turned away.

'Yes and no?'

'Well, we do have the dress and Lizzy loves it but now she is quite distressed, needs some medication and says you will know what it is. I think I can guess what's happening but she doesn't want to talk to me about it. I assume she's having her period.'

Ryan sighed into the phone. 'She gets embarrassed and doesn't like to talk about it. I'll catch a cab to you. She won't be able to go anywhere. Where are you now?'

Molly looked around to quickly find a landmark Ryan might know. 'We're two stores down from the information kiosk. Not too far from the valet parking entrance.'

'Okay,' he began. 'Please stay put and I'll be there

in less than ten minutes. Please stay by her side. I don't want another episode.'

Molly heard the line go dead.

'Is Dad coming?'

'Yes,' Molly told her in a calming voice. 'He's on his way. He won't be long at all.' Molly wasn't sure what Ryan meant by another episode. She assumed it was that time of the month for Lizzy, but she wouldn't ordinarily call that an episode. She sat by the young girl's side and chatted about things that would keep her distracted. A puppy passed them by dressed in a matching outfit to her owner and that made Lizzy smile for a few minutes until they disappeared into one of the upmarket boutiques and out of sight. Suddenly Lizzy's stress began to escalate again. Molly wondered what was causing the panic attack as at nineteen she surely would have experienced numerous periods. Perhaps it was that combined with the idea of attending the dinner, she mused. It was disappointing that Lizzy was feeling so unwell, as she had been quite excited to buy shoes to match her princess dress.

'You know, Lizzy, I had terrible periods too. The worst and then as I got older they improved.'

'They did?'

'Yes. It's still not a fun time but it's not so awful any more.'

Lizzy seemed a little happier with the news Molly had given her but she was still terribly distressed.

'There you are.' A familiar husky voice coloured by concern came from behind them. Ryan knelt down in front of Lizzy and affectionately stroked her forehead.

'I want to go home,' Lizzy said loudly as she looked at her father with eyes so sad they melted Molly's heart.

'That's why I'm here. I'll take you both home. Let's get you both to my car.'

Molly knew she shouldn't be embarrassed by her home but she still had some pride so she was horribly embarrassed and she couldn't change the way she felt. 'Truly, it's okay, you take Lizzy and I'll get a cab.'

Ryan looked at Molly and she felt a shiver run up and down her spine. She was being drawn towards him once again and it was unnerving. He had rushed to his daughter's side like a knight in shining armour and that only compounded feelings that were already growing for the man on one knee.

'It's the least I can do.'

'No, seriously, you take Lizzy home, get her settled and get yourself ready for the dinner.'

Ryan shook his head. 'I'm not going to the dinner. My date's unwell.'

'But you're getting an award,' Lizzy replied.

'An award?' Molly asked Ryan with a curious frown.

'Well, an award of sorts.'

'Of sorts?' Molly replied, taken aback by his casual response. 'The AMA don't give awards of sorts at their annual dinner. It must be something special.'

He reached for the shopping bags. 'I'm being presented with the AMA State Award but I can call through my apology tonight and send a thank you email tomorrow. They can courier it over next week.'

Molly knew how prestigious it was to be nominated, let alone win an award that was voted by medical peers. 'Then you have to be there,' she said. 'I can stay with Lizzy and keep her company and you can go and collect your award.'

'I'm not going to fly solo. Besides, you have to be

home for your brother.' Ryan kept his eyes on Lizzy. 'I assume you parked the car underground.'

'Yes, in the bay nearest the escalators.'

The three of them walked in the direction of the exit to the car park. Ryan's arm was around Lizzy.

'Tommy would be fine watching television for two or three hours,' Molly added. 'I just like to make sure he's had a good dinner, but then I could head over to your place in time for you to leave and keep Lizzy company.'

'Sooty can stay. You can get your award,' Lizzy announced.

'Sooty?' Molly said with an enquiring tone, having no clue who Sooty was or what Sooty might be. Perhaps it was the family dog. There was clearly so much that Molly didn't know about Lizzy and Ryan, and that wasn't surprising after such a short time, yet she also felt an unexpected level of ease being with them. A realisation swept over Molly that it felt almost natural to her for the three of them to be together outside Ryan's practice. It was a strange feeling but she couldn't deny she liked it.

'Sooty is Lizzy's grandmother. Her real name is Ann.'

Molly couldn't help but wonder how Sooty was an abbreviation of Ann. It didn't come close.

As if he read her mind, Ryan continued as they walked together. 'Lizzy adored the British television show *Sooty*. She and Ann would watch it together regularly. One day Lizzy told Ann that she wanted to call her Sooty instead of Grandma. It just stuck. All these years later she calls her Sooty and she even signs messages to Lizzy with that name.'

'That's wonderful. Is she your mother?'

'No, she is Lizzy's maternal grandmother,' Ryan told her as they stepped off the escalator and headed towards the car, which was just outside the sliding glass doors.

'She's a lovely lady, we get on well now, but there were some issues early on. Fortunately, we moved past the challenges we faced.'

Molly assumed it had something to do with Ryan and Lizzy's mother parting ways but she wasn't going to ask questions that weren't her business.

'Ann's house is about fifteen minutes away from ours so she stays over if Lizzy needs her and I have to work back and the three nights that I visit St Clara's.'

Molly reached into her bag and handed the keys to Ryan without him asking. She knew that St Clara's was the residential care for single mothers where Ryan consulted three nights a week.

His fingers brushed hers as he took the keys from her upturned palm. Once again, his touch made her heart skip a beat.

'Please let me drive you home,' he implored as the remote unlocked the car doors. 'Lizzy will be fine once I get her settled in the car and give her some analgesics. She just panics if I'm not around when this happens.'

'No, honestly, I want to pick up some fresh bread to have with dinner anyway. I'll get a cab from over there.' She pointed towards the cab rank and began slowly walking in that direction, then paused to check that Ryan and Lizzy were okay. She wanted to ensure they got away. Molly's maternal instincts were kicking in where Lizzy was concerned. She felt a bond had formed from the moment they met. She couldn't explain why and it defied logic but it was there nonetheless.

'I want Sooty,' Lizzy announced as Ryan held the car door open for her and she climbed in. The pain was clearly growing and, with it, an increasing level of distress.

Molly watched as Ryan secured his daughter's seat

belt and then, standing upright again, he paused. Molly couldn't hear the conversation but he kept raising his eyes and glancing over in her direction and nodding. Then she watched as he made a very brief phone call. Molly shifted a little, feeling slightly uncomfortable. She didn't know what was happening and whether she should go or stay.

Molly noticed Ryan's expression suddenly change from concern to something she didn't quite understand as he shut the car door, then slipped his mobile phone in the inside pocket of his overcoat and crossed to her without saying a word. He looked almost nervous, his eyes randomly roaming the car park. It was an expression she hadn't thought a man like Ryan would ever wear.

'Molly,' he began, then paused as his fingers ran thoughtfully across the cleft in his chin. 'I have a second favour to ask of you today.'

'Sure, anything,' Molly replied without hesitation, in a way that completely surprised her. She had not imagined she would ever think let alone say those words to a man after everything that had happened to her.

Ryan looked relieved by her reply. 'Is there the possibility...that perhaps *you* might accompany me to the awards dinner at the convention centre tonight? I know it's short notice but I'm hoping you might consider it.'

Molly had to steady herself. She had no idea what to say. But by the intense look on his handsome face only inches from hers, he was clearly not going anywhere until she gave him her answer.

CHAPTER SIX

Molly couldn't think what to say as she stood in stunned silence. Her mind was again spinning and Ryan McFetridge was again the cause.

'I must apologise,' Ryan said ruefully, bringing the silence to an end. 'It was presumptuous of me to think you would be free, it's just that Lizzy suggested it to me in the car and I had to agree it was a great idea.'

'I'm not sure… I mean, it's just not something I was expecting you to ask…' Molly hesitated and then decided, like Lizzy, she needed to be upfront. No game playing or hiding her situation. 'To be honest I'm not sure I can. It's just that I don't think I have anything suitable to wear on such short notice for a black-tie event.' Molly didn't think, she knew very well that she didn't have anything in her wardrobe close to what she would need for a black-tie dinner. With the pay rise she could go to a department store and find something but only if she had a few days to search the sale racks. 'I don't want to let you down but perhaps there is someone else you could ask.'

'Perhaps…but I would very much like to take you,' he told her. 'Please be honest, is the dress the only reason you can't make it? Would Tommy be okay alone?'

Molly knew the answer to both questions. 'Tommy would be fine, as I mentioned to you before, as long as I go home and prepare his dinner. He spends most nights watching his television programmes in his room but, that aside, I just don't have time to find something suitable. It's the AMA dinner, not dinner at a local café, so I would need to head into the city to find something and it's already almost three.' She paused. 'That reminds me—you will need to cancel Lizzy's hair appointment.'

Ryan tilted his head a little to one side. 'Do you always make sure others aren't put out?'

'Well, the salon might have a waiting list for clients and I don't want you to be charged for an appointment that Lizzy won't make.'

'I'm not sure how you manage to keep everyone's schedule stored front and centre, Ms Murphy.'

'It's in my job description.'

'I have to disagree on that. I'm beginning to think that you go over and above.' He smiled. 'But if the dress is truly the only issue, then I have already solved that and I can pick you up at seven.'

'What do you mean you've solved that?'

'Well, Lizzy told me about a green dress that, according to her, made you look like a *princess*. I wanted to give you something in appreciation for you helping me out this afternoon and taking care of Lizzy, so I bought it for you.'

'What are you talking about?' Molly gasped. 'You bought me a dress? But I was very happy to spend time with Lizzy. You don't have to give me anything.'

'I wanted to give you something.'

'Fine, that's a lovely gesture, but chocolates or a longer lunch break one day this week would have more than been enough. A dress is definitely too much.'

'No, it's not, and apparently it looks lovely on you, according to my daughter. I must say she has impeccable taste like her father. It was going to be delivered to you at the office tomorrow but it's now on its way down here,' he said, looking behind him towards the escalators. 'Actually, perfect timing. I think this might be it coming down now.'

Molly turned around to see the sales assistant making her way down the escalators towards them.

'But, Molly, honestly, I do understand if you can't make dinner tonight. Let me know how you feel when you get home and if Tommy wants you to stay in or you're too tired after today's running around. Just call or text me…but I want you to have the dress anyway,' he told her as he stepped away towards the car. 'I better get back to Lizzy and take her home before the cramps set in. And thank you again. It would have been a disaster if this had happened when she was on her own.'

'Ryan, I'm not sure…'

'It's fine, Molly. If you can't make tonight, I'll see you at work tomorrow.'

Molly watched as Ryan quickly climbed into the car and then drove away, leaving her mouth gaping slightly.

'Hello again, Molly,' the sales assistant greeted her and handed Molly a black fabric garment bag and a white gift bag, both emblazoned with the store insignia. 'I put a pair of nude pumps in there as well in your size and a small matching clutch as Dr McFetridge said he wanted you to have everything you would need. He's such a lovely man.'

Molly was speechless as the smartly dressed sales assistant smiled and walked away in her very high black patent stilettos, leaving Molly with her own thoughts. So much had transpired in a few short hours. Molly wasn't sure how she felt about Ryan McFetridge except confused.

Very confused.

Staring straight ahead, a garment bag across one arm

and the other holding the gift bag along with her handbag, she followed the signs to the cab rank. Her gaze was just a few steps ahead of her as she climbed the half a dozen cement steps to the street and the line of cabs waiting. Feeling overwhelmed and undecided as to whether she should even consider accepting Ryan's gift, let alone the invitation to attend the dinner, she kept glancing at the bags. Her steps were as considered as her thoughts as she put one foot in front of the other and made her way into the bitterly cold breeze.

She approached the first cab in line and the driver hurriedly jumped out, and, looking up at the heavy grey clouds and the imminent downpour, quickly took her bags and opened the door for her. Molly climbed in, still in a dazed state, and he shut the door and made his way to the other side and placed the bags on the seat beside her.

'Where to?' he enquired as he jumped inside the cab himself, secured his seat belt and pulled out into the traffic.

Molly gave him her address and collapsed back into the seat. Her mind was still spinning and she didn't much like where her thoughts were heading. She just hoped that Lizzy would be okay.

Three hours later, Molly dialled Ryan's mobile. It was almost six in the evening. It was dark outside as it always was in winter at that time, and Molly had the heater warming the living room and another on in Tommy's room. As she pulled back the drapes Molly could see the stars were sparkling in the midnight-blue sky.

Her first question was about Lizzy.

'Lizzy's fine, thank you for asking,' Ryan answered. 'She's tucked up in bed, and I've given her strong pain relief and she's resting her back on a hot-water bottle, with another one on her stomach. She finds the warmth comforting and it helps her to relax. And I called Ann over as she does seem to be able to make Lizzy feel less stressed about the whole situation. I guess it's a woman thing and Ann's the only mother figure Lizzy has in her life.'

Molly learned so much about Ryan and Lizzy in that one statement. Lizzy had no mother or other female relatives in her life. And if there was a girlfriend, she wasn't filling the role.

'It's wonderful to hear that Ann is so close to Lizzy but I had no idea that Lizzy suffered from such chronic painful periods.'

'It's been like that from day one, but I must admit she is becoming increasingly anxious each month.'

'She's very lucky to have such an understanding father who just happens to be a doctor to help.'

'I'm not so sure she's the lucky one, but let's not go there,' he replied, then changed the subject. 'So, you made it home and out of the terrible weather? Battened down for the evening with a roast in the oven?'

Molly hesitated for a moment before she drew breath. 'Actually,' she began, 'I have prepared Tommy's dinner. Not quite a roast—it's soup and shepherd's pie.'

'Sounds delicious. I hope you enjoy it.'

'I'm not eating it…'

'Not hungry?'

'Yes, a little, but I thought, if you would like, I could accompany you to the AMA dinner.'

Molly waited for a response but there was nothing. Ryan's end of the line was silent. She suddenly felt very foolish. Perhaps he had already invited someone else. Her stomach dropped and she wished with her every being that she had not just told him she would like to be his dinner date. She thought she could hear the faint sound of his breathing but no words. She strained her ears but there was nothing. She had never felt that uncomfortable.

'Of course, if you'd rather not go or you already have another date, I understand—'

'No, Molly,' his deep, suddenly serious voice cut in. 'I would very much like you to attend with me. I just don't want you to feel pressured because you work for me or because of the dress. It was a gift and accepting my invitation isn't part of the working conditions. I want you to know that.'

Molly was taken aback by the change. His mood had morphed into something professional and considered. While she thought it was also very gallant of him to let her know there were no strings attached, he seemed to be putting distance between them. Making sure she knew where he stood.

'I was not accepting because you bought the dress… well, actually that's not true. I mean, I have an amazing dress hanging in my closet and nowhere else to wear it and you bought it, so technically I suppose I'm accepting because you bought the dress, but mainly because I think you should attend to accept the award. Lizzy would want you to attend so we can make her happy together. I mean, you can make her happy by attending and I can attend with you.'

Molly felt as if she was speaking at a hundred words a minute. And she was. It was her way to cover the nervousness and vulnerability she was feeling.

'Then, you're my date,' Ryan answered, then quickly amended his words. 'I mean, my guest.'

Molly was relieved that Ryan hadn't left her hanging again as she had initially felt borderline silly for calling and accepting his invitation, but she also picked up on his rapid correction from date to guest. 'I'm happy to be your *guest* and step in for Lizzy so you can accept your award. I'm sure she will be thrilled to see it when you get home.'

'No doubt. She's quite the organiser of my life at times.'

'Women can be like that,' she answered, and then continued. 'Speaking of that, I think it might be more time efficient for me to meet you at the convention centre. By the time you get through the traffic to me and then we get back to the venue, the canapés might be cold.'

Molly wished she weren't so self-conscious and embarrassed about her accommodation but she was and she didn't want Ryan's pity. The time was a factor but her suggestion was also to save face.

'I don't feel right about you finding your own way there. At least let me book a car to collect you.'

'Truly, it's not necessary. I will call a cab when I'm ready and meet you there.'

Molly convinced Ryan to meet her at the entrance to the convention centre at seven, then she hung up and quickly proceeded to get ready. She had forty-five minutes to shower, do her hair and apply light make-up. Molly Murphy was determined not to turn up looking like a drowned mouse in a nine-hundred-dollar dress.

Ryan checked in on Lizzy. She was tucked up in bed, having soup that her grandmother had prepared. Ryan had given Lizzy analgesics and Ann was sitting in a large reclining armchair beside her as the two of them watched television. It was the way it had been for many years. Ryan had bought the very comfortable chair as either he or Ann would sit there and read to Lizzy when she was younger and then as she grew older they would sit and talk about their days. Her room was large and yet still cosy.

'How are you feeling, Lizzy?'

'My tummy still hurts but not so bad as before.'

'Good, I'm sure Sooty's soup will help too.'

'Mmm, it's chicken noodle.'

Ryan looked at his daughter, who was half-distracted by the television and the soup. The pain relief had taken effect but it worried him that each month seemed to be getting progressively worse. He knew that he needed to talk through the options with Lizzy after their consultation with her GP and the gynaecologist. They both needed to seriously consider the options. While a hysterectomy was radical and something he had been wanting to delay or avoid altogether, he wasn't so sure now they could put it off for ever if the pain continued to be so debilitating for her. Together they had to make a decision that neither would regret.

While she hadn't mentioned getting married or wanting a baby in the future and her chronic pain was not going to improve, it still wasn't easy as a father to make the irreversible decision to take away that option for her. At times like that, he wished that Lizzy had a mother in whom she could confide and he had someone to help him make an important and life-changing decision with his daughter. He could not get it wrong. While his medical expertise was leaning towards ensuring her physical health came first, his fatherly concerns were around the future should she change her mind and decide she wanted children. Just when he got it straight in his head, sorted, decided...he questioned himself and decided being a single father to a nineteen-year-old girl was not that easy.

'Molly's agreed to accompany me to the dinner tonight if Sooty can stay and you're all right with me going out.'

Ryan watched as Ann nodded. 'I'm happy to stay and

happy to see you finally get out and enjoy yourself,' she told him.

'Good, you get your award. I want to see it,' Lizzy said, then took another spoonful of the hearty soup. 'And Molly can wear the princess dress. She looks pretty.'

'And Molly is?' Ann enquired with a knowing smile and a sparkle in her eyes.

'My temp office manager.'

'And a pretty office manager by the sound of it. Princesses are always pretty.'

Ryan couldn't help but agree silently. Molly was a very pretty office manager.

'Then it looks like I'm going to dinner,' he told the two women, choosing not to confirm or deny Ann's statement or his own thoughts. Directing his attention back to Ann, he added, 'I'll leave the ibuprofen in the kitchen. Lizzy needs them four-hourly so another dose at eight o'clock and then hopefully she will sleep through the night. If you need me, don't hesitate to call my phone and I can be here in fifteen minutes.'

'Go and enjoy yourself,' Ann said, waving her hand. 'You don't get out enough. Go have some fun with your lovely date. It's about time you enjoyed company with someone closer to your own age. Lizzy and I'll have some quiet time and with any luck she'll be feeling better by morning and if not I'll stay with her tomorrow.'

'She's my guest, not my date.'

Ann raised her eyebrow. 'Let's not be pedantic, Ryan. A date or guest, it's the same in my books.'

Ryan chose to ignore her comment. 'Remember, call if you need anything.' His face was lined momentarily with concern. 'I mean it, please call if you need me and I will come home immediately.'

'Go, scat,' the older woman said with a grin. 'You're

distracting us. We don't know who she's about to choose for her date.'

'What do you mean, choose for her date? Who's going on a date?'

'The bachelorette,' Lizzy said, pointing at the television with her half-eaten bread roll. 'She's pretty.'

'Okay, you're talking about a television programme,' Ryan muttered to himself and nodded with relief. He had thought for a moment that Lizzy was planning a date and that Ann was in on it. And his daughter dating was the last thing he wanted to think about. Lizzy meeting someone and potentially falling in love was something he did not want to deal with for a long time. A very long time.

'Molly, you look absolutely stunning. Lizzy was right, that certainly is a *princess* dress.'

'Thank you,' Molly replied as she alighted the cab. Ryan had not met her at the entrance to the venue, instead he had been waiting at the cab rank for her. The night air was bitterly cold but Molly was not about to cover the beautiful gown with a black woollen overcoat, so she had a silk wrap that had once belonged to her mother around her shoulders. It was one of the few things she had kept for a special occasion and that night suited the bill. It wasn't the most practical accessory on a cold winter's evening but that night Molly had decided to throw being practical to the wind quite literally. Her curly dark hair was held back on one side by an antique silver hair clip, also a gift from her mother, and she had small pearl earrings. They were costume as she had sold her real jewellery but they looked very pretty and nothing too elaborate was needed. The dress was a statement on its own.

'Let's get you inside, quickly. You look gorgeous but I don't want you to catch pneumonia.' He extended his hand and Molly didn't hesitate to take it. It was a firm, warm hold as his fingers securely enveloped hers and it felt like nothing Molly had ever felt before. She swallowed nervously as her heart picked up speed. They didn't need to rush inside, she thought, as his touch was warming every part of her body. And she suddenly felt safer and warmer than she'd thought possible.

She lifted the hem of her gown with her hand that also held her clutch bag and the pair walked together to the entrance with all the other guests who had arrived like them right on the stroke of seven. Molly suddenly and unexpectedly felt at ease and as if she belonged there. Ryan had slipped his hand free of hers once she had both feet on the pavement but had offered his arm as her support and Molly had accepted. Her hand had rested there until they reached the doors. It all felt so surreal to Molly yet so surprisingly natural.

Once inside Molly pulled her silk wrap from her shoulders. It was a Cinderella moment as she walked among the guests with her very handsome and wonderfully considerate dinner companion. The expensive dress was making her feel so special and with little effort Ryan was doing the same.

'Would you like some champagne, wine or sparkling water?' the black-and-white-attired waiter enquired of both Molly and Ryan.

Ryan waited for Molly's response, which was champagne. She watched as he took a flute filled with bubbles from the tray for her and a red wine for himself.

He introduced her to a number of people as they made their way through the crowd. He didn't say how they knew each other or that she was his employee. She was simply his guest. The noise was building as the crowd grew. The doors to the banquet hall were still closed and the guests were all chatting and greeting each other. Molly could hear many talking shop and others speaking of their last vacation, their children or their impending retirement. It was a diverse audience but each somehow connected to the field of medicine, some on the periphery and some right in the middle of it. There were pharmaceutical executives and heart surgeons, Theatre nurses and podiatrists, paediatricians and medical students.

Ryan and Molly made their way to one of the large seating plans displayed on mobile boards. Ryan ran his eyes down the list until he found his name. Ryan McFetridge and Lizzy Jones were seated on table one. Molly saw it at the same time. It was the VIP table. Ryan's award really was something quite special, she realised immediately. And she was so happy he would be there to accept the honour.

'I just wanted to thank you again for accompanying me tonight, Molly,' Ryan stepped closer to tell her before they moved away for other guests to find their names and table numbers on the lists. There were twelve hundred in attendance that night and thankfully more than half had already been seated by the roaming stewards with mobile seating apps.

'My pleasure. And I wanted to thank you for…' She began looking down at her gorgeous gown. She still felt a little uneasy that he had bought the gown and she wished she had been in a position to buy it for herself but she wasn't about to allow regrets of the past colour that evening. She had a gorgeous gown and an equally gorgeous date for the night. And she would deal with the rest tomorrow. The way she always did.

'Please, you have nothing to thank me for at all. It was my pleasure and I can see by quite a few of my colleagues in the crowd tonight it is their pleasure to see you in that gown.' He had an impish smile that Molly had not expected to see but it was a pleasant surprise. 'By the way, I have to admit I'm one of them. From a man's point of view, it's rare to find intelligence, humility and kindness in a woman, and for that matter the population in general, let alone all three qualities along with looking so gorgeous.'

At that moment, the doors opened and the crowd slowly moved en masse in the direction of the banquet hall. It became quite congested, and without warning Molly felt a warm hand in the middle of her bare back, gently guiding her into a clearer pathway.

'Over here,' she heard him whisper in her ear. His breath was warm on her neck and she felt a little shiver run all over her body as she followed her escort for the night down a different route to their table. His flattering comment seemed genuine and, she trusted, without an agenda, and it made her feel special. And it had been a very long time since a man had truly made her feel special.

'You've navigated this room before, I assume?' she asked with a smile as they avoided the crowd and headed to the front of the room. Her heart was beating so fast and she hoped her face wasn't flushed by the effect he was having on her. Silently she admitted she didn't want the feeling of his hand on her skin to end. She would have gladly walked around the room twice just to have the feeling continue.

Alarms should have been ringing but they weren't.

Part of her still wanted to fight her feelings but a bigger part wanted to give into them.

'Maybe once or twice,' he replied with a wink.

Molly's heart picked up more speed as he looked at her so intently she felt as if he were almost touching her soul. The skin around his dark eyes wrinkled softly and a sparkle emanated from somewhere deep inside. Suddenly she was the furthest thing from the damp mouse. Molly Murphy felt like a desirable woman on a date with a chivalrous man. An extremely handsome, chivalrous man who was taking control of the situation, and her feelings were at odds with everything she had thought for the previous twelve months.

And she liked the feeling very much.

And she liked *him*.

CHAPTER SEVEN

THEIR BEAUTIFULLY DECORATED table was positioned directly in front of the large stage and lectern. The stunning centrepiece of sharply angled frosted glass panels surrounding a tall vase of white lilies was lit by a dozen small tea lights. Molly had noticed one arrangement on each table but as she drew closer she appreciated the detail and effect, and thought it was the most spectacular centrepiece she had ever seen.

Ryan pulled out her chair for her to sit before seating himself, and immediately began introductions. Molly quickly found out he knew everyone at the table.

'I'm so glad you could make it, Ryan,' said one of their fellow table guests, who Ryan had introduced as Martha Zontos. Molly imagined the beautifully groomed woman to be in her early seventies. Her powder-blue satin dress was the perfect soft contrast for her short silver-grey hair and the delicate crystal necklace and earrings completed the look.

'The board of St Clara's are so grateful for what you have given to the young women and I know acknowledging you is very important to them.'

Ryan nodded. 'It's a good cause, Martha, and I'm in a position to support them.'

Molly watched as the woman cast her eyes around the

room. 'Many in this room could provide support, Ryan, but they don't, and that sets you apart. You are one in a million.' She patted his hand and then turned back to continue her conversation with her husband.

Molly eyed her boss curiously. She realised that there was even more to appreciate about Dr Ryan McFetridge. Including the fact that he was philanthropic as well as gallant.

'So,' she began as she reached for the glass of water in front of her. 'You're a sponsor of St Clara's.'

'Of sorts.'

'It's a great initiative.'

'Couldn't agree more. Young women need to have a place after they give birth for a few days, a week or even longer, and a place they can call in at any time for advice. There are so many pressures facing a single mother, like family opinions, immediate financial issues, not to mention the fear of the future and the unknown. St Clara's helps them to navigate through what they will face with assistance from professionals instead of their peers, who generally know very little and sometimes add to the overwhelming fear some young women face or make light of very real struggles that someone their age without a child can't fathom. The objective is to prevent them from finding themselves at that point where they feel that they have nowhere to turn and have to consider giving up their babies.'

Molly couldn't help but notice Ryan's demeanour become more serious and a little distant after he spoke. His attachment to the words was palpable. She could sense immediately that there was something very personal in what he was saying.

'I wish it'd been in existence twenty years ago but it wasn't, and perhaps it wouldn't have changed every baby's fate, nor should it as there are wonderful couples who want to adopt.' He shifted in his seat as he spoke and then reached for the glass of wine that the waiter had filled moments before. 'And there's no point wanting to change the past. It's quite pointless.'

'Cheers to that,' Molly answered, watching him throw back his drink and raising her water glass in response. She didn't want Ryan to know just how much she agreed with his sentiment although from a very different perspective. She had not faced being a single mother. But as the carer of her brother, she was a *single sister*, she thought, and at times she had struggled and still did and on so many occasions she thought she could and should have done so much better.

And on her choice of a fiancé, she definitely wished she could change the past but knew it was pointless to waste time dwelling on that disaster. But it still seemed to find its way into her every waking moment.

'The food is always lovely here,' a voice whispered as Molly had turned in the woman's direction, snapping Molly out of her melancholy and back to the wonderful evening that lay ahead. She was there to support Ryan and make Lizzy happy that her father would collect his *award*. An award that Molly now assumed had something to do with a generous donation to St Clara's.

Molly was seated at a table filled with VIPs of the medical profession and she quickly reminded herself just how honoured she felt to be there.

And equally honoured to be Ryan's *guest*, although by the minute he was making her feel far more like his *date*. And past mistakes deserved no headspace tonight. She intended to enjoy herself and forget everything else for just a few hours.

* * *

The evening was perfect, the food and wine delicious and Molly could not possibly finish each course. There was a neonatologist keynote speaker from the Netherlands, and as the applause finished Ryan leant in towards Molly. 'With your background that must have been quite informative. The surgical intervention, I mean.'

'Yes, Dr Swinton is brilliant and the new methods are revolutionary. It will change the outcome for many neonatals.'

'Do you miss it? Theatre, I mean.'

'I guess, hearing about progressive procedures does make me excited and a little sad not to be a part of it, but—' she turned to meet Ryan's gaze '—I wouldn't risk Tommy's peace of mind for my career. Not now or ever.'

'You're an amazingly selfless and beautiful woman, Molly Murphy.'

'I don't think so...'

Without warning, she felt Ryan's mouth drawing closer to hers, cutting short her words as her own lips instinctively reached up to accept his kiss. Then she stopped. She froze and moved away.

'I'm sorry,' Ryan said, moving away. 'I overstepped the line. Please forgive me, Molly.'

Molly couldn't speak for a moment. She wanted to kiss him but she couldn't. Something was holding her back. And that something was her past.

'There's nothing to forgive, Ryan. It's difficult to explain...but please believe me, it's not you.'

Molly could see that Ryan wasn't convinced.

'Would you like to dance?' she asked as the band began to play.

'Perhaps later,' he said, putting distance between them

as he pushed his chair back from the table and she could see him preparing to stand. 'I might just step outside and make a call. I'd like to check up on Lizzy if you don't mind. I won't be long.'

Molly nodded. 'Absolutely.'

Molly wasn't sure what to think as she watched his broad suited shoulders disappear into the crowd. She wanted so badly to give into the feelings Ryan was stirring but she wasn't sure if she was ready. She felt as if they were moving so fast and, while it was wonderful and unexpected, it was like standing on a precipice and suddenly looking down when all the while she wanted to look up to what might be.

'I would like to present the Australian Medical Association lifetime achievement award to Dr Ryan McFetridge, the founder of St Clara's Respite Hub for Single Mothers.'

Molly's mouth dropped open a little. Ryan was not purely a supporter of St Clara's. He had single-handedly founded the initiative. As she watched him stand and button his tuxedo, then make his way to the stage, she suddenly felt her eyes lift upwards a little more. Perhaps she was right to feel the way she did. Perhaps it was time to let go of the fear. At least a little.

'Congratulations, Ryan. I had no idea,' Molly said when Ryan returned to the table, his stunning blue-crystal award in hand. It was etched in gold and standing on a base of black marble and clearly heavy as he placed it on the table with a slight thud.

'Thank you,' he returned with a half-smile, but still Molly could feel there was a distance between them. A distance she had put there by rejecting his kiss. His banter was light-hearted but he was no longer leaning into her. His body language was telling her where she now stood.

And she couldn't blame him. She had set the boundaries by moving away from his lips.

She had never felt so torn. There were moments when the man she had only known for five days made her feel as if she had known him all her life. Or perhaps she had been looking for him all her life. He was an amazing human being but she was scared. He was so humble in downplaying his involvement in a cause and yet the medical association thought it deserved a lifetime award.

She was so proud as she watched Ryan's peers give him the congratulations he deserved. They all knew him or of him. He was the man of the moment in the room, being swept up by the throngs of people wanting to connect, and she felt overwhelmed just watching him manage the conversations. Now and then he took time out between handshakes to look in her direction. To check in with her. But when she caught his glance he looked away. As if he didn't want to be watching out for her and didn't want her to know he had been.

'Nurse Murphy…' a voice broke into her thoughts. 'Well, you certainly look very different without a Theatre cap. Perhaps they should change the dress code in Theatre—that gown is so much nicer. Not at all practical, but so much nicer.'

Molly turned to see Dr Victor Rodriguez. He was one of the state's leading vascular surgeons and Molly had been in the operating theatre with him on more than a dozen occasions.

'Dr Rodriguez,' she replied, not masking her genuine elation at seeing him again. It had been over a year since she had been at the Eastern Memorial Hospital.

'Please, you make me feel so old—call me Victor.'

'Of course.' She smiled as she stood and extended her hand to greet him.

Victor stood and, ignoring her hand, gave a hearty laugh and a gentle bear hug.

'How long has it been since I've seen you?' he asked. 'Actually, I know exactly how long. It would be close to a year since you left the Eastern Memorial. That's when Gertrude came on staff as your replacement. Good God, that woman can talk, and has an opinion on everything that she insists on sharing.'

'Are you talking about Gertrude Rodriguez? Your daughter?'

'Yes, one and the same, and, yes, she's my daughter but she takes after her mother. Drives me mad with that incessant chatter.'

'I studied with Gertrude, Victor. She's so lovely and a great anaesthetic nurse.'

'I'd never debate her skills. It's the non-stop talking. She could talk underwater, a bit like that ex-fiancé of yours, what was his name, Norman? No, that's right, Nigel. I always struggled with his name on the few occasions that I met him. Anyway, he was quite the talker, and a bit pretentious.'

Molly suddenly felt violently ill. Her stomach dropped and her heart felt heavy. The lightness of the evening was quickly disappearing.

'I guess...' she replied, feeling disturbed with the direction of the conversation. As much as she had been happy to see Victor Rodriguez, she did not want to talk about the past right now. It had been a wonderful night and she wanted to stay in the moment and not be drawn back into sadness or regret.

'So how is everyone at the hospital?' she asked, hoping to steer the conversation away from her personal life. She wasn't sure where she wanted it to land but it wasn't on her failed relationship.

'Everyone's great, a few newbies on the roster.' He paused as he ran his fingers through his silver beard, then continued, 'You know, we'd love to have you back there. You're one of the finest anaesthetic nurses, hands down, and we miss that level of expertise—'

'I'm sure you have other anaesthetic nurses, including Gertrude,' Molly cut in, trying to end the conversation without appearing rude.

'They're all very competent, including Gerty, but still not close to your skill. I mean it, Molly, just mention you're interested and you'd be back on staff within a heartbeat.'

'I have family priorities, Victor, so, as much as I appreciate your offer, I won't be thinking about returning for quite a while.' Her tone was kind but firm. She really did not want to travel back in time that night or have her decision to change the direction of her career questioned. That chapter was closed. For now, at least. She wanted to get back on track without causing any further disruptions to Tommy's life. It had been difficult for Tommy when Nigel had left their lives so abruptly and, while Molly knew he was a bad man, in fact the worst, she felt immensely sorry for Tommy as he too felt the sadness of losing someone.

'Is your family commitment your brother? Is he all right?'

'Yes, on both counts,' she answered quickly, disappointed that Victor was delving into her personal life and not leaving well enough alone. She had never remembered him to be so intrusive but it hadn't bothered her before the break-up. Previously she hadn't had too much to have embarrassingly unpacked by others the way Victor was doing at that moment. Her life had not been without the usual sadness along the way but there had been no scandal prior to Nigel.

Hoping she could bring the conversation to an end she added, 'Tommy likes me to be home every night at a set time, so as I said it will be a while before I can return to the hours of an anaesthetic nurse in a busy teaching hospital.'

'I understand but take or leave this fatherly advice. I heard you lost the house when Nigel left your life and the Eastern Memorial is yours for the asking...and the remuneration of the position would get you back on your feet quite quickly. I don't want to see you struggle, Molly. It's no secret you lost your home because of him.'

At the exact moment that Victor's inappropriate and unexpected words poured from his mouth, Ryan returned.

Molly felt her heart sink and her body stiffen. She couldn't believe that Victor would speak so openly about her personal life in a public forum. She suspected she looked like a deer in headlights with the shock of his announcement to all and sundry. Up to that point the evening had been a fairy tale but it had just ended. The whole ugly episode in her life that she had somehow managed to forget for a few wonderful hours came rushing back... and it had happened at the moment Ryan had come back.

She had hoped the wonderful evening might have continued but suddenly the clock had just struck twelve.

CHAPTER EIGHT

'CONGRATULATIONS, RYAN. IT'S been a while. Well deserved on the award.'

Molly couldn't believe her luck or lack thereof. Not only had Victor, with his fatherly intentions, emptied her dirty laundry onto the floor of the elegant event for everyone within earshot, including Ryan, to hear, he also knew Ryan. She suddenly wanted to run from the room. But she didn't want to lose a slipper along the way. She didn't want Ryan to feel obligated to hunt her down. She didn't want or need his pity. Her Cinderella moment was well and truly over. She just wanted to be alone as quickly as possible. She edged away from the two men, her finger absent-mindedly tracing a line on the table, listening intently to the conversation but not really wanting to hear very much. She hoped against all hope her name would be left out of any further discussion between them.

'Thank you, Victor. It has been quite a while since we've caught up. How are you?'

'Good, very good, just trying to convince this young lady to return to the Eastern. We miss her and her skill set terribly.'

Molly froze as two pairs of eyes looked in her direction. She shrugged in response and attempted to smile politely, but it was more like a slight curling of her lips that quickly fell flat again. She felt at risk of breaking down and wasn't sure how long she might be able to delay the welling tears. It didn't seem to matter how much she tried to move past everything that had happened, it seemed to be only two steps behind.

'Best damned anaesthetic nurse I've worked with hands down.'

Ryan shot Molly a knowing look. 'I told you, Molly, there would be offers to take you away from…my practice.'

'So, you know each other?' Victor enquired curiously, obviously unaware they had been seated next to each other the entire evening.

'Yes, Molly's temping in admin at my practice.'

'Well, young lady,' Victor continued, as all the while Molly hoped more than ever that the surgeon and his pearls of wisdom would just leave, 'it would appear that you're in demand. I'm not surprised but, at the risk of sounding disrespectful to you, Ryan, Molly runs the risk of being wasted and losing her skills if she doesn't use them.'

'I will take that under advisement, Victor,' Ryan replied. 'However, there's somewhere Molly needs to be so I'll have to steal her away.'

Molly sensed that Ryan had seen how anxious she had become. She was unsure if he'd heard anything but appreciated him coming to her rescue.

'I'm hoping you don't mind me taking you away from Dr Rodriguez, aka the best-meaning but most times inappropriate advice provider of the Eastern Memorial,' Ryan said as they walked away.

'Not at all. I'm relieved, to be honest, but where do I need to be exactly?'

'I'd say anywhere but with Victor.'

Molly's lips curved into a smile that remained without any hint of fading. 'Would you like to go somewhere else for a quiet drink?'

His voice was deep and husky and his eyes intense and focussed just on her.

'That sounds wonderful.'

Suddenly the memories that Victor had stirred began to fade. She was aware the evening would end in a few hours but she didn't want to dwell on that. She felt more special than she had in a very long time and she felt protected. And it was the best feeling in the world.

Taking off his jacket, Ryan draped it over Molly's shoulders and they left the event without any goodbyes or further ceremony and made their way down North Terrace to the large hotel that had a quiet coffee lounge and bar.

The concierge greeted them both with a nod. 'Are you guests staying with us or are you just looking for a quiet late-night drink?'

Molly was taken aback by the question and she could see that Ryan was equally confused by the remark.

'Just a drink…or coffee… I'm not sure we've decided yet,' he answered, looking at Molly for confirmation.

'I'm fine with either.'

'It's just that there's a visiting rugby team celebrating in the hotel tonight and if you're looking for a quiet place, I'll be honest, it might not be in the bar,' the concierge told them with a concerned expression.

'Thanks for the heads up,' Ryan said with a grin as he directed Molly inside. 'We might settle for a coffee, then, in the lobby.'

Ryan stepped into the warm lobby and quickly settled Molly into a chair near the large water feature that reached up into the four-floor-high atrium. Molly craned her neck to see the flow of water gently running over the copper backdrop from such a height. It was strikingly beautiful.

Scooping up his tuxedo jacket that Molly had placed over the arm of her chair, he placed it on the back of his own chair and was just about to seat himself when another elegantly dressed man approached them. He had a clean-shaven head and a neatly trimmed beard and Molly hadn't noticed the man at the event but suspected, with his tuxedo and polished appearance, that there was a good chance he too had been at the AMA dinner.

'Ryan, good to see you.'

'Brian, great to see you too,' Ryan responded, then, standing again, he turned his attention back to Molly. 'I'd like to introduce Molly Murphy. Molly, this is Brian Chesterman. Brian's a GP practising not too far from me in Erindale. To be honest, I'm not sure how long we've known each other but it's been a damn long time.'

'Pleased to meet you, Molly,' the man responded and extended his hand to Molly.

'Pleased to meet you too,' she replied, meeting his hand politely.

'So, Ryan, how's Lizzy?'

'She's good. In fact Molly took her shopping today to buy a dress to wear this evening, but then she wasn't feeling well so Molly graciously accepted my invitation to attend in her place.'

'That was very kind of you, Molly,' Brain remarked with a smile in Molly's direction before returning his attention to Ryan. With a frown dressing his brow, he continued. 'Nothing serious with Lizzy, I hope.'

'No, just the usual problem she suffers every month, but she'll pick up in a day or so and be back to her happy self. We're seriously considering our options as each month she experiences heightened anxiety and chronic pain. It's a difficult choice. I don't want to rush into it but nor do I want to see her suffer every month the way she does.'

'Of course, the myriad changes that girls face as they become young women…and the choices we all need to make. On that topic, any boyfriends on the horizon? I remember how I dreaded the thought as both of our girls were growing up. They're both married now, the youngest only three weeks ago, but the very word boyfriend strikes fear into the core of every father at some stage.'

'No boyfriends, thank goodness. I'm hoping that I won't have to deal with that issue. Lizzy's happy with her life the way it is and I don't see that changing. She has work and her dog and I'm home most nights with her, so she has a pretty full life and that's why I'm contemplating referring her for the surgery. It would, without doubt, improve her quality of life. She hasn't given any indication of having an interest in boys, let alone marriage in the future.'

'Ah, the ramblings of a man who doesn't want to face the prospect of his little girl falling in love.'

'Lizzy's case is a little different, so I may not have to worry about that.'

'Don't be so sure,' Brian remarked. 'Everyone needs love. Lizzy's no different. And you, my friend, might just have to accept that fact one day.'

'We'll see,' Ryan said, studying the floor for a moment as he shifted on his feet.

'Yes, you will.'

'By the way, I didn't see you at the AMA dinner but I'm assuming you were there?' Ryan continued, brushing aside the comments about Lizzy and prospective suitors.

Molly could see Ryan was becoming a little anxious

about the topic and could tell he wanted to change the subject and shrug off Brian's comments. She knew it would be a difficult decision for a father to make. A hysterectomy was major surgery and there was nothing reversible about it. Ryan would have the weight of the decision on his shoulders. There was no easy way around it nor no right or wrong decision. But she knew in her heart, Ryan would do what was best for his daughter.

Molly suddenly felt awkward knowing that Lizzy did in fact have a boyfriend already. She had confessed as much to Molly the day they first met at the practice. She hadn't taken it seriously but she now wondered if Ryan would, as this wasn't going to be a future scenario Ryan would need to face, it was already on his doorstep; he just didn't know it. And could Lizzy having a partner potentially alter her mind about the surgery?

It was becoming a little complicated. Molly had had no idea when she'd made the promise to keep Lizzy's secret that Ryan was her father. She'd assumed Ryan would soften on the subject once Lizzy told him but now she wasn't so sure. She just hoped Lizzy told him sooner rather than later. Christmas was still quite a way off.

'Yes, Jane and I were there. We were on the table with the board of the university.'

'Interesting company.'

'Of sorts. It can get a bit dry at times and Jane is great at making conversation with everyone. That's the joy in having a wife in the same field. While it can be challenging with two careers in one household, the mutual passion for medicine is what's kept us so close all these years. Speaking of which, it's our twenty-eighth wedding anniversary tonight so I booked a suite here for the night, but unfortunately we won't be staying.'

'Congratulations on your anniversary but why are you

leaving? I hope there's nothing wrong,' Ryan asked with concern clear in his voice.

'No, nothing wrong per se, it's just that our son-in-law called about fifteen minutes ago to say our eldest daughter's in labour in the Fleurieu Community Hospital so Jane and I are heading there now. Jane's with the concierge having the car sent around and I'm about to check us out. There goes an exorbitant amount of money for a room we were in for all of thirty minutes. But our first grandson is on his way and that's more important. The obstetrician estimates the birth is a few hours away but you never can tell with these things, *as we know*, and Jane wants to be there and I'm not about to argue with a grandmother-to-be. She's already booked us a hotel room in Victor over the Internet so we're off. It's just over an hour's drive from here but at this time of night there's no traffic so we'll be there before eleven. Anyway, I'll catch you at the next dinner, Ryan, if not on the golf course. And it was lovely to meet you, Molly.' Brian extended his hand to Molly as he spoke.

'Very nice to meet you, Brian,' Molly added.

At that moment a number of the rugby players spilled from the bar into the lobby restaurant and with their appearance came the noise. They were all large men, clearly chosen for their athletic build, and had been drinking. While they were not offensive in their language, their antics and voices were overpowering.

'Ryan,' Brian began, pausing mid-step as he played with the key card to the room. 'I just had a thought. I've already paid for the suite and we just ordered a late supper and charged it to our room and they can't cancel it. Why don't you and Molly head up and enjoy the martinis and tapas or order some coffee? There's no point letting the room go to waste and I don't think this crowd is leaving any time soon. It could get worse, by the look of the tray of drinks heading this way. You could escape up there for a while and can check out after you've had supper or stay the night. As I said, it's all covered anyway and there's a fantastic view of the Torrens river and the Adelaide Oval bridge from the room. In fact I'm quite sure I paid a significant amount extra for said view! It's quite spectacular and completely going to waste tonight.'

Ryan did not respond, although Molly suspected by the expression on his face that he appeared to be considering the offer. Or perhaps the ramifications of the offer.

'Here's the key card to the room,' Brian said, leaning down and dropping the card on the low gunmetal and glass coffee table. 'Clearly your call, and if you don't want to use the room I'll call in the morning and check out online but the offer's there. It's all paid up, so you can take it or leave it, but I better run as I'm getting the death stare from Jane standing outside in the freezing cold. And it's going to be colder at Victor so we're going to call into home on the way and collect some warmer and slightly more practical clothes. The poor child might take one look at me and mistake me for a penguin in this outfit.'

Ryan laughed and shook Brian's hand before the excited grandfather-to-be crossed the atrium and exited the hotel to where his wife was standing beside the late model European sedan. Ryan and Molly watched him climb inside and drive away. Before either could make mention of the room, one of the rugby players close by suddenly collapsed. He had been sitting on the arm of a large armchair and, without warning or obvious cause, he toppled over, hitting his head as he crashed to the marble-tiled floor.

Ryan and Molly jumped up in unison, crossing to the lifeless figure sprawled across the floor. Blood was seeping from a deep wound on the top of his shaven head. Mindful of not moving the victim, and without saying a word to each other, Molly checked his airway was clear while Ryan attended the wound. It was a deep gash and Ryan suspected his skull had been fractured when the weight of his head hit the hard marble flooring.

'He wasn't fooling around,' one of the other players called out. His words were slurred but the panic in his voice was evident. 'He just collapsed. I swear no one touched him. He just fell sideways. He's not dead, is he?'

Ryan and Molly both shook their heads as they continued their assessment of the man who was breathing but unconscious. A concerned concierge swiftly crossed to them. 'What's happened here?'

'We need an ambulance. We have an unconscious male, pupils are dilated and non-reactive,' Ryan announced as he lifted the young man's eyelids. 'I don't think it's alcohol alone that caused this accident. There's something else at play here. I need clean white sheeting immediately and a first-aid kit until the paramedics arrive.'

The concierge called triple zero immediately and then called Housekeeping without questioning Ryan or Molly further.

Molly had her fingers resting gently on the carotid artery in the man's neck to check his pulse while she observed his other vital signs. 'Respiratory patterns don't appear altered and he has reasonable skin colour. What I wouldn't do for a non-rebreather bag to keep his pulse ox reading at ninety-five per cent.'

A uniformed hotel staff member appeared almost immediately with the sheeting and the first-aid kit, which the concierge opened and placed beside Ryan.

Ryan quickly sterilised his hands and then passed the

solution to Molly before he reached in for some sterile bandages. He ripped the packaging open and wrapped a bandage loosely around the open wound. The lack of hair made it easier to keep the wound clean.

A crowd of the patient's drunken friends began to gather around. 'I need the most sober of you to step forward,' Ryan said loudly and firmly. 'And the rest of you get back and give us room to help your friend.'

A tall, well-built man moved towards Ryan. 'I'm Jack. I'm diabetic and don't drink.'

'Did you see what happened?'

'Yes, Dave fell sideways like they said. He wasn't drunk or messing around. I think he only had one beer because he had a headache. He'd been complaining of it all day.'

'Did he receive a blow to the head during a game today?'

'No, he didn't play today but he did take a hit two nights ago at training and, yeah, he did last Saturday too. He was complaining today about it so the coach kept him on the bench.'

'So, this man suffered two blows to the head a few days apart?'

'Yes.'

'How old is he?'

'He just turned eighteen last week.'

'Perfect age for it.'

'Are you thinking second impact syndrome?' Molly asked as she kept a watch on his pulse and breathing.

'Yes.'

'Will he make it?' came a deep voice from behind them.

'I damned well hope so,' Ryan said as he began CPR.

At that moment, two paramedics came rushing

through the atrium with a barouche. They collapsed it down to almost floor level and dropped to their knees beside the patient. Ryan moved away for them.

'Can you bring us to speed?'

'Dr Ryan McFetridge, GP, and Molly Murphy, anaesthetic nurse. We've been monitoring the young man for about five minutes now. Eighteen years of age, he's suffered two blows to the head sustained during sport a few days apart, a recent headache and a collapse without cause. I suspect second impact syndrome and potentially a subdural hematoma. His skull may have been fractured during the fall here tonight and it may have relieved some pressure as there was blood from the head wound. He has dilated and non-reactive pupils so I would advise you to hyperventilate.'

'Hyperventilate with suspected brain injury?' the paramedic asked.

'Yes, the benefit of temporarily reducing cerebral blood with mild hyperventilation may outweigh the harm from less oxygen delivery. My advice is to titrate the respiratory rate to maintain a reading between thirty and thirty-five or twenty breaths per minute until you reach Emergency.'

'The young man is lucky you were both here. If he makes it, then he'll owe his life to that fact,' the older of the two paramedics told Ryan and Molly, then turned to the younger paramedic. 'Call it in once we're on board. ETA the Eastern Memorial four minutes.' Placing a brace around the young man's neck, the paramedics moved swiftly to transport the patient to the ambulance. Molly and Ryan watched as they exited the hotel entrance.

'Will Dave make it, Doc?' Jack asked.

'I can't say. The fact that he didn't collapse directly after the second blow is a better sign but he probably never recovered from the first injury so the second blow is a more serious complication.'

'But why? They weren't even related. The first one happened a week ago.'

'When an athlete like your friend suffers a second concussion before the first concussion has fully healed there are serious consequences. The fact that he cracked his skull may have in fact saved his life as the pressure building in his skull was released slightly.'

There was no siren as the ambulance drove off and Molly felt herself being pulled into Ryan's strong embrace. This time she didn't pull away.

CHAPTER NINE

MOLLY WASN'T SURE what Ryan was thinking. And she was even less sure what she was thinking about what had transpired.

The players made their way one by one over to thank them for helping their friend. While Ryan and Molly appreciated the show of gratitude, they were both drained by the experience and there were more of the players coming from every direction towards them.

'What do you think about slipping away and having a quiet drink and exhaling in Brian's suite?' he whispered to her. 'I think we deserve it and I don't think we'll get any peace here. They mean well, but it's been a long night.'

Molly nodded, feeling the adrenalin still surging through her body but wanting to escape from the commotion around them. 'That would be lovely.'

Ryan swiped the key card, opened the door to the suite they had been so generously gifted and stepped back for Molly to walk inside. The room was softly lit, and the curtains open, allowing them both to see the stunning panorama of the city lights. As she crossed to the expanse of windows, Molly looked out and down to see the reflection of the lights twinkling in the meandering city river below. It was picture perfect but she wasn't really seeing the view, she was thinking about what had transpired moments before in the foyer. She couldn't deny to herself that saving the young man's life had brought more purpose to her own. It was what she had trained to do and what she loved.

'You miss it, don't you?' Ryan asked her as he closed the door.

'What do you mean?' she said, turning away from the view and towards Ryan, but not wanting to admit to him he was right.

'The rush. The way you have to fire on all cylinders, think on your feet. The way it would be in surgery for you.'

'I guess. Yes. Theatre was my life but that career choice is not possible now. It doesn't mean it won't be one day, just not now.'

'Why not?' he asked as he dropped the card on the coffee table and made his way to the sofa. 'Would you like to sit for a while? Maybe tell me what's changed so much in your life that you have to put your career on hold? I know you want to be there for Tommy, but I'm assuming you were there for him before. What's different now?'

'It's a long story, Ryan,' she told him, trying not to make eye contact and give too much away of how she really felt. 'Let's just say, I had more support before and none now.'

'I certainly can't sleep after what we just went through, so I'd be happy to hear more if you're willing to share it. I'm not going to hide the fact—I think you're an amazing woman, Molly, and I want to know more about you.'

Molly was taken aback by Ryan's honesty about his feelings. He was certainly a straight-shooter and it made her feel safe to open up. At least a little. She sat down on the sofa with him. There was enough distance that she could curl her feet up and spend the next fifteen minutes recapping her life, including her high school years, her study to become an anaesthetic nurse, even the pain of losing of her parents in a tsunami in Indonesia. She wasn't sure how much she intended on telling him, and decided to let it unfold and stop if and when she became uncomfortable.

'I'm so sorry, Molly. That must have been devastating for you and for Tommy.'

'And it was so unfair, it was my parents' trip of a lifetime. They had been planning to travel abroad and finally they felt okay about leaving Tommy with me. He encouraged them to go and gave them a list of souvenirs he wanted. Key rings from each of the places they visited. I took three weeks' leave from my role so that I could be at home for him to make sure he was all right and make sure they could relax and actually enjoy themselves and it all ended so horribly. Tommy's come to terms with it but it's taken a while. They were so young. Mum was only fifty-eight and my father was sixty-five. He had just retired two weeks before they headed off together. Life just hasn't been the same without them. It all went downhill not long after they died.' Tears began to pool in Molly's eyes and she quickly turned her head in the other direction, looking out of the window into the darkness. Suddenly she felt Ryan reach for her hand and encircle it in the warmth of his own.

'Life can be unfair. You can search for reasons and oftentimes none of it makes sense.'

Molly sighed. Ryan was right about that, but she also had to take responsibility for her choices in life as well. 'Sometimes we make stupid decisions too. We can't always blame the universe.'

'You sound like you're speaking from experience,' Ryan replied steadily, but not letting her hand slip from his.

Molly didn't want the process to be like pulling teeth for the man who had stated he valued honesty above all else. She hadn't thought she would share her stupidity with anyone else, ever, let alone Ryan. He was so sensible, his life so planned and thought out. And hers had been changed for ever by one stupid, avoidable mistake. But she couldn't change it by hiding it from Ryan. And it would be best to have it out in the open. If he thought poorly of her, then better at that moment rather than later when she had even more feelings invested.

'I became involved with someone, who wasn't good for me, or for Tommy. He was a bad man, plain and simple. I won't try to make excuses, or blame it entirely on him. I'm a grown woman and I should have known better but I think I was a little lost and, instead of getting stronger over the years after my parents passed, I think I became lonelier. I missed them terribly and that made me vulnerable and I didn't see the warning signs. In me or in him.'

Ryan's look intensified and Molly could see anger simmering behind his charcoal eyes. 'He didn't hurt you or Tommy? Physically, I mean.'

'No, not at all,' she said, putting his fears of violence to rest immediately. 'No, he was a conman. A professional, completely unscrupulous conman who had worked me from day one but I was too silly to see it. I was too caught up in the fairy tale he was spinning to notice that it was all a cleverly planned charade to empty my bank account and more.'

'I'm sorry you went through that. I hope he was caught.'

'By me, yes, only after it was all too late, but he didn't

pay any price with anyone else. He disappeared into the night and left Tommy and I without a roof over our heads. And that's why I'm angry with myself because I put Tommy at risk becoming involved with a man like that.'

'You didn't put him at risk intentionally.'

'Not intentionally, but that doesn't change the fact I behaved irresponsibly and we lost the house and the money that our parents had left us. It would have been enough to ensure Tommy never went without. I can't forgive myself for that. And that's why we live in a not so great part of town.' Molly rolled her eyes.

'I'm sure Tommy wouldn't care where you live as long as he's with you,' Ryan replied.

'That's true,' she said, shooting him a sideways smile that disappeared as quickly as it had arrived. 'But it still doesn't make any of it okay.'

'I don't mean to pry and you can tell me to butt out, but can't you pursue the man, your...ex, through the courts?'

In an instant, a myriad emotions washed over Molly. Rage, guilt, thoughts of how sweet revenge might feel and then sorrow. She knew it was hopeless.

'No, he walked away scot-free after taking everything he could and I had no means of retribution. I wanted to pursue him and make him pay for what he had done, but he left me in such debt that I didn't then and still don't now have the funds or the time to try to find him, let alone take him to court. He's over in Europe now. His father is Swiss, his mother Portuguese so he's hiding out in one of those countries or one somewhere in between, no doubt scamming another vulnerable woman.'

'Well, at least he might not be allowed back in Australia if you alert the authorities.'

'It's complicated because he made it look like I was complicit in everything.' She closed her eyes, wondering if she wanted or needed to go into the detail. Would it make him understand her true financial situation or make him doubt her previous judgement? She didn't want pity but it didn't seem to be on offer, which made her happy.

'After my parents died,' she began, turning back to face Ryan, 'Tommy and I were living in our family home in Burnside. It had been left to us along with insurance money, their savings and superannuation. All in all, we were very comfortable. Tommy worked at a not-for-profit organisation that provides employment for people with a range of intellectual disabilities. He still does. He could enter the regular workforce but he loves the support staff and they know what he's been through losing our parents, so they allow him to stay there and constantly build on his skill set, giving him more responsibility. He's in a supervisory role now.'

Ryan nodded in agreement. 'I'm sure Lizzy could take on a more challenging role too but she loves where she works three days a week, so I don't want to stress her unnecessarily.'

'I agree. There's no need. Those facilities go a long way to raising their confidence and independence and Tommy didn't need to bring in an income as I could support us both, but it was good for him to have that interaction. I was working at the Eastern Memorial. If I had a late shift, one of the elderly neighbours who adored Tommy would wait with him until I got home and, if I was caught up in Theatre, she would prepare his dinner and stay and keep him company. She was a wonderful woman and we both felt blessed to have her in our lives.

'Then about three years after we lost our parents, I met a man while having dinner alone after a medical conference here in Adelaide. He was also eating alone that night at an adjacent table. He struck up a conversation and he asked to join me for coffee. He was new in town, an engineering consultant contracted to deliver advice on a billion-dollar infrastructure project. We hit it off, he seemed genuine and, although I was hesitant at first, we began dating.

'To be honest he was my first serious relationship, as it was difficult to even think about dating between my study and then taking on the carer's role for Tommy and work. I was naive and inexperienced but still at times I knew the decisions he made weren't right, and I should have listened to my gut. But I didn't. Six months into the relationship he proposed and we began planning the wedding. He said that he wanted to buy property together. He didn't want to live in our family home as he wanted a fresh start in a new home that we owned together. I wasn't sure about it but Tommy had grown to like Nigel, and when he saw the house that Nigel had found had a pool and a home theatre he was excited about us having such a big house and living together as a family.

'After much deliberation and hesitation on my part, I agreed and I sold our family home and we bought the new home in the Adelaide foothills. It was quite expensive, but he said using the funds from the sale of my home and the money I had put away we could afford it, and then after he sold his home in Madrid he would deposit the funds in my bank and we would have put equal shares into what would be our for-ever home.'

'It sounds like a reasonable plan and, with the added pressure from Tommy, I can see why you agreed.'

'Well, Nigel had made it impossible for me to say no without appearing as if I didn't trust him. But after I sold my home Nigel insisted he had his name on the title as he said it would cost a fortune to add it after settlement when his money arrived. Again, my gut instinct was to say no, particularly as I thought the new house was overpriced, but he kept allaying my fears. He showed me his home online with a sale price of one point five million dollars and said it would only be a few weeks before it would be snapped up. Of course, that never happened because it wasn't his home. He had apparently found it online and claimed it to be his as it was in his hometown.'

'So effectively he gained a house in his name with no intention of providing any funds to you.'

'Yes, sounds stupid of me, doesn't it?'

'To someone who didn't know your fiancé and having no idea just how experienced a salesman he was, that's easy to say in hindsight. He manipulated your feelings to his advantage. It sounds like he rushed you off your feet and then cornered you. You really had no chance with someone like that. It was a chess game he was going to win.'

Molly stopped still for a moment. Suddenly and unexpectedly, the weight she had carried for the last year had eased from her shoulders a little. Instead of adding to her feelings of guilt, Ryan had somehow almost validated why she had made the decision that had impacted so badly on her life, and Tommy's. With a few words, he had made her feel less culpable and more a victim of another's actions. He was a stranger looking in and he saw it very differently from her viewpoint laden with remorse.

'But I'm still not sure how he took everything.'

'He forged my signature and borrowed against the house—'

'Why?' Ryan cut in. 'What did he do with the money?'

'He gambled it. All of it. And he left. He was gone. He left a note saying that he missed Madrid and his family and felt I was rushing him into marriage. It was one week before our wedding. I thought that he may have had a change of heart when I was woken the day after he left by loud knocking on the door. I thought he'd come back and misplaced his keys and wanted me to let him in. But instead it was a sheriff's officer. I was behind in payments on a mortgage that I didn't know I had. I knew all my money had been sunk into the house but I thought I could sell it, downsize to a similar home we had previously and we would be fine, but we actually had nothing. I collapsed in shock. There was no way I could possibly make the payments on my wage. I was forced to sell before the bank foreclosed. Within six months he had gambled more than half the value of the home. The market had crashed…'

'So, the already overpriced home he had made you buy was worth much less.'

'A lot less and with legal fees and paying for the wedding venue, flowers and car as it was too close to cancel there was literally nothing left in my bank. He'd assured me he had taken care of the wedding costs too and I had no reason not to believe him. But he hadn't. He'd only paid the deposit, so I had to fire sale the furniture and even my car and the jewellery my mother left me for the bond on this house because my credit rating had been ruined in the process. Oh, and cherry on top…when I tried to sell my engagement ring as I thought it would help, I found out that was as fake as his promises. A great copy of Harry Winston he bought online from China.' She sipped on her drink, took a deep breath and continued. 'I can't ask our former neighbour to travel to the wrong side of town at night. I made my bed and I must lie in it and make sure I am home every night in time to meet Tommy. And I wouldn't have it any other way.'

Molly was surprised that she managed to get it all out without tears. Tears of regret and anger at her ex-fiancé and herself. But she knew why. It was Ryan's reaction that made it possible to bare her soul and not react the way she had expected. She felt stronger with every word and that was because of him.

Without saying a word, Ryan leant into Molly and brushed away a tendril of her hair. 'The world has thrown the worst at you and yet you're still the most caring person I think I've met. At the risk of overstepping the mark, again, I wish I could kiss away all the pain you've been through. You're the most amazing woman, Molly.'

Molly felt her heart begin to race and she didn't want to turn away. She didn't want to hold back. She felt as if she belonged in the room, in the moment with him. And she felt safe. Leaning into him, she knew that whatever the night brought, she was welcoming it with her eyes wide open.

And her heart a little vulnerable. 'You wouldn't be overstepping the mark.'

Within moments Ryan's mouth reached for hers. His kiss was passionate and still tender. She felt his hands caressing the bare skin of her shoulders. Her eyes closed as the sensation of his fingers on her body rippled through her. Her mind was filled only with desire for Ryan.

Her eyes opened to find him looking expectantly into the soul she was laying bare.

'Are you sure about this?' he asked.

'I couldn't be more sure.'

Upon hearing her answer, Ryan didn't hold back. His lips were demanding as they met the softness of her mouth. Molly felt the urgency in his kiss and it took her breath away. It was nothing like the kiss before. His kiss told her that he was not a man who intended to wait for even a moment longer. Nor did Molly want him to.

His hard, powerful body lifted her up and pressed against her. She had no doubt in her mind that he wanted her as much as she desired him. His touch was strong yet gentle. His kiss was tender yet reckless. Her mind was spinning and her heart was racing with anticipation as his fingers searched for the zip of her dress and then the clasp at the nape of her neck. With both skilfully undone, he slowly slid the slinky dress from her body. Pulling his lips from hers momentarily, he began to discard his own clothes.

Molly's fingers struggled to untie his bow tie, and quickly his own hands came to the rescue, helping hers, and once it was undone, he tossed it to the ground. Molly unbuttoned his shirt as he used one foot to slip the other free of his shoes and then unbuckled his trousers. The kisses continued fervently. His shirt was open and her hands glided over his chest. She heard his heavy cufflinks drop to the ground. Within moments his clothes were littered on the floor beside her dress. He pulled his mouth from hers and his arms scooped her up, her shoes falling from her feet as he carried her into the bedroom. She had one tiny piece of lace clothing on her body and as he lay her on the bed, Ryan slipped that from her too.

There was nothing between them any more. Nothing to stop them from becoming one.

Where the night would lead the next day was irrelevant. Nothing else mattered. Nothing but the hours they were about to share together in that room. In that bed.

With sleepy eyes Molly looked across the crumpled pillow to the man who had spent hours making love to her. The man who had opened her eyes to what she had not known she had been missing before. His hands had caressed her body as if it had been made for him, as if he had read a book written about her, one that told him everything he needed to know.

Ryan pulled Molly gently and purposefully towards him and into his embrace. Her hand instinctively reached across his toned chest as her head rested on his shoulder. He turned his body towards her and his fingers moved the curls falling over her face as he leant in and kissed her.

'I must apologise,' he muttered.

'For what?'

'Not coming good on that drink.'

Molly smiled. 'I think I can forgive your poor hospitality under the circumstances.'

Ryan kissed her again and his hands began trailing over her body. She could feel the urgency in both his kiss and his hands but she became very aware of the time. She had promised to be home by twelve and she was sure it was getting very close to midnight.

She pulled away. 'I would love to continue this all night but I have to go home.'

His hands cupped her face. 'I would love to continue all night too. Are you sure you have to leave?'

'Absolutely… I need to be at home before midnight,' she replied as she sat up, tugging the sheet up with her to cover herself. While she had shared her body with Ryan and shed her inhibitions, she suddenly felt a little vulnerable and self-conscious.

'Of course,' he said. 'I understand.' He sat up with her, pulling her body to his for a moment longer. 'You're a special woman, Molly Murphy. I'm not sure I will be able to sleep alone after lying in this bed with you.'

'I doubt that very much.' She laughed. 'It was quite the workout on your behalf, so I think you'll sleep very well. Even collapse perhaps.'

Ryan kissed her again. 'I met my match, so you should sleep like a log too. The most gorgeous, irresistible log.'

Molly slipped from the bed and raced into the sitting room of the suite to find her dress.

'I'll drive you home,' Ryan called from the bed.

'Don't be silly. You have the room until morning and if Ann is staying with Lizzy you should stay here.'

'No, Molly. I'm not putting you in a cab this late at night.'

Molly felt her heart sink as she heard him walk into the living-room area in search of his own clothes. She didn't turn to face him. She didn't want him to see the worry on her face but equally she didn't want to spoil the night by letting Ryan see where she lived. While she had told him, seeing was quite another matter. It was the wrong side of town and their time together had been more perfect than she could have dreamed possible. It would be the worst ending to the best night of her life.

'Seriously,' she began as she turned to find him doing up his trousers. He was the most perfect man. The best lover and as she looked over at his sculpted chest softly lit she wanted to freeze time and have the night go on for ever. To have him hold her all night long, but she couldn't. She had to get home to Tommy. To her ramshackle home. 'I will slip downstairs and grab a cab from the rank. I'm only ten minutes from the city.'

His frown had eased as he made light of the situation but his eyes had not moved from hers. She suspected there was a serious side to his question. 'I know you live on the wrong side of town, according to you. But is there more to it than that?'

'No...but compared to this...' she looked around the suite '... I'm embarrassed. I don't want you to see the house and feel sorry for me. It's truly dreadful.'

'So, you'd rather hide it from me?'

Molly bit the inside of her cheek and nodded.

'It can't be that bad. Please let me be the judge,' he told her. 'There's one thing you need to know about me, Molly. I can handle almost anything but I don't want anything hidden from me. I'm not sure where we are heading with…this, but wherever this goes, whatever it becomes, it has to be built on honesty.'

Molly took the shoes he held out to her and crossed to the large sofa. She sat down and dropped the shoes on the floor, slipping her feet inside.

With her head facing the ground, she confessed the reason she wanted to catch the cab. She lifted her eyes to see Ryan's face smiling back at her.

'You don't know how bad. I have no central heating and I live near a train line, a freight-train line. All one hundred and twenty-two carriages pass by twice a day.'

'You count them?'

'Sometimes…'

'If you'll let me, I will gladly take you out more often so you don't have time to count the carriages.'

Molly smiled. 'You might not want to drive over there to pick me up.'

'Molly, some of the coldest people I know live in palatial, centrally heated homes and some of the warmest have no heating at all. And I can safely say that you are the warmest woman I have ever met.'

He walked to her, knelt down on one knee and, cupping her face in his hands, he kissed her. 'I don't give a damn, Molly Murphy, about the suburb, the condition or anything else about your home. As long as there's no man other than your brother living there with you, then there's nothing to hide…but before I take you home, and I am taking you home, I have something for you.'

'What?' she asked, completely taken off guard by the fact he was on one knee. Her curiosity was heading into overdrive as she watched him reach into his pocket.

'You might need these,' he said as he slipped her lace panties into her lap. 'It's cold out tonight.'

Ryan left Molly to stay warm in the room while he walked back down to the convention centre car park and then drove his car back to the hotel. She took only five minutes to tidy her hair and make-up enough to be seen by other guests and then she headed back downstairs. She was barely seated when she saw his midnight-blue sedan pull up and before she could step out he jumped out with the engine running, raced inside, threw his jacket around her shoulders and escorted her back to his car.

'That was very sweet of you but you didn't have to do that. I could have made the dash out to you,' she told him as she secured her seat belt and he did the same.

'I am not going to have you freeze on my watch,' he replied with a kiss before he slipped the car into gear. 'So where exactly do you live?'

'Like I said, I live in a not great part of town but, since you insist, you should take a left at the King William Street lights and I'll guide you from there.'

Ryan winked and Molly couldn't help but notice on the dashboard clock that it turned midnight as they pulled away from the hotel. And she felt more like Cinderella than she'd thought possible although the idea of Ryan seeing her home still played heavily on her mind.

As they pulled up to her house she noticed Ryan's expression didn't alter. Not at all. Not even a flinch. She'd imagined a look of horror might monopolise his expression as they drove into her suburb and then her street but there was nothing that altered from the time they left the hotel to that moment. No visible change at all. Perhaps again, she thought, she had been the one guilty of judgement. Judging herself and her circumstances more harshly than anyone else. And in the process, judging Ryan.

'This is it, home sweet home,' she said without looking in the direction of the house.

'Molly,' Ryan said. 'Is it normal to have every light on in your house?'

Molly turned to see Ryan was right. The house looked as if a party had started; almost every light had been turned on.

'Oh, dear Lord, Tommy must be up and perhaps looking for me. His anxiety will escalate if he can't find me at this time.'

'Of course,' Ryan said, reaching for his door handle. 'Let me walk you to the door.'

'It's better you don't—it might make it worse. Introductions after midnight won't be good and might make Tommy quite anxious,' she told him, and then leant in and kissed him goodnight. 'Thank you, Ryan, for a wonderful evening.'

'No, thank you, Molly. Truly, one of the best nights in a very long time.'

With that Molly wrapped her thin shawl around her shoulders and alighted the car, not giving Ryan time to open the door for her. She raced to open the rickety gate, then rushed down the path to her front door. She waved to Ryan as she stepped inside. As she closed the door, she heard his car drive off into the night.

She knew he was taking a little piece of her heart with him.

A piece she was very willing to give.

CHAPTER TEN

'ARE YOU ALL RIGHT, Molly? I was very worried. It's late and the television was off and everything and you weren't here.'

'I'm sorry, Tommy. I was sitting in the car outside talking to my boss. He drove me home after the dinner.'

'All right, Molly. But don't worry me again,' Tommy told her, then left and went back to his room and closed the door.

Molly felt guilty about worrying Tommy but had no regrets about the rest of the evening. Ryan was everything she had been looking for in a man but had never dreamed even existed outside a movie or romance novel. He was kind and considerate...and the most amazing lover, she added to her mental tally of his praise as she turned off all the lights, except the night light in the hallway, and made her way to her room.

Carefully she slipped out of her dress and hung it on the hanger behind her door. The care she took with the gown was at odds with the way Ryan had discarded it in his eagerness to have her only hours before. She smiled as she hurriedly threw pyjamas and woollen socks on, brushed her teeth and climbed into her bed. She would deal with her make-up in the morning. The brushed flan-nelette sheets were nothing close to the Egyptian cotton that she had shared with Ryan but they would quickly warm up and that was all that was important. That and reminiscing about the best night of her life as she drifted off easily into the deepest sleep she had enjoyed in more than a year.

Ryan drove into the night thinking about Molly. She was nothing close to the office manager he'd had in mind when he'd called the temp agency and he couldn't have been happier about that. When he'd asked her to attend the dinner with him, he had certainly not dreamed they would end up making love in a hotel suite. He'd thought he would have a lovely evening with an intelligent woman. Maybe even learn a little more about her. Which he had, but it was so much more than he'd ever expected.

Images of her body filled his mind as he pulled into his driveway wishing he were not alone. Wishing she would be in his bed all night. What had happened between them happened quickly. His feelings had escalated and apparently so had hers. While he certainly had not planned the way the evening had ended, he wouldn't have changed anything about it.

He knew his reputation sat as somewhere between recluse and playboy and he had never bothered to prove anyone wrong. And he realised in many ways perhaps they were right. He was either at home with Lizzy, working or occasionally spending an evening with a woman who wanted nothing more than that one night. No strings attached.

He accepted, although did not agree with, the general consensus that a man who didn't have a permanent partner in his life by close to forty was either somewhat withdrawn or playing the field. Ryan was neither, but he was a father first and foremost and, for good reason, a man who didn't and couldn't trust women, so he didn't feel the need to have someone on his arm. If the opportunity to sleep with an available woman with no expectations of more arose he would accept it, but he didn't go in search of women to fill that void. He had been hurt in the worst possible way and until that night had never met a woman with whom he suddenly felt that there might actually be a reason to open up, to risk being hurt and to want to share his life. He knew it was crazy to feel that way so soon but Molly was so different from anyone he had ever met. She was feisty, yet caring, emotionally intelligent, not to mention beautiful. And the most giving lover.

He wanted her in his life...with strings attached.

He felt himself trusting a woman for the first time in more years than he cared to remember. Against everything he had believed for the longest time, he suddenly realised that he might just have a future with someone. Molly Murphy was an amazing woman and one who could seduce him with the smile in her eyes.

Dr Ryan McFetridge had not noticed the ramshackle houses in the dubious suburb, nor the unsightly graffiti on the run-down buildings near the vacant rail yard, because he had been focussed on the beautiful woman who had captured his heart.

He opened the front door of his home wishing more than anything that he could carry Molly upstairs and hold her in his arms all night long.

Suddenly it hit him. He might just be falling in love.

'Good morning, Molly. I hope Tommy was not too upset that I got you home late.'

'Tommy was a little worried and told me not to be so late again,' Molly said into her phone.

'That was my fault and I take full responsibility.'

'I take equal responsibility. I could have asked to leave the hotel at any time.'

'Well, I hope that you slept well.'

'I slept wonderfully well, in fact I slept in until about twenty minutes ago and didn't even hear the silly side gate that has been banging for the last two nights. When the wind picks up it's like it's possessed.'

'I can come by and fix it if you like.'

'Thank you but there's no need. I called the landlord to do it. He can do something for the rent I give him.'

'Is he on his way over to do it now?'

'God, I hope not. I'm still in my pyjamas.'

'I wish I didn't know that.'

'Why?'

'Because I can imagine how desirable you look...and I want to hold you in my arms again.'

Molly suddenly felt warm all over. The idea was completely impractical but delicious nonetheless. Waking in Ryan's arms would have been the only way to make the night any more perfect than it had been. Ryan was definitely not holding back and playing games. He said it as he felt it, and she loved that level of openness and honesty. He was very different from the closed, guarded man she had first thought him to be.

'I hate to disappoint you but I think the look is more cosy than sexy, to be honest.' Molly brought her thoughts back to reality and confessed as she looked down at her odd socks with lint from the dryer, mismatched pyjamas and oversized dressing gown and screwed up her face. There was nothing sexy about any of it but she didn't have to let on just how bad she looked and spoil his early morning fantasy.

'I'm sure if I was there I would disagree,' he told her,

then continued. 'I know it's early to be calling and I do apologise but I wondered if you and Tommy would like to go on a picnic. It's cold today but not going to rain so I thought we could rug up and head up to Waterfall Gully. I could swing by and pick you up at about noon. I thought if I give you plenty of warning then it's more likely to be a yes.'

Molly chuckled at his line of thinking. It was considerate, and also not hiding his intentions. As Ryan had already seen her home and still wanted to venture back into the suburb, she was not about to decline but she had to consider Tommy's view of the invitation as she had already left him alone the night before and wanted him to be happy about the outing. 'That sounds wonderful but I will have to check with Tommy and get back to you,' Molly told her early morning caller. 'Is Lizzy up to coming?'

'No, she's still not good. It's usually two days before she's feeling up to doing much but Ann's here with her for the day. I told her what I had in mind and Lizzy's actually encouraging me to go out with you. She really likes you, Molly. To be honest, if it wasn't for me knowing that she really was unwell last night, I'd think she set the whole thing up. Looks like she's dabbling in a bit of matchmaking.'

'I'm not sure about that but I think Lizzy's a very special young lady.'

'I'd have to agree with you,' he replied before returning to his original question. 'Please ask Tommy if he's up to it. And take as long as you need. I've packed the picnic lunch already with enough for the three of us so just let me know by, say…eleven-thirty.'

'I will have an answer for you before then, and thank

you, Ryan, for the invitation, and thank you for including Tommy.'

'You're very welcome and of course I would include Tommy. I'm looking forward to meeting him and, since Lizzy doesn't have a brother, it might be nice for them to hang out in the future too. There's not a big age difference so they might become famous friends.'

'That would be great. I'll get back to you as soon as I know.'

Molly hung up with her heart as light as air. She didn't think anything could wipe the smile from her face. Thinking way too far ahead, Molly wishfully thought they had the potential to be like the Brady Bunch with Tommy and Lizzy and Ryan and herself. Could it be possible that she and Ryan could be more than just a fling? She had never thought she would learn to trust a man again, let alone contemplate falling in love, but that was exactly what was happening to her and she wanted to rest back and enjoy the feeling.

Could Ryan be her happily ever after and a stable male figure for Tommy? He had an understanding of the special needs of a young man like Tommy as he was successfully raising Lizzy and, to the best of her knowledge, coping with those challenges. She was daydreaming and in bliss as she walked past Tommy's door that was still shut. He too must be sleeping in, she thought, and she gathered her things to have a shower.

The warm water felt wonderful running all over her body but not as good as Ryan's hands the night before. The heat in the steam-filled room was heavenly on a cold morning but Ryan's fingers had been ecstasy. Life had certainly turned the corner for her and Tommy. Perhaps, she mused for a moment as she lathered her hands with the cake of soap, both Murphys might be lucky in love after all.

* * *

'Tommy, are you on the telephone?'

'I was but I'm not now. My girlfriend had to go,' Tommy called from behind his closed door. His voice told Molly he was grumpy.

'Well, it's lovely that you can call her and talk,' she replied, hoping to lift his spirits. 'She must be very special because I know you like her very much.'

'I love her.'

Molly quickly took stock of her words and her attitude. She kept forgetting that Tommy was a twenty-five-year-old man in love.

'Of course, you do. Do you have plans today or would you like to come on a picnic?'

'No. I want to stay at home.'

'May I come in, Tommy? It's difficult to have a conversation with your door closed.'

'Yes. You can open the door.'

Molly slowly opened the door to find her brother sitting on his bed. His head was hanging down and he looked very forlorn. 'I thought you might like to go out and have a picnic,' Molly said, still hoping to cheer him up with the idea of an outing. 'Ryan asked us both out for the day.'

'He's your boss.'

'That's right.'

'He took you out to dinner.'

'Yes, he did and we had a lovely time.'

'You came home late and made me worry.'

Molly chewed the inside of her cheek for a moment. She was slap bang in the middle of a grilling from her baby brother. 'I know I did.'

'Do you like him?'

'He's very nice.'

'Is he your boyfriend?'

Molly was taken aback by the line of questioning. It was unlike Tommy. She could see he wasn't happy and she wasn't sure about the answer to his last question. Was Ryan her boyfriend? She didn't know herself. The fact he had called so early and planned a date for the three of them could lead her to assume they were dating but she wasn't sure and she wasn't ready to tell Tommy anything until she was sure.

'Tommy, Ryan is a friend and a very nice man and I think you would like him.'

'I was going to see my girlfriend today but I can't. She's staying home. I wanted to go to the mall and get a ring and then ask her to marry me.'

Molly almost dropped her coffee cup and some colourful language with the shock. She knew that Tommy had spoken of a girlfriend but had assumed it was a fleeting crush. He had a big heart and it had been filled with romantic thoughts about pretty girls before but after a few weeks he usually found the girls to be silly and he stopped talking about them. She had suspected this wouldn't be any different but it clearly was very different. Molly doubted Tommy had ever kissed or been kissed. His crushes had been platonic and innocent up to that point.

Molly's head had been in the clouds with her own romantic thoughts and she had forgotten to enquire further about Tommy's girlfriend, but talk of marriage was the last thing she'd expected to hear from her little brother.

'She's so pretty and we've worked together for over a year. I was her boss for a few weeks but now she's a boss like me. I have four people who work for me folding the mail and she has three. She started there on May the second last year. I remember because it was her birthday the next day,' he continued happily, completely unaware of the panic washing over his sister.

'And you want to get married?'

'Yes, and I want to buy a ring. A pretty one that she will like so she says yes to me.'

Molly steadied her breathing so her brother didn't notice her reaction. Everyone deserved to find someone to love and she didn't want her brother to think he deserved anything less but she couldn't help but be surprised and apprehensive. It was all happening so very fast. The week before she hadn't known Tommy had a girl in his life and now he wanted to get married. It was a lot to absorb. And she needed to know he was sure about his feelings before he got too involved.

Suddenly she pulled herself up. Her relationship with Ryan had moved even more quickly. She had met, fallen in love and slept with a man she had known for only a week. It was against everything she had thought she would have done. In fact, she'd never thought she would get that close to a man again, let alone in seven days.

'Do you want to come and sit on the sofa with me? I can put on the heater and we can chat. I want you to tell me everything about her,' Molly said as she headed in the direction of the living room. She needed to give her complete attention to her brother as this was a life-changing decision he was about to make. She turned on the gas heater and closed the door to keep the heat in the room, then dropped to the floor and sat cross-legged with her coffee cup in her hand. She could hear the side gate banging again against the wrought-iron fence in the strong wind. Molly had tied it up so many times but it always came free. She made a mental note to put one of the broken red house bricks on either side once the rain stopped. The thought of going outside and getting wet through once again that week was worse than the incessant and annoying noise. They were snug and warm inside and there were so many questions Molly had for Tommy, but she wanted to take it slowly.

'Honey is like the prettiest flower in the garden, only better,' he said, holding his arms out wide with a smile to match. 'She's the prettiest girl in the world and if she says yes then we'll get married.'

'Do you think she knows you're going to ask her?'

'No, but we love each other. I told her that I love her and she told me that she loves me.'

'I know you've worked together for over a year but how long have you been together as boyfriend and girlfriend?'

'Six weeks.'

'I see, and how old is she?'

'She's young. She doesn't have wrinkles like the lady that drives the bus.'

Molly was glad to hear that, since the bus driver was a retired volunteer in her early seventies.

'Do you think you might like to get to know each other for a little bit longer before you get married?'

'Do you think she will say no?' Tommy's face suddenly became overcome with sadness.

Molly couldn't bear to think she had made her brother sad. Not for even a second.

'I'm sure she will say yes. She would be lucky to be married to you. It's just…' Molly hesitated, not wanting to say anything that would create doubt in Tommy's heart about how Honey felt about him, but she did have some reservations. 'It's just that I'd like to meet her too. And maybe her parents, and you don't have to rush. You might like to take things slowly. It takes time to know that you are really in love,' Molly said, and immediately felt like the world's biggest hypocrite. She was telling her brother to take things slowly and she definitely had not. Clearly she wasn't listening to her own advice. Never had there been a better case of *Do as I say, not as I do.* She didn't want to have two sets of rules and hated that her first reaction was to do just that. It wasn't right but she was so accustomed to being protective and she was struggling to step away from that role and feel the same level of excitement that her brother felt.

But she had to do just that. She knew in her heart that she had to be happy for Tommy. No matter what the future held, she needed to push away her reservations and doubt and find happiness for him. Real happiness. He needed to know that she was sharing his joy.

Tommy tilted his head a little. 'You mean sleepovers? Like Nigel did?'

Molly almost choked on her warm drink. She hadn't been expecting to hear that. Being reminded that Nigel had slept in her bed was upsetting and equally the thought of her little brother having a young woman in his bed would take a little getting accustomed to by Molly. Marriage, sleepovers, all of it had been sudden and she was struggling to know how to feel about it.

'You will like her, Molly. She's neat.'

Molly smiled. She loved her brother and she would support him however she could, but she knew there could be challenges ahead for him and his future bride if he was to marry his girlfriend. 'I know I will like her very, very much.'

'Can she come for dinner one night?' Tommy asked, smoothing down his hair as if his prospective bride were in the room.

'Of course, she can. I told you that I would love to meet her.'

'You promise, she can come over.'

'Definitely.'

'All right, but it can't be today. She can't see me today but she still loves me.'

Molly could see the potential for heartbreak but she could also see the potential for love and she was well aware she couldn't influence the outcome. Just be there to support the one she loved no matter what. She was yet to meet the young woman who had claimed her brother's heart. While he was sensible and relatively independent, Molly still wanted to ensure that this young woman had his best interests as well as her own in mind.

The guilt she felt in losing the family home played heavily as well. Tommy wouldn't have very much to offer his bride-to-be and the sheer practicality of getting a home would be difficult. Fortunately, there was some insurance money still in trust for Tommy that would be accessible to him when he turned thirty, not sufficient to buy a big home, but he could purchase a modest home in a nice suburb. But that was more than five years away and she wasn't sure his bride-to-be would be happy waiting that long.

Her mood became sombre for a moment as she looked out of the window and thought back to what she had done. A wolf in sheep's clothing had come knocking on her door and she had let him in. Taken him at his word and allowed him to become part of the family and with that allowed her financial security to be exposed and put at risk. Suddenly she worried if she had done the same in trusting Ryan. Was it too soon to really know him? Should she have waited before falling into bed and potentially into love with her boss?

She tried to push her negative thoughts aside and remind herself that Ryan was in a different league. He was the kindest, most chivalrous man she had met. She wanted the doubt to disappear, her fears to leave, but there were traces and, while she suspected they might always be there lurking in her mind, she couldn't and wouldn't allow her past to cripple her future. Ryan McFetridge was not like Nigel and never would be. He was not the type of man who would pull the rug out from under her. She hoped with all of her heart that Dr McFetridge was there to stay…no matter what.

'What if we have the picnic lunch together and then go with you to the mall and pick out a ring?'

'With your boyfriend?'

Molly ran her fingers through the unruly curls as she wondered how to answer her brother. She decided to brush over the reference to boyfriend. 'We could ask Ryan if he would like to come along, but only if you want that.'

'Maybe. What will we have for lunch?'

'Something delicious, I'm sure.'

Molly smiled. Tommy was bending to the idea. She wanted so much for Ryan and Tommy to meet and then Tommy and Lizzy to meet. For the first time in a long time she thought she might only be a few steps away from her happy ever after.

Ryan came exactly on noon and Molly and Tommy were ready and waiting by the door. It was cold outside but the sun was shining and the sky was the most vivid blue. They were rugged up with scarves and gloves and winter coats, and Molly thought it would be lovely to be out in the fresh air. Particularly with her two favourite men.

'Hi, Ryan, please come inside,' Molly said as she opened the front door to her tiny home. She kissed him on the cheek, mindful that she hadn't confirmed to Tommy the status of her relationship with Ryan yet and she didn't want to rush anything in front of her brother. Ryan gave her a knowing smile that told her immediately he understood how the day would play out for the three of them.

'Tommy, this is Ryan McFetridge,' she began the introductions as soon as Ryan stepped inside. 'Ryan, this is my brother, Tommy.'

Ryan extended his hand and Tommy chose not to meet his handshake. Neither Molly nor Ryan said anything and quietly accepted that Tommy was not yet ready to greet him favourably. Molly hoped that would change in time but understood, after losing Nigel abruptly, that he would be hesitant to get close to Ryan in a hurry. Tommy had liked Nigel. Why wouldn't he? He had said and done everything to make Tommy like and trust him all the while stealing his inheritance. This time they needed to take things slowly so Tommy could really get to know Ryan and feel safe.

They needed to take things a day at a time and see if this was a for-ever relationship. While it seemed wonderful, Molly knew there was another person to consider in any decisions she made about seriously dating Ryan.

'If you're ready, I have the heaters on in the car and we can head up and have a picnic.'

'Okay,' Tommy answered matter-of-factly, and stepped outside to see a shiny red SUV at the front of the house. Suddenly his face lit up. 'That's a neat car.'

'Glad you like it,' Ryan replied. 'It's our weekend car. We like to get out for long drives and head into the hills and, when I get holidays, we go to the Flinders Ranges to stay. My daughter chose the car. She loves the colour red.'

'Me too.'

Molly was surprised to hear Tommy say that. She didn't know he liked red. She'd thought blue had been his favourite colour for a very long time. But she was just happy to see her brother happy so didn't question his new colour preference.

Tommy climbed into the back while Ryan opened the car door for Molly. She was relieved to see a level of enthusiasm from her brother.

'You have a DVD screen,' Tommy said gleefully before Ryan closed Molly's door.

'Yes, Tommy. I'll start it for you as soon as I get in.'

Ryan kept his word and the moment he was seated inside the car, he lowered the ceiling screen. 'I have a few DVDs here or a cable so you can stream from your smartphone.'

'I don't have a smartphone,' Tommy told him bluntly. 'Smartphones cost too much money so Molly and I don't have one.'

'I agree. I just have one because I'm on call,' Ryan replied. 'But don't worry, you can stream from mine. Let's get you set up before we head off.'

Molly watched as Ryan did just that. Tommy chose a science fiction movie he wanted to see even though the trip was only thirty minutes, and the three of them headed off for their picnic. Molly was so happy to be spending time with Ryan, and having Tommy along with them made it a perfect day.

The picnic lunch was wonderful. There were wooden tables and benches in the small park at the foot of the gully climbing trail. Ryan had packed everything they would need, right down to a checked tablecloth and thick woollen blankets to throw over their legs. There were two home-made salads, one was pasta and the other Greek with feta cheese and olives, a loaf of fresh crusty bread, bottled water, a still-warm rotisserie chicken that Ryan didn't take credit for as his local chicken shop did better than he could by a mile, and roast potatoes, again courtesy of Charlie's Chickens on Portrush Road.

They all tucked into the food and, once it was finished, they enjoyed piping hot chocolate from a flask.

'That was good, Ryan,' Tommy said, pulling the serviette free from his collar. Then he turned to Molly. 'Can I make a call to my girlfriend?'

'Sure,' Molly said.

'If you'd like privacy, you can make the call in my car, Tommy. Here's the keys,' Ryan added, pulling the keys from his coat pocket and handing them to Tommy. 'The top button on the remote unlocks the doors.'

Tommy nodded, took the keys and headed to the car only twenty metres away in the almost empty car park.

'Thank you for that,' Molly said, squeezing Ryan's hand under the table and out of view of Tommy. 'That was very sweet of you.'

'He's a grown man. I think he deserves privacy,' Ryan reasoned.

'Sometimes I forget that. I try to make sure I don't treat him differently, but when he told me this morning that he's going to ask his girlfriend, Honey, to marry him, I have to admit it freaked me out. He's twenty-five but I still think of him as my little brother.'

'Wow, marriage. I can see it would. Marriage is a big step. Have they been together for a long time?'

'Six weeks, but apparently worked together for a year.'

'That's moving fast but sometimes you just know.'

Molly felt her heart race yet again with the way he looked at her as he spoke. She wondered if that was how he felt about her.

'Have you met this mystery young woman?' he finally said.

'No.' She was shaking her head. 'Which is making me a little anxious. I'm sure she's lovely but I don't know anything about her. Tommy's been waiting for that special someone and he always spoke about getting married and settling down. I guess I never thought it would really happen.'

'Well, I think you need to get to know the young woman and her family before the lovebirds set a date. There's lots for everyone to think about, but if they're in love then you may not be able to stop them becoming engaged and it's not your place to try,' Ryan remarked, then, looking over to Tommy chatting happily in the car, added, 'But you can make sure there's plenty of time between the engagement and the wedding so they don't rush into anything that they're not ready for.'

'Let's hope I can stall them. On that subject, Tommy would like to go to the mall later. I've suggested the Eastern Hills Mall as it's open until late tonight with the mid-winter sales.'

'Would you like me to accompany you or is this brother-sister time?'

'If you don't mind, it would be lovely for you to go with us. Perhaps a man's opinion would help. He actually wants to buy the engagement ring today.'

Ryan ran his fingers across his forehead. 'He's not wasting any time. He's a man on a mission.'

'Apparently.'

'If he'd like me to be there, I'm happy to do so. Does he have a budget? The jewellery shops in the Eastern Hills Mall are quite pricey.'

'He's been saving hard and now wants to spend it all on the ring.'

'She must be quite the catch.'

'Honey is apparently *a princess*,' she said.

'Then I'm sure I can help to haggle a little. Even in those stores there's room to move on prices.'

Molly looked into the warmest, most caring eyes and wanted so badly to kiss the man sitting beside her. He was so wonderful and understanding. A true knight in shining armour who made the best pasta salad she had ever eaten. She could see Tommy in the car glancing up at them now and then, so she refrained from acting on her impulse. She didn't want to surprise Tommy by making it obvious Ryan was more to her than a friend too soon.

But with little effort Ryan was becoming more and more to her with every passing minute they shared.

And the winter picnic was no exception.

CHAPTER ELEVEN

RYAN DID JUST as he promised and managed to have the price reduced on the very pretty ring so it came in under Tommy's budget. While the diamond was quite tiny, the white-gold setting was pretty and Tommy particularly liked the red velvet box.

The three of them then headed to Molly's home. Molly had suggested Ryan stay for dinner and Tommy seemed keen on the idea too, but Ryan declined as he wanted to check in on Lizzy.

As they pulled up in front of their home, Ryan turned in his seat. 'Good luck with the proposal, Tommy.'

'Thank you, Ryan. I'm going to work hard and save my money and buy a house so we can be happy. And you can live with us too, Molly, so you won't be alone.'

Ryan shot a sideways smile at Molly.

'You're a good man, Tommy, and any girl would be lucky to have you.'

Molly and Tommy ate dinner together and, after the dishes were washed and put away, Tommy went to his room leaving Molly alone with her thoughts. He was tired and also excited. He told her he would guard the ring with his life until he proposed.

Molly hugged him goodnight and sat by the heater.

Her week had certainly been monumental, she thought as she stretched her pyjama-clad legs out in front of her and rested her head on the sofa. Closing her eyes, she thought back over the previous seven days. She had started a new job, received a pay rise, attended a black-tie dinner with her boss in the most gorgeous new dress, they'd made love, had gone on a second, picnic date...and she accepted that she had fallen for him. A week ago, she could never have imagined her life turning around like that.

She had paid her rent, health insurance and they'd enjoyed salmon for dinner. She hoped it was not too good to be true and the bubble burst but she couldn't see how it would. Common sense was telling her to tread carefully but her heart and gut were urging her to throw caution to the wind and enjoy the happiness the universe was gifting to her. While an argument raged in her head between logic and emotions, with emotions the favourite to win, she was startled by a dragging sound outside. She stood to investigate. Pulling back the drapes, she saw a figure outside holding the side gate in place with his foot while he put bricks on either side. Her stomach dropped. She couldn't make out his face as he was hunched trying to sort out the loose gate but she suspected it was the landlord's son. She shuddered at the thought of him coming to her home late in the evening. What was he hoping to achieve? She had already told him she was not interested in him and the rent was fully paid. She suddenly remembered when she paid the rent she had told him that the gate was banging all night and she wanted it fixed. She'd meant in the day when she wasn't at home, not late in the evening.

She peered into the darkness and as the stranger turned his head under the dim street light she realised it was Ryan.

She rushed to the door and then mid-step realised she was wearing her pyjamas.

Suddenly she didn't care. She was curious as to why he was back there but excited to see him and her state of dress didn't matter.

'Ryan,' she called out from the open front door. 'What are you doing out there?'

'Stopping your side gate from banging all night and keeping you awake. I remembered when I got home that I had wanted to sort it out so I'll do that and leave…'

'Are you serious?'

'Absolutely not. I'm hoping to come inside. I brought a bottle of wine and some chocolate-dipped strawberries that Ann made with Lizzy today. I thought we could spend the evening together since Tommy already knows about me. I hoped it would be okay.'

A little while later, with Molly still in her flannelette pyjamas, the two of them sat side by side on the floor by the heater in her tiny lounge. Tommy had stepped out of his room to get a glass of milk, said hello to Ryan, took two strawberries and then headed back into his room. Molly was pleasantly surprised at how quickly he had accepted Ryan in their home almost like a piece of furniture. The day together and Ryan's help in finding a ring for Tommy's soon-to-be fiancée had made all the difference. Ryan's support had been unconditional even though Molly knew he had a few reservations about the proposal and the marriage. But for Tommy's sake, he kept that to himself.

Molly sipped her wine and leant back into Ryan's arms as she nibbled on the very ripe strawberry coated in the darkest Swiss chocolate. It had been for ever since she had enjoyed a glass of wine in her own home or such a delicious fruit treat. It was a luxury her situation had not afforded but, she conceded silently, being in the arms of Ryan would have made vinegar taste like champagne. They were facing the television but it wasn't turned on.

'I have to say, Molly, after everything you told me last night, I think you're even more amazing.'

Molly shook her head.

'I mean it—you are so strong. Others might have crumbled with the disappointment of being left and the struggle that followed but you chose to fight on.'

'Everything I did, I did for Tommy. I could never walk away from him.'

'And when you came to work for me, despite what you were going through, you found a way to make improvements to the running of my practice.'

'Clearly I wasn't doing that well… I turned up looking like I'd been caught in a monsoon, not to mention the odd shoes…'

'But you turned up to a job that was not using your skills and well beneath your pay grade to put food on the table and be here at home at the right time to keep Tommy feeling secure. Some women walk away from anything that hard. And they feel nothing for those left empty and hurt by their actions.'

Molly turned her face towards Ryan. The conversation had taken a detour to a place that confused her. It was a side of him that seemed quite dark. 'That sounds like you're speaking from experience.'

'You're more than just a pretty face…'

Molly brushed aside the joke he tried to use to cover up his feelings. 'I'm serious, Ryan. What happened to you?'

Ryan drew a deep breath and pulled away slightly

from Molly. She could feel him retreating but knew he needed the space.

'You know Lizzy's my daughter but what you don't know is that I only found out that I had a daughter seven years ago. Lizzy was twelve when I discovered I was her father.'

'Lizzy was twelve before you knew?' Molly asked, her confusion at his announcement not hidden.

'I only found out that I had a daughter when her adoptive parents both passed away within three months of each other. They say that her adoptive mother had a stroke and passed, and her adoptive father died of a broken heart.'

'You must have been quite young when she was born.'

'Two months short of twenty. Lizzy was born on the third of May and I was born on July third but I didn't find out until I was almost thirty-two. I dated a girl, Madeline, in my hometown of Port Lincoln and we broke up when I was nineteen. We'd started going out in high school and dated for close to three years. I would travel back every few weeks from Adelaide where I was in my first year of medicine and call every day but it wasn't enough. She didn't like the long-distance relationship and I wasn't prepared to throw in my studies to live in a tiny town and work for her father's prawn-trawling business. We came to a stalemate and she gave me an ultimatum that I needed to move back home and marry her or she would end it. She was calling my bluff, thinking I would move back, but I was young and decided I needed to stay in Adelaide, finish my studies and think about marriage down the track. We broke up. It was inevitable when two people can't compromise. We were too young to really understand what compromise even meant.'

'Even though you were young, it still must have hurt. Three years is a long time.'

'It was hard for a while, but again I was so young and my focus was on getting my medical degree and then deciding where I wanted to live. Maybe it would be a country doctor, but I hadn't lived anywhere but Port Lincoln so I wanted to spread my wings before I nested.'

'That was a sensible idea. Nineteen is so very young to get married and settle down for life.'

'She clearly didn't think so,' Ryan said, glancing back at Molly and then back to the black television screen. 'It was about three months after we ended it, Madeline discovered she was pregnant. She decided not to tell me as she was already seeing a local lad and she decided that he would probably marry her and they could live happily ever after with no one the wiser.'

'Three months…then could the other young man have been the baby's father.'

'No, they had only been seeing each other for about six weeks and as she'd irregular periods she hadn't paid much attention to being late. She thought it must have been the upset of the break-up and teenage hormones and we'd always been careful, as much as teenagers could be, so she had no reason to think she was pregnant, but the doctor told her she was already close to three months. So, she decided it was going to be her secret.'

'But how did she think she could keep that kind of secret?'

'She planned on telling everyone the baby was premature.'

Molly was shocked by the level of deception at such a young age. 'But that's wrong in so many ways.'

'She was young, angry with me and wanted to get married and settle down and thought that the baby would cement things with her new boyfriend. She was scared I wouldn't come back to live there and she'd be raising the baby alone.'

'I'm sure she was wrong. Even only knowing you for a week, I think you would have done the right thing.'

'I've thought about that over the years, and I say now that I would but I can't say with any certainty what I would have done at nineteen. Perhaps I would have married her, perhaps not, but I know that I would've taken care of my child financially.'

'I don't believe for a moment that, at nineteen or any age, you would have left her to raise the baby alone.'

'I appreciate your belief in me,' he told her and, pulling her close, he kissed the top of her head.

'How could I not believe in you? I've seen how much you love Lizzy. You would give her the world if you could and I doubt that's just because you're older and wiser. I think it's because of who you are as a man. And the way you relate to Tommy after only just meeting him.'

Ryan said nothing but Molly could see the past was preoccupying his thoughts. She drew her legs up underneath her body as she faced him.

'If you don't mind me asking, how did her new boyfriend take the news of the baby?'

'He apparently was surprised, very surprised, but at Madeline's request her father offered him a job with the family business and he took it. He was a local farmhand so it was a step up for him. They planned on getting married after the baby was born. She wanted her figure back to walk down the aisle and felt secure, with the new boyfriend on the payroll and a baby on the way, that he wouldn't leave her.'

'But didn't she worry the baby wouldn't look like her boyfriend?'

'She had a type. He pretty much had my height and colouring. It seemed like a flawless plan to her.'

Molly was stunned by everything she was hearing. For a teenager to be so calculating and cover all her bases to get the outcome she wanted disturbed Molly. She also worried how Madeline's personality had evolved over the years. She hoped she might have looked inside and discovered a moral compass but she had her doubts.

'Unfortunately for Madeline, it didn't work out the way it was planned,' Ryan continued. 'Elizabeth was born on her due date and with Down's syndrome. The young man then made enquiries with the doctor if the prematurity had anything to do with Lizzy's condition and the doctor told him that Lizzy had been born on the date she was expected.'

'She didn't have antenatal check-ups and discover Lizzy's condition before she was born?'

'The chances of Down's syndrome in a woman under thirty are about one in twelve hundred and there was no one in the family with the condition so no one thought that would be a consideration that justified the testing.'

'So, what happened?'

'Well, the relationship went south after he discovered she had been lying to him. He left Madeline and the family business. Her father was close to disowning her for lying to everyone as they were good people. They quickly realised it was my baby.'

'Did they contact you?'

'I wish they had but they didn't. They put Lizzy up for adoption. The couple who adopted Lizzy were a couple in the country. They were childless and in their late forties. Bob and Laura Jones knew Lizzy would have special needs but Laura had nursing experience and they were prepared to provide her with whatever she needed and more. Madeline's mother, Ann, had wanted to raise the baby but her husband, while a good man, was practical and said it was not in anyone's best interest to hold on to Lizzy. He said it was too much to take on. Their daughter's life had fallen apart after the lies were exposed and Madeline wanted nothing to do with the child, so Ann had no choice but to agree that the baby be put up for private adoption.'

'Ann who's now called Sooty?'

'Yes, one and the same. She would send birthday and Christmas presents along with money to the agency to be forwarded on. The adoptive parents were not wealthy and they accepted the gifts on behalf of their daughter. Ann felt it would be disruptive to meet Lizzy so she never asked for the new parents' details, but she left hers if they ever asked for them. While it was a strange relationship, it allowed Ann to keep her sanity and Bob and Laura Jones had the additional financial assistance to raise their much-loved daughter.'

'So that is why Lizzy's surname is Jones.'

'Yes. I didn't change it when she came to live with me. By twelve, she had learnt her name. While coming to live with me brought a lot of challenges, as you could certainly well understand, changing her name would have been very confusing and unnecessary.'

'What happened after her adoptive parents died, before she came to live with you?'

'Ann received a letter from the agency telling her that Bob had passed a few months after his wife.'

'That's so sad. And poor Lizzy.'

'Well, Lizzy had been taken in by the neighbours but they were unable to offer her a home long-term as they had five children of their own. They offered a month so a new family could be found to adopt or foster Lizzy. This broke Ann's heart and she didn't want Lizzy to ever live in foster care. She genuinely loved the child she had never met but her circumstances had changed. In the twelve years since Lizzy was born, her husband had died and she was getting older and worried if something happened to her then Lizzy might once again be facing fostering.

'If she had been ten years younger, I know she would have taken Lizzy into her home. Anyway, in desperation she reached out to me. She tracked me down through networks on the Eyre Peninsula who knew where I was practising in Adelaide. I received a call out of the blue asking if I could travel to Port Lincoln urgently. While I had no clue what to think, I flew over there. I thought perhaps something had happened to Madeline, but I quickly found out that she had long moved away and forgotten everyone and everything that had been a part of her life in Port Lincoln. Ann poured out everything to me.'

'That must have been such a shock for you. Trying to absorb everything at once. I can't imagine what you went through that day.'

'It was devastating in so many ways and I felt so many emotions that day. A bit like I had been run over by a bus. Twelve years of deceit came undone and I felt enormous pressure, as if I was just supposed to ride in and sort it out. I left Ann's home not sure what to think or do. I was angry beyond belief, and hurt and disappointed, but the next day the concern I had for the daughter I never knew became the strongest emotion and driving force behind my decision. I called the agency, undertook a paternity test to prove I was Lizzy's father to the authorities and began the process of bringing Lizzy to live with me.'

Molly did not know how to react, except to reach for Ryan's hand and gently squeeze it. He didn't pull away.

'I guess the rest is history and I have spent the last

seven years getting to know Lizzy. I struggle every day with the years I lost, the years I was shut out of Lizzy's life, and for that I guess it's no surprise that I have little time for anyone who's not upfront with me. I can deal with anything, bad news, horrific news, but not secrets. It does my head in.'

'And Lizzy's mother?'

'Last I heard she's living in the US, married to a marine she met while he was on shore leave in Australia and they have three boys. Sending Lizzy to live over there would have been wrong on so many levels, including the fact the life of a military family has no stability and we both know that a child with Down's syndrome needs routine. Quite apart from the fact that Madeline didn't want her daughter.'

'How can a mother not want her own child?'

'Apparently, it was relatively easy for Madeline,' Ryan said, shrugging his shoulders. 'But I have to admit the disaster she left behind wasn't easy for anyone. It was a daily challenge for Lizzy to settle with me but we worked very hard over a long time and Ann helped when I finally let her back into our lives. She felt guilty for not reaching out to me, but to be honest, with all the deception from their daughter, neither Ann nor her husband had been thinking clearly. He'd just wanted what was best for Lizzy and I think to have the scandal fade away by Lizzy not being there. And Ann knew their daughter was not the type to provide the care that Lizzy needed. And they were right.'

'What do you mean by "finally let her back into our lives"?'

'I blamed her for the longest time. About a year, actually. I didn't respond to her calls or emails after Lizzy came to live with me. I told the agency to return any gifts that were sent to them and I returned anything sent to my practice. I wanted to punish someone for what had happened and I couldn't punish Madeline or Madeline's father so I took it out on Ann. In hindsight, it wasn't fair but Lizzy didn't know her grandmother and at the time I was not thinking logically.'

Molly feared her judgement of his actions would be evident on her face but she couldn't prevent it. It was understandable but still harsh.

'I finally realised that I was punishing the wrong person. If she hadn't kept in contact with Lizzy's adoptive family over the years, and also reached out to me and risked my wrath, then Lizzy would be God knows where now. It just took me a while to accept that I needed to let go of the blame and move forward, so I reached out and apologised for what I then saw as cruel. Ann had no family in Port Lincoln as Madeline was in the US and Ann's husband was gone, so I suggested she move down to Adelaide so she could be closer to Lizzy and myself.'

'Well, that was pretty wonderful of you.'

'I don't know about wonderful, but I thought it was the right thing to do. We all needed each other. And I wanted her to finally get to know her granddaughter. Now Ann is a patient at the practice and for her age has very little to be worried about. She's in great health.'

'I don't know what to say. It's an incredible story… with a happy ending.'

'It's better than it could have been, but not as good as it should have been if everyone had just told the truth nineteen years ago. We've all come through it, but I can't say unscathed and it could have been avoided.'

Molly had never expected Ryan to talk about his past to her so openly and honestly. She had never met a man so willing to share his thoughts and his experiences, good and bad. Each word brought him closer to her.

But it also cast a dark shadow over the two of them.

Sitting there holding the hand of a man who had been deceived by so many, she suddenly realised that she might be doing the same. While she had not taken Lizzy's secret boyfriend too seriously at the time, knowing now how Ryan felt about his daughter dating, would he find her silence on the matter as betrayal? But if she came clean about it, then she would be breaking her promise to Lizzy.

And could she ever win Lizzy's trust again?

Molly sat wrapped in the warmth of a wonderful man's embrace, silently debating her options. She quickly realised they were limited. She had to pray Lizzy's infatuation ended quickly and, when it did, swear to herself that she would never again make a promise she couldn't keep.

Because she knew in keeping her promise to Lizzy she might be taking a huge risk in having a future with Ryan.

CHAPTER TWELVE

It was Saturday morning and the weather had eased a little with no rain scheduled for the day. The breeze was still bitter and the dark clouds hung low in the sky like a dull canvas. Molly wasn't sure if the bureau of meteorology had it right or not, but she dressed in jeans and a sweater.

She wasn't planning to go out until late in the day so it didn't much matter what was happening outside. There was so much happening inside her own head she would deal with rain if and when it eventuated. Molly had just cooked a hearty breakfast of bacon and eggs to share with Tommy. It was a Saturday morning ritual to relax and eat a nice breakfast because the rest of the week they would be rushing to get to work.

Molly had not seen Ryan outside the practice all week as he had late-night rounds and spent three evenings consulting at St Clara's, but the time they spent at work he did not hide his feelings for her. When they were alone at the end of the day, he pulled her close and his kisses were as passionate as the night they'd spent together. She melted in his arms and couldn't wait to spend another night in his bed. But they were both very professional in front of patients and his nurse Stacy when she was rostered on. Molly liked Stacy but they were both so busy they didn't have much time for social chit-chat, which was probably for the best because Molly didn't like her chances of hiding how she felt about Ryan if questioned by her colleague.

They'd made plans to have dinner that night. Ryan was going to pick Molly up at seven o'clock. He had asked her out on the Monday morning, so with plenty of notice she had managed to find a lovely little black dress on sale at a department store in town. She would wear the same nude patent shoes and bag. And while she wanted to look nice, she wasn't stressing about impressing him—he had seen her in her flannelette pyjamas and hadn't bolted so she felt a little more secure about her appearance.

But while she was excited and so looking forward to being alone with Ryan again, Molly felt torn between keeping Lizzy's confidence and being honest and open with Ryan. She made a promise to herself that she would give Lizzy one week to tell her father. After that she would have to take it into her own hands. She wasn't entirely sure how she would manage the situation but she would find a way.

Molly served breakfast and called out to Tommy. He came quickly to the table and was wearing a big smile.

'You look happy this morning.'

'Because I am happy… Lizzy said yes. She will marry me.'

'Lizzy?'

'My girlfriend, Lizzy.'

'But your girlfriend's name is Honey.'

Tommy laughed as he tucked his serviette into the neck of his jumper and reached for his knife and fork. 'I call her Honey. She calls me Sweetheart. Her name is Lizzy. We sat under the trees yesterday. I asked her to marry me and she said yes and she kissed me and I kissed her back.'

'Oh, my God, I had no idea her name was Lizzy…' Molly dropped her own fork and stopped mid-sentence. She was aware of the sudden shrill tone to her voice and needed to calm down. She didn't want to upset Tommy, who was clearly thrilled his proposal had been accepted. She also reminded herself that Lizzy was not an unusual name.

'I told you,' he said, before he took another mouthful of the scrambled eggs.

'No, Tommy, I would have remembered.'

'Are you cross, Molly?'

'No, not with you. Not at all. It was my fault I didn't ask,' she said, patting his hand over the breakfast table. Molly wondered why she had never questioned Tommy more about his girlfriend before that day. She'd had a lot on her mind and Tommy had called her *Honey* and Molly had thought that was her name. Not her pet name. Everything had been travelling at lightning speed the previous week and Molly hadn't read between the lines.

And clearly Ryan hadn't doubted that Honey was Tommy's girlfriend's name when they'd all shopped together for the ring.

Her head had been in the clouds with her own relationship and battling how to deal with Lizzy's boyfriend confession. She suddenly thought she had been selfish with the time she had devoted to Tommy's life. Up to that point she'd always known everything about Tommy, but he had become a little mysterious and paying more attention to his grooming and she had become preoccupied at the same time. She had been focussed on her burgeoning relationship with Ryan and had forgotten to question further the most basic information about

Tommy's relationship. Could Tommy's relationship and Lizzy's relationship be one and the same?

'What's her last name?'

'Lizzy Jones,' came Tommy's reply. 'But it will be Murphy when we get married.'

'And Lizzy's favourite colour is?'

'Red.'

Molly had been grasping at straws. Narrowing it down and hoping with each question she would find something that didn't match, but it all matched. Perfectly. She collapsed back in silence onto her wooden chair. Her eyes closed as tight as her chest felt at that moment. And to make matters more complicated, Ryan had helped to buy the ring for his own daughter. The daughter he didn't want to be going on dates, let alone getting married. The secret that Molly had hoped would go away had just got so much worse. It all seemed so overwhelming. How she wished Lizzy had not confided in her, but she had.

Molly wanted to be happy for Tommy, but her mind was torn between being excited for him and the potential for an emotional roller coaster of the worst kind playing out in her mind. The carriages were about to be flung off unless Lizzy told her father everything. Immediately. He couldn't find out second-hand. It would be the worst way for him to know and it would bring back too many painful memories of being shut out of his daughter's life before. Another father, in a different situation with no previous trauma, could deal with a hidden boyfriend, but with Ryan's past a hidden fiancé would be a recipe for disaster.

Lizzy was the sweetest girl and Molly felt sure that she and Tommy could be happy together, but only if Ryan accepted it. If not, then he could, with the best protective intentions, tear them apart before they had a chance.

But now Ryan had to be told that Lizzy not only had

a boyfriend, she had a fiancé and not just any fiancé, Molly's brother. Which Molly doubted Lizzy knew. Nor did Tommy know, apparently, that Lizzy was the daughter of Ryan. They hadn't made the complicated connection. Molly was the only one who knew the whole story. Everyone else knew bits but not everything. So, who should really be the one to tell him? Her thoughts were becoming more jumbled by the moment. Layering one problem on top of the next and then sandwiching questions in between until she had a giant, precariously tipping sponge cake of trouble.

There were so many ways to look at the problem. And then there was the ever so small chance it wouldn't be a problem. Perhaps Ryan would think it was a lovely coincidence and be happy for the couple. Unfortunately, Molly didn't believe that for a moment. After everything he had been through, being the last to know something that involved Lizzy was not going to sit well with him. Someone needed to tell him immediately.

But who?

Lizzy?

Tommy?

Molly?

Nothing in her head or her heart was making her feel confident about a happy outcome for anyone. It was already two weeks after Lizzy's confession so it probably wasn't going to help him with his trust issues as she had kept something about his daughter from him. But if she had broken a promise to Lizzy, how would that fare for any future relationship with the young woman, who might now be a part of her family? And poor Tommy might be caught in the crossfire and have his heart broken if Ryan tried to stop them seeing each other. The idea of them ever being a happy family was further from her grasp than she'd thought possible.

She was going to let someone down. It was just about picking the person she hurt.

Molly picked up the telephone. She could see it was Ryan's number. With bated breath she answered.

'Hello.'

'Hi, Molly. I was wondering, at the risk of becoming a nuisance, if you might enjoy lunch here at home with Lizzy and I in a few hours. You could bring Tommy along too. Finally, they can meet. And then later tonight I can have you all to myself when we enjoy our candlelit dinner.'

Molly swallowed the lump that had formed in her throat. If all four of them were in the room together it stood the chance of being the meeting from hell. She could picture it in her mind. Lizzy and Tommy saw each other and within a minute started holding hands and kissing. Ryan would be more confused than any man had ever been. And then it would all come pouring out in the worst way possible.

No, Molly knew she had to delay the meeting until Lizzy had confessed. She wondered if perhaps she could speed up the process by taking Lizzy aside and encouraging her to tell her father. If it came from Lizzy, then he might just accept it.

Molly wasn't convinced, but it was the most logical scenario.

'I'd love to have lunch with you but I don't think Tommy will make it this time.' It wasn't a lie; Tommy wouldn't make it because Molly would omit to invite him until she had spoken with Lizzy. Woman to woman, she would explain the value in sharing her good news with her father. And even if it wasn't accepted as good news initially, he might warm to the idea.

But Lizzy had to tell her father before he found out.

Just before twelve, Lizzy caught a cab to Ryan's house. She insisted so he gave her the address again in case she had misplaced it since the shopping expedition. Tommy was watching television when she left home and she promised to be back before dinner. He had a corned beef sandwich, an apple and a glass of milk and he was happy in his room as the weather was still dismal outside. He said he would call his fiancée some time during the afternoon because they had plans to make.

Molly just hoped she could manage the situation that afternoon so Tommy still had a fiancée at the end of the day.

'Come in.' Ryan greeted Molly with a tender but brief kiss as she wiped her feet on the doormat and stepped inside. Ryan's home was a hundred-year-old gentleman's bungalow. The cab had driven in the sweeping return driveway to drop her at the front door.

Ryan's mouth returned to hers and lingered after he had closed the door on the cold breeze. She felt safe in his embrace but also feelings of guilt were building. It could all be so temporary if she couldn't get Lizzy to tell her father what he deserved to know. It couldn't wait six months for Christmas.

'I'm so glad you could come over but I really wish you would have let me come and pick you up.'

'Honestly, there was no need.' Molly felt her heart racing and hoped that Ryan did not pick up on her anxiety.

'Let me take your coat,' he said as he pulled away slightly. 'I'll hang it up for you...'

'Molly!'

Molly turned to see an elated Lizzy skipping down the hallway to her.

'I haven't seen you all morning and you only come out of your room because Molly's here,' Ryan said, laughing. 'Well, I know where I stand.'

Molly felt Lizzy's arms wrap around her waist as she leant into her. 'I like you, Molly.'

'And I like you, Lizzy. I'm so happy that I get to spend the afternoon with you both.'

'Me too.'

Ryan hung Molly's coat on the ornate hall stand. 'Would you like to come into the sitting room? I lit a fire a few hours ago and it's nice and warm.'

Molly nodded and followed behind with Lizzy, as Ryan led them down the hallway. The home had been restored perfectly, or perhaps maintained over the years rather than restored. The dark antique furniture was pristine and looked stunning against the off-white carpet. There were modern paintings in the hallway, which worked as they were framed in an older style. It was like a picture from an elegant homes magazine and a long way from the home she shared with Tommy.

'Please take a seat and I'll put the soup on to warm and we can have a casual lunch on our laps in here.'

'Yum,' Lizzy said, rubbing her tummy. 'What soup?'

'Sooty dropped over home-made minestrone soup yesterday.'

'I like Sooty's soup.'

'I know,' he told her, then disappeared into the kitchen. 'I'll only be a few minutes.'

Molly sat on the sofa nearest to the open fire and Lizzy sat right next to her. Molly looked down and suddenly her worst nightmare was realised. Lizzy was wearing the engagement ring that Tommy had picked with Ryan's help.

Molly thought she might have a heart attack.

Molly sat staring straight ahead in contemplated silence. She could bolt from the house claiming a fake emergency; she could confess everything to Ryan; or she could hope that Lizzy told her father. But with all of the options, Molly couldn't hide from the fact that she knew. All of it now.

And well before Ryan had any clue.

'I've got another secret. Shh. I'm engaged.'

'Uh-huh,' Molly replied, and added softly, 'Have you told your father yet?'

'Has she told me what?'

Molly almost jumped from her skin. Ryan was standing behind them holding a small table for each of them.

'As I said, it's so cosy in here I thought we could sit and eat our soup and chat in here,' he continued as he put down the two folding tables in front of Lizzy and Molly. 'What's the secret? Do you want to go shopping together again?'

Molly sighed. His question was so sweet and naive. She wished with all her heart that a shopping date were all that Lizzy was hiding.

Before Lizzy had a chance to answer Ryan froze on the spot. His body went rigid and Molly could see his eyes were focussed on the engagement ring on Lizzy's finger.

'Lizzy, is that a new ring?' he asked, moving the small tables out of the way before bending down in front of her. His voice was not raised but it was firm and coloured by concern.

'Yes. It's pretty.'

'And who gave you that ring?'

'My boyfriend.'

'It's a pretty ring,' Ryan replied with a hint of recognition in his eyes.

Ryan then shot a sideways glance at Molly. She could see that the pieces were falling into place in his mind and by his expression they weren't landing favourably. She knew he would have recognised the ring. How could he not? He had helped to choose it.

'It's beautiful,' Lizzy said with a beaming smile as she twisted her finger to hit the light and make the tiny diamond sparkle.

'I didn't know you had a boyfriend, Lizzy. What's his name?' Ryan's voice was calm and in no way threatening but Molly knew behind the calm there was a storm brewing. And she suspected the storm was heading her way.

'Tommy. He's nice. He asked me to marry him.'

'Tommy? Well, that's a surprise.'

'He's my secret boyfriend. Only Molly knew.' Lizzy giggled as she smiled up at Molly.

Ryan's glance at Molly was no longer sideways. It was face to face and more intense than Molly would have thought possible.

'I need Molly to help me in the kitchen with the soup, Lizzy. You can stay here in the warm room and we'll be back in a minute.'

Ryan did not need to ask Molly to follow him. In silence, she stood and walked behind him to the kitchen. Nervously she smoothed her jeans as she walked. There was no purpose in her actions but the adrenalin surging through her body forced her to do something with her hands. He closed the door behind them and stared at her in silence for the longest moment, then turned away and looked out of the kitchen window, still not saying a word. Molly suspected he was trying to choose his words but she didn't think any of them would be something she wanted to hear.

Finally, he turned back to her. His eyes were cold and unflinching, at odds with hers as they blinked nervously. The tension in his jaw was clear. His voice was a loud whisper with anger and disappointment both simmering close to the surface.

'You knew about this?' he started and then, without waiting for any response, continued. 'When did you decide to set your brother up with my daughter?'

'I didn't set them up,' she responded at a similar volume, aware that Lizzy was in the next room.

'You expect me to believe it was a coincidence?'

'It was. I didn't know that my brother and your daughter worked together. I just found out this morning that Tommy had proposed to Lizzy. I didn't know he was her boyfriend. I didn't know who she was dating but I didn't think for a minute it would be my brother. It just never occurred to me.'

Ryan rubbed the back of his neck. 'Not that I do believe you but, even if I did, you're still admitting that you knew she was dating someone and you didn't think I should know that? I'm her father. I should have been told.'

Molly chewed the inside of her cheek. That part of his rant was true and his anger with the situation was justified. Molly should have told him and would have told him under different circumstances.

'It wasn't my place to tell you.'

'Why not? You couldn't have been blind to my feelings about Lizzy dating. Didn't you think I should know something as important as that?'

'Yes, I know, but Lizzy had sworn me to secrecy. I couldn't break her trust.'

'That is so convenient. Such a tidy way to round it all up.'

'It's the truth.'

'I'm not so sure I can believe that word coming from you.'

Molly couldn't help but notice he wasn't using her name. He was keeping the conversation impersonal.

'You let me help your brother choose my daughter's engagement ring without knowing it was for her. Did you think for a moment that was okay?'

'I didn't know it was for Lizzy. You have to believe me.'

'I can't. It all seems way too convenient. I'm not blaming Tommy or Lizzy…'

'Great, so you're blaming me…' she countered, her hands on her hips.

'No, actually I'm blaming myself, Molly.'

She shook her head. 'Now I'm really confused. What have you done?'

'I've been too preoccupied with work and St Clara's…'

'Me?'

'Let's leave it there. I think you know where I stand on all of this.'

'Lizzy's nineteen, Ryan. She's not a child.'

Ryan rubbed his forehead in frustration. 'Lizzy isn't like other nineteen-year-olds. She has an innocent way of looking at the world…'

'As does Tommy. They are two wonderful souls who met each other and fell in love.'

'Do they really know what love is?' Ryan countered. 'Do they truly understand what marriage is all about? It's a lifetime commitment. It's more than a ring, a kiss and setting up home.'

'Don't sell Lizzy short now. From what you've told

me, and Lizzy's outlook on life, you've never done it before. You've always encouraged her and never limited her. You've always been there to support her. Don't stop now when she needs you the most. They're engaged and I don't think either would be expecting this reaction to their happiness.'

'Can you tell me, when did my daughter confide in you? On your shopping trip?'

'No, actually it was my first day on the job. When she arrived for her appointment.'

'You expect me to believe that Lizzy told you this secret within minutes of meeting?'

'She did. And it surprised me too. I only agreed to keep the secret because I didn't know you were her father. I had no idea. I thought her father was parking the car or delayed. How could I have known when you have different surnames?'

'It doesn't add up to me. You made a promise to a young girl you barely knew.'

'To a young *woman*, not a girl, a young woman who wanted to confide to another woman about something she held precious. There's a difference.'

'Precious? They barely know each other either.'

'Nor did we, and I thought what we shared was something precious.'

Ryan looked down at the ground in silence for a moment. 'We got that wrong, didn't we?'

Molly felt her heart sink.

The door swung open without warning. 'You are talking a lot. Is the soup ready? Tommy will call me soon.'

'It will be ready in a few minutes, sweetie. You stay in the warm room and we'll both be right out.'

Lizzy disappeared back into the sitting room, leaving them alone. Molly didn't think there was any more she could say.

'I think I should leave.'

Ryan nodded. 'That would be best for everyone.'

'I'll talk to you on Monday when you have calmed down. Unless you'd prefer I didn't come back to the practice.'

While she was effectively offering him her resignation, she hoped he would see that was not necessary and that they could work it out between them.

Ryan turned back to her, staring for the longest moment.

'Maybe you're right. It was only a four-week assignment and I'm happy to pay you out for the next two weeks. You can get on your feet and find something suitable.'

She couldn't help but notice he looked sad more than angry and that broke Molly's heart further. She really had messed up everything.

CHAPTER THIRTEEN

RYAN'S NEW OFFICE MANAGER, Gemma Potts, arrived bright and early on Monday morning. Molly had called the agency and said she wasn't feeling well enough to continue the assignment and needed a replacement.

Ryan acknowledged the young woman briefly and then went about his business of seeing the patients Molly had booked in on Friday, along with those that the automated booking system had booked in over the weekend. The week passed slowly and the nights even more slowly. He was angry with himself for being naive and allowing himself to trust again and for being too busy to notice what was happening in his daughter's life. He barely knew Molly and yet, for some now unfathomable reason, he had thought she was someone she wasn't. He was angry for almost falling in love with her.

He couldn't deny to himself that he felt empty but that was how it had to be. He had to concentrate on Lizzy. He would cut back his roster at St Clara's to one night a week, and pay a locum to call in the other two nights. He might not be able to deter Lizzy from seeing Tommy in the future, but he would not be encouraging it. They had other issues at hand. They had to decide on the treatment plan for her and if that did or didn't include surgery.

* * *

It was three in the afternoon on Friday when George rushed into the practice, demanding to see Ryan.

'I left two messages for you,' George told Ryan when he appeared in the waiting room.

'I'm sorry, Dr McFetridge. I didn't want to interrupt your last patient,' Gemma offered apologetically.

'That's okay. I'll take it from here.'

'What's wrong with you? You should have returned my call,' George said, waving an accusatory finger at him.

Ryan could see the older gentleman's blood pressure was on the rise as he walked him into a consulting room and sat him down. He was sure he knew the reason.

'George, I can see you're upset.'

'Dorothy's in hospital.'

'I know, George. I'm so sorry. The doctor at the Eastern Memorial called me late yesterday with the news. I'll be calling in today after I finish here.'

'But she wasn't sick, she was fine and not having her stupid cakes. I don't understand what went wrong.'

'It was a stroke. No one could have predicted it, George, but Dorothy's a strong woman and she'll pull through this.'

'She has to. I love her. I even love her stupid cat. I know I'm not the easiest man to live with but I love her and our family with everything I have. I wish I'd told her that more often. I think my military upbringing made me a hard man but Dorothy made me the best version of myself. She made me see that there's always two sides to everything. I know I stressed her at times, but she always found a solution to every problem. I'm not as cluey as her. I can't live without her. I'll stuff up everything with the family. They already think I'm a grumpy bastard and probably only tolerate me because they love her. They have no idea how much I love them. Women are so much better at the messy stuff than us.'

'Sometimes,' Ryan replied to George's ramblings, then asked him to take off his jacket and roll up his sleeve so he could take his blood pressure.

'You know, it's hard having daughters too. I have four of them and I swear they've always spoken to their mother about everything. What are they going to do without her?'

'You're thinking too far ahead, George. By all accounts Dorothy will recover. I'll see her tonight and get an update and I'll call you.'

'But if she's not okay the girls won't cope. They can't talk to me about the stuff Dorothy manages. They've all had so many secrets over the years and they knew their mother would hide that stuff from me and just deal with it.'

'You were okay with them hiding things from you?' Ryan asked.

'Sure, it's a woman thing. Girls need to confide in someone they think will understand and that's always another woman.'

Ryan thought about George's comment but wasn't convinced. His situation was different he tried to tell himself as he noted the blood pressure. As he became concerned with the reading, he changed the subject. 'You're one-fifty over ninety so we need to get that down. Make sure you take your antihypertensive medication this evening and I'd like to see you again tomorrow.'

'Sure, Doctor. Dorothy normally arranges that and I guess I must've forgotten it today.'

'You can't forget medications, George, particularly

your blood-pressure tablets. You're a grown man and you need to take some of that responsibility away from Dorothy. When she gets home…'

'If she does.'

'No, George, *when* she does. As I said, there's no indication that Dorothy won't recover, but she'll need rest and you need to step up and take charge of running the house a little.'

'Running the house? I wouldn't know where to start,' George admitted, shaking his head as he rolled his sleeve down and slipped his tweed jacket back on.

'Then, George, you need to find out. And in a hurry.'

Ryan drove home that night thinking about George's remarks, but Lizzy had Ann; she didn't need to confide in someone she barely knew. But then he had also confided in someone he barely knew and made love to that same someone, he reminded himself. Taking a deep breath, he brushed those thoughts aside as he turned into his driveway. He had to let it go. He had to let his feelings for Molly go.

Ann was waiting with Lizzy when he got home. She had a small leg of roast lamb in the oven for the two of them to enjoy. The smell of rosemary sprigs on the slowly cooking meat filled the house.

'I'll be off, then,' she said. 'The potatoes and pumpkin are in with the meat and the gravy's in a small pot and the string beans are already in the steamer.'

'Can't you stay and have dinner?'

Ann smiled. 'Thank you for asking but I have bridge tonight. I have a few newbies coming along to my class. I do love it and they have a lovely supper for us so I won't go hungry. But don't forget to turn on the heat under the saucepan and it will all be ready in ten minutes.'

'What would we do without you?' Ryan replied as he dropped his jacket on the arm of the sofa.

'You'd manage, but I'm just grateful I get to see so much of Lizzy and you. It could have been so very different and I'm just so happy we worked through everything.'

'That makes two of us,' he said, nodding. 'So where is that wonderful daughter of mine?'

'In her room. I was going to speak to you about Lizzy tomorrow. She seems quite down at the moment. She mentions Tommy and Molly a lot, and I understand you want her to take things slowly with him. You did explain the boyfriend situation and the marriage proposal, and I know it was all a bit messy the way it came out, but she misses Molly terribly. I never met her but she sounds very nice.'

'Well, she's gone and we have to move on.'

'Pity, a young woman needs another woman to talk to at times. You might need to perhaps arrange a lunch for the two of them because she really is very sad not being able to see her.'

Ryan walked with Ann to the front door. 'I think Lizzy can confide in you quite enough, and I've lightened my workload so I'll be having more time at home, so she can open up to me whenever she needs. There's not so much happening in her life that she needs to find someone else to share the load.'

'Quite the opposite, actually. She's worried about the thought of the hysterectomy and wanted to chat to Molly about it.'

'She said that?'

'Yes. Lizzy doesn't want to talk to me or Tommy or you about it. Perhaps let them chat on the phone. She said that the pain is bad and she wants to have the operation. She is quite sure she doesn't want babies as they cry and they're messy, so she doesn't mind that she won't be able to have them, but she's a bit scared and she wants to talk to Molly about it.'

'I don't understand how she formed such a strong bond with her so quickly.'

'By the sound of it, you did too, didn't you?'

'It wasn't anything serious.'

'I might be seventy-six, but I'm not silly. I know when a man has fallen in love and is still in love, and that's you. You can choose to say it never happened but I can see it in your eyes.'

'It was just one night,' he replied, rubbing his neck. 'A fling, nothing more. It didn't work out.'

'I don't think it was a fling. I know you've had many flings over the last seven years, but Molly wasn't one of them. There was more to it than that. It can be as complicated or as simple as you make it, Ryan.'

'She kept something from me. And you of all people know I've been lied to in the worst possible way before and she did the same.'

'I don't know any such thing, Ryan,' she said. 'Tell me, who was she protecting?'

Ryan stood up and walked to the window and pulled back the heavy drapes to look out at the night sky.

'What do you mean?'

'You're punishing Molly for protecting the person you love most in the world by keeping her confidence. Molly risked her relationship with you to make sure she didn't let down Lizzy. She behaved like any mother would, under the same circumstances.'

'That's a romantic version of the situation.'

'No, it's the realistic one. Lizzy needs a mother figure, Ryan. She's at that age when it's important to be able to share things with someone closer to her age, not with her grandmother.'

'She can share them with me…'

'She can't. You won't accept that she is a young woman who wants the chance to love and Molly accepted that. And didn't judge her.'

'Her life is full without the complications. What if she gets her heart broken? How will I heal that for her?'

'That's what this is really about, isn't it? You want to protect Lizzy. Well, you can't, and shutting Molly out is making four of the sweetest people in the world suffer because of the actions almost twenty years ago by of one of the most selfish women in the world. You and Lizzy were both hurt by my daughter and I can see her for what she was then and still is. She has the life she wanted and she doesn't want her past to ever interfere with her new family. She knows that you have custody of Lizzy and can't understand why you would want to adopt her. Madeline doesn't have a selfless bone in her body and her deceit ruined lives and robbed us all of Lizzy for a long time, but you can have everything your heart desires now if you just let go of the past. She hid a secret to benefit herself, not to protect anyone else. There's a big difference.'

With that, Ann stood up and walked to the front door and prepared for the cold weather that would hit her when she stepped out to her car. 'I love you, Ryan, like you were my own son, so I have to be honest. You, and you alone, are the only one standing in the way of everyone being happy. Including yourself. Stop trying to protect Lizzy from people who love her…and stop protecting your own heart from feeling the same happiness.'

Ryan didn't put the heat on under the string beans that night. Instead he sat in the dark for an hour thinking about everything Ann and George had said. He hated to admit it at first but, alone in the darkness, he soon realised they were both right. He had been hiding behind the pain. Pushing Molly and Tommy away to protect Lizzy, when in fact his own actions were hurting her more. While he didn't have the power to change the outcome for himself—he had single-handedly ruined that—he knew he had to make things right for Lizzy and Tommy.

It was late at night when he drove to Molly's house with Lizzy in the car. He had explained to her that Molly was Tommy's brother on the drive over and that they were going to visit them. He also explained that since they were unannounced they might not be able to stay, but that he wanted to try. When he pulled up, he left Lizzy locked in the warmth of the car and, unsure of what he would say and how Molly would react, he walked up the front path. He was taking a risk, but he had been a fool. He had brought the hurt from the past into his present and ruined everything wonderful. There was no one else to blame but himself, he knew, as he knocked on her door. While Tommy and Lizzy would have their struggles, Molly was right in wanting to support them.

'What are you doing here?' Molly demanded as she opened the door. Her emotions were still raw and she did not invite him in out of the chilly night air. Instead she pulled her dressing gown across her chest and stood her ground against him and the icy cold breeze.

'I'm here to apologise and let you know that you were right.'

'I'm confused, Ryan. Where's this sudden change of heart coming from?'

Her brow was wrinkled and her eyes squinting in his direction and he didn't blame her for her reaction.

'What you said and did, all of it came from your heart, from pure intentions. I just couldn't see it.'

'A week ago, you told me you didn't want to see me, you showed no desire to support Lizzy and Tommy's relationship, oh, and that's right, let's not forget you fired me.'

'I was stupid and there is no excuse for what I did.'

'Yes, you were, and no, there's not. So, if that's it, goodnight.' With that Molly half-closed the door.

'Wait, Molly. Please hear me out.'

'Why should I?'

'For Lizzy and Tommy's sake…and for us.'

Molly flinched. 'Us? I trusted you, I let you into my heart and you threw that away. There is no us. It was over before it began.'

'No, it began and it was real for both of us. There has never been anything more real to me than what we shared that night. But if it's over for you, then I will understand and respect your decision, but you need to understand why I did what I did,' Ryan said, not taking his eyes away from Molly for a second. 'I've spent the last seven years feeling guilty for not being there for Lizzy. The thought of my baby daughter being alone in the hospital and then being adopted when I should have been protecting her from the moment she was born has driven me to protect her at all costs. I didn't want her to get hurt like that ever again.'

Molly lifted her chin and took a deep breath. 'But I would never hurt Lizzy, not for anything in the world.'

'I know that. I was just scared if she fell in love she would get hurt and I worried you were encouraging her to be in love. Not that there's anything wrong with that anyway.'

'I wasn't encouraging her, I was supporting her. And being hurt is part of life, Ryan.'

'I know, and you were strong enough to risk that hurt when you put your trust in me that night in…our hotel room.'

'Well, that was a bad decision on my part.'

'No, it wasn't, in my mind. My knee-jerk reaction was the bad decision. You did everything you could to make everyone happy. I didn't know how to deal with the idea of my daughter falling in love. It scared me to the core but the way I reacted was wrong and what you did was right. I've realised that I've been an idiot and, while I thought I had put the past behind me, in fact I was still hiding behind it and using it as a shield.'

Molly looked past Ryan, still unsure what to think. 'Is there someone in the car?'

'Yes, Lizzy's out there. I'm hoping that you will allow her to see Tommy and she's excited to see you. She's missing you both so badly and nothing will cheer her up. If you slam the door on me and choose never to forgive me, I would understand. And I'd deserve it, but, please, can you consider allowing Lizzy to stay here with you for an hour or so. I can go and come back later.'

'You want Lizzy to spend time with Tommy?'

'Yes.'

'And me?'

'Yes.'

'So, you approve of their engagement, then?'

'Yes. Tommy's a wonderful young man. There was never any doubt in my mind about that. And, by how unhappy she is without him, I know she loves him too.'

Molly turned her head to listen to what he had to say.

'There's no guarantee they'll survive the challenges

ahead. I know now they both deserve a chance at love and our support. And Lizzy wants and needs you to help her make a very big decision. It's a woman's issue and I would appreciate if you would talk that one through and perhaps meet with her specialist if you have time. A father can only do so much.'

He stepped back a little to give Molly space to think.

'Are you sure about all of this? Really sure?'

'I have never been so sure. If you would see Lizzy and let her see Tommy too, then one McFetridge would be very, very happy.'

Molly looked at the man standing before her. She could hear the honesty and anguish in his heartfelt words. She hadn't fully understood the guilt he had been carrying for seven long years. She had assumed it was anger and bitterness, but she had been wrong. Guilt had been driving him and he should never have felt any level of guilt. None of what had happened to Lizzy had been his fault. He had done nothing wrong up until now. And he wanted to make what he had done wrong right again for everyone. He was taking the biggest risk, reaching out and putting his trust in her...and in Tommy.

'And what would make the other McFetridge happy?' she asked with her head tilted slightly.

Ryan looked at her standing in front of him, with her hair a gorgeous mess around her beautiful face and a dressing gown that had seen better days hiding the body he had loved that night they had shared together.

'I would be the happiest man alive if I could have you back in my life. Not for a night, not for a month, but for ever. Waking up to your beautiful face every day and telling you how much I love you is all I will ever need.'

Molly drew a deep breath and stepped from the warmth of her home into the warmth of his arms and the beginning of her fairy-tale ending. With her lips only inches from his, she muttered, 'Then I guess you need to bring Lizzy inside and there will be *two* happy McFetridges tonight…and for the rest of our lives.'

* * * * *

MILLS & BOON

Coming next month

THE SHY NURSE'S REBEL DOC
Alison Roberts

She had to catch his gaze again and she knew that her curiosity would be evident. What surprised her was seeing a reflection of that curiosity in *his* gaze.

'It was a one-off for more than the fact that neither of us do relationships,' she said. 'We work together. It would be unprofessional.'

Blake snorted softly. 'It's pretty unprofessional to be thinking about it all the time.'

Again, Sam seemed to see her own thoughts reflected in those dark eyes. He had been finding this as difficult as she had? Wow…

Could Blake hear how hard her heart was thumping right now? 'Um… maybe we just need to get it out of our system, then.'

His voice was a low, sexy rumble. 'Are you suggesting what I think you're suggesting? Another… one-off?'

'Or a two-off. A three-off, if that's what it takes.' She took a deep breath and then held his gaze steadily as she gathered her words. Yes, she did want a real relationship that was going somewhere but it had to be with the right person and that person wasn't going to be Blake Cooper because she could sense that his demons were even bigger than hers.

But, oh… that didn't stop the *wanting*, did it? The lure of the bad boy…

'We both walk alone, Blake,' she said quietly, 'for whatever reason – and at some point we'll know it's enough.

Maybe we just need to agree that when one of us reaches that point, the other walks away too. No regrets. No looking back.'

Somehow, she had moved closer to Blake as she'd been speaking, without realising it. Her head was tilted up so that she could hold his gaze and he was looking down.

Leaning down… as if he couldn't resist the urge to kiss her.

Then he straightened suddenly and Sam could feel the distance increasing between them with a wave of disappointment. Despair, almost…?

But he was smiling. That crooked, irresistibly charming smile of a man who knew exactly what he wanted and was quite confident he was going to get it.

'What are you doing tonight, Sam?'

Her mouth felt dry. 'Nothing important.'

'Give me your address and I'll come and get you. You up for a bike ride?'

Sam could almost hear her mother shrieking in horror at the thought but her rebellious streak wasn't about to be quashed. She might only get one more night with this man so why not add an extra thrill to it?

She could feel her smile stretching into a grin. 'Bring it on.'

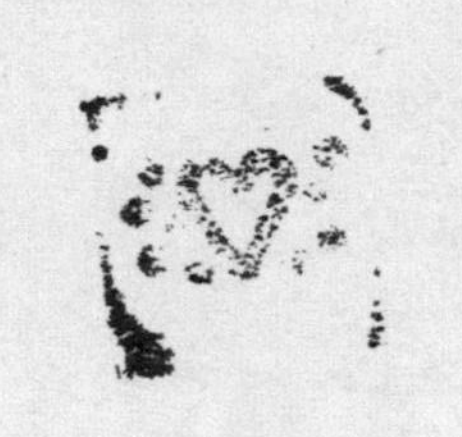